Hair Tea

Barbara Yakov

Cover art by Mandy Garlick

ISBN-13: 9781505785890
ISBN-10: 1505785898
Registered with BooksinPrint.com

For encouragement,

I thank my loving father David Woroft;

for sparkle, my mother Debby;

for always being there, Renee;

for laughter, Isobel;

for spirit, Jordan David Hoffmann;

for vitality, Natan, Emmi, and Lea;

for love and strength, Dror

FOR generous support upon reception of this book, I thank Esther Fox, Renee Fox, Natty, Nicole Somers, E.B., Jerry Manas, Ola Sypien, Laura Hoffman, Valaree Cash, Mengyin Chen, Naida Moss Kroll, Jan Horwitz, Adina Raucci, Shari OBlon Biagi, Melissa Young, Marc Kaman, Stacy Scherr, Brad Silver, Alex Baum, Linda Champion, Brennan Mault, Jennifer Chalal, Caroline Wolk, James Traub, Marissa Silverman, Lorella Parrillo, Jessica Gordon, Shelly Anapol, Donald Spencer, Rose Lee, Isobel Sollenberger, Deneen Mack, Vin Gyo, Jill Paikin, Wanona June, Ellen Barnett Bluestein, Stefanie Siegel, Jill Levy, Mindy Feldman Nachsin, John Fox, Jordan Erika, and Devyn Rey. I thank Mandy Garlick for the cover art. And I thank Adam Mazer (9850) for the guiding light.

iii

CONTENTS

To My Sister,
Renee

CHAPTER ONE

For The Cause

Done for the day – I strolled by the Bell Tower, inhaling a freshly lit Marlboro red. Students gathered and scattered in and out of crowds along the way, dotting the landscape of Temple University's campus life in Philadelphia. Just overhead, the lush green leaves of summer had already transformed into brilliant shades of autumn, inspiring my imagination: *An earthly umbrella of gold leaf latticework ... A heavenly spice rack of cinnamon and saffron, crimson and clover, over and over ...* Vibrations of change seasoned the air.

Although I walked alone, I belonged to the scene – a speck in the picture – a focal point that balanced the composition for no one else, perhaps, but me. And then, through the silent stare of contemplation – as though from nowhere – Jordan emerged. I spotted him running towards me fast, waving his muscular arms through the sparkling sky. The Bell Tower was our meeting place.

"Bree! ... Bree! ... I need your help!" He shouted breathlessly as he neared. "The model *died* yesterday!"

"What?" I squinted, emphasizing the *t* in *what*.

"Remember the old man I told you about?" he

asked, panting as he spoke. "The model – from my painting class – who's around ninety years old – *old Uncle Sam* – Remember?" Jordan's face turned a deep shade of razzmatazz. Every time he panics, it looks like a gallon of blood flushes up to his head.

"Uncle Sam? – Uh – I *guess*," I muttered, trying to recall the details, but Jordan's beet-skin sense of urgency hijacked my attention aboard a train of red images: *a ruby ring ... a cherry pie ... a bowl of borscht ... old veins.* I found his colorful expression much more interesting than his words. That is — until his words involved *me*.

"We don't have a model today," he continued. "My class starts in twenty minutes, and there's no one to model for us. Will you do it? – Do you have a class? – Can you do it?" He seemed to be speaking in riddles.

"Do *what*?" I asked with confusion, dragging hard on the cigarette, as though I'd inhale a better understanding of what he was trying to say.

"Model," he explained in a calmer tone, "for my class."

"Me? – Model? – Now? – Are you *nuts*?" I dropped the cigarette.

"Come on, Bree. You can do it. Do it for *the cause*: For *Art*." The puppy in his bright-green eyes seemed to bark at the word: *Art*.

And just like that, in less than an instant, the word *Art* had transformed from sound and air into something more tangible, something with shape and texture that turned my mind and opened my thoughts: *Art is a bone in the shape of a key, designed to unlock the very nature of my soul. It defines my life in the*

2

ninth degree: ART.

An ancient three-letter alarm rang and sang to my spirit. I existed for the sake of *Art* – as did Jordan. We always shared the same excitement when it came to color and form and texture and expression.

Even so, I struggled to resist the impromptu task of modeling in the nude. It's not that I had total reservations about it. In fact, it appealed to me on many levels. The idea of involving myself in the creative process in such an intimate way was a real turn-on. But posing for Jordan's painting class wasn't what I had in mind. He was my best friend – My best *male* friend. It was fun hanging out with him and his artsy buddies on campus. I imagined us all having a smoke after class: *I'll be fully clothed, but they'll be looking at me through XXX-ray vision – naked – in full detail – not exactly the image I want to plant in their minds.*

"I don't know, Jord. I was all set to go home and take a nap," I whined. "I'm really tired and —"

"That's the beauty of it," he interrupted. "You don't have to do anything. Just sit there. You can even take a nap if you want. Come on, Bree … Just do it. You'll get paid seven bucks an hour," he practically begged on all fours.

It must have been the puppy in his eyes that got to me because somehow I caved. *"Fiiine,"* I stretched with the word, waking up to resolve. "I'll do it."

"You will?" he beamed.

"Uh-huh."

"Great," he chuckled. "You're the coolest … I love you." And on that, we embraced. The April-fresh scent of Downy fabric softener in his shirt was comforting as I nestled into his canine hug.

"What the hell happened to old Uncle Sam?" I asked, ready for the hug to be over. His arms tightened around my back.

"I didn't have class yesterday, but Eric and Paul said that he died right there in the painting studio."

"*What!* While he was modeling, for God's sake?" I broke free from his grip.

"I don't know all the details of it, but he was in there when it happened. Listen, it's getting late. Just run up to the studio, and tell Mr. Spade that you're the new model for the class. I have to go meet someone real fast."

"What?" I kept saying the word *what* and grew annoyed by the sound of my own voice for doing so. "You're not even gonna walk me over?"

"I would, but I have to go *hook someone up*. You understand. It'll only take a few minutes." He made it seem so simple, but it felt more like an act of betrayal. Jordan had convinced me to sacrifice an afternoon of relaxation, only to abandon me to my own fears and insecurities. I wasn't thrilled, yet I agreed to the arrangement.

"Okay. I'll see you in there," I said, rolling my eyes.

"You should hurry. Mr. Spade doesn't even know what's going on." His voice trailed off as we separated in opposite directions. Five bells of the tower chimed, announcing to all that another quarter hour of time had passed.

I smoked half a cigarette before entering Anderson

Hall. With a bit of reluctance and a stream of smoke still in my lungs, I took the elevator up to the second floor. *Ding.*

In the lobby-like space between the elevator and the studio, the air was thick with turpentine and linseed oil, a Renaissance scent I instantly favored. I breathed it in as though my life would expire without it. It was the scent of genius. The scent of rebellion. Of justice and love. It carried a message, reminding me that my current task had more importance than any personal inhibitions. In less than an instant, I exhaled some leftover smoke and followed my instincts.

Students continued to enter and exit the studio through one of the double doors that was propped open by an old sable suitcase. *Rocky Raccoon* was playing inside the studio, blasting through the paint-splattered speakers of an oversized boom box. I knew every word and sang quietly as I entered: *"Rocky Raccoon (beat, beat), checked into his room (beat, beat), only to find Gideon's Bible ..."*

"Hi. I'm here about the modeling job." I spoke with an animated confidence to a skinny man wearing salty glasses and a peppery moustache. I just figured he had to be Mr. Spade since he was the only person in the studio holding a clipboard.

"Oh, good," he said, happily surprised. "We're in *desperate* need of a model today." His moustache twitched as he pulled a form from his clipboard and handed it to me. "Just write your name down here ... your signature there ... and make sure you fill in your social security number on this line, so you can get paid." He offered me the pen to get me started. "By the way, what is your name?"

"Bree Yeager."

"Nice to meet you – *Bree*." The way he said *Bree* gave me the impression that he'd never heard the name before. He seemed nervous. "Where've you modeled before?" he asked.

"I did some modeling over at the Academy," I lied. I wanted to sound like an experienced model, and I knew I could pull it off because my best *female* friend, Jessie, studied at The Academy of Fine Arts, and she modeled in between classes to help pay for her tuition. I thought that stripping down to nothing in front of an entire class was fantastic. One time I waited nearby while Jessie did a private job for one of the seniors. I watched as she posed in the Grand Stair Hall of the museum, surrounded by spectacular ornaments of lavish décor. The freedom that her nudity conveyed aroused my curiosity: *What would it be like to free myself of all inhibition and shame in the name of Art?*

Although posing nude was something I'd considered, something I'd fantasized about, I never actually looked for a modeling job. The job found me ten minutes before I found myself face to face with Mr. Spade.

"You can get undressed in there," he said, pointing his hairy finger towards the curtained-off area on the stage. I get nervous around hairy fingers but played it cool as I climbed into the dark, tiny space that closely resembled the shabby makeshift dressing rooms at I. Goldberg Army & Navy store on Chestnut Street.

I took off all my clothes, dropped them into a sloppy pile in the corner, and stood there naked – butt

6

naked. An unexpected sweat broke out all over my body as conflicting thoughts pervaded my mind, bringing into question my quick decision to turn a fantasy into reality:

Get your clothes back on you idiot! You're not walking out there – in front of all those people – naked! They're all going to look at you in a sexual way: The instructor. Jordan. His friends. Get dressed and get the hell out of here. Don't look back. You're not Jessie. You're Bree. Jewish girls don't take their clothes off in public ...

Slightly shaking and a bit numb, I stepped out of the dressing room through the dark linen curtains, which somehow served to magically erase my former thoughts. I stood upon the stage, feeling as though I'd emerged through some sort of birth canal, completely reborn.

Students were busy setting up at their easels. My eyes searched for Jordan. It was a big studio. I didn't see him. The door remained open and students continued to enter. People in the hall passed by. Some glanced in my way. It was somewhat awkward, but I was fascinated by my own boldness – proud of myself – liberated as could be. Pearls of silver sweat dried all over my body, chilling and tickling my skin.

The final verse of *Rocky Raccoon* concluded just as Mr. Spade climbed onto the stage with an expression of horror upon his face. "Uh – there's a robe – hanging up – back in there – on a hook." He pointed his hairy finger at the curtained-off area again. "I guess you didn't see it. *Please* put it on until we're ready to begin. Classes are *still* changing." He was talking to me, but he was staring at my body. He couldn't help himself. My body's great. I felt like an idiot.

A robe? DUH! How could I be so pathetic? I changed into a purple satin robe and sat upon a long wooden box that was draped with a thick piece of cherry-red silk. On top of that was a mustard-yellow corduroy pillow full of lumps. The arrangement of colors and textures provided something for me to focus on while I attempted to regulate my breathing — and hide my embarrassment.

Looking down at the purple robe, I suddenly felt like royalty. Earlier that day in my Shakespeare 101 class, I learned that royalty were the only people allowed to wear purple clothing in Elizabethan England. For anyone else, it was illegal. And anyway, the commoners couldn't afford it. The only way to get the purple dye back then was by crushing thousands of tiny seashells.

Then I had a horrible thought: *Is this the same robe that old Uncle Sam put on before he uncovered his shriveled frame? Maybe he was wearing it when he died!* I had the sudden urge to take it off again. *Where the hell's Jordan? How long does it really take to hook someone up with a bag of weed?*

Mr. Spade began lecturing the students on color and how it sits in space. "Yellow is the most saturated of the colors ..." They were listening to him, but I knew what they were thinking: *Old Uncle Sam is dead, and a hot, young girl is taking his place.*

The music started up again. This time it was Indian: Ravi Shankar.

"*Now* you may take off the robe and get into position, Bree. Stay seated if you like." Mr. Spade spoke to me as if he knew I had no idea what the hell I was doing.

I let the robe fall to the floor and didn't bother picking it up. Everyone smiled to make me feel welcome, I guess. I didn't really care one way or the other. My thoughts were on Jordan: *Where is he? I'm only doing this because* he *asked me to, and he's not even here. Asshole.*

But he was there. On the other side of the double doors, out in the hall, Jordan was there, pacing with worry. He had seen me in my bikini hundreds of times, but never saw me naked. The whole *naked thing* made him anxious. Five minutes went by. The door opened. He walked in but didn't even look at me. My eyes followed his every move from the supply area to the easel. He set up his palette. And just as the sitar was beginning to annoy the crap out of me, Shankar changed to Mozart. Our eyes met. He let a smile peek out of his mouth as he began stroking color against the canvas.

About fifteen minutes later, our eyes met again. He blew kisses at me, Italian style. I gave him the finger with a straight face. A kitchen timer went off. Mr. Spade shouted, "Ten minute break!"

I quickly slipped back into the royal purple robe and grabbed my Marlboros. Most of the students filtered out of the studio onto a side balcony that was covered with cigarette butts.

"Are you okay?" Jordan asked.

"Yeah. You're giving me a ride home after class,

right?"

"Of course," he smiled. "You look great up there. Your body's fantastic. Wait till you see what I'm working on. The nipples are magical."

"I'm glad you like them." His use of the word *magical* was a bit much, but I didn't feel like discussing my nipples, so I let him do the talking. The sun glowed lower in the sky. The cigarette was so damn good. I had been a nervous wreck, and now I was getting used to the whole modeling thing. Only half an hour had passed, but I already felt like a professional.

Mr. Spade played The Rolling Stones album *Sticky Fingers*, as Jordan created his "favorite painting of all time." Then we headed back to Northeast Philly. Jordan smoked a joint between shifting gears in his Volkswagen van on Route One. I'd quit smoking pot right before that semester had started, but I got a contact high anyway.

*

At home, my mother called everyone into the kitchen: "Dinner's ready!"

My oldest sister Mona took her seat at the table. Our middle sister Jackie gave me a *wedgie*. She loved pulling my underwear way the hell up out of my pants. "Bitch!" I laughed, re-adjusting myself. Everyone quietly chewed on salad vegetables.

"I got a new job today," I proudly announced, not knowing exactly how they were going to react.

"Oh, yeah?" my mother said, looking up from her salad bowl.

"Well?" my father asked, "What is it?" I could tell from the look on his face that he sensed something questionable about my new profession. He often has sixth-sense capability.

I explained the extreme circumstances that led to my employment by really emphasizing the cause-and-effect aspect of the story: "The man who modeled for Jordan's painting class *died* yesterday. He just dropped dead in the painting studio in the middle of class, so they didn't have anyone to model for class today. They were *desperate*, so Jordan looked all over campus for me. When he finally found me, his class was about to begin. He begged me to do it. At first, I was like, *no way*. But then I reconsidered because, first of all, it's easy money. And second of all, it's great experience. And third of all, I'm entirely dedicated to the world of Art. Who was I to refuse my fellow artists in need? So, I just got up on stage and did it!"

"You're modeling *nude* for an art class?" Jackie asked, intrigued.

"Uh-huh." I proudly nodded my head as I chewed on a cucumber.

"You're so *weird*!" Mona said with a scowl. "You and your friends are all a bunch of *freaks*!"

Mona's the real conservative type. I don't know how she got into our family. No one in our family is conservative.

"And just how much are they paying you for modeling *nude*?" my father asked, controlling his tone, keeping his cool.

"Seven bucks an hour." I grinned from ear to ear.

"Isn't that great?"

"Seven bucks an hour! That's all?" he shouted in a tone of intense opposition. "That's an outrage!" His hand slammed down on the table. Food came out of his mouth as he spoke. "You should be making triple – no – quadruple that amount for taking off your clothes!"

"It's good money, dad. Jessie only gets paid six bucks an hour at the Academy." I really had no idea how much Jessie was earning, but I had to say something to strengthen my argument.

"It's *still* not enough," he affirmed, returning back to a controlled temper.

I chewed on a thick tomato wedge covered in Russian dressing and didn't dare say another word as my father digested the news. I'm pretty good at knowing when to shut up.

Jackie, on the other hand, has no regard for awkward kitchen silence and immediately broke it with her own announcement: "While we're on the subject, I just want to let everyone know that I might get a job dancing – at *Visions*!"

"You people make me sick!" Mona shrieked. "I can't believe you're my family!" She stormed out of the kitchen and slammed her bedroom door.

Visions is a go-go bar.

CHAPTER TWO

Fortune Cookies

During the third week of my modeling career, I got my period. As usual, I walked through the curtained-off area on the stage, wearing the purple satin robe, but I didn't feel quite like royalty. I had horrible cramps and was on eight hundred milligrams of Motrin.

"I'm keeping the robe on today. It's that time of the month," I informed Mr. Spade. I felt so bloated and awkward and didn't think that the bright aqua string of my o.b. tampon would look very classy on canvas.

"That'll be fine," he agreed.

Keeping a frozen pose was getting harder and harder. While Cat Stevens was diaphragm deep into *Wild World*, I got the idea in my head that the whole *modeling thing* was silly. There were at least twenty young artists intensely working on the image of me, and I decided that my job was a big waste of time and money. *Why don't they just take off their own clothes and paint each other.* I imagined the whole class standing naked at their easels. *That would be much more interesting.*

During the breaks, I'd walk around and check out the paintings. It was fun seeing so many different interpretations of the same exact image. It reminded me of a poetry assignment I had to do back in high school during my senior year. My English teacher, Mrs. Sylvia, wrote nine words on the chalkboard: *Mountain, Whisper, Sweep, Blackberry, Mother, Song, Leaves, Storm,* and *Knife.* She instructed the class to create a ten-line poem that included all nine words. Then she made each of us stand and recite our work. Although a few of the poems were similar, most were outstanding originals. I liked that assignment because it framed each individual's perspective. Walking around the studio, I felt like nine words on a chalkboard.

While I was checking out one of the more interesting paintings, some guy was checking me out.

"How ya doin'?" He sounded exactly like Rocky Balboa.

"I'm feeling about nine words long," I replied. He didn't know whether to smirk or smile. I can be so annoying when I have my period.

Jordan continued to drool all over his palette and make love to his canvas when he painted. As his interest in my figure peaked, my interest in the job hit an all-time low. I knew I wouldn't be modeling much longer. I could never sit still for too long. Even during my regular classes, I'd fidget in my seat like a butterfly in a box. And during those restless moments, I always think I have ADHD or something of that nature, constantly adjusting myself, never quite comfortable. Every once in a while, I get real paranoid and glance around the room to see if anyone notices. They never do though.

That night I sat on the futon in my bedroom, studying the difference between the uses of the words "you" and "thou" from the time when Shakespeare was busy writing verse in iambic pentameter.

"You" is formal. "Thou" is familiar – Oh! I get it! It's just like the words for "you" in Spanish: "tú" and "usted." That's easy! As I was relishing the *aha! moment*, Jackie barged into my room.

"I'm doing it tonight!" she proclaimed, wearing a satin-gold, second-skin dress with pointed breast cups like Madonna's, and matching five-inch heels. "I'm gonna dance tonight at Visions. Do you believe it? Oh my God, I'm so excited! How do I look?"

How did she look? Fantastic! Jackie has the most incredible body I've ever seen up close. People say that I have a great body, but they wouldn't just say that Jackie has a great body. The word "great" isn't strong enough an adjective to describe her; there aren't enough syllables. Jackie's body is incredible, amazing, flawless. One time I overheard some guy in a bar talking about her. He said, *"She's built like a Playboy Bunny!"* It struck me in a curious way when he said it.

But it's not just her body. There's a lot more to Jackie than her figure. Her facial features are also incredible, sort of like a cross between Cindy Crawford (without the mole) and a young Sophia Loren. If either of those beauties saw Jackie from a distance, they'd consider what I just said a compliment. If they saw her up close, they'd consider her a threat. She's as hot as a bomb. And when you're *that* hot, you have to explode.

"What're you gonna do?" I asked her.

"Dance and strip," she answered with a beaming smile.

"Do you know anyone who works there? I mean, how did you get into the whole thing?"

"I do their nails – some of the strippers come into the salon to get their daggers done." Jackie worked as a nail technician in a hair salon a couple blocks away from Visions.

"What're you wearing under your dress?" I asked, a bit concerned. My *Riverside Shakespeare* text was still wide open on my lap. I glanced down at it. A line glanced up: *"I have lost the immortal part of myself, and what remains is bestial ..."*

Jackie pulled up her dress and revealed a hot-pink G-string, studded with rhinestones. "What do you think? Does it look good?" she asked.

"Yeah. It looks great," I said, studying her whole ensemble. Her eyes were painted like an Egyptian queen. Her hair was full like the mane of a lion. "Does daddy know?" I asked.

"Not yet. Come with me to tell him. He's watching an opera in the living room. At least he'll be in a good mood."

I followed her down the hall, and, sure enough, his attention was immersed in *La Traviata*, his favorite Italian opera. He's always watching operas, ballets, musicals, or anything else on PBS that has to do with the Arts. We grew up on his favorites and know them all by heart. Jackie did a triple spin in front of the TV set. His mouth opened as wide as Pavarotti's.

"What're you doing?" he asked with excitement.

"I'm dancing tonight – at Visions," Jackie replied with equal excitement.

"Are you sure it's a good idea?" His voice flooded with concern.

"Of course it's a good idea – I'm gonna make a *lotta* money." She did a few more spins around the room. I stood there watching my father, hoping he'd say something like *"Get thee to a nunnery."* But he didn't.

"I'm just worried you'll get caught up in it … It could lead to prostitution … or *worse –*"

"Oh, daddy, don't be ridiculous! I'm just gonna dance," Jackie reassured.

"Well, be careful. You look gorgeous." He put his index finger up to his cheek and tapped it twice – his own special way of saying, *"Give me a kiss."* She ran over to him and planted a big one on his cheek. Then he hugged her – as if for dear life. "Don't do anything stupid," he warned.

"I won't," she promised.

While Pavarotti hit another high C, Jackie changed her clothes and was out the door. I returned to my room, to Shakespeare.

*

Sometime around three in the morning, a Bon Jovi album was playing on low volume in Jackie's room. I could hear it because her room was right next to mine.

Her door wasn't locked, so I went in. She sat on her bed in a pile of cash – a bunch of dollar bills all folded up like the small notes my friends and I used to pass around the classroom when the teacher wasn't

17

looking. Some of the bills were folded into different things, fans and rings and such. Some were balled up.

"Help me straighten these out," she demanded. "I already counted over four hundred bucks."

I helped her unfold the fortune. Our hands moved fast, like workers on an assembly line, and I discovered that money is oily. It smelled like perfume and cigarettes and alcohol while she told me all about her night:

"I was so nervous. The DJ played the wrong song at first, and I couldn't move. I walked off the stage and told him, 'I didn't request this song. You better change it. NOW!' I think I scared the shit outta him because he changed the song right away. After that, I started dancing and the cash started flying, literally." She pointed to a twenty-dollar bill that was folded into a paper airplane. "I made all this in only three hours."

"Are you serious?" I asked. It didn't seem possible. But by the time all the money was unraveled, we were staring at a healthy wad of six hundred and sixty-six dollars. Jackie freaked out because of the number 666.

"Oh my God! This is the devil!" she shouted, gazing at the money as though it were cursed.

"You don't even know what you're talking about," I insisted. "In my World Religion class, last semester, we learned that the whole 6-6-6 thing is a fluke. Don't even worry about it."

"Cool," she said, relieved. "You're so smart."

I crossed my eyes and stuck out my tongue as if to say: *Anyone could be smart, for* that *matter.*

"Do you believe I made all this money in just three hours?" She sounded so proud of herself.

"Yeah, I believe it," I said. If you saw my sister, you'd believe it, too.

"Some of the dancers I met do it full time. They say the best money to be made is downtown at The Lion's Den. It's real classy there – well – classy in terms of go-go bars. The dancers at Visions are pigs. They're disgusting. One girl shoved a *Blow Pop* up her crotch; then she shoved it into a customer's mouth. It was nauseating. I wanted to puke when I saw that. I *definitely* can't work there, so I'm getting an audition at The Lion's Den tomorrow night. Wanna come with?"

"And do what? Watch you?"

"Audition," she clarified.

"Me? Are you out of your mind? It's not for me."

"Why not? You're already modeling *nude*, aren't you? If you dance, at least you'll be in a G-string." She was serious, but I was laughing. The only G string I was interested in was the G string on my violin.

"Modeling's one thing, dancing's another. And besides, aren't you worried about bumping into someone you know? This is Philly. You're bound to see someone." I had a point there.

"I don't care. I'm auditioning tomorrow night."

"I'll stick to modeling. You do the dancing ... Listen, I have an early class in the morning, so I should get back to sleep now."

"Here, take this before you go." She handed me two twenties and a ten. "It's a tip – for helping me straighten out the money."

"Cool," I said, quickly accepting the cash. "That's the easiest fifty bucks I ever made in my life."

"Yeah, and now I can say I made 616 instead of 666."

I fell asleep and dreamed I was in a Chinese restaurant, opening piles of fortune cookies full of dollar bills.

CHAPTER THREE

Dictionary Skills

I had an awful itch on my butt while posing for the art class during the fourth week of my employment. All through the music of Simon and Garfunkel, Antonio Vivaldi, and Andreas Vollenweider, I refrained from scratching while silently rehearsing my resignation.

During the breaks, I'd go into the bathroom to see what the hell was on my ass, but I couldn't get a glimpse of it in the mirror – too low. Convinced that I'd caught some sort of infection from either the mustard cushion or the purple robe, I grew completely disgusted with the job. The itch was unbearable.

After class, Jordan asked me to go with him to an art opening at PCA (Philadelphia College of Art) on Broad Street. Even though the invitation was optional, I really had no choice. Art is my passion. It's a window through which I can see the world with new eyes; it's like a drug. There was a magical force embedded in the idea of an entire show. Perhaps I would gain a fresh understanding of nature, of time, of anything. The infinite possibilities were impossible to resist.

Jordan found a parking spot right away, which was pretty lucky in that part of the city, only a few blocks from PCA. It usually takes much longer to park the van. And since the show wasn't scheduled to open for another forty-five minutes, we took our time strolling up Spruce Street.

We turned onto Broad and continued. Then we stopped at the corner of Broad and Pine in front of a health food store called Natural Foods. I gazed the many advertisements in the window. One stood out: *Homeopathic Cures for Skin Conditions.* I scratched my ass. Next to it was a *Help Wanted* sign. "Let's go in," Jordan said. "I'm hungry." He was a big guy, and he was always up for a meal.

It smelled like health in there – not the sweaty health of a spa, but rather the aromatic health of naturalists, hippies. The place was small and cozy and filled with many products that I happened to be familiar with, thanks to Gina, Jessie's mother. Gina joined up with the health-food fanatics in the '70s – around two decades earlier – because Jessie and her little brother had been pretty sick when they were kids. They both had childhood diabetes, and health food became something of a religion in their house. Gina filled up wooden salad bowls with vitamins twice a day. Jessie could swallow fistfuls at a time. I can barely get one Motrin down my throat without gagging. They drank carrot juice and spinach juice every twenty-four hours, and when the trays of wheat grass in their living-room window grew tall enough, they'd juice that too. I could handle most of what they consumed, but that wheat-grass juice tasted exactly like my front lawn. I gagged on it.

Gina taught Jessie how to control her diabetes, but she didn't follow through too well. She liked to smoke and drink and ended up in the hospital pretty often. In fact, it was during one of her low-blood-sugar episodes when we first met at The High School for the Creative and Performing Arts in South Philly. I majored in Instrumental Music; Jessie majored in Visual Art.

One day in the school library, Jessie was screaming and cursing: "Where're the fuckin' books on the Holocaust?" She was doing research in the throes of a major attack. The Art Department participated in a Holocaust project each year, and all the Art majors were required to enter the contest for a grade. Jessie needed references: "The fuckin' Nazis! Fuckin' Germany! Could somebody fuckin' help me?" She fell into a shelf, knocking an entire row of books onto the floor. I ran over. Her eyes rolled into the back of her head like marbles. "Food," she whispered softly. No one else around seemed to hear the word. I had a roll of cherry Lifesavers in my pocket and popped one into her mouth as quickly as I could manage it.

The reason why I had those cherry Lifesavers is because I love anything cherry. When I find something with a cherry on it, I buy it. About a month ago, I found the *softest* tank top with a tiny cherry pattern on it at a thrift store in West Philly. Now it's my favorite shirt, and it only cost me forty cents! My favorite pair of underwear has giant cherries printed on the butt cheeks. I've been wearing a pair of jeans for four years that have cherry patches stitched onto the knees. And, when I was a little girl, my favorite pajamas had five cherry buttons: four on the shirt and one on the bottoms. I wore those pajamas every night

– for as long as I could – even after the knees ripped.

It's a good thing I had those cherry Lifesavers in my pocket. I didn't really know what diabetes was at that time. My grandfather had it, and I knew he had to monitor his sugar, but that's all I knew.

Jessie came back to life. "You're beautiful," she said in the *cherriest* voice I'd ever heard, and we immediately became best friends. We rode the subway together that day. She injected insulin into her belly, right in front of all the passengers. Her belly looked pregnant, but it wasn't. It had been that way her whole life, extra skin or something. I nicknamed her *Jezebelly*. She nicknamed me *Brie Cheese*. She pointed the syringe into her cheeseburger belly and looked like a heroine addict. Everyone on the subway stared. I always love a good dramatic moment.

During our lunch periods at school, I'd spend my money on pizza, cheese steaks, or any other greasy crap they served in the cafeteria. Jessie always had a packed lunch, and she'd trade her tofu-tahini-and-bean-sprout sandwiches on seven-grain whole wheat for any slop I was eating. I'd slurp her organic soymilk while she downed my can of Coke.

As our best-friendship grew, I'd often visit her house, and from her mother Gina, I learned all about vitamins, juicing, and health-food nuts. So I felt at ease asking the skinny guy behind the counter of Natural Foods, "Are you still hiring? I saw the sign in the window."

"You'll have to speak with Niomi," he replied in a British accent. "Wait here. I'll see if she's available." He walked to the back of the store, strutting his *stuff*

24

like a fashion model down a runway. I tried not to laugh out loud.

Jordan ordered two veggie burgers at the lunch counter. I wondered if one was for me. While we waited, the owner came over to see about my inquiry. She was a very short, knock-kneed woman with dark hair who squinted through outdated Sally Jesse Raphael glasses. "Hi. I'm Niomi – I'm the owner. Are you looking for a job?" She seemed to be smiling too much and caught me off guard.

"Hi, I saw the sign in the window. My name's Bree. I'm interested in working here, part-time, if you're still hiring."

"Are you an art student at PCA?" she asked. There was a good amount of five-o'clock shadow on her chin and around her cheeks. It reminded me of the bearded witches in *Macbeth*.

"No, I'm an English major, over at Temple University. Actually, I started out as a music major at Ester Boyer – I play the violin – but I recently switched majors."

"*Cool*," she said, slipping comfortably into a hippy tone of voice. "I graduated from Temple with a degree in English. Isn't that *cool*?" She perked right up and acted as though we were cosmically connected by this coincidence. I immediately felt the need to change my major again, but I smiled and acted like I was impressed by her English degree. "We're in need of kitchen help. Is that the kind of work you're interested in?" she asked. Her whiskers were so distracting. It was difficult to stop myself from staring at them. In an effort to look elsewhere, my eyes rested upon her bulging pregnant belly, and I was surprised that I hadn't noticed it sooner. Everything about this woman was strange.

"Sure. I'd love to work in the kitchen," I said, glancing from her stomach back up to her stubble.

"Do you have any experience with health food?" she asked.

"Oh yeah. I grew up on it," I lied. I had been raised on meals of meat and potatoes, TV dinners, and macaroni and cheese from a box. My favorite green vegetables were cut string beans from a can that had a picture of the Jolly Green Giant on it. Most of my childhood memories of food products have visual images attached: the Campbell's Soup kids, the Keebler Elves, the Little Debbie girl, the Morton Salt girl, the Sun Maid raisin lady, Chef Boyardee, Mary Jane … "I'm a bona fide granola girl," I smiled.

"*Cool*," she said again, smiling and squinting all over the place. "I'll get an application from the office."

The application was full of questions, like a test: *What's the difference between a vegetarian and a vegan? Why is white flour bad for you? What does organic mean?* I did my best and got the job while eating a veggie burger with Jordan at the lunch counter.

"What time does your sister's wedding start?" he asked.

My sister Mona was getting married that weekend. The gala event was only three days away. Jordan was my escort. He thought he was my date.

"One o'clock," I said. "Don't forget to pick up

your tux."

It felt like we were going to the prom again, in a way. But this wedding wasn't nearly as exciting for me as the prom had been. The wedding wasn't about me; it was Mona's big day. I was excited for her, but there was so much momentum building up at home. The tension was gaining. Proms are much simpler than weddings.

After the art show – which didn't impress me the way I had hoped – I convinced Jordan to take me to The Lion's Den to see Jackie dance. Her audition had gone well, as I knew it would, and she was hired to dance there five nights a week. She proudly told me that they only hire the *best* dancers to work there five nights a week. It was a real honor or something. Most of the dancers only got scheduled two times a week.

In addition to the salary from her full-time job doing nails, the cash she earned from dancing quickly turned her into quite the breadwinner. The money poured down upon her. Drenched in cash, she couldn't keep up with it, so I received the task of unraveling the oily green bills. She paid me fifty bucks each time I helped her out. Her fortune was my fortune. Sometimes I'd count over a thousand dollars and never less than eight hundred.

The money turned me on. There was so much of it. I'd often fantasize about how I'd spend it if I were to make that kind of cash. But I didn't feel as though I had enough confidence to dance around a bar without a stitch of material covering my top. And what really frightened me were the spike heel shoes and boots that the dancers wore. My idea of thigh-high boots was moccasin-style: flat, suede, and full of fringe. I had been alternating between wearing them and my Birkenstock clogs since high school. I dressed in ripped jeans and Guatemalan sweaters, beaded earrings and cowboy hats. Go-go dancers had long, painted claws extending from their fingertips. My nails had been short and stubby for as long as I can remember, mainly due to the many years I spent practicing the violin. Jackie gave me nail tips once, just for fun, and I couldn't do anything with them, couldn't even button up my Levi's 501 jeans. The idea of go-go dancing in high heels and long nails seemed equivalent to eating a dessert of ice cream and pickles. They just don't go together. Working at the health food store was more my speed.

*

Although Jordan's not the kind of guy who hangs out in go-go bars, he grew awkwardly stimulated once we were in The Lion's Den. "This place is like a Manet painting," he said with a quiver in his voice. I didn't really want to go there with him, but they don't let females walk in unless a male accompanies them. It's definitely some form of discrimination. I don't know how it's legal.

The lights were all lavender and blue, beautiful. The dancers were all over the place, all topless. There were at least five different stages. The place was cavernous. *Wow, Planet Go-Go!* I thought, as I looked around for Jackie.

Men were placing dollar bills in between the dancers' breasts, behind their G-strings, and in their

28

panty crotches. There was an art to the placement of the dollar; everyone was a master of the art. They all looked professional, dancers and customers alike. I felt completely out of place, completely thrilled.

Jordan's silence was unnatural for him. I could tell he felt both turned on and embarrassed at the same time. My eyes surveyed the place. My stomach tightened when I thought I spotted my brother-in-law-to-be in the crowd. The tightening of my stomach was quickly accompanied by a slight dizziness as his face came into focus each time the disco ball threw a spotlight on it. It was Mona's fiancé, Steven, surrounded by all his friends, enjoying his Bachelor Party. "Holy shit," I uttered. And before I had a chance to fully interpret the peculiarity of the moment, the DJ announced the next dancer: "Jackie." She didn't even use a stage name.

Pour Some Sugar on Me by Def Leppard poured through the Den. As the patrons witnessed the lioness on stage, they were mesmerized. As was I. Jackie flashed through the purple and blue rays of light, wearing a black cowboy hat, double-strapped high heels, a leather biker jacket, and a pair of shredded daisy dukes. *I'm gonna borrow that cowboy hat tomorrow*, I thought.

Slowly and provocatively she unbuttoned her shorts. Slowly and provocatively she lowered them off, revealing a silver-studded G-string. The short, leather jacket she wore had an airbrushed portrait of Jackie sprayed onto the back. It was pretty tacky, but *man* could she dance, kick, and wrap herself around the pole like an X-rated angel.

29

When she took off her jacket, I shot a glance over at Steven and his squarer-than-square buddies. They were settling the tab with the bartender. I didn't let Steven see me as he left. His face was a fire engine.

Jackie beamed when she spotted Jordan and me in the crowd. She came right up to us and bought us a round. Jordan ordered a beer. I ordered a glass of red wine. I only drink red wine. I didn't tell Jackie that Steven had been there. Just didn't want to.

On the way back home, we passed by Visions. There was a neon sign on the building that flashed "sTOPLESS GO-GO." The s in "stopless" was lower case, and all the other letters were upper case.

"Stopless" isn't even a word. I looked it up in the dictionary.

CHAPTER FOUR

White Wedding

On Friday afternoon, I became the assistant to the chef behind the lunch counter at Natural Foods. She was a redheaded, orange-skinned woman named Nanette who was wholeheartedly devoted to the Macrobiotic cause. Health food is one thing; Macrobiotics takes it to another level. Nanette taught me how to roll *Mock Sushi*, how to bake a dish called *Not-a-Drop-of-Tuna Casserole*, and how to mix *Un-Chicken Salad* with "positive energy." She also taught me that almost everything *white* is unhealthy. No white flour. No white sugar. No white rice.

It was pretty ironic that the owner's husband Nick, who also worked there, was busy snorting *white* powder up his nose every chance he got.

In the back of the store, the door to the bathroom wasn't really a door, only an accordion-style piece of white plastic that barely reached the frame. While passing by it on my way to the walk-in fridge, I couldn't resist a peek. I saw Nick seated backwards on the toilet seat, cutting through white lines with a rusty razor blade on the lid of the ugly toilet. Then he emerged from the bathroom like a newly charged Energizer Monkey.

Nanette rolled her eyes as he passed by. She knew what he was up to. Everyone knew, except for his hairy, pregnant wife Niomi. She was too busy counting the money in the register drawers, and too busy plucking the hairs on her chin to notice her dope-fiend husband. He was dopey – kind of like Barney Rubble from *The Flintstones*. And it was this dopiness that always made Niomi laugh. If she'd known about his other dopiness, she wouldn't have been laughing so much.

By the end of my shift, my fingers turned a bright shade of orange from juicing carrots. There were so many orange-skinned juice addicts who patiently lined up for it all day long, treating me like some kind of carrot-juice goddess. As a result, I acquired orange hands.

The customers, for the most, were a polite bunch, extra kind in their *hip and groovy* ways, but there was this one guy who got banned from the store when evening arrived. He aimed to buy a product called *Guarana*, some type of herbal speed. When he discovered that the store was out of stock, he threw a fit:

"You people are stashing it somewhere for yourselves. You're hiding it from the costumers. You better get it out from your hiding spot. I'm a paying customer!" he clucked, all plumped up like a rooster.

"You better hit the road man, or this bat's gonna hit your face." Nick pulled a baseball bat from behind the register counter and chased the guy out of the store, down the block. We all watched from the door. Addicts are funny like that.

I told Nanette about the rash on my ass. She said that it sounded like ringworm and suggested Witch

Hazel. I took a bottle off the shelf before leaving for the night.

*

A war had erupted at home, but I knew it would end as a comedy. Shakespearean comedies always end with a wedding, and Mona's wedding was quickly approaching — but not quickly enough. There was too much conflict to work out in the meantime. After Steven witnessed Jackie stripping on stage at The Lion's Den, my father insisted that she find somewhere else to work as a dancer. The pressure was on:

"Eh, maybe dancing in Philly's not such a good idea. People are saying that they've seen you. You better find somewhere out-of-state if you want to dance," my father argued.

"No way!" Jackie shouted. "If people aren't comfortable around dancers, then they have no business being in a go-go bar in the first place."

Jackie's not the type to be easily pushed around. But when my father received two more calls that same night about her dancing at The Lion's Den – one from his nephew, and one from a guy who belonged to his lodge – I could tell she began to consider other options. The whole thing was shaking up our house during the stressful time before the wedding.

Then my old boyfriend Matt-the-Drama-Major from high school called. I hadn't heard from him in over a year:

"Hey, Bree. It's Matt. How've ya been?"

"Great," I said. "What's up?"

"I saw your sister last night at The Lion's Den, and was wondering if maybe you could get me a date with her. She's *so* hot."

"Oh yeah? You really think so?" I asked, not knowing what else to say.

"Your sister could wake up in a pile of dirty laundry and *still* look great. Whaddya say? Will ya hook me up?"

"I don't know, Matt. She's pretty busy these days, but I'll see what I can do." I couldn't believe he actually said that bit about the dirty laundry.

"Do you still have my phone number?" he asked.

"Of course, I do."

"Thank you *so* much ... but don't forget."

"Don't worry. I'll talk to her," I assured him, although I knew I wouldn't.

"You're the best!" he exclaimed.

Whenever someone wants you to do something for them, they always say *you're the best.*

I was kind of bothered by the call, but didn't tell Jackie about it. I wasn't about to burst her bubble. Her out-of-control confidence level was admirable, and the fifty bucks she paid me for straightening out her dancing money was adding up nicely. My hands were getting quicker and quicker each time. Why would I mess things up? I was on her side. And besides, she surprised me that same day with a pair of sunglasses that had red frames in the shape of cherries with green stems at the top. They were the coolest sunglasses I'd ever seen.

"Leave her alone, dad," I rebelled. "She's right. If people can't handle seeing her dance, then they should just stay the hell out of the bar. She's only doing what she wants. Shakespeare would've agreed … like in the play *Hamlet* … when Polonius gave advice to his son. He said, 'To thine own self be true.'"

"Polonius was a *fool*, you *idiot*! You better shut your mouth and keep it shut," he said in a rage.

I quickly got out of the kitchen, went into the bathroom, and bent over by the mirror on the sliding shower door. Peering through the space between my knees, I inspected the rash. *What the hell is ringworm?* I wondered as I applied the Witch Hazel. It calmed the itch for about a half a minute. I applied some more. It calmed the itch for about ten seconds.

The next morning the rash was worse: redder and puffier.

I wasn't scheduled to work that day, but got a call from Niomi, asking me to come in. "Nanette has to leave after she cooks the specials, and I need someone to serve in the kitchen. Can you do it?" she asked. I agreed because I wanted to escape the insanity of my household. I also wanted to tell Nanette that the Witch Hazel wasn't working.

I took the El, got off at 15th Street, and walked down Broad. Some guy sitting across from me on the train was jerking off with his pants on. I felt bad for him, so I acted like I didn't notice. He was mentally disabled or something. I stared out the window through a Jerry Curl stain and dreamed of owning a used Jeep Cherokee, forest-green with red pinstripes.

If only I could dance with Jackie, I could buy a jeep for cash in just a few months. Then I wouldn't have to witness crazy people jerking off in public.

Nanette was really sick. She'd been fighting leukemia for five years, and her cancer had just come out of remission. Macrobiotics had been working like a charm since her initial diagnosis, but now her health had been thrown a curve ball. The regular doctors wanted to try experimental chemotherapy when they received her most recent round of blood count results. That's why she was leaving the store early. She had an appointment with Jacob Wellerstein, the local macrobiotic guru. Nanette was determined to hit that curve ball out of the ballpark. She figured that macrobiotics had more potential driving power than experimental chemotherapy.

Before she left the store, I told her about the Witch Hazel. "Try some Tea Tree Oil. And stay away from foods that are yon," she suggested. "Okay," I agreed, without any clue as to what *yon* foods actually were.

There was this Italian guy who walked around the store, scribbling notes on a clipboard. He was in charge of stocking the shelves and taking inventory. Every so often, I'd catch him staring at me. His name was Dante Arrigucci. He had smooth olive skin, soft black curls, and large blue eyes. And in his super-tight sweatpants, an extra-large bulge was firmly stocked for all to ponder. His bulge was a constant distraction that I had to contend with. Watching him work was sort of like watching one of the male ballet dancers – like Baryshnikov or Nureyev. My father would often call my sisters and me into the living room to watch them dance on TV: *"Girls! Get in here ... Watch how he leaps through the air."* I always ended up staring at their bulges.

Dante wasn't really my type, though. He wore heavy-metal concert shirts and looked more like someone who might interest Jackie. But that afternoon, after I put a small bottle of Tea Tree Oil in my pocket, he put his hot mouth in my ear and whispered, "I love you." My palms broke out in a sweat. The space between my legs vibrated. *Romeo?* I thought.

My ears are highly sensitive. They were still sending flaming red messages to my limbic center as Dante exited the store. I watched his Baryshnikov butt disappear into a long, white car left over from the '70s.

The next day it snowed for the first time that year. Everyone threw white rice at the bride and groom. Everything was white. There were white roses, a white wedding canopy, white tablecloths, white candles ...

The bride and groom fed each other white wedding cake and danced to Billy Joel's *Just the Way You Are.* I knew that Mona would never change the color of her hair or try a new fashion. She and Steven would stay just the way they were, for always, like wax people behind glass in a museum.

I gazed at Steven in his tux and Mona in her white wedding gown. They had been together for so many years, and now they were having their white wedding. It was nice seeing them so happy in love, but I kept thinking about what Nanette had said ... about *white* being bad for people. I recalled the tragedy of *Othello* and the way he described Desdemona's skin just before he smothered her to death: " ... *That whiter skin of hers than snow and smooth as monumental alabaster."* I almost started a conversation about it with Jordan.

Then I took my father's advice, and kept my mouth shut.

CHAPTER FIVE

In Lust

The Tea Tree Oil wasn't working either. The whole thing was pretty embarrassing, so I gave up on finding a cure and just scratched my ass like a dog with fleas.

Dante made a hobby of whispering triple-X nothings in my ear. And although the tickling sensations that raced down my spine seemed to put me on the edge of torture, I didn't stop him. I never pulled my ear away from his mouth. I liked it. And besides, it gave me something to look forward to.

Then there was Kate Jones, my lesbian admirer. She worked the cash register at the front of the store and bore a striking resemblance to Melissa Etheridge. Kate called me "Hon" or "Love" whenever she spoke to me and gave me an occasional friendly slap on the butt, like the football players. She always smiled my way with sparkles in her eyes. Whenever the store wasn't busy, her hands somehow managed to settle themselves upon the back of my neck, gently applying pressure, easily working out all the spots and knots that had settled within. Her talent as a masseuse impressed me, and I sort of flirted with her a little. At first it seemed harmless because I really enjoyed her massages. I didn't think she was *serious* about me. I certainly wasn't serious about her. I was just kidding around a little – big mistake.

Later that week, Kate asked me out on a date. I laughed out loud at the thought of it, but she wasn't joking. When I told her that I wasn't gay, she scolded me and said I had led her on. She lectured me on the cruelties of deception, and acted like I had hurt her in a deeply personal way.

At first I felt bad about it and tried to smooth things over. But Kate didn't let up. She blew the whole thing out of proportion, and acted exactly like a woman scorned – moping around the store – refusing to make eye contact with me when I spoke to her – playing the role of the heartbroken victim – as though we had actually had a serious relationship! It was absurd!

And when Kate realized how much my affection for Dante had grown, she was furious. She accused me of being a closet lesbian, and made no effort to hide her outrageous jealousy. I didn't even know what to say. She was so bitter. So I just acted like nothing had happened, because *nothing did happen*!

It only took a week's worth of employment to produce so much ado about nothing at the health food store. Drama wrapped itself tightly around my world, like a straight jacket.

Located in the "gay section" of the city – the "gayborhood" – Natural Foods had a steady stream of gay clientele. Most of them were just everyday people who possessed an abundance of gay pride and an awareness of the constitutional phrase that "all men [and women] are created equal." Some were overt with regards to their sexuality, and some were reserved.

One guy named Tommy Cavicoli shared with me

the personal details of how his father disowned him when he "came out." I could tell it was a very painful yet important memory for Tommy as he relayed the details to me at the lunch counter. Tommy was a rather short and very good-looking man, who radiated with physical and mental health. I was impressed by his honesty. I was honored by his trust. Although I was a stranger whom he had just recently met, he somehow sensed that he was safe with me. That he was in the presence of a true human being, free from judgment. The way he'd open up and tell me his stories made me feel like a bartender, even though I was only serving carrot juice.

Tommy was a professional actor and a published writer. He inspired my creativity and my self-esteem. He made me feel as though any aspiration that went through my imagination was attainable. And although Tommy Cavicoli was the brightest star among the gay clientele that I met at the health food store, there were many others who left such an impression upon me.

But then there was Kate Jones, my lesbian admirer who seemed to take pleasure in my discomfort. And there were others at Natural Foods who had similar convictions. A few individuals made it a point to draw a thick line of distinction between the hetero and homo worlds we inhabited. Even though they were the exceptions, they bothered me, and they seemed to do it on purpose.

There was this guy named Lenny, one of the regulars, who always said something crude about his personal interests. He was very tall and extremely skinny, and he didn't look healthy at all. During one of my afternoon shifts, he sat at the lunch counter, sipping a Knudsen's Boysenberry Spritzer. As he held up the beverage, he asked me, "Do you know why this is my favorite flavor?"

"No," I replied.

Using his fingers, he covered up a portion of the word *Boysenberry* printed on the can, revealing just the first four letters: *Boys.*

"That's why it's my favorite flavor. Get it? BOYS! *Hee-hee-hee!*" Lenny giggled like a little girl.

"You're sick in the head," Dante said, smacking Lenny over his head with the clipboard. Then Dante covered my ear with his hand and made out like he was telling me a secret. Then he made out with my ear. My body responded with the usual organic reaction.

*

In the kitchen, Nanette persisted in her struggle against cancer. Her diet was limited to brown rice and Bancha tea, a combination that was supposed to cleanse her body. But in spite of this special formula, she continued to hemorrhage. I admired her willpower and her strength. She was unstoppable. She swam at the JYC for an hour each morning before she cooked and served the lunch specials.

And then one day, to my surprise, she decided to set up an after-store-hours cooking class for people with HIV/AIDS, to teach them about foods that strengthen the immune system. She hired me to be her assistant. I was excited. Natural Foods provided me with an endless supply of stimuli and excitement.

42

Our first cooking class consisted of four me
bald and bearded bus driver who worked for SEPTA
arrived in uniform. He was a Black man, but he
looked Orange and very sick. The second guy also
sported a dark beard. He stood tall and gorgeous and
looked like a Greek god. "I got AIDS from a blood
transfusion in Beirut," he said, letting me know he
was straight from the start. The remaining two men
were short, thin, and well dressed, closely resembling
a pair of Latin-American bookends. Channel 12
showed up to film the class.

I did all the chopping. Nanette did all the cooking.
She steamed carrots, daikon, and kale for the class,
demonstrating how to chop the roots and leaves in a
way that maximizes the energy of each slice. She
taught the men how to properly cuff their hands for
rolling Japanese Brown Rice Balls, counting to thirty-
three as they formed each wad. With her index finger,
she demonstrated the correct way to drill a hole into
the center of the sticky rice ball, just before shoving
the required amount of purple Umeboshi Plum Paste
in there. The plum paste looked like the rash on my
ass and reminded me to scratch. *I hope the camera
guy didn't record that*, I worried. The men wrapped
the rice balls, like little presents, in black sheets of
Nori seaweed, and rolled them again, thirty-three
times. "The number thirty-three has healing power,"
Nanette informed the audience.

There was so much enthusiasm, and everyone
seemed to enjoy the class, but a few disturbing
thoughts rolled around my mind during that hour. I
know it's unfair to say, but I felt like I was surrounded

by a pestilence. In order to combat the upsetting feeling, I imagined there was a plastic bubble all around me – protecting me – just like the one in the movie *The Boy in the Plastic Bubble*. I also imagined myself deep inside the rice ball, protected by walls of seaweed. *I'm The Girl in the Rice Ball.* It was a relief when the class finally ended. I was happy to go home.

*

Mona and Steven returned that day from their Mexican honeymoon and moved into their new house. They had bought the house some time before the end of the summer, but they wouldn't move in together until they were officially married. That's how they ran their lives, prim and proper all the way, navigating from one ninety-degree angle to the next.

The not-so-proper Jackie took my father's advice in the end. One of the dancers at The Lion's Den told her about a go-go bar out in Princeton, New Jersey called Studio 67. It's illegal to dance topless in the county of its location, so all the dancers have to cover their tops. It's a real conservative, affluent town. Jackie made more money there than she'd made at The Lion's Den. She kept telling me to go up with her, but I was having too much fun at Natural Foods. And aside from that, my rash was spreading, growing, getting redder and redder like a strawberry. *What kind of go-go dancer runs around with a strawberry on her ass?*

The following week, our cooking class was down to three. One of the Latin bookends had died, but not from AIDS. He was killed in a plane explosion on his way back from London. We had a moment of silence for the dearly departed before preparing Silky Squash Soup, Tempeh-No-Meat-Loaf, and Sesame Kuzu Pudding. Nanette could make a rag taste good. I loved working with her, but felt awful about the Latin guy. In the middle of the lesson, I began to cry. The man from Channel 12 peeked out from behind his camera, uncertain about what to make of my tears. Nanette tried comforting me with a hug, but when I wouldn't let up, she got real serious: "The energy you exude will flow into the food you're preparing," she advised. "So be careful about sadness or anger. Your food will taste awful." I forced myself to stop crying, but it wasn't easy. I really am much too sensitive.

When I left the store that night, Dante was waiting for me alone by the dumpster. We walked down Broad Street arm in arm, leg in leg. It was cold outside, but I was in heat.

"When are you coming home with me?" he asked.

"Where do you live?" I was ready.

"In Overbrook."

"Where's that?" I didn't know anything about Overbrook. When I was younger, I used to watch an after-school show called *Dancin' On Air*, and a lot of the dancers would introduce themselves to the audience. *Hi, I'm Tina Marie. I'm 16 and I go to Overbrook High.* That's all I knew about Overbrook.

Dante explained, "I take the El train, westbound to 69th Street. My house is just a few blocks from there."

"I take the El, too. But I go *eastbound* to Bridge and Pratt in the opposite direction." *Damn it!* I thought. *We live in opposite directions. I'll never get a chance to go to his house. It's too far.*

"Well, I'm having a party in a few weeks. A bunch of friends are coming over to celebrate before I go to Europe. It's gonna be a big send-off. You should come," he said.

"You're going to Europe?" My heart ripped and sank like the Titanic.

"Yep, I'll be there for about a month. Do you think you can make it to the party?"

"I don't see why not. Will anyone else be there from Natural Foods?"

"I'm inviting everyone. But I don't know who's coming yet."

We arrived at the giant clothespin on Market Street and descended the spiral concrete staircase. As we inserted our tokens and passed through the turnstile, I got a strange feeling, like I had passed through a threshold of some sort. It was pretty quiet down there. One of the vendors was burning purple sticks of incense. The station smelled like a church.

We pressed against each other and kissed. It was the kind of kissing where time is a tunnel, and all I could do was travel down, down, down. I couldn't hear anything except the sound of the ocean, as though my head were trapped inside of a giant conch shell. My body drifted far in the feeling. I wanted to buy a big white dress and marry Dante right then and there in that leaky subway station. Our kissing continued through the roar of an approaching train, growing louder and louder, piercing the whirlwind in my pituitary gland. People ran to get on board as we kissed and pressed. His Baryshnikov bulge was delightful. His mouth tasted like pepperoni pizza.

I was wearing my favorite cable knit sweater-jacket over a pair of black spandex leggings. They were soaked through the crotch. I was so hot for him. We said our goodbyes while two more trains arrived and departed. *"Parting is such sweet sorrow ... "*

I fell asleep on the El and dreamed I was making love to Dante high up on an ancient balcony. It was weird because he was wearing a mask.

*

At home, Jackie modeled two large bags of costumes for me while I made another fifty bucks, unraveling another pile of money. She had been shopping for go-go attire that day at Erogenous Zone on South Street. I ranted and raved about Dante Arrigucci during her game of way-too-sexy dress-up in fishnets, sequins, pleather, leather, and lace.

"I hate to tell you this, but you're in lust," Jackie informed me. She had just gotten out of a long, destructive relationship and was convinced that being in lust was equivalent to being possessed by the devil. Bent on recognizing the difference between love and lust in her own life, her concern spilled over into mine.

"I'm not in lust. I'm in *love,*" I assured her.

"How can you be in love when you don't even know this guy?"

"I know him! What are you talking about?" Instead of sharing my excitement, she was questioning it. *How dare she?* I thought.

"If you know him so well, then tell me, what does he do?" It was hard to take her seriously while she posed in an erotic version of the American flag.

"He works at the health food store where I work, DUH."

"Okay, what does he do *besides* work at the health food store? You go to college. What does *he* do?"

"I don't know," I admitted. She had me on that point.

"You see what I mean. You don't even know this guy and already you think you're in love with him –"

"Wait, wait, wait … I know what he does." I suddenly remembered something. "He plays the guitar in a heavy-metal band. See. I know him," I beamed.

"You better find out more. I just don't want you to get hurt, Bree."

"Don't worry. I'll be okay." Her exaggerated concern began to annoy me, so I quickly changed the subject. "*Look, Jackie!* Look at how much money's here!" There were more big bills than I was used to handling, more fives, tens, and twenties. Jackie counted over thirteen hundred dollars.

"Princeton's awesome. You really should come up with me. They'll hire you in a second. The managers love me."

"Thanks, but no thanks. I'm staying right where I am."

CHAPTER SIX

Catching Flies With Honey

The SEPTA driver died the following week. Nanette called Channel 12 and cancelled the class. The whole thing depressed me. I didn't want to work in the kitchen anymore. *Everyone's sick in here. Not just pretend sick,* real *sick.* I got it in my head that all the people who ate at the lunch counter were unhealthy, diseased, dying. *It's the "Sick-Food" Store.*

I entered Niomi's office to speak to her about changing jobs. She was busy plucking herself. She had one of those tri-fold electric make-up mirrors plugged in with the *daylight* intensity bulbs turned on. Three different types of tweezers sat on her desk as she plucked away at her whiskers. It was a pretty unpleasant sight.

"You could work the register and stock the shelves," she suggested, pivoting the mirror to the magnified side.

"Great," I said. And it dawned on me that I'd be working alongside Dante. Then my *daylight intensity bulbs* lit up.

Niomi finally pulled out the whisker she'd been struggling with, and we both relished the satisfying moment.

A guy who looked like a Rastafarian was hired to

replace me in the kitchen. He called himself Amminadad, but his real name was Cecil Jones. I saw it on his paycheck. Amminadad tried to convince me that I wasn't really Jewish because I was white. "The true Jews are Black," he said.

"Maybe the true Jews are both Black *and* White," I responded, trying to even things out.

"*No, no, no!*" he laughed, shaking his overflowing-with-dreadlocks tam beret from side to side. "The true Jews are Black ... *ah-free-KAN* ... black. Not White."

"Oh yeah, try telling that to my parents." My family is as Jewish as Jewish gets, and no one could convince me otherwise, especially not some Rasta-head who puffed reefer in the walk-in fridge with Nick whenever the store wasn't busy.

Nick offered me drugs on a regular basis: cocaine, marijuana, Quaaludes. I'd already quit smoking marijuana, and wasn't about to start experimenting with coke or pills. Besides, I was already high on Dante Arrigucci. He was the only drug I needed – Couldn't get enough.

Early one evening while I was busy in the smallest compartment of the stock room, loading gallon-sized jars of honey onto a high shelf, two Wild West Wildflower jars rolled off and hit the floor, cracking open like giant glass eggs. The honey oozed out, thick and sticky. There was so much of it. I found Dante. "Will you help me clean up some honey?" "Sure, honey." We couldn't figure out exactly how to clean it up, but enjoyed tasting it for a while. The sweet potency of the honey was powerful, and, in the midst of enjoying the taste, I was reminded of the advice

50

that Friar Laurence gave to Romeo and Juliet at their secret wedding ceremony: *"The sweetest honey is loathsome in its own deliciousness ..."* What did he mean by that? We had analyzed the line earlier that week in class, but I couldn't remember a strand of the discussion. Love is so confusing.

I dipped my finger into the honey and spread it gently onto Dante's tongue. He did the same to me. I sucked his finger. He came in his pants. We were really getting off on each other when I realized we weren't alone. Kate Jones the lesbian was watching.

"You *heteros* make me sick!" She turned sharply around and marched towards the register. She reminded me of my sister Mona, in a twisted kind of way. Mona often made nasty comments to Jackie or me before disappearing into the silence of her own world. Then she'd hold an eternal grudge and ignore us.

One time, when I was around eighteen, while my parents were down the shore at the casino for the weekend, Jordan and I had been hanging out in the basement, smoking a joint. A little while later, we went up to the kitchen to satisfy our *munchies* with a bag of chips. Mona passed by and mumbled under her breath, "*Druggie.*" She said it just loud enough for me to hear. The way she said the word *druggie* was comical, and I laughed out loud, but her little comments often made our household very uncomfortable. So did her silence. I wouldn't hear another comical word from her until it was absolutely necessary for us to speak again.

But that wasn't the last we heard from Kate Jones

that night. She immediately found ways to communicate without speaking. Dante had been playing a Tesla cassette over the stereo system. Kate turned it off in the middle of a song and put on the Indigo Girls. In her lunatic lesbian way, she was trying to make a point.

She was *always* trying to make a point. No matter the weather, she wore the same denim jacket that was covered in buttons of varying sizes and colors; each had a *gay saying*; each conveyed a symbolic message that Kate assumed would affect her viewers in such a way that either their lives would be forever changed for the better, or they'd just realize what "lowly heteros" they really were, and, therefore, unworthy of being in the presence of such a grand display of "righteousness" – or so she thought. In reality, her jacket looked more like an airport security nightmare than anything else, bearing metal buttons with pink triangles and the double female astrological symbol. Buttons with sayings, such as *"She's With Me"* or *"Sorry I Missed Church, I've Been Busy Practicing Witchcraft and Becoming A Lesbian."*

I couldn't understand why she had to be so adamant about proclaiming her sexuality. Should everyone walk around with sexual-preference slogans pinned to their outerwear? I could just imagine the whole city rushing from place to place wearing buttons with proclamations, such as *"I Like It On Top"* or *"Doggy Style Works For Me"* or *"I Swallow."*

Maybe my thoughts about Kate were a little too harsh. I'm not totally insensitive. I understand that gays and lesbians are a minority, and that gay pride is real, but I couldn't figure out why Kate's lesbianism had to exude from every ounce of her being. She clearly resented me because I was a heterosexual woman in love with a man, and she had failed in her attempts to convert me. She tried to make me feel like I was really missing out on something. She actually told me: "If you're not gay, then you're *not* hip." Harassing me with her belittling remarks was like a game for her, but I tried not to let it bother me too much.

All I needed was my honey and a broken jar of honey in the wild corner of a stock room – and I was a happy hetero.

CHAPTER SEVEN

The Big Barbie Head

"Excuse me," Nanette interrupted, clearing her throat. She rarely ventured past the walk-in fridge, but there she stood in the stockroom, holding a large pair of scissors. Dante and I had been making out behind the empty water jugs. He tasted like an Italian hoagie.

"I know this is going to sound like an odd request, but can I cut off a piece of your hair?" Nanette asked.

"Whose hair?" I asked, confused. "His or mine?"

"Both. My blood count's off the chart, and I need to drink some hair tea."

"Hair tea!" Dante shouted. "Are you serious?"

"I know it sounds crazy. But I was told that if I combine yin and yon hair types, and boil them down to a powder for tea, then it might help. I'm desperate for a cure. I'll do anything they suggest down at the Macrobiotic Center. You can say no if you don't want to do it. But when I saw you two kissing, I realized you're the perfect yin and yon combination. You really are a cute couple."

"I'll shave my whole head if it'll help you, Nanette," Dante offered.

"Thanks, sweetie. But I only need a piece."

We bent our heads over. Nanette snipped off a chunk of each. His black curl and my brown wave looked intriguing through the tight grip of her orange hand. I still don't know which was yin and which was yon. Nanette thanked us as though we had just made a sacred sacrifice. It was nothing, really. You couldn't even see that any hair was missing. Having shared this pagan experience with Dante felt special, like an ancient ritual before marriage.

Speaking of hair, Jackie was ready to give up doing nails and started training for a hair license. She wanted to be a Colorist. Ever since we were little girls, she had wanted to be a hairdresser. Her favorite toy was the big Barbie head. It was supposed to be a present for all of us, but Jackie immediately possessed it and declared, "It's mine." And that was that. You couldn't even try reasoning with her either. She was the manic middle child who always got her way. Now she was ready to mix color and leave the comfort zone of the nail station. Ready to play with the big Barbie head again. I was her first guinea pig.

The whole thing made me nervous. I had never messed around with the color of my hair. My best friend Jessie was always changing her hair color. When I met her in the school library it was Eggplant – and shortly after that it was Fireball. One time she drenched her hair in Peroxide, and it turned Albino White. And after that she dyed it Blue-Black. But my favorite was when she soaked her head in a bowl of Kool-Aid and walked around looking like a human candy apple. Right now she's Platinum Blond – and not only does she color it herself, but she also cuts it herself. Sometimes her hair is real short and uneven and looks like a choppy work of art. Whenever the roots start growing out, she changes it again. Being her friend is so much fun because she's a true artist, always treating herself like a living canvas. I'm often surprised when we meet for coffee or something like that. I'll be searching around for a dome of Sunrise Gold only to find a ring of Crimson Violet hallowing her head. I've never even seen her natural hair color, but I bet it looks just as good as any of the other shades she's had. Jessie is gorgeous. Her eyes are trippy, like sky-blue kaleidoscopes overloaded with crystals. Most people are taken in by her beauty – probably because she looks more like a cheetah than she looks like a human – except for her blue eyes.

Jessie and I hadn't seen much of each other lately. After high school graduation, our best-friendship evolved into another realm. High school had afforded us the opportunity to see each other every day. And when the school week was over, our fun extended into the weekends with sleepovers, parties, family vacations, concerts, festivals, and more. We were inseparable. We identified with each other. We had the same taste in clothes, music, art, boyfriends, food, everything. In short, we were the archetypal pair of teenage best friends. A cliché in all its glory. But when high school ended and college began, we slowly grew apart and separated, like the branches of a tree. The divide was inevitable, sad yet exciting. We knew we had to grow as individuals, and we discovered that like the individual branches of a tree, we shared the same roots, the same well of inspiration. Although we were no longer addicted to each other's company on a daily basis, there were times when we'd end up together for a solid twenty-four hours. We'd get our

56

fill of each other, and it kept us afloat.

*

When my shift ended that afternoon, I said goodbye to Nanette before leaving the store. "What did the hair tea taste like?" I asked her. "Just use your imagination, kid," she said. I imagined it tasted like a delicious magic potion, since it was made from *double love.* But the expression on Nanette's face told otherwise.

Jackie picked me up from the health food store in her black 280 ZX sports car. Dante thought we were twins. Everyone thinks we're twins at first. We're two years apart, yet we've always looked exactly the same age. Mona's two years older than Jackie, and she doesn't look too much like us. She looks more like my mom, except she has my dad's curly hair. Jackie and I both look like my dad, except we have my mother's wavy hair.

Jackie drove me to the salon where she worked, and some gay guy named Omega coached her through the process. It was fun sitting there, feeling the paintbrush gliding down my hair, but the smell of the place was dizzying. I'd grown accustomed to the healing aroma of Nanette's cooking. The sensation of entering Natural Foods was delicious. You could immediately taste something good before you even ate anything. In contrast to that pleasurable event, I choked on chemicals the moment I entered the salon. Hair spray, nail polish, even the cigarette smoke bothered me, which was odd because I'd always been a smoker. Even before I was born I was a smoker. But since I'd been hanging around with Dante (who didn't smoke), rather than hanging around with Jessie (who always smoked), I had cut back a great deal. I never completely stop, though. It's awful. When my mother was pregnant with me, she craved cigarettes the entire time. "I smoked more cigarettes when I was pregnant with you than I ever smoked in my life," she told me. "We didn't know smoking was bad for you back then. The doctors never said anything about it." Thanks to the negligence of the medical field during 1970, nicotine is part of my chemical make-up, but it was really bothering me in the salon. I tried to concentrate on happy thoughts about Dante.

Jackie took an eternity while coloring my hair. She pushed my head down so hard that my chin bumped my clavicle. "*Ouch!*" I howled. "Do you have to be so aggressive?"

"Why is there a CHUNK of hair missing back here?" she demanded to know.

"There is?" I asked. I'd almost forgotten that Nanette had made tea out of my hair earlier that day.

"Yes, there's a HUGE chunk missing." She sounded so cocky.

"Oh, that. My friend Nanette needed it to make some kind of medicinal tea for her cancer," I said. It sounded reasonable.

"She made TEA out of your HAIR?"

"Mine *and* Dante's," I proudly added. "We both let her cut off a piece."

"You better quit that job. It's weird. It sounds like voodoo or something," she warned. Omega excused himself to the bathroom.

"Nanette is dying, Jackie. Wouldn't you give *your friend* a piece of *your hair* if she were *dying*?" I had her there. I knew she wouldn't deny it.

"Okay, just shut up. I need to concentrate," she insisted, and the conversation was over.

Omega returned with light-pink Shimmer on his wide, African-American lips. It looked good on him. He and Jackie talked about "sectioning" and "foil placements" over my head as though I didn't exist. I was just a head of hair for the day. The big Barbie head with a missing chunk.

I thought about Jordan. I'd been neglecting him. He left three messages on my answering machine that week, and I hadn't called him back once. I felt guilty about it while my highlights processed for twenty minutes.

Jackie took off the foils and washed my head. She scrubbed so hard it hurt. "Ouch! Take it easy!" I yelled.

"Shut up! Don't complain so loud. I don't need Omega hearing you complaining." Jackie gets real bitchy when she's under pressure. Then she adjusted the water. It was scalding hot, but I didn't say anything. Then she scratched my neck with her fingernail and squirted me in the eye with the hose. It was torture being her guinea pig.

After suffering over the sink, which felt more like a guillotine, Jackie straightened my hair with the blow dryer, burning me twice and pulling too hard with the big, round bristle brush. Again I suffered in silence. In the end, it was worth the pain.

"You! Look! Amazing!" Jackie sliced each word

into its own sentence.

I couldn't believe my reflection in the mirror. My used-to-be-just-brown head of hair looked fantastic, highlighted with caramel streaks and a few blond pieces. It reminded me of all my favorite fudge flavors in the candy store: chocolate fudge, vanilla fudge, peanut butter fudge. I never knew I could look that glamorous. I couldn't stop from staring at myself in the mirrors.

Everyone in the salon was impressed by Jackie's first attempt. They were sure she'd fail miserably, wanted her to fail miserably. People are always jealous of Jackie because she's gorgeous *and* talented. She showed me off around the salon as if I were some kind of prized canine at a dog show.

*

I called Jordan that night. "Hi, *Jordy*," I said with maple sweetness because I felt guilty about neglecting him.

"Hey! Where've you been?" he asked.

"Just busy. Between my new job and school, I barely have time to study."

"I miss you, Bree," he said.

"I miss you, too. Why don't you meet me tomorrow for lunch at the health food store around twelve o'clock? I have an early morning class. Then I'm working the afternoon shift. We can meet before I start."

"Sounds great, but first I have to stop at *Utrecht* for some art supplies. Wait for me if I'm a little late," he said.

I didn't mention anything to him about Dante. Jordan had always loved me more than just a friend. I felt guilty for being in love with someone else.

Mona and Steven came over that night just as Jackie was lugging her suitcase out the front door.

"What's in there?" Mona asked.

"My go-go costumes," Jackie proudly answered.

"I don't know *how* you do it!" Mona snipped.

"I don't know *how* you don't!" Jackie snapped.

"Ugh!" Mona groaned as she entered the house.

"Why do you let her *dance*?" She directed the question to my father. Challenging his authority is not something we do in the Yeager house.

"She's over eighteen. She can do whatever she wants," he declared. "And anyway, do you have any idea how much money she's making?" My dad was trying to convince Mona that go-go dancing was acceptable. That's like trying to convince a vegan to eat a greasy cheese steak.

Remembering the futility in arguing with my father, Mona changed the subject. "Your hair looks good, Bree," she said.

"Thanks. Jackie did it. She's a Colorist now. You should let her do your hair. You'd look great with some highlights," I said.

"No way. I'll never change the color of my hair."

"I love her just the way she is," Steven added.

They were holding true to the words of their Billy Joel wedding song, just like I thought they would.

"Hey Mona," I said. "Don't you work on Broad Street?" I knew she worked downtown in some kind of marketing agency, but wasn't sure about where.

"Uh-huh, I work at the Bellevue … on the 11th floor," she said.

"I'm working on Broad Street, too. I got a job at a health food store on the corner of Broad and Pine. It's called Natural Foods. If you're ever up that way, come in and eat some lunch."

"You mean, you're not *modeling* anymore?" she asked.

"No, I quit modeling. Sitting still was driving me crazy."

"Good. At least I can say I have *one* normal sister." She sounded so relieved. "I'll come up and get a salad when I have some extra time. Just give me the phone number, so I can call and make sure you're working."

I scribbled down the number on a piece of newspaper.

Normal sister? Was I the normal sister? I was having orgasms over honey with someone I barely knew, donating my hair for tea, and praying for a cure for the rash on my ass so that I could possibly become a go-go dancer. I didn't feel very *normal,* but it was nice knowing that Mona thought I was.

CHAPTER EIGHT

My People

The following day, my universe simultaneously collided and expanded. Jordan met me for lunch at *Natural Foods*. I stored his art supplies from *Utrecht* in the stock room. The bundles were heavy. He wasn't thrilled with my new hair color.

"I can't believe you changed your hair. It's nice, but I like you better the way you *naturally* are," he said, petting my head. Even though he thought he was giving me a compliment, he sounded a lot like my brother-in-law Steve, which put me off a bit.

Nanette served us the day's special: Sesame Udon Noodles with Ginger-Scented Vegetables. I couldn't wait to ask her about the hair tea. I wanted it to be the magic cure she'd been searching for. I kept wondering if it was working, but the dark crescent moons under her eyes didn't look like a good sign.

"I have something important to tell you," Jordan said. He smelled like Downy fabric softener again. I loved that about him. No matter how often we'd hang out together, the fresh scent of his clothes was always surprising. It lifted me up, but the "important" message he was about to deliver weighted me down with dread. I got the feeling that he was about to declare his love for me.

"What is it?" I asked through an udon noodle. He

handed me an acceptance letter from the Tyler School of Art. I read the first line.

"Wow, Jord! Congratulations! – I didn't even know that you applied to Tyler – Oh my God – I'm so happy for you! – You really deserve it – You're such a good artist." I threw my arms around his neck.

"Hold on, Bree – there's more –" he added. "I already registered for a semester in Rome – at Tyler's campus over there."

"You're kidding! This is such great news." I was happy for him and relieved for myself. I had dreaded his important message in vain.

"But that's not the *most* important thing I wanted to tell you," he quickly added. His puppy-dog eyes lit up. A noodle fell off my plate.

"What is it?" I asked, but already knew.

He cleared his throat and held my eyes with his. "I'm in love with you, Bree," he proclaimed, reaching for my hand as my smile fell off my face. "I've been in love with you ever since seventh grade. I had to finally tell you because – lately – I've been feeling like I'm gonna explode –"

Nanette was listening to our conversation from behind the lunch counter as she adjusted the setting on the pressure cooker. She shot me a look of distress.

"I can't believe you're saying this now – after all this time – since seventh grade!" I was surprised by that part despite my former premonition. "Why did you wait so long to tell me?"

"I don't know, Bree – I really don't. If you feel the same way about me – that I feel about you – then I won't go to Rome. I'll stay here and we can be together. If not, then don't worry about it. I'll survive – Life goes on – I'll just travel around and do my own thing."

I didn't know how to react or what to say. The moment was cliché, full of awkward silence. I needed another cliché to occur, to be *saved by the bell*, or something else unoriginal.

And then, in a flash, Kate Jones was hanging over my shoulder. "Your sister Mona's on the phone," she said. *The bell saved me. It's a miracle!* I thought.

I told Jordan I'd be right back and headed towards the front of the store to take the call. Kate accompanied me down the aisle, making her usual narcissistic small talk.

"What did you *do* to your hair?" she asked.

"I painted it," I answered.

"It looks good on you, but I didn't think you were *the type*."

Type? What type? I wondered.

Kate was up, way too high, on her lesbian mare named Superiority Complex. Since she didn't mess around with her own hair color – and since I did – it gave her a reason to judge and label me as some other *type*, some *inferior type*, and she actually had the balls to say it. *Who does this girl think she is?* I felt like slapping her across the face as she handed me the phone.

Mona told me she was heading up to the store for lunch right away. *Crash!* Then Dante walked in. *Crash!* He grabbed me as I hung up the phone, pushing my weak spots in all the right places. "I'm in love with you," he said, blowing the words into my highly sensitive ear. "Your hair looks beautiful." He stroked my new colors. I glanced over to see if Jordan could see us. He was looking directly at me. *Crash! Boom! Bam!* I returned to the lunch counter.

"I don't want to hurt you, Jord. You're the last person on earth I'd ever want to hurt. But that guy … the one you just saw me with by the phone … he's my new boyfriend … But you're my *best* friend. You'll always be my best friend. I love you so much. Please don't hate me." A pressure cooker whistled and steamed in the kitchen. I felt like shit – like a crap-covered, pressure-cooked cliché.

"I love you, Bree. You're my baby," he smiled. "I'll always love you, no matter what." I buried my nose in his hug, inhaling the Downy again, and I knew that as soon as I let go of him, the empty space between us would start to grow and expand.

As I picked at the food on my plate, I loathed the expanding emptiness. There was nothing I could do to stop it, like the red shift in space after the Big Bang.

Mona arrived. She ordered a garden salad and ate it as though it hurt.

"What's the matter? Don't you like it?" I asked.

"I'm not really used to grated beets in my salad," she said. "This really is the worst salad I've ever eaten."

We'd grown up on salads made of iceberg lettuce, tomato wedges, cucumber slices, and a touch of diced onion lathered in either Russian, Italian, or French *Seven Seas* dressing - nothing more, nothing less. The salads that Nanette prepared at *Natural Foods* contained beets, carrots, bean sprouts, and several leafy greens we Yeagers weren't accustomed to eating. But because of Jessie's mother, I'd become familiar with the health food staples. Mona made it clear – with every forkful that entered her mouth – that the salad didn't please her. I acted like I didn't notice.

If the tables were turned, and it were Mona who worked in a health food store, I would just act like I enjoyed the damned salad, for her sake, to make her feel good. That's the difference between us. If Jackie didn't like the salad, she wouldn't even try to pick around the beets. She'd let everyone in the whole store know she didn't like it; then she'd try something else, anything else, everything else. We're all very different when it comes to reacting to foods we don't like.

While Mona struggled to eat around the beets, Jessie entered the store. I knew she was there even before I saw her because I heard her laughing. Jessie's the only person who shocks me with her laughter. It's as though I'm listening to music with headphones on and someone suddenly turns the volume up all the way. It jolts me.

Her unexpected laughter was quite a relief. I had been contending with Jordan's declaration of love for me, and with Mona's declaration of hate for the salad. Jessie's laughter was like another cliché bell, ringing in the nick of time. I jumped up and gave her a kiss. Her hair was Copper Brilliant. Her lips were loaded with Banana-Coconut Lip Smoothie.

Kate Jones was stocking the organic produce bins under the sign that said, *"Why Panic? Go Organic!"*

She stared at Jessie and me as we hugged for a few seconds. Then she gave me this cockeyed look, as if to say, *Hmm. Closet lesbians.* Kate would probably think I was in love with my own mother if she saw me give her a daughterly kiss. She acted like such a screwball. I tried not to let her bother me, but I wanted to slap her again. *Why did I ever let her massage my back?* Kate was the first person I had ever encountered that inspired me with violent urges (except for Mona, but she doesn't count, because she's my sister).

Jessie's presence cut a lot of the tension and made the afternoon much lighter. She was still my best friend, would always be my best friend.

"I just moved into a studio apartment in Chinatown," Jessie said. "It's *soooo* cool. It used to be a factory. If you ever want to move in and share the space, let me know. It's huge ... about the size of a football field. I could really use some help with the rent, even though it's dirt cheap."

"Maybe one day," I said. Jessie ordered a carrot-beet-celery juice. Her clothes smelled like Camel cigarettes.

I sat down again. The whole lunch counter was full of my people. It was weird.

"How's your mother?" Nanette asked Jessie. Everyone in the health-food business knows Jessie's mother. She's sort of famous because she does colonics, and they're all running to get colonics. One time, when I was serving behind the lunch counter, I wanted to puke my guts up listening to people discussing that crap: *"Oh, I just got a colonic, and it's so wonderful. I feel ten pounds lighter."* ... *"Well, I had my colon cleansed last month, and I couldn't believe what was passing out of me. There was so much of it. Unbelievable. Unbeliveable!"* It was an awful thing to have to listen to at a lunch counter.

After a few minutes of sitting around, chewing on health food and listening to colon therapy chitchat, Kate Jones came over arm-in-arm with some girl I'd never seen before. "I'm going out for pizza. It's time for my lunch break," she announced. Kate's a vegetarian, but she never ate at the store.

"I'll be up at the register in a minute, right after I say goodbye to my people." I liked saying *my people.*

"Sure. No prob. Take your time."

She sure looks gay (happy) *next to that girl,* I thought.

"This is my new girlfriend, Sam." Kate's proud announcement turned every head at the lunch counter in the same direction, like a tennis audience.

Sam's head was shaved down to peach fuzz, and when she swirled around to give Kate a hug for introducing her in such an "open" way, she displayed an airbrushed painting of a bald Sinead O'Conner on the back of her black leather biker jacket. I recognized the artist's signature in the lower right-hand corner: Frank Baldi. He's the same guy that painted the back of Jackie's pornographic jacket. *Strange coincidence.* I thought.

"Isn't she beautiful?" Kate asked. "I'm gonna marry her."

Sam was plug ugly. Plugly. Like a scratched-up, dirty old bowling ball that no one wants to use anymore.

69

"Congratulations," said Nanette.

"Don't forget to invite me to the wedding." I smiled, happy that Kate had a new object of interest.

"I have to get back to work now," Mona said. "How much do I owe?"

"Don't worry about it," I insisted. "It's on me. I'm glad you came up for lunch. Come again some time soon." We walked down the cereal isle toward the door.

"Thanks," she whispered, "but no offense, I don't think I'll be coming back. The food isn't really for me, and the people are so *weeeird*." The word "weird" was a mile long coming out of her mouth.

"I know, Mona. I'm one of them," I admitted and laughed.

"Maybe we can have lunch together somewhere else one day!" Mona got all excited about this new idea that just lit up her cerebrum. You could almost see through her head to that glowing part of her brain where the idea was born. I'm not kidding. She really excites herself over stuff like a lunch suggestion. She's in love with her own ideas. It's kind of funny.

"That's a great idea!" I pumped her ego a little.

"I'll call you next week," she said. I knew she wouldn't though.

Jordan left and Jessie shopped for a while. I took over the register and followed every move that Dante made in his tight, navy sweatpants.

While I was weighing a customer's bag of nuts at the checkout counter, he asked, "Did you ever model over at Temple?"

"No," I replied.

Some girl was flirting with Dante in the back of the store by the bulk bins. I tried to see what was going on, so I couldn't concentrate too well on what the customer in front of me was saying. He had a giant spiked Mohawk. I kept trying to see over it, around it, between it. All the pretty, horny girls from PCA would come in the store and flirt with Dante.

"Are you sure?" Mohawk Man continued. "There was a model there who looked exactly like you."

"You must be confusing me with someone else. People do that pretty often. I have one of those familiar faces," I assured him.

*

L-Arginine 500 mg Vegetable Capsules; Vitamin B12 100 mcg tablets; Norwegian Cod Liver Oil Soft Gels ... "Shit!" I shouted out loud when it finally dawned on me that I *had* modeled at Temple. I was in the middle of stocking vitamins on the back shelves of the store, wondering if I should start taking some of that Ginkgo Biloba Leaf Extract for memory enhancement because, surely, I was losing my mind.

The store was quiet. It was getting late. Niomi worked the register. I glanced up from a bottle of Evening Primrose to the big round security mirror hanging in the corner of the store, under the ceiling. It reflected the image of a rather small man pointing a medium-sized gun at Niomi's large pregnant belly. She silently placed the register money into a recycled brown paper bag. He grabbed it and ran out the door. I flew to the front.

"Are you okay?" I panicked. "I saw the whole

71

thing in the mirror."

"It's only money, Bree," she said, cool as an organic Kirby cucumber. "Insurance'll cover it."

CHAPTER NINE

"Achtung Baby"

Getting dressed for Dante's going-away party was like dressing for a high-stakes burglary. I sneaked into Jackie's suitcase of costumes. I wanted to drive him mad with desire. My life had turned into a series of soap-opera clichés. I hate soap operas. When I was still too young to go to nursery school, my mother watched at least three daytime soaps in one sitting. In turn, so did I. – Between these early childhood soap opera influences and my current fascination with Shakespearean five acts, it was no wonder that my life had turned into chapter drama.

A black fishnet one-piece hooked onto the red glass of my silver bangle. I carefully slipped into it. My nipples practically popped out of the mesh. *Is this what it means to "cover up" in Princeton?* I wondered. The costume was definitely a violation. The thong went right up my ass, and I hoped that Dante wouldn't notice the strawberry rash back there. But I didn't care too much. I was so damn horny. And anyhow, the rash was only noticeable if I bent over.

Everyone gave Dante a going-away present. I bought him a pair of Bolle sunglasses. They cost a hundred bucks. Thanks to Jackie's fifty-dollar tips, I had plenty of money to throw around. I was saving up to buy a Jeep, but I was in love (and allegedly in lust) and, as a result, I temporarily lost my mind. The thought of Dante nailed me down into the frame of addiction. I like being obsessed. No matter how unhealthy it is, I always enjoy it for a while.

During most of the party, Dante and I were in the bathroom making out. After everyone left, we were alone.

"Don't even think about leaving." He grabbed my jeans by the belt loop. It snapped off.

"What about your mom? Won't she be mad?" I asked.

"Nah ... she's *hep*," he said. "She doesn't care." Dante's Overbrook slang was new to me. I'd never heard of "hep" for "hip."

He lived with his mother and his older brother. His parents were divorced. Their house was very Italian with a great big Christmas tree decorated in red and white lights. "That's an Italian tree. It's the colors of Italy." Because I was Jewish, Dante felt the need to explain things like that about his house.

We passed a stairwell Crucifix on the way up to his room. I knew that the Catholics had rules against premarital sex, but I couldn't recall any Jewish law forbidding it and smiled at the Crucifix.

Dante turned on a lamp that had a sexy red light bulb. I immediately got out of my jeans, took off my sweater, and felt like a centerfold in that fishnet piece. "Your body's sinful," he gasped. We fooled around half-dressed for a while, then got busy in bed, kissing each other all over the place. It was a thousand degrees in the red bed, and just as I was about to mount the Italian stallion, he sat right up and asked,

"Do you have any condoms?"

"Condoms? ... uh ... no ... I don't have any condoms." I was no virgin but had never been asked for condoms before. I thought it was something that guys were supposed to take care of in advance.

"Get dressed. We're taking a walk." He pulled his pants up and over his Baryshnikov bulge, which looked like it wanted to leap back out.

"Where are we going?"

"To Wawa. It's just a few blocks away."

Wow, I thought. *This guy is so responsible. He's able to stop himself in the midst of passion.*

I sure wasn't. At that point, I didn't care if he wore a condom or not. I'm such an idiot. People in the health food store were dropping like fruit flies from the AIDS epidemic, but it hadn't occurred to me that my own life could be at risk. I felt so irresponsible.

We walked through Overbrook, heading towards the nearest Wawa. The lights were blinding in there. It was way past two in the morning, yet there were still lots of people around. My hair was disheveled. I felt like I had the words "Bitch in Heat" printed on my forehead. It was awfully embarrassing, standing there next to Dante, as the cashier rang up the condoms.

The sex was great, but I really hate condoms. I could never be a prostitute.

Dante served me a bacon-and-eggs breakfast in bed while serenading me on his acoustic twelve-string. I didn't even know that he could play classical guitar. It was heavenly. All my loving and lusting had paid off. It was the most romantic I'd ever felt in my life – bacon and eggs and all.

The morning grew brighter and brighter. I still wanted more satisfaction. Something was missing. But what? I couldn't quite figure out what the missing thing was exactly. It had been a perfect night – a perfect morning – Why did I feel so empty?

After breakfast, Dante walked me to the El station on 69th Street with his guitar by his side. "I want you to keep this for me while I'm in Europe," he said, handing me the case.

"Are you sure?" I was surprised, flattered.

This is a true gesture of commitment, I thought. *This is the* thing *that was missing*. I felt as though he had just given me an engagement ring. Guitar … Ring … What's the difference? *"How well my comfort is reviv'd by this!"* Shakespeare's lines were alive on the stage of my life.

"I'll feel better knowing my guitar's in your hands. I love you, Bree. I'll send you a postcard as soon as I get there. I promise."

"I love you, too."

And there it was, completely beautiful. I wanted to go back to his house and make love all day, but my train arrived and that was that.

My father was furious when I got home. I had forgotten to tell him that I was staying out for the night.

"Where the hell were you? Do you know how worried I was? I thought you were deadinanalley!" He always said "dead in an alley" as though it were one word whenever any of us were late getting home. His voice shook the house. I stood there clenching the handle of Dante's guitar case, thinking of what to say.

76

"I was at a party … and I fell asleep … I'm sorry."

"You're such an idiot," Jackie shouted from the kitchen.

"Where'd the guitar come from?" my father asked.

"It's Dante's. He asked me to hold on to it for him while he's traveling in Europe. He'll be there for about a month. I'm going to learn how to play it."

"Who's Dante?" he asked. I had forgotten to tell my father about Dante.

"She's in love with him," Jackie shouted from the kitchen.

"Would you shut up in there!" I shouted back, before returning to my usual relaxed tone. "He's a guy I met at the health food store. We work together."

"Dante? What's he, Italian?"

"Yup."

"Would it hurt you to find yourself a Jewish boyfriend?"

"What does it matter if he's Jewish or not?" I was getting testy.

"It might matter when it comes time for marriage."

"Well, I'm not marrying him, so you don't have to worry." I would've married Dante in a drumbeat.

"Then what the hell are you doing with him all night that you can't even remember to call your poor old father who's worried sick about you, you little bitch!" His bass crescendoed into a full roar as he got up from his chair. His roar is always humbling.

I ran to my room and tried to play Dante's guitar using some violin fingerings. It sounded pretty good once I worked through the odd spots. *"Deny thy father and refuse thy name …"*

*

Jordan was busy getting organized that week. I didn't hear from him at all. On his way to the airport, he stopped by the house and handed me a cassette tape of U2, *Achtung Baby*.

"I listened to this all week, over and over, and thought about you the whole time. I want you to have it."

Then he handed me a single, red rose. A thorn cut through my flesh.

CHAPTER TEN

Out With A Bang

Two postcards came from Jordan. None from Dante.

Jordan had fallen in love in Rome with another art student named Lisa. I was happy for him, but couldn't help feeling sorry for myself.

During the winter break, I took on more hours at the health food store and hung out with Jessie in Chinatown. We bought Chinese chewing gum and porcelain Buddha babies for good luck. I acted happy as I sunk further and further into depression. I tried to keep the Depression Monster at bay, but there was no use. My life had become dull. No classes to spark my mind. No Dante to spark my libido.

Then one day, in the middle of my shift at the health food store, something exciting happened. Niomi ran out of her office. "My water just broke!" she shouted. Everyone in the store turned into an instant ice sculpture except for Nanette, who grabbed an empty glass pickle jar from under the counter. She escorted Niomi into the bathroom. It was odd and suspicious to involve a pickle jar. They were up to something. It all seemed rehearsed, like they had a secret plan. I casually acted as though I had to get something from the stock room, but aimed to peek in through the accordion door to see what they were up to in there.

I saw everything. Nanette held the glass jar between Niomi's bare legs. They both stood there waiting for something to happen. "I feel another pain," Niomi said. And a rush of amniotic fluid overflowed the pickle jar.

"Thank you so much," Nanette said, screwing the lid on tightly. "This should be enough. I'll go get Nick."

I ran to the front counter and landed behind the register out of breath. Nanette looked around. "Where's Nick?" she asked.

"He went to the bank. He's not back yet," I answered. Nick always took the cash register money to the bank, but he was taking too much time that day.

"When did he leave?"

"Over an hour ago. He should've been back by now."

A minute or two later, Nick flashed into the store like white lightening. I saw him round the corner from Pine Street to the store's only entrance on Broad. He wasn't coming from the direction of the bank, though. The bank is on Broad down by Chestnut. He was coming from Walter's house. Walter's his dealer.

"Call the cops!" Nick shouted. "I was robbed. Some guy grabbed the bag of money with the receipts and ran down into the subway with it." Nick was out of breath. I could tell he was lying. He was high on coke, and he smelled like ammonia.

Your wife's in labor," I said.

"Oh shit!" he replied. *This guy is such a loser*, I thought. He darted to the back of the store. "Call the cops, Bree, and make a report," he shouted.

"How much was stolen?" I yelled back.

He zipped to the front of the store. "Eight thousand fuckin' dollars!"

"Eight thousand?" I questioned in disbelief.

"Yeah, don't forget."

That store never did over twelve hundred in a single day. Nick's whole life was a lie. I wondered if Dante was a liar too.

Daniel and I worked the registers that day. Daniel is one of the funniest people I have ever met. He's tall, blond, and skinny – like a brand new No. 2 pencil. He's the guy I first spoke to the day I applied for the job. He spoke with a proper English accent, even though he's from New Jersey. I never bothered asking him about it. I just enjoyed the way he pronounced his words.

Niomi's friends kept calling the store to find out if she'd given birth yet. And then she did – at one o'clock that afternoon. A speedy delivery.

"*Hiiii*, this is Niomi's girlfriend *Aaaaby*. Did Niomi have the *baaaby* yet?" Even though Niomi sounded like a hippie when she spoke, all her friends sounded like Valley Girls.

"Yes, she did in fact," Daniel softly replied.

"Oh *mi Gawwwd*! What is it?" Abby inquired. Daniel shared the phone with me; our ears touched.

"It?" he asked. "*It* is an eight-pound eggplant. She delivered an eggplant! Absurd, isn't *it*?"

Click.

We laughed at that for a while. Then there was another call.

"Hi, this is Gloria. Did Niomi have her baby yet?" Gloria ordered take-out from the lunch counter everyday, and Amminadab always flirted with her. You could tell that Amminadab made her nervous.

"Yes, Gloria. She had the baby half an hour ago." Daniel's voice was soft, like a cloud.

"Is it a boy or a girl?"

"It's a WHITE girl. Our kitchen chef, Amminadab, is extremely relieved. So is Niomi, as you can imagine."

"Oh … my … well … Can you tell me what the lunch special is today?"

"We're serving steamed umbilical cord and fried placenta."

Click.

I got such a kick out of Daniel. I laughed like a fool the whole afternoon and forgot to call the cops. Daniel enjoyed having such a receptive audience.

"If I had to have sex with a girl, I'd want to do it with you," he told me. For some weird reason, I have that effect on gay guys. I don't know why. When I was in high school, my friend Brian said something similar to me. We were walking down South Street one day, and out of nowhere he started French kissing me. "What are you doing?" I asked. "Tell me if I'm a good kisser," he said. He kissed me with the passion of Cupid. "You're a great kisser," I assured him. "Thanks, Bree. I would never kiss a girl. But there's something about you that makes it okay." And when I was seventeen, my boyfriend's brother was gay, and he tried to *rape* me! I can't figure out why gay guys find me attractive.

Later on I watched Nanette as she removed the pickle jar from the fridge. She unscrewed the lid and drank all the fluid, bottoms up.

"Are you drinking what *I think* you're drinking?" I asked.

"It's only amniotic fluid. No biggie. Wanna try some?" she joked.

"Nanette! Why are you drinking that? Is it for the same thing as the hair tea?"

"Yup. Please don't tell anyone. It's pretty embarrassing. But let me tell you something, my dear. I'm getting better. Ever since I drank the hair tea, I've stopped hemorrhaging. And my blood count is getting back to normal. Jacob Wellerstein said that if it was possible to ingest some of Niomi's amniotic fluid, then it might help out, too. So, when the opportunity came, I figured, what the hell. In two days, I'm having my blood tested again. Say a prayer for me, willya kid?"

"I'll say a hundred prayers for you."

"Have you heard from Dante?" she asked.

"Not a word. He said he'd write, but who knows?" I shrugged.

"Don't worry. He'll be back soon."

I went into the stock room and began unloading a box. There was a new brand of liquid moisturizing soap for hands: *Cotton Flowers with Shea Butter*. I unscrewed the pump and took a whiff. The freshness of Downy flew into my nose. I inhaled until I was full of it. I took the tester bottle into the bathroom and washed my hands with … the scent of Downy … with the scent of Jordan. I missed him for the first time. I washed and whiffed my hands a thousand times that week.

*

Niomi was back in the office almost immediately, counting money and plucking herself and breastfeeding her baby. She'd sit in there all day long with her boobs hanging out. They looked like white watermelons with brown nipples.

Soon enough, Dante returned. He dropped by the store to let us know that he was back. A bunch of his friends waited outside next to the big white car from the 70s. I recognized most of his friends from his going-away party, but there was this girl with them who I'd never seen before. She looked like a South Philly chick – big hair and big earrings. She kept staring in the window at Dante, then at me, then at Dante. I knew something was up. He seemed happy to see me, yet the general feeling between us had changed. The light was out. The flamed had fizzled. Again the words of Friar Laurence from *Romeo and Juliet* echoed through my mind. *"These violent delights have violent ends. And in their triumph die, like fire and powder ..."* But this time, I got it. I understood.

"Sorry I didn't write. I was so busy sightseeing and stuff," Dante said. I hate when people say *and stuff*. It sounds pathetic.

"That's okay. My friend Jordan's over there studying in Rome, and I got *two* postcards from him. At least *someone's* thinking about me." My tone was obnoxious.

"Don't be like that, Bree. I thought about you. I just don't think we should be so serious. We can be together … but we should see other people, too. What do you think? Aren't we too young to be serious?" He had a nervous smile on his face, and he sounded like he doubted his own words.

"Seriously," I said, "Fuck off. I'm outta here. I'll drop off your guitar tomorrow." I surprised myself because I don't usually curse at people to their faces.

I ran to the back room, stuffed three containers of hand soap that smelled like Downy into my bag, grabbed my jacket, and stormed out of the store before anyone could see me crying. "He's gonna fuck you too! Enjoy it while it lasts!" I screamed at the South Philly chick.

I marched down Broad Street in a whirlwind of emotion. The tops of the buildings were all I could focus on. Looking down or straight ahead was too upsetting. I could only look up. On top of a building at the corner of Broad and Walnut, I saw Jessie painting a Jack Daniel's advertisement onto a billboard. It was a picture of a special whiskey bottle commemorating the Riverboat Captain. That was her new job: painting billboards. I knew right then and there that I wouldn't be working at Natural Foods anymore. *It's time for me to change jobs, too,* I decided. I wanted to buy a bottle of Captain Jack and drink it with Jessie (even though I didn't know what whiskey even tasted like). I wanted Captain Jack to get me high that night – like in the song. I wanted to scream up to Jessie and tell her – but I couldn't find my voice.

I rode the El that day for the last time. When I got

home, my mother was rolling chicken cutlets in white flour next to a sizzling frying pan. I pulled down my pants and bent over in the middle of the kitchen. "Mom, look at this rash on my ass." She gave me a tube of over-the-counter, generic anti-fungus cream. I rubbed it on before I went to sleep.

When I woke up, the rash was barely visible. After one more application, it was gone. It was finally gone!

Dante Arrigucci and the annoying strawberry on my ass were both gone. The curtain was down.

CHAPTER ELEVEN

Game Over – Insert Coin

The next day I called the health food store.

"Hi, Nick. It's Bree."

"Holy shit! I was just about thinking about you. Why didn't you call the cops? The insurance company said I can't claim a thing if a report wasn't made," he whined.

"I guess I forgot. You should fire me," I said.

"I'm not gonna fire you. You're a part of the family here. And anyway, Niomi loves you. She'd never let me fire you."

"Well, then I guess I have to quit. I can't work there anymore."

"Oh, come on! Are you *shitting* me?"

"No. I really called to let you know that I won't be coming back."

"Why? Whaddya do, get a new job?"

"Yeah, I figured if I have to work around a bunch of sex-crazed drug addicts, I might as well get paid a lot of money for it. So I'm gonna be a stripper. Tell Niomi I said thanks for everything, and tell Nanette I'll be in touch … Oh, and, my sister's dropping off Dante's guitar at the store later today, so do me a favor and give her my paycheck."

"Are you quitting because of Dante?"

"Yup. He acted like a creep, and I'd rather not be

around him. When I saw him yesterday, I felt like I was suffocating. So, that's it. It's over. I'm not coming back. Even if Dante quit working there tomorrow, I still wouldn't come back. I'd be miserable."

"Shit, Bree. We're really gonna miss you."

"I'm gonna miss you guys, too." I hadn't even thought about that and started getting a little choked up.

"Well, don't be a stranger. Stop by and check in every once in a while. Niomi's gonna go nuts when I tell her you quit."

"Just explain it to her. She'll understand … Bye, Nick."

I hung up the phone and felt miserable.

*

I went into the living room and plopped down on the sofa next to my father. He lowered his newspaper for a moment, acknowledged me, and resumed his reading. My mother was lying on the other sofa watching *The Price is Right*. She's a real gamester. If she's not playing, she's watching. And, as a result, when I was still too young for nursery school, I spent a good deal of my early childhood viewing the TV game shows that streamed into our home (in addition to the soap operas). Sure I got my daily fill of *Sesame Street*, *The Electric Company,* and *Captain Kangaroo,* learning about language, numbers, and society through age-appropriate programming. But I also gained another type of education about the world by absorbing the game shows that my mother watched before and after lunchtime:

The Wheel of Fortune taught me that any random person, who seems to have it all, could easily go "bankrupt" in a second flat. I learned that total strangers, who paired up on *The $10,000 Pyramid,* often understood each other far better than the married couples on *The Newlywed Game*. I also learned that there are always more losers than winners.

As the familiar sounds of *The Price is Right* brought my childhood back into focus, I felt like a loser at the end of a game. I had played *The Game of Love* and risked it all on Dante. Everything ran so smoothly at the start. It seemed simple, logical, and easy. But then my luck changed. I picked a bad card. I spun the wheel too fast. I said the wrong word. I lost and didn't even get a consolation prize.

I used to feel sorry for the contestants on the game shows who lost the first or second round and weren't given the chance to compete in the final round. I felt extreme sadness when they exited the studio – because the game wasn't really over. It was only over for them. I suffered through many game show moments as such. Fortunately, there was always a light at the end of the tunnel: the commercial breaks. I'd forget my *Match Game* sorrows as soon as the *Slinky* commercial jingle came on. If watching *The Joker's Wild* was hell; then listening to *"Plop plop, fizz fizz"* was heaven. It all evened out. Life was simple. I was a happy-go-lucky little girl. And by the time my sisters returned from school in the afternoon, I had already forgotten about my sadness and concern for those who suffered in between commercial breaks.

My game show blues had been neatly tucked, deep within the folds of my subconscious mind, sleeping safe and sound. But the day I quit my job at the health food store, my game show blues returned. Only this time, I was the loser.

When Bob Barker directed the next contestant to "Come on down!" I realized that I was still waiting for a commercial break to end my suffering. I looked at my mother and could tell she was getting ready to place a bid on the next item. I looked at my father and knew that he would never place a bid on the next item. He doesn't watch game shows. He ignores them and reads the paper. My mother never reads the paper. She just plays the crossword puzzles and cuts out the coupons. My parents have nothing in common, as far as personal interests go; yet they love each other. Something strange dawned on me as I sat there watching them:

I love Jordan. He loves me. He would never hurt me the way Dante did. But now he loves Lisa. That's all he ever writes about. Lisa this... Lisa that. Lisa, Lisa, Lisa! I drove him out of Philly into the arms of another woman. On another continent! And now I have to pay for it. Emotional bankruptcy. Game Over.

My thoughts turned grimmer and grimmer. I needed to talk to my sister.

I slowly opened the door to Jackie's room and tiptoed in. Surrounded by darkness, I couldn't see a thing until my eyes adapted. Jackie was completely naked, sound asleep on her heated waterbed. It was the middle of a cold afternoon, in the middle of a Philadelphia winter, but Jackie appeared as though she were sleeping in the midst of a hot summer night in the tropics. Even though she looked so peaceful, I wanted her to sense my presence and wake up. No such luck.

I went to my room and called Mona.

"Hi, Mona. It's Bree."

"Hi, Bree. How are you?"

"I just quit my job at the health food store, and I'm really upset."

"Oh my God! What happened?" She sounded so interested, which was a relief because I never know how she's going to react when I get personal.

"I was in love with this guy Dante who worked there, and he broke my heart after I had sex with him. Now I'm really upset because I just realized that I'm in love with Jordan. But he's in Italy, and he has a new girlfriend –"

"I can't talk about this!" Mona interrupted. "I'm busy. I have to go."

Click.

She hung up on me. I was in need of sisterly comfort, and Mona's rejection only added to my woes. I returned to Jackie's room.

"Jackie … Jackie … Wake up … I need to talk to you." I seated myself on the frame of her waterbed.

"What time is it?" she whispered.

"It's around one in the afternoon. Listen, I quit my job today."

"Good. What happened?" She yawned and stretched, gaining more and more consciousness.

I cried, panted, and blew my nose twice as I explained my dilemma.

"I'm so sorry, honey. Don't let it get to you. You deserve better," she said.

"I know. I deserve *Jordan*. But like an idiot I turned him down. And now that I want him back, he's gone. I really screwed things up. How could I have been so stupid?"

"We all are."

The way she said *we all are*, in such a matter-of-fact kind of way, made me feel as though I had experienced a universal rite of passage for females. As though a piece of hidden knowledge about becoming a woman had been revealed. I felt a little better. Jackie always makes me feel better.

"How's Studio?" I asked, sucking back my tears.

"Great, but I think one of the dancers stole one of my costumes out of my suitcase in the dressing room. I can't find it anywhere."

"Are you talking about a black fishnet one-piece? I asked, a bit nervously."

"Yeah, how do you know?"

"I borrowed it the night before Dante went to Europe. I wore it for him, that asshole. I forgot to put it back. It's in my room." I almost started to cry again.

"I was going crazy looking for it. You need to tell me if you borrow my costumes."

"I'm sorry. I won't do it again." I felt bad about the costume and how I made her go crazy looking for it, but there were still other issues of importance to discuss. "Listen, I need you to do me a favor. Will you take a ride up to the health food store today and give Dante back his guitar and get my paycheck from Nick? I'm never going in there again."

"Fine, whatever you want, just let me sleep a few more hours," she yawned.

"Maybe I should go up to Studio with you and —"

Before I could finish my sentence, Jackie sprang out of bed like a jack-in-the-box and tugged three times on the bottom of the window shade. It snapped up too quickly. Blinding white light paraded into the room and stung my eyes. The sky was as white as a clean sheet of paper.

"You're coming up with me *tonight*," she insisted. "I'm calling the manager right now." She grabbed the phone and began dialing. I stared at her in disbelief; partly because a lot of black make-up was smeared around her eyes and she looked like a raccoon, and partly because I didn't stop her from making the call. It was all happening so fast. I was fearful, but excited.

I ran into the living room. My parents were still busy being opposites. A *Nike* commercial was silently ending with the words "Just Do It" printed on the TV screen. I love those commercials.

"I quit my job at the health food store," I announced.

"Does that mean you quit your *boyfriend,* too?" my father asked, folding his newspaper in his lap.

"Yup. It's all over. I'm getting a job at Studio. Jackie's on the phone with the manager right now. She wants me to go up with her tonight."

"That's even better," my father said with a smile. "I'm glad you're going with Jackie. I don't like the idea of her driving out there by herself, all that distance. And it'll be a good experience for you. You'll make a lot of money. Just don't piss it away.

Oh, and don't tell your sister Mona. She's having a hard enough time handling the fact that Jackie dances. There's just no point in telling her. She's too immature. It'll only upset her."

"Whatever you say, daddy. You're the boss." I agreed to keep it a secret from Mona and acted like it didn't faze me at all, but a few fleeting thoughts on the matter disturbed me:

Mona had been completely inconsiderate when I called her less than an hour ago. I reached out to her for solace and comfort, and what did she do? She hung up on me. She shot me down and shut me out. And now I'm supposed to be considerate to her? I'm supposed to shield her from the fact that she now has two sisters who dance for money? Give me a break. What's the big deal? It's not like dancing at Studio is a crime. Who cares if it bothers her?

The fact of the matter was that my father cared, and I cared about my father. I wasn't about to argue with him. Like I said before, whenever he tells me to shut up, I always do.

And anyway, I had already had enough conflict playing *The Game of Love*. I was ready to move on. Ready to insert the coins and start a new challenge.

CHAPTER TWELVE

Snow Globes

We were ready to go. Jackie had an overstuffed suitcase and a loaded make-up case. I had nothing. "What should I bring?" I asked.

"Don't worry about packing anything for now. You'll wear my costumes and use my make-up until you get your own." I could tell by her tone that she enjoyed her role as my role model. She was ready to mold me, to melt me down into liquid and pour me into the cast of her world. It was a relief to be guided by such a confident leader, but I felt so unsure about the whole thing.

"I hope I don't make a fool out of myself," I said with worry.

"You'll be fine. Let's go. It's getting late." She looked at the clock with a fearful expression. "Oh shit! It's later than I thought. I don't think we have enough time to go to the city. Can't we return the guitar tomorrow? Why do we have to do it tonight? It's totally out of the way, you know."

"I have to get Dante out of my life. The whole thing's so painful. I'm not keeping his guitar another night." I started to panic.

"Fine," she said. "It's just that it's getting late, and is it really worth it to go forty minutes out of our way?"

"Will you stop giving me a hard time? I'd do it for you. I just went through hell with this guy."

"All right, all right. We'll go." Jackie agreed because she understood my pain. She understood that Dante's guitar was more than just a guitar. It had become a part of me. It was a symbol of love. It was Cupid's misguided arrow, stuck in my heart, poisoning my mind. In order for Jackie to take me under her wing and teach me to fly, I had to drop the heavy load weighing me down.

Snow clouds lit the night sky with intensity as we made our way to the car. Jackie threw her suitcase into the hatch. I threw Dante's guitar into the back seat. I didn't handle it very gently. I had been trained to treat instruments as though they were newborn babies. When I was eight years old, I got my first violin. I loved that violin and used to tuck it into the case, each night at bedtime, with the tender love of a mother. I'd place a rubbery green humidifier into one of the f-holes as though it were a pacifier and cover its body with a soft little *blanky*. Then I'd give it a good night kiss. I really did. I loved that violin. Banging Dante's guitar around made me feel like a lunatic.

When Jackie pulled up in front of Natural Foods, she looked me straight in the eye and said, "You're going in."

"No, I'm not. You said *you* would," I reminded her.

"You're gonna go in there and face him. Don't be afraid."

"I'm not afraid. He disgusts me."

"Go in there, NOW!" she demanded in her

perfectly pitched bossy tone, leaving me with no other choice.

I got out of the car and pulled the guitar case out of the back seat, banging it some more.

The store smelled the same. Dante popped out of the cereal aisle with a price gun in his hand and his usual Baryshnikov bulge in his pants. "Hey, Bree," he said with surprise, beaming from ear to ear.

"Hi. Here's your guitar. You can have it back," I motioned, expressionless.

"Aren't you even gonna give me a *hug*?"

"No, I'm not giving you *a hug*." I put the heavy guitar case on the floor and pushed it towards him with my moccasin. I felt myself shaking a little. My palms broke out in a sweat. I didn't understand what was happening to me. Although my mind was set on getting as far away from Dante Arrigucci as possible, my body desperately resisted a huge magnetic force pulling me towards him.

"Don't you love me anymore?" he asked in disbelief.

Is this guy crazy? I thought. *What's he trying to pull?* Without saying a word, I broke free of his invisible hold on me and rushed out of the store.

"What took you so long?" Jackie asked, accelerating down the street.

I was about to go into a detailed explanation, but it suddenly dawned on me that I forgot to see Nick. "Oh shit," I grunted. "I forgot to get my paycheck."

"Well, we're *not* going back. And anyway, you're gonna make so much money at Studio, you won't even need that paycheck."

97

"Oh, I'm getting that paycheck. It's a big one. I worked a lot of hours during the break. There's no way I'm handing my hard-earned cash over to Nick. He'll just buy a lot of white powder with it and snort it up his nose."

Jackie focused on driving fast. We were supposed to arrive at Studio by seven o'clock, and it was already six thirty. I could tell she was tense because she was silent for a little while. But as soon as we got onto Route One, she turned the volume up on the radio and began singing *Patience* along with Guns N' Roses. By the middle of the song, it started to snow, and within the next few minutes, the snow thickened and accumulated on everything. Large, fluffy snow flakes flew down from the sky like angels, like millions of beautiful little angels coming down to save me. My thoughts traveled far with the snow: *This is a good sign. I'm on the right path. Nanette was wrong about white being bad for people. White is good for people. Even for her. When she boiled my hair for tea, it eventually turned into a white powder. She used the white powder to make the tea, and it worked. She said it helped her fight the cancer. Her blood count was almost back to normal. White can be good. Some white is bad, and some is good.*

It looked like the trees were covered with chunks of white icing. Highway signs were hidden beneath mounds of white frosting. Cars and trucks were suddenly dressed in the same white coat, driving on the same white road, as the world transformed into a white work of art.

Around half way there, just before the bridge, there

was a car in front of us that slowed Jackie down. Instead of switching lanes and passing, she flashed the high beams a few times. The car remained in front of us. She flashed the high beams again. Still nothing.

"What the hell! Why won't this car get out of my fuckin' way? This is the fast lane. And look! It's slowing down on purpose just to be obnoxious." I wondered if Jackie was talking to me or to herself. She turned off the radio and flicked on the bright headlights. She carefully tailgated the car in front of us and leaned on the horn.

"Why don't you just pass it on the right?" I suggested.

"No way! This car's supposed to get out of *my way*." Stuck in one of her I'm-Right moods, she leaned on the horn again. I didn't bother arguing. That would be pointless.

Jackie tailgated the car for a long stretch of road. It finally pulled into the right lane and let her pass. She turned off the high beams and zipped down the highway. Just as I was about to turn the radio back on, a flashing blue light grew brighter and brighter behind us. It was on the dashboard of the car we had just passed, which was now behind us, tailgating us, and flashing the high beams on us.

"Shit! It's a goddam State Trooper!" Jackie said, adjusting the rearview mirror.

"How can you tell?" I asked. "It's just a regular car with a light on the dash. What if it's one of those freaks who dresses up like a cop and rapes women?"

"I'll try to outrun him. Jersey's right over the bridge. I don't think he can ticket me in Jersey if he's a Pennsylvania Trooper." Jackie adjusted the rearview mirror again and kept checking it as she quickly gained speed. Her snow-covered car blasted like a bullet through the snowstorm at eighty-five miles per hour. The speed limit was fifty-five. The car behind us stayed on our tail. We were only five minutes from the bridge. "I could get arrested," Jackie worried. "Shit! I better pull over." She veered to a stop and locked the doors.

The State Trooper stood next to her window in a funny hat with a strap that pressed against the dividing line of his double chin. He looked like Smokey the Bear.

"Open the window," he demanded, rapping on it with a flashlight. Jackie lowered the window about half an inch. "Let me see your license and registration, young lady," he said, pointing his flashlight my way, stinging my eyes.

"Let me see your badge!" Jackie insisted. "I'm not showing you anything until I see a badge."

"You better show me your license, young lady."

"I'm not fuckin' showing you anything until I see some ID." I couldn't believe she was cursing at Smokey the Bear. Then she turned to me and spoke to me, but her words were for him. "I'm not showing him anything. How do I know he's really a cop? He's in an unmarked car. He could be one of those freaks they talk about on the news!"

The State Trooper grew frustrated. Jackie has a way of doing that to people. He reached into his pocket and pulled out his badge. I thought he was reaching for a gun. "Drive away!" I screamed. "He's got a gun! He's gonna shoot us!"

"Calm down, Bree. It's not a gun. It's a badge," Jackie said.

She studied his badge while he pressed it against the window. It appeared authentic. She rolled the window down some more and completely changed her tone. "My license is in the back, officer. I have to get out and open the hatch to look for it."

"Go right ahead," he said, satisfied that she had finally agreed to cooperate. By that time, his funny hat was covered in snow.

She popped the hatch, got out of the car, and opened her suitcase. Her driver's license was hidden somewhere among dozens of costumes. After several minutes of searching through the sequins ... and silks ... and satins, she found it playing peek-a-boo inside a hot-pink pump. Smokey the Bear gazed on in disbelief. He told her to wait in her car.

"I'm dead. He really *is* a State Trooper. Shit!" Jackie worried. The snow came down harder then. Jackie's hair was full of flakes. She looked like the Sugar Plum Fairy. We waited for ten long minutes before he returned.

"Excuse me, Ma'm." He rapped on the window again. She opened it all the way. "Do you know why I pulled you over, Ma'am?" he asked.

Why's he being so polite all the sudden? I wondered. *Why's he calling her Ma'am?*

"Yes, Officer, I know why – I was speeding – because I'm late for work," Jackie said.

"Where do you work?" he asked.

"At Studio 67."

Are you going there to *work* – or are you going there to *dance*?" he asked, changing his polite tone to one of arrogance.

"I *work* there – Get it? – I go there *to work*." Jackie's tone firmed up again. She looked at me and grunted a few more curse words under her breath.

"Well, Ma'am – I'm giving you a warning this time – but don't let me catch you speeding again. It's very dangerous, especially in the snow."

"Thank you." Jackie grabbed the yellow warning slip from his hand. "Thank you so much." She smiled and drove away and didn't speed again until we were in Jersey. "I am so lucky!" she shouted. "That guy could've arrested me!"

"He probably liked your sexy costumes. I bet he was jerking off in his unmarked car the entire time we were waiting. How long does it really take to write a warning?"

"Maybe he knows the owner of Studio, Joe. He's a cop, too," Jackie said.

"The owner of Studio's *a cop*? – Are you serious?" I asked, finding it hard to believe.

"Yup – All his cop friends come in and hang out there."

"Is that legal?"

"I guess so."

The snow came down in a mysterious way. I felt as though I was inside of one of those snow globe shaker toys that you can buy in a souvenir shop. I have one with the Golden Gate Bridge in it, which makes no sense because it never snows in San Francisco.

I don't know how Jackie drove through it.

CHAPTER THIRTEEN

The Dressing Room

We pulled into a shopping center parking lot, just twenty minutes late. Studio 67 was comfortably wedged between a Shop-n-Bag supermarket and a pizza joint. The sign said "NON-STOP GO-GO." *At least they're literate in Princeton*, I thought, recalling the "sTOPLESS" sign that loomed over Visions.

"The parking lot's empty," Jackie said with concern. "I hope there's business tonight."

The parking lot looked pretty full to me, but I didn't say a word. My mouth was stopped by my nervousness. The feeling was familiar. It was the same uncertainty of spirit that had accompanied me when I first stood nude upon the stage of Jordan's painting class. My adrenal glands pumped. My heart raced. My muscles tensed. I loved the thrill of being overwhelmed by adventure, but I couldn't find my voice.

We pulled around back and unloaded the hatch. I followed Jackie to a large metal door that had no handles or knobs on it. She rang the doorbell twice, and complained about having to wait in the snow. I didn't mind though. The moment was nice – silent and peaceful. The snow looked like big flakey angels, flying down all around. As I gazed upward, to get a better look, my eyes fixed upon a blinking red light, flashing from a security camera above the door. For a split second, I sensed the presence of the devil, but the thought quickly vanished when the metal door popped open.

A bald guy with a thick goatee smiled at Jackie as she entered. "Hey, sexy." "Hi, Joe." They greeted each other with a friendly peck on the cheek. Then the formal introductions began:

"This is my baby sister, Bree," Jackie proudly announced, smiling at me as though I were *her* joyful creation – the successful product of *her* guidance. I smiled and played along, but I felt more like a lab experiment that was about to fail.

"Wow! – Are you two twins?" Joe asked. He had big wide eyes and a deep raspy voice – a whiskey voice.

"No, she's my *baby* sister – We're two years apart. She's auditioning tonight," Jackie explained.

"Hey, 'lil sis. I'm Joe, the night manager." He smiled and gave me a peck on the cheek.

"Nice to meet you." I managed to squeeze the sentence out with a smile, eluding my anxiety.

"Do you dance, or is this your first time?" His scratchy voice reminded me of someone, but I couldn't place it.

"She danced with me at The Lion's Den," Jackie quickly fabricated. "She's really good."

"Well, if she's anything like you, then I'll hire her in a sec … You girls better get dressed – You're up on stage at 7:40 sharp," he said to Jackie. "And *you*, 'lil sis, can go up right after her, at 7:50."

I figured it out. He sounded like a wailing Janice

Joplin, only deeper.

*

We entered the dressing room. It was a nice-sized room, but the clutter made it seem smaller. There were suitcases all over the place. Some were closed. Some were open. Some were super sloppy with costumes and shoes and boots sticking out all over the place, while others were impressively neat with everything folded and organized into dozens of zip lock plastic bags. The open suitcases reminded me of my hand-me-down Barbie dolls. They were the original dolls from the '60s, passed down to my sisters and me in the '70s. When we received them, they had been sloppily stuffed into a crooked cardboard suitcase that was fully stocked with a steady stream of wardrobes, wigs, and waistlines. It was always a lot of fun dressing up the dolls and entering an imaginary world of innocent fun. But the very last time I played with them, it wasn't so innocent. My friend Jan and I drew ink tattoos all over their plastic Barbie skin and had them simulate sex scenes with the Ken doll. After that, I stuffed everything back into the crooked cardboard suitcase and never opened it again.

Standing at the entrance of the dressing room, I got the feeling that I was trapped in some kind of weird dream in which my Barbie dolls had come to life – and I was turning into one of them. I closed the door behind me, ready to face my new reality.

The dressing room walls were lined with brown basement paneling, which inspired a homelike atmosphere, but it smelled more like a smoke-filled hair salon in there. A bunch of dancers sat jammed together on a sofa, counting their piles of money. The sofa looked exactly like the sofa in the opening scene of *The Simpsons* when the whole family crowds together on it to watch TV. In the center of the room, one of the dancers was passed out on an old vinyl recliner. Some of the dancers sat on the floor, searching through their suitcases for a costume to wear. Some lined up in front of a giant mirror that was framed with naked light bulbs, fixing their hair and adjusting their make-up like Hollywood showgirls. A few leaned way over the long counter to get a better look in the mirror, stretching their asses way out. One girl had a tattoo of a red strawberry with the words "Eat Me" written below it in green cursive. It was tattooed on her butt in the same exact place where my itchy strawberry rash had been. I chuckled at the familiarity of the strawberry.

Jackie greeted many of the dancers, and another round of introductions began. "Come here, Bree. This is Betsy, but her real name's Mercedes. This is Porsche, but her real name's Betsy."

"Hi," they said in unison.

"Are you serious? They're really your names?" I asked. They smiled and nodded as though sharing a uni-brain. One had braces on her teeth. The other had fake boobs that popped out like oversized cupcakes.

"Isn't that hysterical?" Jackie beamed. She seemed happier than usual.

Then there were three loud knocks on the door. "It's 7:30, Desiree! Get your ass on stage!" shouted Joe's unmistakable voice. The girl on the recliner

106

woke right up and sprang out of her seat. The girl with the chest full of cupcakes pounced onto the recliner.

Jackie opened her suitcase. It was the sloppy variety. "Pick out something to wear," she instructed.

"Will you pick something for me?" I asked. The task of going through her suitcase seemed too great.

"How's this?" She held up a red-hot, meshed one-piece that was more like a two-piece strung together like the web of a spider. "That's fine," I nodded, and she tossed it over. I was glad to finally get out of my clothing because everyone in the room was either naked or half-dressed. It was a much more comfortable feeling than I had formerly experienced while getting undressed to model for Jordan's painting class. *What will Jordan think of my new job?* I wondered.

"Are they *yours*?" one of the dancers asked me, breaking my stream of thought.

"Are *what* mine?" I asked, as I was still unfamiliar with the flow of go-go dressing-room conversation at that time – I didn't know what she was talking about.

"Your tits!" she clarified.

"Oh ..." I looked down at them. "Yeah ... they're mine."

"No, they're *not*," Jackie interrupted. "They're *mine*."

I gave a look. Our perky boobs looked the same in the mirror. We're both C cups, and the difference is slight. Mona's chest was always significantly larger than ours. She's a D cup – not that anyone would ever know it by looking at her because she hides them behind her bulky clothing.

"Oh *mi gawd*!" one girl shouted. "You guys're so lucky. I already have stretch marks, and I ain't even got kids yet! Look at 'em." She pulled off her costume as her breasts sagged out into a series of silvery stretch marks, like a roadmap. "I'm gettin' 'em fixed … soon as I save up enough cash."

"Heather got 'ers done," another girl added. "They look great. D'jya see 'em yet?"

The conversation wasn't exactly university caliber, but it was intriguing. Jackie handed me a pair of red pumps. I put them on. They were half a size too big, so I stuffed the front with some tissue and tripped on my way over to the counter. Aerosol hair spray cans, perfume bottles, cosmetic cases, hair dryers, fully heated curling irons, and ashtrays full of half-smoked cigarettes lined the long counter. To me, it looked like a fire hazard waiting to happen. To everyone else, it was just business as usual. I put aside my fear and followed Jackie's lead, applying the exact amount of eyeliner, mascara, lip-liner, lipstick, and bronzer powder that she did. I felt like her clone. She puffed out my hair with some hair spray. For a second I thought the hair spray was going to act as a trigger, and I imagined the whole place blowing up in an explosion. I tried to ignore my apocalyptic thoughts.

"You look great," Jackie said with satisfaction. "Put this on." She handed me a white leather, fringy jacket to wear on top of my costume – a cover-up that barely covered up anything at all. "Let's get a drink while we're waiting," she suggested, ready to exit the dressing room.

I followed her out and practically broke my neck

while stepping around all the suitcases. I couldn't walk in high heels. The last time I'd worn high heels was at my Bat Mitzvah when I was thirteen years old. I vowed never to wear them again and never did. Not even to the prom. Ballet slippers are my dress-up shoes of choice. I wore ballet slippers to Mona's wedding, too.

When I agreed to go up to Studio, earlier that day, I hadn't even considered the fact that I'd be dancing in high heels. I was so relieved that the strawberry rash on my ass was finally gone – other obstacles hadn't even occurred to me. But there I was, once again, going through a rite of passage in five-inch stripper shoes.

CHAPTER FOURTEEN

"My Favorite Go-Go Action Pop-Up Book"

Jackie opened a black door that led into the bar. When I stepped through, I realized just how much I didn't know about go-go bars. I had expected Studio 67 to look exactly like The Lion's Den, but it was completely different. I just assumed that all go-go bars looked the same – that there was some sort of established standard or business code that required all of them to have several small stages, a variety of bars, and many different platforms for seating and viewing options. But what did I know? Studio was nothing like that. It was much simpler. It felt like a better fit for me than I'd expected. I let out a sigh of relief and found even more comfort when I saw the St. Pauly Girl glowing on a neon sign on the wall to my right. I always loved the St. Pauly Girl commercial.

The barroom was huge – like a football field. Counters and stools wrapped around in a giant rectangle. It looked like the bar on the TV show *Cheers,* only much, much bigger. In the center of the room, a big wooden stage rose out of the floor. There were two shiny golden poles extending from the stage to the ceiling, one at each end. The smoke machine let out a puff from a hole in the middle of the floor. One of the girls I had just met in the dressing room danced through the smoke. She was up on the stage doing these horrible ballet turns – the kind where your eyes focus on a specific point, and then you spin around quickly to end up staring at the same focal point. My sisters and I learned how to do it in ballet class when we were younger. It looks all right when a bunch of little girls are practicing in a ballet studio – or when a good ballet dancer does it the right way – but this girl looked awful. She was the one with the braces. Her horrible performance made me feel more at ease because I knew I could dance better than her. But I couldn't wait to get some alcohol coursing through my veins.

"It's dead in here," Jackie said. "It *is*?" I asked. It didn't look dead to me. There were plenty of customers seated around the bar.

We got comfy at the closest corner, and Jackie introduced me to a few of the regulars: Mike, Bob, Tim, Jim. They all had one-syllable names. I never remember one-syllable names. I can remember someone named Eustacious or Reginald, but I forget all the Toms.

I just smiled and tried to act like a *bimbo*. Everyone called me "Lil' Sis." It didn't bother me, though. I had been called "Little Jackie" or "Lil' Sis" my whole life and kind of liked it – I love Jackie.

"What'll it be girls?" the bartender asked. All of the bartenders sported black tights and thongs up their butts. Jackie introduced me to Bobbi the Bartender and ordered a Cranberry Vodka. "Same for me," I said.

In any other situation I would have ordered red wine, but I had developed an immunity to its effect. I needed to be drugged instantly.

A single Cranberry Vodka wasn't enough to calm my nerves. Two minutes after I ordered the first one, I ordered another. Some guy with a one-syllable name paid for our drinks. I couldn't focus on anyone in particular. There were these large red numbers on a digital clock right next to the St. Pauly Girl that held my attention strong, as did the pathetic dancer on stage. I studied her every ungraceful move just to be sure I wouldn't do anything similar when it was my turn to go up.

Jackie took me into the DJ booth for introductions. We had to walk to the opposite end of the bar (football field), and I was sure I'd fall on my face at any moment. Jackie walked too fast. I couldn't keep up in those heels.

The DJ was a short guy who looked exactly like Doogie Howser, real geeky with a button-up shirt and wire-framed glasses. He even had a pen case in his shirt pocket. "This is my sister, Bree. She's going up at 7:50."

"Wow – are you twins?"

"She's my *baby* sister," Jackie smiled again. "Baby Bree."

"You two should do a sister act. They'll pay a lot for that." He searched through his collection of CDs. "What would you like me to play for you?"

"I don't know. Play something sexy," I said. I couldn't think of a song.

We went back to our bar stools. I bummed a

cigarette. Jackie coached me: "If the customers want to tip you while you're on stage, get down and take the tip. Then get right back up and continue dancing until the next girl comes out."

The digital clock changed to 7:40. *"... And next up on stage is the lovely Jackie."* Doogie Howser's voice sounded pretty smooth through the speakers. *Dream Weaver* came on. Jackie ducked under the bar, placed her pocketbook on the stage, and started dancing. Everyone stared in amazement. She was incredible. Her perfect turns, kicks, straddles, and highly advanced moves around the pole made me wonder: *How am I ever going to follow this act?* Before her ten minutes were up, she had the whole place drooling. Then it was my turn.

"... And next up on stage is ... Barbie."

Barbie? Who's Barbie? Is he talking about me? I stood still in confusion, and for a moment, I thought it wasn't my turn. Jackie came right over to me. "Get on stage!" she demanded.

"But the DJ said 'Barbie.' I'm not *Barbie*. I hate that name," I winced.

"I guess he got confused when I told him you were 'Baby Bree.' He probably thought I said 'Barbie.' Just get up there and you'll straighten it out later."

I wanted to kill Doogie at that moment.

He played *Sweet Little Sister* by Skid Row. Everyone at the bar, who knew that I was Jackie's little sister, laughed and thought it was a clever song to play. I ducked under the bar and placed my pocketbook on the stage next to the pile in the corner – just like Jackie had done. When the dancers couldn't hold on to their large wads of cash, they'd run over to their bags and make a deposit.

I climbed onto the stage in the red high heels and grabbed the nearest pole as though it were a life raft. Slowly and carefully I did some sexy moves around the pole. Then I leaned my back against it and lowered myself down into a *grande pliete* – a more appropriate ballet move than the horrible turns that Miss Crazy-Brace-Face had attempted. I caressed myself with my hands exactly the way that Jackie did when it was her turn on stage. As I bent over, I imagined I was a Victoria's Secret model. A patron in the corner held up a dollar. I got down and jiggled my boobs together as he placed the bill in my cleavage. *My first tip!* I thought. I wanted to frame it. I was about to get back on stage, but he held up another bill. I placed my knee up on the edge of the bar. He tickled the dollar along my thigh. The exchange was taking entirely too long, so I slightly lifted the part of my costume just above my bikini line. He gently placed it in. My lips puckered. I blew him a kiss before climbing back on stage and placing the bills in my bag.

I stood up again and attempted to make my way across the miles of stage that stretched before me. It felt like I was walking on stilts. Every second posed a threat to my balancing act, but I managed to get to the other pole. I took off the fringed cover-up and did the same sexy turns and bends around the pole that I had done before. Another guy summoned me with his cash. After he placed the first two bills exactly where the other guy had, he motioned for me to turn around and placed a bill behind my G-string. I climbed back on stage feeling sexy as hell.

I'm doing it! I'm pulling off this act of being a dancer. These people are under the impression that I know what I'm doing. They really think I'm a dancer.

As soon as my confidence level started to rise, I decided to try a spin and a kick – Jackie style. The spin was okay. But as I kicked my leg up, the red shoe went flying across the stage and over the edge. The paper I had stuffed in the shoe flew out, too. *Shit! What the hell do I do now?* I tried not to panic and acted as though I'd intentionally kicked off the shoe by kicking off the other one. Then I slowly crawled over to collect them. Some guy with a foot fetish got excited. He held up a twenty.

"Hi, *Barbie*," he said with a plastic smile.

"Hi," I smiled back. "Havin' a good time?"

"Sure am," he nodded. "My name's *Ken*."

"What a coincidence," I said with enthusiasm. *Freak*, I thought.

"If you let me hold your shoe, I'll give you this." He waved the twenty. I handed him the shoe. It seemed like a reasonable exchange.

Before meeting *Ken*, I had been thinking about a stage name while dancing around, and was certain I'd tell Doogie that my name was *not* Barbie before my next set. I'd tell him that it was Cherry. Cherry seemed like the best choice for the situation. Cherry is my middle name. It's supposed to be pronounced with an initial "sh" sound, but I always say it the other way. After Ken handed me the twenty-dollar bill, I reconsidered. *Maybe this Barbie theme will work in my favor.*

I returned to the stage barefoot and danced around, enjoying the feel of the stage beneath my liberated feet. I decided to slide down into a straddle, unaware that I was directly above the hole in the floor. Doogie switched on the smoke machine. A blast shot up, engulfing me in a cloud. I tried my best to keep from choking without much success. When the smoke finally cleared, I retrieved my shoe from Ken and started the whole routine of trying to get around in heels again.

Quickly and awkwardly, I made my way across the stage from pole to pole. Jackie rushed over to me. "Stop running! Slow down!" she whispered firmly in my ear. I did my best, but it was a mess. I had no control of my body in those power pumps. Still, my turn ended and I had made thirty bucks in ten minutes.

It was much easier collecting money in the red shoes than it was dancing in them. Each dancer had to walk around the entire bar at least once before she could take a break. Most walked on top of the bar, carefully – very carefully – navigating around the drinks and ashtrays, bending down to squat or sit or lay while entertaining the customers and collecting the cash.

During that set I made three trips over to my pocketbook; the money kept falling out of my hands. After collecting an entire round of tips, I was ready to return to the dressing room. Jackie was still busy working the bar. The St. Pauly Girl smiled at me on my way.

Joe the night manager stopped me before I reached

the door. "Hey *Barbie*, you have a great ass."

"Thanks. Does that mean that I'm hired?"

"Sure does," he rasped with a smile and patted my butt as I walked past him. In any other setting, I would've had a confrontation with him over the ass-pat. But this was a go-go bar, and I was in character, playing the part.

My feet were red and throbbing. Searching through Jackie's suitcase, I found a pair of thigh-high leather boots that were black and smooth as butter. The heels weren't quite as high as the red pumps. I knew I'd have more success in them on stage. I shimmied back into the black fishnet one-piece that I'd worn for Dante during our night of ecstasy.

Over at the counter, the girl with the strawberry ass-tattoo reapplied her make up. I bent over to make sure that my strawberry rash was really gone – not a trace of it was left. I fixed my hair and freshened up, listening to the other dancers' complaints about the empty bar. I couldn't figure it out. Money seemed plentiful. After reapplying just the right amount of black eyeliner, I took a pair of silver hoop earrings from Jackie's cosmetic case and liked the way they looked on me.

"Your nipples are fantastic," said the girl with the strawberry.

"Thanks." I looked at them in the mirror. My nipples practically popped right through the fishnet. I needed to find a cover-up in Jackie's suitcase. A faded denim vest and a pair of shredded Levi's cut-offs worked well over the fishnet.

The girl with the strawberry stared at me. She

117

reminded me of Kate Jones, in a "dykey" kind of way. I didn't want to lead her on and give her the wrong impression – like I had done to Kate – but I couldn't resist a quick compliment about her tattoo. She got real excited. I got the hell out of there.

I sat next to Ken at the bar and ordered a glass of red wine. His ear-to-ear plastic smile was still painted on his face. "I'll give you another twenty if you let me massage your feet," he offered. My feet were killing me. I removed the long leather boot. He went to work. It felt great – better than great. I bummed a Marlboro red off the guy to my left and sipped the wine.

Wow, what a racket! I thought. *You usually have to pay for treatment like this. And here I am, making money for nothing.*

Jackie stepped up to collect a tip from Ken. I couldn't figure out how she managed to stay on her feet for so long.

"Are they my earrings?" she asked.

"Of course they are."

"They're my *favorite* earrings," she said, agitated.

"You told me to use your stuff," I reminded her in a singsong kind of way.

"Well you're going to have to start bringing your own stuff." Jackie has such a pathetic attachment to her things and gets out of sorts when I borrow them, even if she offered in the first place.

"Shut up, Jackie," I said as politely as possible, giving her the get-back-to-reality look.

"I'm only kidding," she grinned, feeling guilty about being possessive.

Our sister quarrel excited Ken into handing me

another twenty.

During a second glass of red wine and a second bummed cigarette, it was Jackie's turn to dance again. *She didn't even take a break!* I marveled. When Doogie announced her name, she ran back to the dressing room and changed her costume in one minute flat.

Everyone stared at the empty stage, waiting for her return. I anticipated my next set with thigh-high uncertainty for the remaining eight minutes of Jackie's knockout performance.

Men with snowflakes in their hair filled the bar more and more. Even in a snowstorm, the regulars remained loyal. I danced to Marvin Gaye's *Sexual Healing.* The boots were much better. They gave me the extra support I needed, and I didn't have to worry about accidentally kicking them off. They stuck to my legs like wet paper.

While on stage, I couldn't help staring at myself in the mirrors, as they visually echoed my every move. Most of the walls in the bar were mirrored. I needed to be sure I looked all right up there – to check and correct any trace of sloppiness – to find a balance between smooth and sexy. But I kept focusing on my form and would often forget to make eye contact with the customers, ignoring the very reason most of them were at the bar in the first place: personal attention. I even danced right past a guy who was waving money at me. The mirrors were very distracting.

By the time my fourth set was over, the thickening snowstorm thinned out the crowd. I was practically dancing for myself during the last set of the night. On my way from pole to pole, I'd bend over and practice my moves in the mirrors. I'd get down and roll around some, stopping every now and then to turn into a split or a straddle, stretching my muscles like a cat upon awakening. It was good exercise, except for the fact that I was breathing in a ton of smoke.

A big banner on the back wall hung above the pinball machines: MEET THE DREAM TEAM, THURSDAY NIGHTS, ACTION-PACKED GO-GO. The words on the banner reminded me of a book I had bought at a Book Fair when I was in second grade: *My Favorite Go-Go Action Pop-Up Book.* It was all about trains and planes and automobiles that popped up from the pages. My favorite image was a city bus that had a little tab in the shape of an arrow attached to the side of the page. When I pulled the tab out, it revealed all the people on the bus. When I pushed it back in, the people disappeared and all that remained were the empty bus windows. That's what went through my mind while receiving a dollar in the shape of an arrow behind my G-string. I still have that book. I never throw away anything that I love.

*

We had to clear six inches of snow off the car before we left.

On the way back to Philly, I ran my mouth about all the people I'd met. Jackie loved sharing this part of her life with me.

"Do you know the guy who says he's a sex therapist?" I asked.

"Oh, God. Isn't he pathetic," she giggled.

120

"Who the hell would go to *him* for sex therapy?"

"He's not *really* a sex therapist, you idiot."

"Yes, he is. He gave me his business card."

"It's a fake. Most of the guys come into the bar to play out their little fantasies."

"They even go as far as making up phony business cards?" It seemed like a step over the edge.

"Yup. At Studio 67 their dream worlds come to life."

"That's so deceptive."

"I know, but they pay enough for it. How much money did the guy with the foot fetish give you?"

"A lot. Ken gave me four twenties," I said, proud to have remembered a one-syllable name.

"Ken? He told you his name was *Ken*?"

"Uh-huh."

"Did you believe him?"

"Not at first ... but I guess he convinced me somehow. He's kind of cute."

"Just so you know ... his real name is Tom. He's a regular and he'll go after anyone that'll let him get near their feet."

"God, they really are sick bastards, aren't they?"

"They might be crazy, but who cares? Wait till you see what goes on in there on Thursday nights. It gets wild ... really *wild*." Jackie's eyes opened as wide as the word.

After driving through the snow for an hour, we finally got home. My father was waiting up for us, reading the newspaper on the sofa. I could tell he was relieved that we made it back without any problems – because of the storm. "Well?" he sat up. "How did your audition go?"

"Fine," I smiled.

"Are you hired?" His concern was sincere.

"Of course she's hired," Jackie replied.

"It's too bad you didn't start dancing sooner. Think of all the money you could've saved by now," he said.

"Dad, I'm lucky I had the nerve to get up on that stage at all!"

"Do you know how well you made out … with the tips?"

"I don't know. But I'm sure it's more than I made at the health food store."

"Aren't you going to count it?"

"I'll count it in the morning … I'm exhausted … I'm going to bed." I gave him a kiss and wondered if he could smell the stench of the bar on me. "Good night, Daddy."

"Good night, darling. We'll talk in the morning."

"Good night, *Barbie*!" Jackie teased.

I took a shower. At first the steam smelled like a wet bar. I lathered up with lemon verbena before spreading the Downy-scented Cotton Flowers with Shea Butter soap all over my skin. Thoughts of Jordan bubbled and foamed. *Ah … relief.* The water was incredibly soothing. I think I fell asleep standing up for a few moments.

That night I dreamed I was in a Barbie doll commercial: Go-Go Action Barbie surrounded by Ken dolls – spinning around and around on a plastic platform between two plastic poles – as tiny plastic money snowed down, covering the floor.

CHAPTER FIFTEEN

Those Shoes!

I woke up with large and small dark spots all over my legs and looked like a leopard from the waist down. Climbing on and off the hard wooden stage – getting on and off the bar – my legs had banged around a lot more than I was aware of. They looked horrible, like I had been in some kind of an accident or something.

Getting out of bed was a slow-motion event. Every move ached. *Shit! Am I going to feel like this every time I dance?* I washed up and headed to the kitchen. Jackie was making her morning cup of tea with a wedge of lemon and five teaspoons of sugar. Upon seeing me, she pulled down another teacup. "*One sugar,*" I uttered.

"Are you okay?" she asked. "You look crazy."

"I can barely move. I'm in pain."

"You'll get used to it. It's just your muscles."

The way she said *you'll get used to it* confirmed my fear of this less-than-temporary occupational side effect. I pulled up the bottom of my sweatpants, exposing my calves.

"Look at this! Look at these bruises!"

"I know it looks bad, but it's nothing. They go away fast." Jackie pulled down her pants and showed me her marks. They weren't as bad as mine. Just then my mother entered the kitchen, followed by my father.

"What's going on in here?" my mother asked as Jackie pulled her pants back up.

"We were just comparing bruises to see who got banged harder last night," I chuckled, unable to resist a distasteful pun.

"Who got banged last night?" my father asked, always willing to keep a distasteful pun rolling.

"*Barbie* did," Jackie joked.

"Who's Barbie?" he asked. My mother left the room.

"I'm Barbie," I said. "The DJ made a mistake and introduced me as Barbie every time I got on stage, all night long."

"Did you correct him?"

"No, the name seemed to excite the customers, so I went along with it."

My mother came back into the kitchen.

"The snow's melting," she announced. "Does anyone want breakfast?"

"I do," I said, feeling hungrier than usual. "I want an omelet. Are you making eggs?"

"I'll make whatever you want," she said.

"I have to work today," Jackie said, referring to her job at the hair salon. "So, will you count my money for me? I don't have time." Jackie asked.

"I haven't even counted *mine* yet," I answered.

"Well, you better get busy. I'm taking you shopping for costumes later. I'll pick you up around four. Make sure you're ready. Daddy'll count my money. Right daddy?"

"I will if I have to," he said.

Jackie placed her puffy leather, cash-filled, go-go pocketbook on the dining room table. My father was more than happy to help her count her money. He got a real kick out of the fact that his daughters were dancing on a stage, even if it was semi-professional work. He had always been a fan of the burlesque theater, and during his senior year of high school, he played hooky more often than not to enjoy the shows at the Trocadero on Arch Street.

I learned about his truant behavior when I was younger: I had been rummaging around the storage room in the basement, searching for anything of interest in my parents' personal history relics. All their pre-marital belongings were stuffed into cardboard boxes. It was one of those boring, Cat-in-the-Hat rainy days when I came across my father's high school commencement book. I looked for his name but couldn't find it at first. Down at the bottom of the Italian, Jewish, and African-American names, listed in alphabetical order, was a line that read: "The following students will graduate after completion of summer school." There wasn't any room left on that particular page for the names of the flunkies, so I turned the page. One name followed: "David Yeager." A whole page was added just for his name.

My father loves anything that has to do with the arts, even if it means failing school or dancing around a pole on stage in a G-string.

When my sisters and I were little girls, he made us watch the musical *Gypsy*, over and over. It was about the life of the famous striptease artist Gypsy Rose Lee. There's this one scene in the musical that takes place right before her very first appearance on stage as a stripper. She was pretty nervous, so the veteran dancers were giving her advice while they're all in the dressing room getting ready. They tell Gypsy that the way to succeed in the business is to get a gimmick. Then they sing this fabulous number about their individual gimmicks. One of them, Miss Electra, has little light bulbs all over her costume like a Christmas tree. She pushes a button and lights up to electrify the audience. Then this other stripper named Miss Mazeppa incorporates a trumpet into her act. She bumps and grinds and blows her horn. It's hysterical. She's my favorite. Tessie Tura, the third stripper in the number, comes on in point shoes as this ballerina type who thinks she's demure because she has poise and grace. She does pretty little pirouettes and dainty little sachet steps before she bumps and grinds her hips as vulgar as the others. Whenever *Gypsy* was on, you could tell my father enjoyed that scene most of all. He'd laugh his head off.

After breakfast we got busy straightening the bills. I made six hundred and fifty-eight dollars. Jackie made nine hundred and ninety-nine.

"How come Jackie made so much more money than you made?" my father asked.

"She works the bar more. She barely even stops to take a break. And anyway, what's wrong with making six fifty-eight in five hours? That's over a hundred dollars an hour, tax-free cash."

"Nothing's wrong with it. I would do it if I could. Just don't forget why you're there, Bree. Get the money. That's what you're there for. And don't forget it," he said.

"I know, dad. But it was my first night, and I could barely walk in those shoes. I had to take breaks. Look at my legs!" I pulled up my sweatpants.

"*Eww*. You better take it easy." He sounded concerned.

"What's the matter?" My mother asked. I'd forgotten that she was in the room because she was playing her pocket poker hand-held game on the silent mode.

"What's good for bruises? ... Her legs are full of them," my father said.

"Are there any lumps?" she asked. The two of them were starting to irritate me in the usual way. I opened the delightful red metallic wrapping of a *Cella's* chocolate-covered cherry and popped it into my mouth. My mother keeps a candy dish full of them on the coffee table – just for me.

"I don't feel any lumps," I answered through a mushy mouthful.

"Well, if you find any, just take a cold knife and press the edge of it down on the lump and leave it there for a while, and if it doesn't go away –"

"Okay, okay," I interrupted. "I don't have any lumps."

"Just take it easy on yourself," my father advised.

I spent the rest of the morning sleeping, completely wiped out. When I woke up, around two in the afternoon, I felt a lot better. The house was quiet. It felt more like a Sunday than a Tuesday. As I prepared a cup of coffee, I heard the mailman approaching and blazed like wildfire to the front door. My dancing pains ached again.

Yes! Another postcard from Italy!

Jordan faithfully wrote to me every week. He may have had a new girlfriend, but it was me who he loved. I sipped my coffee in the quiet afternoon, brewing over each and every word he had written:

Dear Bree,

You would love Rome. It's a feast for the senses. I wish you were here, by my side, right now.

Every day, around this time at dusk, I sit and watch as the sun sets pink on the Eternal City, and gets buried under centuries of chestnut gelato.

My mind swims around in a flood of pleasures. I am studying the life of art, and living the art of life. I am sketching all that I see, painting all that I feel.

And all the while, I think of Love, I think of Beauty, I think of You. How I've missed you, Bree.

Looking forward to a new semester and to the day when I'll be with you again, my lovely best friend.

Forever Yours,
Jordan

As I read the postcard – over and over – the sounds of children playing outside in the sun-glistened snow delightfully accompanied Jordan's poetic message. It was the first time that he didn't mention his girlfriend Lisa's name at all. *Maybe they broke up,* I thought.

I took another shower just to use the "Downy" soap again. Thinking about Jordan and the future we could possibly have together gave new meaning to the day. Like me, he too was excited about resuming classes. I had had enough of the winter break. The idea of being a full-time student/part-time dancer held the promise of charm and mystery.

I spent the rest of the afternoon marching around the house in Jackie's heels like a five-year-old who had just emerged from her mother's closet. Determined to get used to them as quickly as possible, I chose to play dress-up in a pair with straps conveniently fastened around my ankles. Even though they were difficult to walk in, at least they wouldn't fly off my feet if I did another kick.

My parents returned home with Mona while I was making a salad. They'd been out shopping for fabric that Mona would transform into curtains for her new home. She's great with the sewing machine. I can't even figure out how to thread it. Mona makes a lot of her own clothes: shirts, skirts, scarves, and such. She even put together an entire bathing-suit wardrobe one summer – crocheted, beaded, and stitched to cotton lining. The bathing suits were special. Jackie thought so too, but Jackie and I weren't allowed to touch them.

"Why are you wearing THOSE SHOES?" Mona shrieked, looking at my feet as though they were on fire.

I dropped the cucumber I'd been peeling and turned around in utter shock. I had forgotten I was even wearing them. Her look was horrifying as she gazed down in disgust. I wasn't thrilled with her white Bo-Bo sneakers either. *Go-Go ... Bo-Bo*, I thought, and laughed as the rhyme filled my mind. "Oh … I'm … practicing," I said.

"Practicing *what*?" she asked.

"What do you think? I'm practicing walking in heels, DUH!" I answered.

"I can see that. But *why* are you practicing walking in heels?" Mona couldn't tell that I was stalling for time to think of an excuse. That's what I love about her. She has no criminal mind.

"I'm applying for a job as a cocktail waitress," I decided. "And I have to wear high heels."

"Oh, where is it?"

"Out in Princeton … where Jackie works," I said, even though there weren't any cocktail waitresses at Studio 67.

"At the go-go bar?" Mona whined, twisting her face.

"Uh-huh."

"Can't you find a job somewhere else? Somewhere *normal*?"

"No, I can't. So why don't *you* find me a job where I can make that kind of money? Okay, Mona? Since you know everything about everything, then why don't you get me a job?"

"Why don't you just get your own job?" she cleverly suggested.

"What do you care anyway? Does it really matter to you where I work or what I do?" I had taken enough of her crap and even considered telling her about last night, but my father's eyes burned out any thought I had of being honest. Having to make up lies about myself started to frustrate me: *All for Mona –*

Mona who was sensitive – Mona who needed protection from the truth. What was she anyway, some kind of saint?

"No," she said, "I don't care what you do. Why don't you just dance like a tramp with your *other* sister? Or better yet, why don't you turn tricks on Broad Street in those whore heels? I hear they're hiring."

"Fuck off, Mona."

"That's enough girls," my father announced from his corner of the ring. And the conversation was over. I started peeling the cucumber again.

"Do you want a salad? I'll make you one if you want me to," I offered. I never leave an argument open with Mona. Like I said before, she holds an eternal grudge.

"No thanks. I'm meeting my husband for dinner tonight at our favorite Italian restaurant in South Philly." Her face lit up at the thought of Steven who she could finally call her husband. I was reminded of another Billy Joel song.

"Are you gonna have a bottle of red … or a bottle of white?" I asked.

"They don't serve alcohol there, but we could bring our own bottle if we wanted to. We never do, though. We're not really drinkers."

"I know, Mona. I was only joking."

"Maybe this time we'll drive up to Princeton for cocktails afterwards," she joked.

"You can if you want. It all depends upon your appetite," I laughed, but she didn't get it.

Later on, Jackie took me shopping at Warrior,

Erogenous Zone, and, of course, Fredericks of Hollywood. Now I had my own suitcase full of costumes and my own kaboodle case full of cosmetics and accessories. Things were looking up, even though I had already spent *all* of what I'd earned.

CHAPTER SIXTEEN

The Cat Walk of Success

The parking lot was full of Thursday night cars. Some were noticeably fancy. I'm not a real looker when it comes to cars, but a Jaguar, a Viper, and a super-stretch limo in one row of a straggly shopping center parking lot caught my eye. "Cool! It's busy!" shouted Jackie. "Thank God the snow melted."

I was excited to try out my new costumes. We entered through the back door, same as before, except the energy was different. The floor vibrated under our feet; the music thrashed; the crowd could be heard, hooting and howling. Joe the night manager rasped to us the same schedules as the last time: 7:40 and 7:50.

"Why are you putting us on so late?" Jackie asked with a righteous attitude.

"They all showed up extra early tonight. You know how it goes. First come, first served," he said.

"Oh, come on. Can't you get us on earlier?" Jackie whined.

"Stop complaining, Jackie. I'm stressed out enough as it is. I had to kick out two guys who were jerkin' off in the bathroom. Do you have any idea how stressful that is?"

"Uh, I really don't," Jackie admitted.

"Well, it ain't pretty."

"Fine." Jackie turned and stomped toward the

dressing room.

"Has she always been a spoiled brat?" Joe asked.

"She has middle-child syndrome. She can't help it," I said.

"Come on, Bree," Jackie demanded with a hint of frustration in her voice. She didn't want to hang around for a whole hour, waiting for her first set to begin. She felt defeated, and defeat is not something she handles well. Even when we were younger, she'd always overreact whenever things didn't go her way. We used to play a card game called "Spit," where the object of the game is to get rid of all your cards. If Jackie's pile grew larger in her hand, rather than smaller, she'd end the game by throwing all her cards at me. Jacks, diamonds, blacks, and reds came flying at my face. The messy pile of cards on the floor translated into my success. It was the same thing with backgammon. She'd slam the boards together and all the chips would collide. Winning was never fun with her.

We went into the dressing room. There were so many girls and not much room for our suitcases. Everyone knew Jackie, greeting her as though a diva had arrived. She went through the routine of introducing me to all the dancers, none of which had been there on my first night.

"Do you want to go next door and get a slice of pizza?" she asked. "We have a lot of time to kill."

"Let's just get a drink and wait at the bar like we did last time," I said.

"It's Thursday night, Bree. There's nowhere to sit. The bar's packed."

"Three deep!" one of the dancers announced. I didn't understand what *three deep* meant. "We're making money tonight, ladies." She fixed her hair in an up-do that revealed a tattooed nametag on the back of her neck: *Sierra.*

My father had forbidden us from getting tattoos. "Not under my roof," he'd say. He was always saying that about tattoos and body piercings. I probably would have ventured into the world of self-mutilating expression had I been allowed. While checking out the hack job on Sierra's neck, I silently thanked my father.

I had never seen a larger set of boobs in comparison to the ones that Sierra had. They were huge – even bigger than Niomi's postpartum milk jugs from which her baby suckled in the back room of the health food store.

"What bra size do you wear? … If you don't mind my asking," I said.

"I don't mind. Everyone asks me that. I got 'em done a few weeks ago, and that's all I ever hear now," Sierra replied, still fixing up her hairdo.

"Well, what size are they?" Jackie repeated. All the dancers in the room stopped what they were doing in order to hear which letter of the alphabet it would be.

"A full H cup," Sierra announced with extreme pride, throwing back her shoulders, displaying her H cups even more. Every eye in the dressing room was on her chest. She looked as though she was standing behind two big balloons. Not regular balloons, though. More like those Hoppity Horses we used to bounce around on as kids.

"An H cup?" I gasped in amazement. "I didn't even know that was a bra size."

"See, ya learn something new everyday," Sierra said with a smile, pleased to have been the teacher of such uncharted information.

"Are they heavy?" I asked with curiosity. They looked like they weighed a tremendous amount.

"*Nah* ... light as can be. Feel 'em." She made her way over to me. *Is she for real*, I thought. *I don't want to feel them!* "Here, put your arm under 'em like this and lift 'em up," she demonstrated. I thought it best not to be rude, so I did as she said, lifting the H cups with my forearm. They were pretty heavy.

"Wow, they're so light!" I lied, acting as though I was very impressed. But really, I was relieved to have been done with the grueling task.

"Are we going for pizza, or what?" Jackie asked.

"Yeah, let's go." I grabbed my bag and headed towards the door. "Nice to have met you and your H cups, Sierra," I said on my way out.

"Pleasure's all mine." She inserted extra large hoop earrings that were almost as big in circumference as her boobs. She sure had a circular gimmick going on around her body. I imagined her twirling a Hula Hoop as part of her stage act.

The pizza place was right next door to Studio. But in order to get there, we had to exit the bar through the front door. On our way out, I came to understand what "three deep" meant. Three full layers of customers filled the barroom, starting innermost from those who were sitting. Every bar stool was occupied. Then there was a second layer of customers who stood individually or in groups, filling the floor space. And the third layer of the *three-deep* was the row of men who leaned against the walls.

Flashing lights cut through the thick smoke, revealing an army of dancers. They were everywhere. Three dancing on stage at a time. A dozen or more collecting tips. Some working directly on top of the bar. Some working the floor inside the bar. Other dancers were sitting with customers, drinking and smoking, chatting and laughing. "Holy shit!" I uttered. "I *told you* Thursday nights were wild. And it's just getting started," Jackie grinned.

So many of the customers turned their heads to catch a glimpse of us as we weaved our way through the crowd to the front door. They eyed us up and down, checking us out in just our regular clothes.

Inside the pizza place, I felt pretty nervous. Everything seemed so normal in there. Teenagers laughed around the game machines without a care in the world for the cheese that was stuck in their braces. Parents sat in cozy booths with their kids, innocently eating pizzas and sipping soft drinks. All this family-fun normalcy sharply contrasted with the greatest freak show in the world that was taking place right on the other side of the wall where grown men got caught jerking off in public. Where dancers vowed to save their tips – to buy larger breasts – to make larger tips. Where guys like Ken or Tom (or whatever his name was) paid extra to sniff the foot of a female. As these thoughts occurred to me, I realized that this was just the beginning of my journey into the world of go-go. I realized that I didn't really belong there. I felt like a puzzle piece that didn't quite fit into the picture. I felt like a freak because I was eating pizza, surrounded by normal, everyday people, and I couldn't wait to get back to the freak show on the other side of the wall. However vulgar it might have been, I found it fascinating.

*

I got dressed in a hot-pink two-piece, slipped on a pair of white pleather, thigh-high boots, and covered up with a little white leather jacket. Jackie slid into a metallic-silver one-piece that gave her a futuristic look, like a go-go dancer from *Star Trek*. We still had ten minutes to wait before it was Jackie's turn, so we squeezed our way into a quick drink at the bar.

The music pumped through my body. I could feel bass vibrations in my stomach. Jackie saw some guy she knew. "I'm going over there to have a drink with that customer. I want to introduce you to him. He's a big tipper. Come with me," she said practically shouting, so I could hear her through all the commotion in the bar. "You go. I'll stay here. I need to take all this in for a minute," I said, trying not to shout. "Are you sure?" "Go. I'm fine." She reluctantly left my side.

The same one-syllable names were seated in the same corner of the bar as before. A *Bob* offered his seat to me, but I insisted on standing. I wanted to get used to standing in high heels again before I went up on stage. Bob sneaked a peak at my ass every once in a while. I could tell that it pleased him to have such a close-up view of it, but he wasn't offensive or rude or

138

anything like that. He was an older gentleman – a mechanic who worked at the corner garage that specialized in foreign cars. In Princeton foreign cars ruled the roads. Bob looked like he had been working overtime. There were fresh grease stains under his fingernails, and he was still wearing his uniform. A patch above his shirt pocket had his name stitched on it, which was good for me because I didn't have to worry about remembering it. I felt comfortable by his side.

Bobbi the Bartender came over, wiped the counter, and emptied the ashtrays. Her hands moved faster than one of the dancers on stage whose legs seemed to zip around at the speed of sound. The dancer was clad in a tightly fitted motorcycle outfit with a thick silver zipper running along it from top to bottom. She looked sharp in a matching leather cap and black sunglasses. I kept thinking that either the glasses or the cap were going to fly off her head because she made some seriously complex moves. But she wasn't the amateur that I was; every piece of her headgear remained in place. I gazed in amazement as she tore up the stage and riled the crowd. "Wow, she's incredible," I said.

"She's a professional," Bob explained. "A lot of 'em come down from the city to cash in on the Thursday night crowd." He pulled a soft pack of Winston cigarettes from his shirt pocket and offered me one. I accepted. The idea of dancing on the same stage as New York professionals was more than a humbling thought. I wasn't half the dancer of the women I'd be sharing the stage with. I was out of my league, but there was nothing I could do about it. There was no magic wand to wave over my head. All I had was a Winston cigarette to puff on in between large sips of red wine.

Bobbi the Bartender continued to clean the counter, exaggerating the task by lifting each glass, napkin, and ashtray two or three times – scrubbing and wiping – then placing them back down with her shaky hands. Each of her fingernails was the size of my whole pinkie finger. "Did you hear about Junior?" she asked Bob.

"Hear what?" he asked.

"You didn't hear about his baby?" she said, ferociously wiping a spot on the edge of the counter.

"No, what happened? Is he working tonight?"

"He won't be in for a while. His wife had the baby." Bobbi stopped scrubbing the counter for a moment. "It died – It was a boy – It died the same day it was born."

"Oh shit," Bob grumbled. He placed his head in his hands, threading his grease-stained fingers through his graying head of Elvis Presley hair.

"Him and his wife don't have enough money for a proper funeral, so we're taking up a collection."

"Here, take this." Bob pulled out a twenty and handed it to Bobbi. He frowned and shrugged his shoulders. I opened my pocketbook and pulled out a ten. I didn't know Junior, but felt the need to contribute to the collection.

"Thanks," Bobbi said. "You're Jackie's sister, right?"

"Yeah. I think we met already. I was here on

140

Tuesday … when it snowed," I said.

"Oh yeah. I left early that night. You guys look exactly alike. Are you twins?" I went through the usual explanation.

"Tell me your name again," she said.

"I'm Bree, but my stage name's Barbie."

"Right – I remember now. My name's Bobbi, and when the DJ said 'Barbie' – when he called *you* up to the stage – I thought he was calling *me* for a second – like he was playing a joke on me or something," she smirked. "Nice to meet you, again."

"You too," I said, forcing a smile past the thought of a dead newborn baby.

"Junior's the regular Thursday night DJ. He'll definitely appreciate this." She placed the funeral funds in her money belt and wiped her way to the other end of the counter.

The crowd hooted and howled like wild animals. Two of the dancers were making out on stage. Then it was Jackie's turn to go up. Another dancer stayed on stage while Jackie danced – and that's how it went on Thursday nights. We all had to share the stage with one or two other dancers at a time. Jackie kept looking my way as if to say she was frustrated about something. She got down and came over. "What's wrong?" I asked.

"The stupid DJ's playing the wrong song. I *told* him to play *Rocket Queen*. The regular Thursday night DJ's not here. He's the best. No one else can keep up with this amount of dancers … I wonder why he's not here … Junior's always here on Thursday nights."

"I know why. I just heard about it from Bobbi. His

wife just had a baby – and it died." The words tasted bitter as they rolled off my tongue.

"Oh my God – That's awful!" Jackie shouted. It was a horrible thing to think about in the middle of all that merriment. Jackie sipped my wine in silence until her song came on. Then she got back up on stage and knocked out the crowd with her long legs.

Five minutes later it was my turn. I was thrilled to be dancing to *Tainted Love*. I'd always loved that song and danced around with ease, even though my new pleather boots were as stiff as could be. They felt like two little raincoats wrapped around my legs. Each time I bent down, they sounded in a series of sharp crunches.

In the middle of the song, the DJ switched on the black lights. For a while, everyone's teeth turned greenish white as they smiled at me. The whites of their eyes glowed, too. I felt like I was in a jungle, surrounded by nocturnal creatures with night vision. During that set, I spent more time getting down and collecting dollars than I did dancing. I tried my best not to look in the mirrors because there was too much money to be made. I kept reminding myself to follow my father's advice: *Get the money. That's why I'm here. Don't forget.* By the time my ten minutes were up, I had more cash than I could hold on to.

Running over to my pocketbook to deposit the bills took too much time, so I stuffed the money in my boots. It was much more convenient. And, as an added bonus, the money helped protect my legs from the bar – like extra padding. Ending up with a new set of bruises in the morning was a fear that kept my every move coordinated, poised, and precise.

Jackie kept pulling me away from the customers I was entertaining and introducing me to the big-tipping, holier-than-thou, Thursday night regular spenders. One was a vice president of AT&T. One owned a fleet of ships. One was a stockbroker. One was a surgeon who worked in the ER. He slammed down a bunch of drinks before heading back to the hospital. Most of the guys were very polite. But then there were the bachelor parties. They got rowdy.

While I was up on the bar, I found it easy to manipulate the patrons for at least three bucks a try – one in the cleavage, one in the crotch, one in the ass. One, two, three … One, two, three ... If a customer started folding another bill, after he'd already given me three, I'd change my position and go for the fourth. It took some getting used to, but after a while, I created a special pose for the fourth bill by sitting on the bar with my back to the customer, resting my head on his shoulder. That way, he'd get a different view of my figure – a landscape view. They usually couldn't resist another three bucks once I got into that position. Sometimes a guy from the second or third row of the *three deep* would reach over and place (or shove) a bill in, too. I didn't really like it when that happened, because I couldn't always see who had given it to me since I was facing the other way.

I assessed the other dancers on a constant basis. No one sat on the bar the way I did. Jackie was impressed that I had been so innovative, so fast. "I like your little pose on the bar," she said.

"Thanks. Does it look okay?"

"Yeah, it looks great. You're really catching on to this, aren't you?"

"It's not exactly brain surgery. It's a racket. I can't believe these guys spend all this money for thrills."

"Believe it."

During my second set, I wore the black fishnet again. I bought one for myself because it looked so damn sexy on me. Jackie wore hers too and got up on stage while I was dancing to INXS, *The Devil Inside*. We wore the same costume, the same boots, and the same earrings. The crowd went wild. A bachelor party on the right side of the bar chanted, "SIS-TER-ACT, SIS-TER-ACT." We got down and went over to collect. They were drunk. One guy tried to slide his hand in my crotch. I pulled away pretty quickly and grabbed his hand before anything really happened. Jackie saw the whole thing. "If you try and pull that shit again, I'm gonna have you and all your friends kicked outta here," she threatened.

"Lighten up, little lady. We're only having fun," he said.

"Well, you're NOT allowed to touch the dancers like that! GET IT?"

"Oh, come on. There's no harm in trying? Is there?" he asked, trying his best to amuse her.

"Uh, it's illegal. You wanna get arrested? The owner's a cop. I'll get him right now," Jackie warned. The guy backed down.

Three dancers were on stage putting on a lesbian act. One had her head buried in the crotch of another while two of them were making out and feeling each other all over the place. The natives grunted their mating calls. The bachelor party started drooling. The guy who Jackie had been arguing with turned a hormonal shade of red. Jackie took a twenty-dollar bill that was sitting on top of his pile of money. He didn't notice. I thought she was pretty bold for doing it. "I'll split it with you later," she said out of the side of her mouth.

"You just *stole* that guy's money?" I asked in disbelief.

"He wasted my time. He *owes* it to me, for one thing – and for *another*, he's lucky I didn't get him kicked out."

"Okay," I laughed. We both ran around making our money. I had forgotten that the owner was a cop, and although Studio 67 was not a topless go-go bar, many of the girls ran around with their tops down while they collected their tips. They'd use their forearms to cover up their nipples, allowing them to "accidentally" pop out every once in a tip. It definitely seemed like a violation of some sort. The lesbian acts also seemed like a violation. Whenever the girls were going at it on stage, the customers would give even bigger tips, completely entranced, brainwashed.

As I witnessed more and more of what went on that night, I realized that go-go dancing *is* a form of brain surgery – metaphorical brain surgery. The dancers cut into the minds of the spectators with the tools of the trade and manipulated their thoughts. Sierra certainly had her tools. You could see her H cups swinging around the pole all night long. She'd climb to the very top and hang upside down from the pole like a bat of erotica. Her boobs were always right in your face no matter where you were in the bar. In between sets, I'd often join one of the customers for a drink and a smoke, and every time Sierra came over for a tip, I was tempted to pop her big balloons with the lit end of my cigarette. I thought they looked absolutely grotesque. The guys loved them, though.

I met a dancer named Sheila that night. She's half Japanese-half Swedish with exotic beauty and phenomenal talent beyond compare. Even Jackie admits that Sheila's the best dancer at Studio. When The Commodore's wrote the song *Brick House*, I imagine they had someone like her in mind: tall, tan, strong, and sexy. Her allure, however, is tricky – like a trap or a riddle: She's so beautiful that you have to stare – but staring is rude and uncomfortable – so you look away – but it hurts to look away because everything else looks so dull next to her – so you have to stare at her again – and so on. Her wild black hair adds to her overall appearance of an enchantress. She's a real femme fatale. I've seen the smoothest-talking men turn into stuttering fools in her presence. She can have that effect. Whenever Sheila gets on stage, the other girls get off to make room, even on a Thursday night. No one wants to get in the way of her incredible routine.

Although Sheila possesses bionic kicking power and bombshell ranking, her intellect is what really sets her apart from the other dancers I've met so far. While we're in the dressing room, she has more to tell than just a *Tale of Two Titties*. She discusses her favorite horror novels, using literary terminology and gothic expressions, such as *protagonist, entrapment, incubus,*

146

and succubus – to name a few. She really blew my mind with her knowledge of the genre, but when she told me about her former job as a Target Girl – a Knife Thrower's Assistant – my eyes just about fell out of my face. Her off-stage personality is even more riveting than her on-stage persona.

Sheila is also a self-declared bi-sexual, and she has a crush on my sister. She physically pulls Jackie up onto the stage whenever the chance arises. They dance together and simulate a sexy scene, but I know Jackie's only acting. They don't do anything too intimate like the other girls do. I can tell Sheila is trying her best to convert Jackie's sexual status.

She's also very friendly with me. I'm probably one of the few dancers she's ever had a university-level discussion with about gothic literature. She was impressed by my insights and immediately took to me, but sometimes I wonder if she's taken me under her wing just to get closer to Jackie.

In many stages of my life, I've often been sheltered by the protection of Jackie and her friends. When I started attending my neighborhood high school, two years before I transferred to the Performing Arts school, Jackie was already there in the eleventh grade. All the freshmen were trying their best to be cool and fit in with the older students, but I didn't have to try to impress anyone. I was Jackie's little sister; therefore, the older girls tried to impress *me*. Having that connection in school made me feel important – higher up on the ladder of social placement, above the peons. It was the same feeling with Sheila. Dancers can be very, *very* catty. They're usually trying to outdo each other to make the money. With Sheila on my side, I didn't feel threatened by anyone. I was already higher up on the catwalk of go-go status. I know it sounds crazy, but that's the way it was.

*

At 1:27 the house lights came on. The music stopped playing. Tabs were settled. The place cleared out.

Dancers counted their cash in the dressing room and packed up their things. Everyone tipped the DJ before leaving for the night.

I straightened my cash on the way home. Eight hundred and twenty-nine dollars, plus the ten bucks I tipped the DJ. Jackie made over a grand.

CHAPTER SEVENTEEN

If You Come Back, I'll Be Your Girlfriend

The spring semester started. One week of classes had passed before I decided to drop Survey English Literature from my roster, and add Painting 101 in its place. At the heart of my decision to switch electives, was Jordan. The discomfort of his absence grew on me steadily – like a giant *Chia Pet*. I had to do something to shake the feeling. *Maybe if I take a painting class, I'll feel closer to him*, I thought. And two weeks later, it was working like a charm. Oil paint had a way of smoothing out my emotional rough spots.

The painting studio served as somewhat of a sanctuary for me. I felt much more comfortable as a student at the easel than I had formerly felt as a model upon the stage. Even though I highly valued the experience of my short-lived modeling career, I discovered an even greater joy on the other side of its reality. For me, painting an image on canvas was, without question, preferential to *being* an image on canvas. Actually, when the class first started, we didn't even use canvases at all. Instead we painted on gessoed paper with palette knives.

The model who posed for the class was a middle-aged man named Pedro. He wore a white cotton bathrobe that hung loosely by his sides. One of my classmates, a Russian girl named Elena, found Pedro's nudity very disturbing. She spoke with a heavy Russian accent: "I can *NAUWT* even *LOOWK* at *heem* below *heez PUPKA!*" she complained, glaring directly at me with wide eyes and clenched teeth. I thought her frustration was funny, and laughed at the way she said "pupka" – the Russian word for "bellybutton."

"When I was younger, I used to call my bellybutton 'my pipic'," I told her. But she wasn't amused, so I tried to think of something else to say: "Just squint your eyes and blur your vision," I recommended. And although I thought I had given Elena some valuable advice, none of her paintings ever displayed anything below Pedro's "pupka." She should have entitled her paintings: "Pedro's Pupka No. 1 ... Pedro's Pupka No.2 ..."

I, on the other hand, found so much joy in the mixing of paint and in the application of color, that anything below Pedro's "pupka" was simply a matter of shades, shapes, and shadows. But, the whole time, in the back of my mind, I kind of felt bad for Elena.

My very first successful study was one of eight medium-sized paintings of Pedro's half-robed body. I included the entire stage and studio background, up to the ceiling. The instructor, Mr. Mault, said that I had "a natural knowledge of color." That comment made me feel like a budding Picasso.

When I brought the painting home the following week, my parents grew with excitement. Their pride was almost tangible, vaporizing above their heads as they gawked. My mother took the painting to a professional framer, and my rendition of Pedro has been hanging on the dining room wall ever since.

I couldn't wait for Jordan to see it. I knew he was going to love the way that Pedro's white bathrobe turned out. The whole painting has this terrific 3-D effect that I wasn't even trying to produce. I think the palette knife had something to do with it. Everyone in the class was impressed. And I loved taking credit for it. But honestly, it happened just by chance. I really didn't know what the hell I was doing. Some accidents are good.

*

Jordan and I sent postcards and short letters to each other pretty regularly. It was nice reading his carefully selected poetic words and messages. But it wasn't enough. I wanted more than fantastic poetic fluff. I wanted flat reality. I wanted to hear his voice and have a regular conversation with him. I wanted to hear him speak to me in plain English. I wanted to tell him what was really going on in my life.

One evening, just as I was about to wash out my costumes, the phone rang and somehow I knew it was him. I don't know *how* I knew. I just did. Maybe the ring of the phone was slightly different since he was calling from overseas.

"I'll get it!" I shouted, dropping the laundry basket on the floor. "Hello?"

"Hey, *Barbie*," said a distant voice that I didn't recognize.

"Excuse me? I said, taken aback by the sound of

my stage name. *Who the hell's calling me Barbie?* I feared it was a Studio stalker.

"Uh ... Is Bree there?" he asked. I smiled at the sound of his familiar voice.

"Hi, Jord! Why did you call me *Barbie*?" I asked.

"I didn't call you Barbie – I called you *Baby*. I said, *Hey Baby*," he explained.

"Oh, I guess the connection was a little fuzzy ... How are you? ... How's Italy?"

"Things are pretty interesting here in Rome."

"What's going on?"

"School's great – I love my classes. And I got a job waiting tables at this really nice restaurant. The tips are actually good. Everything's gotten much better since me and Lisa broke up."

"What happened? Why did you two break up?" *(Yeah!!! Clap! Clap! Clap!)*

"She needs a total commitment, and I'm just not ready – at least not with her. But enough about her ... What's going on with *you*? You never say much about yourself in your letters. Are you still working at the health food store?"

"No, I quit during the break – and I broke up with Dante. My whole life has pretty much changed since then."

"Really? ... Are you seeing someone else?"

"No way – I'm not interested in anyone right now. I don't want a new boyfriend. I'm so busy with school ... and I got a new job. It's really exciting."

"Cool ... What is it?"

"Uh ... It's kind of hard to explain ... so I'll just say it as plainly as possible ... I'm working as a

152

dancer ... a go-go dancer."

"At The Lion's Den? – With Jackie?"

"No, not there. Jackie doesn't even work there anymore. She got a job dancing in Princeton, and I went up with her a few weeks ago. It's not topless and the money's fantastic. I feel like I'm dancing around in a bathing suit ... except there's a lot of wild, freaky, erotic stuff going on ... I don't really feel like I fit in. Sometimes I feel like an outsider – looking in through a window – watching another episode of the human condition. But the weird thing is ... I really like it. I have a lot of fun when I'm dancing."

"That's amazing, Bree. I'm so glad you're telling me this because I've been going through some freaky, erotic stuff too."

"You have? ... Like what?" I asked with excitement. Even though Jordan was on another continent, he was experiencing life in a way that paralleled my personal universe, even the X-rated part of my universe.

"Are you sure you want to know?" he asked.

"Yeah ... I'm sure."

"Okay, but promise me you won't judge me about this. It's pretty crazy."

"You know I won't judge you ... Just say it already!"

"Okay. This is what happened: I was riding on the bus one night last week, going back to my flat, and there was this really pretty Italian woman sitting next to me. She was around thirty years old or something. I started drawing in my sketchbook, just the usual stuff: the sky, the rooftops, people on the bus ... So anyway, in this very thick Italian accent, she asked me if I wanted to go to her house and sketch her nude. I couldn't believe what I was hearing! She was *really* hot, so I said yes. Then I didn't know what to do, so I continued drawing in my sketchbook. Then all of the sudden, she leaned over and started kissing my neck … then my ear … she was all over me right there on the bus!"

"Holy shit, Jordan! It sounds like a movie – like a *hot*, Italian movie, just like that one that –"

"Wait, I'm not done. There's more. It gets better: There was this *other* woman sitting behind us. She was a little younger than the first woman, but just as hot. I didn't even know she was there. It's like she came out of nowhere and moved herself to the seat in front of us. Then she turns around and starts watching us – and then *she* starts kissing me, too! I didn't know what the hell was going on! Then, she gets up and slides in next to me, practically on my lap, and then *they* start kissing each other! I thought I was losing my mind. I swear. I actually pinched myself just to make sure I was really awake. So, then somehow a decision was made, and we all got off the bus and went to the first woman's flat – the older one. It was a full-blown *ménage à trois*. I still can't believe it happened. I swear to God, I don't even know their names."

"Wow, Jord. That's a crazy story. It sounds like you're having the time of your life –"

"Wait. There's more. Check this out: These two women were *really* hot for each other, and while they were getting into it, I sat on the floor with my

154

sketchpad and drew them. I filled the rest of my book with sketches of the two of them in all their erotic positions –"

"You said it was a *ménage à trois*. What about the *"trois"* part? If you were just sitting there drawing them, then it wasn't *actually* a *ménage à trois*. Was it?"

"After a while they remembered I was there, and made me put down my pencils and join in. But I swear to God, Bree – it was just as good sketching them as it was making love to them."

As Jordan shared this part of his life with me, I started thinking that my go-go dancing experience was just a small shadow in the bright light of his erotic tale. I felt as though my story wasn't really mine to claim, as though I'd been casted as an extra in a movie with no significant role of my own, just a face in the crowd. Jordan's story was his – featuring him as the star. It was full of passion and lust … art and expression.

"You better send me some of those sketches," I said. "That's an incredible story."

"I know, but it doesn't really end there."

"What! There's still more?"

"When I got back to my flat, Lisa was waiting for me. In all the excitement, I completely forgot that I had plans with her. She was really pissed off. I didn't know what to say, so I told her the truth and showed her my sketchbook. She gave me back the key to my flat and broke up with me. I felt bad about it when she started crying. But I have to admit … it was worth it … God, was it worth it."

"Well, I'm glad I'm not the only one experiencing the benefits that this triple-X rated world has to offer," I said.

And then, just for a moment, I recalled the first time that I had modeled for Jordan's class. I recalled how much more innocent the world had seemed back then. I decided to change the subject –

"I want to tell you something before I forget – I'm taking a painting class at Temple."

"That's great. Who's teaching it ... Spade?"

"No, it's that skinny guy, Mr. Mault."

"Mault's a really good teacher. He used to teach out here in Rome before he got married –"

"I know, I know, I know. That's all he ever talks about. He's always droning on during class about his depressing family life and how he traded in his freedom as a painter for 'little league' and 'parent-teacher conferences.' He told the whole class that we should all stay single and happy, and he said we should *never* quit smoking. He's nuts. Sometimes I feel him breathing down the back of my neck in class. It's awful. I'll be lost in whatever I'm painting, and all of the sudden I smell his cigar-and-coffee breath coming from directly behind me ... I think he's in love with me or something."

"Everyone's in love with you, Bree ... present company included."

"Are you still ... you know ... in love with me ... the way you were ... like you said before you left for Rome?"

"I don't want to bother you with that, Bree. I don't want to make things uncomfortable ... Let's just keep talking about your class. What made you decide to take a painting class anyway?"

"You did, Jordan. I took the class because of you. I know this might sound crazy, but I thought that I'd feel closer to you if I was in the painting studio. I really miss you … really … more than you can imagine. When are you coming back?"

"I don't know. Everything's going great here. I'm supposed to come home during spring break for a visit … but I might not. I can't say for sure."

"If you come back, I'll be your girlfriend," I said, surprising myself.

"Don't tease me like that," he said, all serious.

"I'm not teasing you – I mean it."

"Don't fuck with my head, Bree. It's not funny. You know how I feel about you."

"I know Jord … but just listen to me for a minute. They say you never know what you have until it's gone. And even though it's corny, it's how I feel about you right now. I don't want to mess with your head. Really … Don't take it like that … I'm just telling you what's in my heart. I've been having different kinds of feelings for you since I broke up with Dante. Feelings that are stronger than … I don't know … I just miss you."

"I miss you, too. I'm gonna be thinking about what you just said all night long … *Oh, shit!* … I'm all out of coins for this call. We're gonna get disconnected in like a minute, so we have to talk fast … I love you, Bree."

"I love you too, Jordy. I just wish I'd realized it sooner … I don't know what happened to me. It was like an epiphany. And now you're all I think about."

"You're always in my thoughts … You always were … Hey, thanks for listening to my crazy story. You really are my best friend, Bree baby –"

Before I had the chance to say *Ciao*, the connection failed.

As soon as I hung up the phone, I wanted to call him back and tell him about my stage name. But I didn't have his number.

CHAPTER EIGHTEEN

Fired

Sheila was alone in the dressing room, sorting and snorting white parallel lines on the make-up counter. Our eyes met in the big mirror as I entered. I was relieved to have finished my second set – ready for a break – but I felt like an intruder. *Shouldn't she be snorting her lines somewhere else ... like in the bathroom ... like Nick did?* I wondered.

"You wanna do a line of crank?" Sheila offered.

"*Crank*? I haven't heard the word "crank" since middle school! Why are you snorting *crank?*" I asked with a sour look on my face as though I'd just bitten into a lemon.

The reason I knew about "crank" was because when I was younger, there was a group of kids in my neighborhood – the kids we called "The Scums" – who snorted the stuff. I didn't really know what it was, but I understood it to be a cheaper version of cocaine, only more toxic, or something like that. Whatever it was, they were hooked. It made them giggly, weird, ugly, and violent. I had a fear of "The Scums" and a fear of becoming addicted to anything I didn't understand. So I never tried crank, and wasn't about to – at Studio 67.

"My dealer's not around," Sheila explained. "This was all I could get my hands on. It's actually pretty good. You sure you don't want any?"

I could tell she was embarrassed about doing middle-school drugs.

"I'm sure. But thanks anyway." I felt bad about making a big fuss over the word *crank* and tried to act casual, like it was no big deal. But my high opinion of Sheila had already crashed on the floor.

She snorted another line as I changed into a turquoise sequined one-piece. Her flaring nostrils reminded me that Nick still owed me money from the health food store.

I opened my kaboodle cosmetic case and began freshening up in front of the mirror for my next set. Although I moved at a regular pace, I looked as though I was in extra-slow motion – next to Sheila. It became grossly obvious that the crank was cranking. Her movements in the mirror were jerky and repetitive. Every time she painted a black liquid line around her left eye, she'd quickly erase it with a tissue and start over, re-applying it again and again. And when she spoke to me, her legs kept moving around in a way that made her look like she was about to run a marathon. She might not have been as cool and collected as usual, but she was still just as pretty.

"How's university life?" she asked, spreading a wad of Vaseline on her fleshy Angelina-Jolie lips.

"It's great. I'm taking a painting class. I love it. I could paint in the studio all day long. I'm really into mixing color. It's like being back in kindergarten." I enjoyed discussing my new interest in oil paints with anyone who would listen – cranked up or not.

"Wow ... I know what you mean ... I'm back in

160

school, too … I'm studying to be a mortician," she said, nonchalantly.

I turned to look at her. We'd been making eye contact in the mirror during our little discussion, but when Sheila said that she was studying to be a mortician, I physically turned ninety degrees to face her.

"A *mortician?*" I asked in amazement. It was like speaking with a grown-up, sexy, Asian version of Wednesday Addams.

"That's right baby *sista*, a mortician. I'm pretty close to getting my license … just a few more months to go. I've always been fascinated by death … Let's go get a drink." She whisked me out of the dressing room as I imagined her snorting crank off the lid of a coffin.

*

The crowd around the bar was thin for a Thursday night. We sipped on two glasses of red wine and sped through a conversation before it was her turn to dance. She did ten thousand turns, fast-forward on the stage. It looked like she was spinning around and around on ice skates. I couldn't tell if the crank was still working or not because she always danced like that.

Sheila was also somewhat of a Yogi – getting into strange positions that were hard to comprehend. There was this one move she did where she straddled her legs from the stage all the way to the bar counter, while her torso was upside down, supported by her hands that extended from the floor where the bartenders walk around. (I know it's hard to imagine, but that's the point.) Then she'd somehow cartwheel her way up to the bar counter, wrap her long legs around a customer's neck, and pump his head into her crotch with her thigh muscles. It was hard to make sense of her performance. She seemed to defy gravity and human limitations. She moved like a killer cat woman. The men feared her just as much as they were turned on by her.

Then it was my turn. The DJ played *Son of a Preacher Man*. For some reason I could really work the audience on that one. The soundtrack of *Pulp Fiction* had just come out. Anything sacrilegious seemed apropos in Studio. But that night, during that very song, a Hasidic Jewish man wandered into the bar. He had a long, dark beard and long, curly ear locks dangling from the sides of his old-world hat. The sight of him made my back arch and stretch like a tiger protecting her young. *What the fuck is this guy doing in here? Research?* Hasidic Jews make me very nervous. It's probably the same kind of reaction a Catholic School girl has when she sees a nun, even when she's not in school. He stood against the wall. I tried not to look directly at him.

Rolling around on stage, going from one straddle into another, I felt something wet and stiff traveling up my leg. I turned my head around and met the dark eyes of a dancer named Pamela. I had only worked with her once or twice before that night. She had jet-black hair, and she was covered in tattoos and body piercings. I thought of her as *Pam the Porcupine Pin Cushion.* Her wet, studded tongue was on the back of my thigh. Her widening eyes gave her the appearance

162

of Gene Simmons from the rock band Kiss, which totally freaked me out. I immediately assumed she'd been snorting crank in the dressing room with Sheila. And, for some reason, she assumed that I was going to go along with her whole lesbian-act thing. She continued sending her tongue up my thigh. I thought of the Hassidic Jewish guy and pulled away, gracefully rolling into another straddle so that my legs were out of her reach.

"Oh, come on – don't be like that," she said, practically pleading for affection. "Get the fuck away from me," I whispered and quickly headed over to the pole. I looked around for Super Jew. He had already left the bar. But all the same, his appearance was so powerful that it cast a permanent shadow on the wall where he had earlier stood that night. It was the first time I felt uncomfortable in my comfort zone, in Studio 67.

The dancers did lesbian acts all the time. Sometimes they were real, sometimes simulated. I wasn't ready to start that stuff – not after seeing that Jewish zealot, and not with someone cranked up like *Prickly Pam the Pin Cushion*. She was too freaky for me. I didn't want to be a part of that aspect of the job. I liked it better when the other dancers got wild. While they were up on stage doing all the work, I'd walk around and make all the cash. The customers would start tipping like crazy when they saw that stuff.

Sheila was back on stage, rolling all over Jackie like a cranked-up tornado. Another dancer named Tex got spicy-hot jealous. Tex was a body-builder from

Texas who was in lesbian-love with Sheila. Tex entered body-fitness competitions. And as a result, there was a Miller Lite advertisement that she had modeled for, hanging in the bar, with her picture on it. She was a typical American girl with long wisps of dirty blond hair, dimples around her full southern smile, and a full figure equipped with double-D saline implants. Tex was a real show-off, too. One time, when a bunch of us were in the dressing room, she started flexing her muscles, showing them off for everyone to see. But it wasn't very appealing: As her pectorals stood straight up high, her saline sacs remained rooted below. When half her chest went up; the other half stayed down. I guess she didn't realize how awkward she looked because she kept on flexing and smiling like she was really fit. I tried to act like I was real impressed by her freaky flexing. But the way I saw it, nothing fit together very well on her body. She looked like an advertisement for horror. The whole thing caused me to shudder.

While Sheila and Jackie were engaged in the moves from the wild, Tex took a pitcher of ice from the bar, got up on stage, and dumped it over Sheila's head. Right in front of everyone, Tex had a temper tantrum. I was ready to fly up there and knock her down because, at first, I thought she had attacked Jackie. At that moment, the whole world disappeared and my natural reflexes kicked in. As the world came back into focus, my muscles relaxed, and I was able to breathe again. It's a good thing she didn't dump it over Jackie's head, or it would have turned into a *Jerry Springer* episode up there.

My sisters and I have violent reflexes when it comes to defending each other. Jackie and I even roughed up some girl back in high school for Mona's sake. It was around the time that Mona had gotten serious about Steven. Some girl named Nikki also liked him and kept calling Mona names, such as *bitch, cunt, whore* … Jackie and I walked right up to her in the court yard, all rough and tough like Pinky Tuscadero and her sister Leather from the show *Happy Days*: "You better stay away from Mona, you little bitch. And if you don't, you're dead!" Jackie warned. "*Yeah!*" I chimed in, with my hand on the hip of my *Sergio Valente,* stitch-pocket jeans. From that day on, Nikki stayed away from us, away from Mona, and away from Steven.

*

Some guy who had just turned twenty-one was celebrating his birthday at the bar with his uncle. He bought a round of drinks for Jackie and me. It was always nice to sit at the bar and take a little break.

"I think all the dancers are on something tonight," Jackie whispered.

"Sheila was snorting *crank* in the dressing room. She offered me a line, but I didn't do any."

"You better not. That shit's gross. She knows better than to offer me any," Jackie said.

"What do you think about Tex and the ice?" I asked.

"I'm not saying a word to her about that shit she pulled … and don't you either. It's not worth it."

"What'll you do if she dumps ice over *your* head?"

I asked.

"I'll kick her fuckin' ass."

"That's what I thought," I laughed.

"But not in here. Not in the bar. *First*, I'll get her fired. *Then* I'll kick her ass. This job's too good to give up for Tex Mex." Jackie sounded more rational than ever.

"I had to get that girl Pamela away from me on stage. She was licking my thigh and –"

"Can I lick your thigh?" the birthday boy interrupted. I hadn't realized he was listening.

"No," I laughed.

"What are you girls gonna do for *me*? For my *birthday*?" he grinned.

"We're *sitting* with you," Jackie replied, smiling. "That's all ya get."

*

At the end of the night, *Pam the Porcupine Pin Cushion* was crying in the dressing room.

"Are you okay?" I asked with concern.

"Joe just fired me," she wept as eyeliner streamed down her cheeks, like the black waters of the river Styx.

"Why?" I asked, shocked that a dancer could actually get fired at Studio. It seemed so extreme.

"You know that guy out there? The one who was celebrating his twenty-first birthday with his uncle?" she sobbed.

"Yeah, I had a drink with him," I said.

"He asked me to do something special for him, for his birthday *(sob, sob)*, so I asked him if he wanted me to suck his nipple *(sob, sob)*. He said yes … and I guess I bit too hard *(sob, sob)* … and it started bleeding *(sob, sob)* …"

"What started bleeding?" I asked.

"His *nipple*," she cried.

"That's crazy," I said. What I really wanted say was: *You're crazy! You're the craziest chick I've ever met!*

"His uncle saw what I did, and he told Joe *(sob, sob)*. So now I'm fired! Do you believe this shit?" She sobbed and sobbed and sobbed as she packed her bags.

Pam The Porcupine Pin Cushion was the first of three dancers to get fired in the time that I worked at Studio.

CHAPTER NINETEEN

Banana Coconuts

Spring break was only two weeks away. Jordan had decided to come home after all. He couldn't resist my promise of love. He was a romantic at heart, and I awaited his return without much patience. The days grew longer, both literally and figuratively. I passed the time by studying for midterms and by paying especially close attention to the changing of the seasons.

Life became dynamic. The snow had melted into the earth, providing a wet palette of color for Mother Nature to play with. The trees awakened. Flowering buds popped open. Bees got busy. Life was full of new promise. Life was full of new life. And even though I was well into my twenty-third year upon the earth, I felt as though I was seeing it all for the first time:

The grass was never that shade of green before ... Those flowers must be a new species because I never saw them before ... That tree never had red leaves before ...

Perhaps I had these revelations due to my new interest in mixing oil paints and experimenting with color. Or perhaps I had these revelations due to the fact that I had just become the new owner of a used Jeep Cherokee, and I was able to travel around a lot more than before. Just as I had imagined, my dream jeep materialized as hunter-green with red pin stripes. I bought it for thirteen thousand dollars, most of what I'd saved of my dancing money. And even though I was the third owner to hold the title, it was practically new, with just seventeen thousand miles on the odometer, with plenty of miles left for me to cruise.

The first place I drove it to? Natural Foods, naturally – to pick up my paycheck. After parking slightly in front of a No-Parking sign, I found the door to Utrecht irresistible. It was great having money. Art supplies cost a fortune, but thanks to Studio 67 I was able to afford high-quality paints, brushes, and oils.

While shopping around in Utrecht, I bumped into Jessie. She was stocking up on supplies. Fate always draws us together from time to time. That's one of the best perks of being her friend. It's a totally-meant-to-be friendship.

"I'm going to a party tonight," she told me while searching through etching inks. "Well, it's not really a *party-party* … just a little gathering at my friend Elliot's house on Brown Street … He goes to the Academy, too … He's an *amazing* artist … Come with me … We'll have so much fun …"

"Where's Brown Street?" I asked.

"North Philly."

"Sounds good to me … And I can drive us there because (drum roll) I bought a jeep this morning!"

"You did! … That's awesome!"

"Wait till you see it. I'll drive us over after I get my check from Nick. He still owes me money."

Going to a party with Jessie sounded like the best

thing I could possibly do that night. I was in need of some good-spirited fun, and driving around the city was going to make it easy. I loved Jessie so much and was so happy to be making plans with her as she found the type of ink she'd been searching for.

"You're going to love Elliot's house," Jessie said. "He bought it for a dollar!"

"A *dollar*? ... How's that possible?"

"The mayor's selling shells for a dollar. And Elliot's fixing it up really nice. He's rebuilding the staircases, the doors, the floors, the walls ... *Everything* needs fixing. That's why it was only a dollar. I think the property was condemned or something. There weren't even any windows when he got it. But the whole place is turning into a work of art. Elliot welded these wrought-iron bars into beautiful shapes on all the ground-level windows. One's a sun with rays shooting out. It looks so cool – so much better than the typical prison bars you see on other house windows ... He's not finished, though ... It's gonna be a masterpiece." I could tell she was over-enthusiastic about Elliot's house.

"Are you in love with this guy Elliot?" I asked.

"I *would be* if he'd come on to me. He's such a gentleman. I'm gonna have to be aggressive if I want to get anywhere with him."

"Wow, Elliot sounds great."

Jessie talked some more about Elliot while we waited in the checkout line. I could tell she was really into him. Their friendship sounded like a budding romance; it was just a matter of time before it would get physical.

"Why don't you come with me to Natural Foods?" I asked. "We can get something to eat ... my treat ..."

"Isn't it late? ... I'm pretty sure they're closed by now," she said.

I looked at my Swatch. "*Whoa* – it's almost seven o'clock," I said with confusion. The transition into springtime always confuses me when the sun remains higher and the days grow longer. I'd spent way more time in Utrecht than I originally planned. Being with Jessie was always an occasion that caused time to fly without warning, especially in the aisles of an art supply store with more cash in my pocket than I needed. Putting Studio's dollars to use was fun, and I insisted on paying Jessie's bill.

Once we exited Utrecht, Jessie seemed like she was in a rush to get home. But I wanted our good time to continue.

"Come with me to the health food store. It'll only take a minute. I just have to get my check."

"I would, but I have to get back to my place and separate my laundry. Elliot said I could use his Wringer."

"His *what*?"

"He has a 1950 Maytag Wringer. It's ancient, but it does the job."

"Why's it called a 'Wringer'?"

"There's no spin cycle. The water just drains out of the basin. So you have to feed the soaking-wet clothes, one-by-one, through these two rollers that *wring* the water out ... hence the term *wringer*. It's a pain in the ass, but it's better than hanging around the Laundromat."

Jessie's life always seemed more difficult than it had to be.

"Thank you so much for the art supplies, Bree. I'm gonna take a taxi back to my place … now that I have some extra cash … Just swing by and pick me up after you get your check," she said, and hailed a cab as I walked a block to Natural Foods.

*

The door was locked, but the lights were on. I knocked … Nothing … I banged on the door like a lunatic. Dante came walking down the center aisle.

Somehow a rock made its way into my throat. Sweat seeped through my palms. A pounding replaced my heart. *Why am I reacting like this?* He smiled and unlocked the door.

"Bree! I can't believe it! What a surprise!"

"Hi … I'm here for my check." I could barely speak. Numbness invaded my frame.

"Sure, come in. Your paycheck's in the office – You look great."

"Thanks. Can I get something to drink?" A feeling of weakness was bringing me down.

"Help yourself. Whatever you want." He led me to the juice cooler. I picked out a Knudsen's Banana Coconut. I usually drink Cherry Cider, but I felt like a banana coconut.

"Is anyone else here?" I asked.

"No. I let Kate leave early because she wanted to go see some *Coming Out* play."

"That was nice of you."

"I *really am* a nice guy, Bree. I'm sorry if I hurt

172

you."

"It's okay. Don't worry about it." I didn't know what to say. I wasn't prepared to deal with the situation and, somehow, I lost my mind. I got so damn horny all of a sudden. I wanted to jump on him. So, I did. Right there, in Niomi's office on her swivel chair, I mounted the Italian Stallion for the last time.

Next to an electric breast pump and an electric make-up mirror, I got a big dose of Vitamin O ... and it felt oh so good. But I knew it was wrong, especially when Dante shouted, "Shit! The condom broke. Shit, shit, shit! ... Damn ... I'm so sorry, Bree. This has never happened to me before!"

"Don't worry about it. I don't have AIDS or herpes or anything," I assured him.

"It's not just that ... I mean ... you could get pregnant," he said.

"Pregnant? I'm not even ovulating so don't worry. There's *no* chance of *that* happening."

"Oh good. I love how women know their bodies. Your body's amazing." He looked me up and down with hungry eyes. I didn't know what to think. I wanted to get out of Niomi's office, away from Dante, back to Jessie. "You wanna grab a bite to eat? Pizza, maybe?" he offered.

"Thanks, but I can't. I have plans with Jessie."

"Can I call you tomorrow?" he asked.

"Uh ... that's definitely *not* a good idea," I said, remembering my promise to Jordan. "I'm sorry Dante but this was a mistake. I don't even know why I just had sex with you –"

"It didn't feel like a mistake to me –"

"Well, it was ... Listen, I have to get going now. Jessie's waiting for me to pick her up." I started feeling claustrophobic, like the walls of Niomi's tiny office were caving in. "Just give me my paycheck, and let's forget this ever happened."

Dante scowled and acted like I was breaking his heart, but I knew better. He just wanted a few more rounds with me before he'd break mine again.

With a Natural Foods paycheck in the amount of eighty-seven dollars and forty-four cents clutched tightly in my hand, I ran like a wild banana coconut down Broad Street.

When I got to the jeep, there was a parking ticket for twenty-five bucks on the windshield. Some guy whistled and called me "Senorita" while I was reading it.

CHAPTER TWENTY

The Maytag Wringer

I beeped the horn in front of Jessie's Chinatown studio apartment. She shoved two overstuffed laundry sacks into the back seat of the jeep. I had some dirty laundry of my own to air:

"I am such an idiot! I can't believe I just had sex with *Dante*! What's wrong with me?"

Instead of finding comfort and compassion from Jessie, she told me that I was "oversexed." It was impossible to believe that Jessie – my best female friend who had never criticized a facet of my being since the day we met – had labeled me, slapped a psychological term on me as though it were a pair of handcuffs.

Oversexed. How dare she? I thought. I decided to bury the idea deep inside the catacombs of denial. If I truly was an oversexed fiend, I wasn't going to let it ruin my night. It's a good thing that my father had made me watch *Gone With the Wind* four different times because, ever since, I've been able to apply the Scarlett O'Hara Method-Of-Coping: *I won't think about this today ... I'll think about my oversexed issue tomorrow ... After all ...*

We parked on Brown Street in front of Elliot's half-built, half-not-built house. Nothing truly finished except the windows and doors. Don't get me wrong though, what he had accomplished was incredible; there just wasn't enough of it. He'd created hand-carved wooden entry doors and several stained-glass windows; the bathroom floor was a marvelous mosaic of broken tiles and mirrors that Elliot had fitted together to form the figures of mythological females: three sirens, two mermaids, and a sphinx. The walls were coated with sand and other scattered mosaics. I found it all enchanting.

The house was coming together in a way that would most likely be the topic of tongue amongst the local art critics. That is, if they didn't break their necks on the way up the steps. The long stairwells were seriously dangerous. They looked like loose rows of rotted teeth. On my way up to the second floor, I almost fell three times. It was impossible to be sure of my footing. Some of the rooms had no floors. Some had no ceilings.

Jessie went down to the basement to start her laundry while Elliot and I discussed the house. "Sorry about the steps," he apologized. "I haven't even drawn the plans for them yet. The windows and doors took precedence … and the master crapper, of course."

When Jessie returned, we got busy in the kitchen baking organic hash brownies. We drank homebrewed beer and smoked Marlboro reds. "I can't believe he bought this house for *a dollar*," I said in amazement. "I could buy the whole neighborhood on one night's salary from Studio."

"Buying is one price. *Fixing* is another," Jessie explained.

"I know. But what about the land it sits on? Isn't

that worth *more* than a dollar?"

"Not around here ... apparently."

Some guy who had just gotten back from Vermont brought half of a dead pig to the party – the back half. He talked about making ham-hock soup, which I'd never heard of before. "You never heard of ham-hock soup?" the Pig Bearer asked. "Nope." I felt like a foreigner from another land, a Jewish land with oceans of Chicken Soup and Cabbage Borsht.

I enjoyed the lesson about pig slaughter and ham-hock soup. And watching their attempts to fit the pig into an old yellow Frigidaire was especially amusing. It almost fit, but the door wouldn't shut. So they put it outside. And even though the official spring season had formally begun, the air temperature on that particular night was certainly cold enough to chill any animal, dead or alive.

Jessie and I cracked up at every little thing. For some strange reason, the sound of the word "pig" had an amusing effect on us. We always laugh and oink whenever we're partying together, but that night was underscored with an unusual abundance of hysterics on our part. Perhaps the homebrewed beer was responsible.

We gathered upstairs on the third floor with Elliot and his friends and their friends. It was warm and cozy up there by the wood burning stove. We snacked and drank and enjoyed the festive vibe.

There were these two Chinese women who laughed at everything, just like Jessie and me; only their laughter was twelve octaves higher and much quicker. Someone put a Buddy Holly record on. By the end of

Peggy Sue, the brownies had taken effect.

"I'm going to get my laundry out of the washer," Jessie announced and disappeared. I found it odd that she was doing laundry in the middle of such merriment.

A short while later, I decided to escape the noise of the party room and explore the house on my own. So I slipped out.

Carefully – *very* carefully – I attempted to make my way down to the second floor. As I descended the decaying staircase, I felt like I was in an Indiana Jones movie, crossing an old wooden bridge, high above an alligator-infested river. It was risky work, but I survived the adventure, and entered the bedroom where Jessie and I had stored our jackets and bags.

Feeling a bit stressed from the stairwell episode, I sat down on the edge of the bed to relax a bit. I lit a cigarette and opened a newly installed window for ventilation. In doing so, my attention was immediately captivated by the fattest moon I'd ever seen. Its bright sparkle against the night's sky inspired me to draw the scene. I searched through Jessie's bag for a sketchbook and a pencil. She always traveled around with a variety of art supplies in her bag.

The graphite wand in my hand seemed to guide itself as celestial energy coursed through my veins. I entered a state of perfect happiness, something like nirvana. The feeling was harmonious and serene – but much too short-lived, because just I started shading in the negative space, I heard a sound that was out of rhythm with the moment. Out of tune. Off color. Like the sound of a siren.

At first I thought it was the Chinese women's laughter. But as it grew louder and louder, again and again, I knew it was bad.

The party noise stopped all at once. And within a moment's time, the silence was cut by a single voice coming from the basement. It was Jessie's voice, though it didn't sound like her. The house quickly filled with one sharp word:

"helP! heLP! hELP! HELP! HELP! HELP!"

Her cries of agony escalated in pitch and desperation. I wanted to HELP her, but I couldn't move. I just sat on the edge of the bed, paralyzed with fear. My heart hammered against my chest. *What the fuck is happening to her?* I wondered. *What type of injury could cause such an agonizing shriek?*

In my search for a logical explanation, I turned to the window and looked to the sky. The imagine of Jessie's body on fire, soaring past the fat moon, appeared in my mind's eye.

Oh no! Maybe the floor in the party room buckled under the heavy weight of the wood-burning stove. Maybe the stove crashed through the crumbling ceilings and landed in the basement!

I believed that Jessie was burning, engulfed in flames. And I was frozen stiff.

Elliot and his friends, however, had a more active response to Jessie's cries for help. They raced down to the basement; they ran to her rescue. The thunder of pounding feet shook the house with great force, and I feared that the entire structure would collapse – or ignite – any moment. *The Fall of the House of Usher* flashed through my mind.

179

When the house stopped trembling, Jessie's screams slowed to moans. Somehow I worked up the courage to make my way down to the basement.

Afraid of what I'd see, I covered my eyes and peeked through my fingers. Elliot's hands were fast at work ripping Jessie's shirtsleeve off. The sound of tearing threads revealed a significant amount of raw and damaged skin on her left arm, which also appeared to be broken.

Jessie's face had turned a dark shade of purple. She foamed at the mouth like an old horse. I slowly removed my hands from my face and gazed at her in amazement. My eyes darted from image to image:

Torn sleeve ... Raw skin ... Purple face ... White foam ...

Seeing her like that was awful. But really, I was relieved that she wasn't on fire.

The injury had occurred when Jessie tried to feed a wet sock through the wringer. Her fingers got stuck between the two rollers – rollers that were designed to wring water out of each garment, one at a time. In just a few seconds, her hand was pulled through. She tried to pull it back out, but it's impossible without releasing the rollers. That was when she started screaming for help. But before anyone heard her, or could get to her, the rollers devoured her arm well past her elbow. Elliot had taught her how to use the release button, but she forgot to bang down on it with her free hand. She never should have done her laundry after eating hash brownies.

It was a pretty common household injury during the time that Maytag Wringers were the only washing machines available on the market. And it's probably the reason that better washing machines were invented.

*

They wouldn't let Jessie drink anything in the emergency room. "Get me water," she pleaded through a whisper. I ran to the waiting room and bought a can of Sprite from the soda machine, but they wouldn't let me bring it back through the ER doors. "You can't bring that drink in here."

I apologized to Jessie, but again she entreated: "I'm so fucking thirsty! Get me some fucking water!" The inside of her mouth looked like there was peanut butter stuck to the roof of it.

I had to get creative. I went back to the waiting room, filled my mouth with water from the water fountain, and walked back through the ER doors, hoping no one would notice. My mouth felt like a water balloon about to explode. I leaned over Jessie's face and gently released the water, through a single stream, into her mouth.

"Thank you, Brie Cheese. I love you," she said with relief.

"I love you too, Jezebelly –"

"More … More water … Get me more," she pleaded.

In turn, I gave Jessie a refreshing drink of water, mouth-to-mouth, eleven times in a row.

There was another accident victim in the bed next to Jessie's. We couldn't see him because the nurse pulled the curtain all the way around his bed. But we could hear him loud and clear. He was a young Italian, mafia man who had numerous shards of shattered glass embedded in one side of his face.

"*Da mutha-fuckas* shot *da fuckin'* window. Me and m'boys were out in *da* stretch, and they fuckin' tried *da* kill me." He explained the situation to a nurse who I couldn't see behind the curtain, as she prepared to remove the glass from his face. She must have been beautiful because he kept calling her *gorgeous*. "I love you, gorgeous ... Marry me, gorgeous." When she picked the glass out of his face, he howled in a stream of curses like a South Philly werewolf.

Another nurse placed three icepacks on Jessie's arm. She closed her eyes and slowly fell asleep, so I went outside to smoke a cigarette. About a dozen of Mr. Mafia's friends were out there. One was smoking a joint. I asked him for a light, and he struck up a conversation:

"I'm Frankie," he said. "What's *ya* name?"

"Bree," I smiled.

"*Ya 'talian?*" The way he said the word "Italian" sounded like there was no initial letter *I*. He sounded exactly like Bugs Bunny.

"No, I'm Jewish. But Italian people always think I'm Italian," I explained.

"I dated a Jewish gal once ... Nice chick."

I think he was trying to give me a compliment. He offered me a hit of his joint and I gladly accepted. It smelled good, like freshly cut happy flowers.

"So *whaddya* do? ... Work? ... Go *da* school?" he asked.

"I'm an Art student at Temple," I said.

182

"Wow, *whatta* coincidence! I'm an *awtist*! I designed *da* menus for my cousin Vinnie's restaurant."

"Oh, yeah? What's the name of his restaurant?" I asked, trying to seem interested.

"It's called Vinnie's. It's over on 12th Street. Ever *hoid* of it?"

"Is it in the basement of a house?" I asked.

"Yeah! Wow! Ya know Vinnie's!" The more Frankie got excited, the more he puffed on the joint.

"It's my sister Mona's favorite Italian restaurant. She eats there all the time with her husband. They've been going there for years."

"*Dat's* incredible! *Don'tchya tink dis* is *kinda weird*? ... *Ya* know ... us having so much in common. We're both *awtists*. Ya *sista's* favorite restaurant belongs to my cousin Vinnie. We're both *he(r)e*, at *dis* hospital, under *dis* incredible moon tonight ..."

As I looked up, the moon was even fatter than it had been before. I was fascinated by the way Frankie spoke and wondered if someone had forgotten to teach him to pronounce his R's. He was cute, but definitely not for me.

"I don't think it's weird," I said. "Philly's a small city."

"I like *ya* style ... eh ... *Whaddya* say *ya* name was?"

"Bree. B-R-E-E." I don't know why I spelled it out. I guess I wanted him to know there was an R in it.

"Bree ... Bree ... Bree ..." He said my name three times before he could think of what to say next. "*Dat's* nice ... *Yaw da* real natural type. I like *dat* in a

183

gal."

"Thanks." I then realized that he didn't pronounce *TH* sounds either.

"Can I *getchya* phone *numba?*" Maybe we could … *eh* … go out some time?"

I scribbled a phony number on Frankie's matchbook just as Mr. Mafia walked out of the hospital with half his face wrapped in bandages, like half a mummy. His buddies followed him into a stretch limousine that had a missing window.

I went back to the emergency room. It wasn't too long before Jessie was discharged. Luckily, her bones weren't broken. Unfortunately, everything else in her arm was crushed and mangled.

CHAPTER TWENTY-ONE

"Ya Gotta Getta Gimmick..."

Too tired to get out of bed the following day, I skipped my painting class. When I finally did wake up, my left arm was bent and refused to straighten out no matter how much I tried. I had a classic case of sympathy pain for Jessie. Whenever people I love are suffering, their symptoms manifest in me. One time I heard my cousin shrieking during childbirth, and later, that same night, my crotch felt like it was on fire. I had to keep an ice pack on it for two hours.

Mona came over for dinner without Steven. He was working late. It was the first time in a long time that we all ate a meal together, just the five of us. My mother made cabbage borsht with meat, beets, tomatoes, a ton of sugar, and beef-marrow bones – yummy Jewish soul food. While Jackie and I were busy arguing about who was getting which bone, my father started a discussion about money. He loved discussing Jackie's money whenever Mona was around, probably because she was so judgmental about the whole dancing thing.

"Do you know how much money I've set aside from your earnings, Jackie?" he asked with a poker face.

"No, how much?" Jackie was busy sucking the marrow out of a bone.

"You're not going to believe it," he teased.

"How much?" I asked between slurps.

"One hundred thousand dollars," he proudly pronounced.

"Are you lying?" Jackie asked in disbelief.

"No, I'm *not* lying. I didn't want to tell you that it was adding up to so much because I was afraid you'd do something stupid with it. But now that it's rounded out to a significant figure, you need to start thinking about investing your money."

My father had opened a savings account for Jackie a while back, and had been making weekly deposits of her go-go money, as well as the cash tips she made from doing nails at the hair salon.

I tried to do the math in my head: *Jackie had been earning at least eight hundred a night in go-go money. She'd been working for six or seven months, four or five nights a week. Was it possible for her to earn that much money in such a short period of time? How much was added in from her earnings at the salon?* The numbers were too big. My inability to do brain-math forfeited any attempt.

"I know *exactly* what I'm gonna do with the money. I'm gonna open a hair salon. My own salon! ... Oh my God, I can't believe it! ... I'm so excited!" Jackie beamed.

I looked at Mona's face and couldn't decide if it expressed disgust or admiration.

"Mona," I said with the best intentions, "You should make costumes for the dancers and sell them at the go-go bars in the dressing rooms. Remember when you made those bathing suits? They were gorgeous.

You'd be great at designing costumes. The dancers pay a lot of money for them, and there's barely any material involved—"

"I don't think so, Bree." Mona didn't even look up from her borsht. She can be so snotty.

"No … really … there's good money in it," Jackie insisted. "A Russian woman sells costumes at Studio every week, and she makes out like a bandit. The dancers drop hundreds on her as if it's nothing. And that's just at Studio. She goes around to *all* the bars. Just imagine what she makes a week –"

"You can all save your breath. I'm not interested," Mona insisted.

"Leave her alone," my father said. "If she doesn't want to make that kind of money, then it's her loss."

"Mom, you're gonna be the receptionist at my salon," Jackie declared. My mother smiled. She never voices her opinion during a meal.

*

The next day I went to my painting class and discovered that I had one day to complete a two-day assignment. They had started a still life in my absence.

Mr. Mault arranged a bunch of objects on a big green table. I had never painted a still life before. There were all kinds of things scattered on the table: a deer's skull, a spaghetti jar, a yellow bowl (that looked like the one my grandfather ate his oatmeal from), a huge ball made of orange glass, a dark-green pumpkin, a navy-blue candlestick that was burning and dripping, etc.

I looked at the paintings the other students had begun. Some of them included all the objects exactly as they appeared on the table. Some included just a handful of objects. One girl zoomed in on the skull.

Without giving it much thought, I painted all of the objects. But, in my painting, I shoved everything into a corner of the table. The rest of the table remained empty, yet full of the fantastic green color I had mixed to the sound of Peter Gabriel. It was a satisfying mission, a satisfying color: Viridian Green No. 10364, a touch of Cadmium Red Medium No. 10644, a smudge of Titanium White, and a splash of my favorite: Crimson Red No.1.

I had to work quickly, so I just shoved everything in the corner and completed the painting before the end of the period. By that time, Mault was breathing his hot cigar breath down my neck.

"This is very interesting," he said. "Is there something you're pushing into the corner of your mind?" he asked. I thought of Dante.

"Actually there is," I answered.

"Painting is a psychological process. You can tell a lot about a person by the choices they make on canvas."

"Wow ... That's pretty amazing. I wasn't even thinking about it."

I couldn't believe how transparent I was. My decision to place the objects in the corner of the canvas was completely subconscious. The more I looked at the painting, the more fascinated I became with it. The empty area of the green table was just as large as the cluttered area. But while I was painting it,

I'd perceived the space differently. I thought that there was a lot less empty table than there actually was. It was perfectly balanced, but it told a tale of how my mind was not. I felt like a true artist when Mault analyzed my mind through my art. I was so proud of my psychotic still life. It was more than a painting. It was me.

While my life came together in the art studio, it came together on the go-go stage as well. I finally got a gimmick. A lot of the girls had their individual gimmicks while they were dancing on stage. And although their gimmicks were entertaining, they were also very trite. I didn't want to be unoriginal, so I stayed away from the whole gimmick thing until it just sort of evolved.

The night before Jordan came home for spring break, I was doing my usual moves on stage, but couldn't stop sweating. Outside, the cold weather had finally broken, but it was still far from summer. I found it unusual to experience such a sweaty reaction to the not-so-drastic change in temperature, and considered that my condition might be linked to allergies or some other seasonal malady. When I finished dancing for my second set, I jumped off the stage over by one of the ice bins, grabbed a piece of ice, and rubbed it over my skin to cool down. The customers at the end of the bar were really turned on. They started tipping like madmen. I walked around rubbing ice all over my body just to stay cool, but everyone thought I was doing it to be sexy. And that's how I got my little gimmick.

The other gimmicks were funny as hell. This one

girl named Sabrina (who looked like Demi Moore when she had short hair) dressed up like a pornographic French maid. In the middle of her set, she'd pull out this big ostrich feather duster and start dusting the pole to the tune of Abba's *Voulez-Vous*. I laughed every time.

One dancer named Maria used to come out wearing an evening gown and long white gloves. She'd do a real burlesque strip tease act to Frank Sinatra's *Summer Wind*, peeling off the gloves, throwing each one to the crowd. Then she'd whip out a Whipped Cream canister that had a picture of strawberries on it and shake it up. After unzipping her long back zipper, she's let her big boobs out of the gown and load them up with whipped cream. The crowd went crazy for that kind of stuff. Maria saved her money and opened up a bridal shop by the time her Studio days were over.

The school-girl act is another classic. Ginger (who looks like Ginger from Gilligan's Island) wears pigtails and glasses, a pleated skirt, fishnet stockings, a white collared shirt and a tie. She dances around in power pumps to Billy Joel's *Only the Good Die Young* while stripping off her uniform, driving the men back to their Catholic school memories, bringing their boyhood fantasies to life.

One girl comes out in a mummer's costume, but she doesn't dance to mummer's music. She requests hard rock all the time. *Hard rock and mummers? Doesn't make sense.*

I used to go to the Mummer's Parade on Broad Street in South Philly with my family every year. We have cousins who live down at Broad and Morris. So after we'd tire ourselves out watching the drunks and the mummers strut their stuff, we'd enjoy a New Year's Day supper at cousin Herbie's house. When Herbie's family competed on The Family Feud (another game show I was privileged to grow up on), they gave Richard Dawson a mummer's doll as a gift. After that, I begged my mom for an entire year to buy me a mummer's doll. She surprised me on my next birthday.

That dumb dancer was spoiling my childhood memories! She looked ridiculous as a stripper mummer. Maybe I wouldn't have minded so much if she had done it with more grace. But she looked awkward and klutzy, like the headpiece was too heavy and she was about to topple over every dumb move she made. The customers didn't seem to notice, though. I never could figure out just why they hooted and howled for her.

Then there's this black girl with a bubble butt who looks exactly like Eddie Murphy. She isn't pretty at all. But what she does on stage really requires guts. She takes two sulfur matches – the kind with the cardboard ends you get for free when you buy cigarettes from a machine – and she separates the ends, wets them with her tongue so they stick to her nipples, and ignites the other end. Then she stands there half naked on stage with flames shooting out of her nipples. The act is always an eye opener. I can't even remember what kind of music she dances to because my brain only processes the visual stuff when fire is involved.

My gimmick might not have been as elaborate as some of them, but it made me feel as though I had finally arrived. I finally had my own thing going on. I was an ice goddess.

CHAPTER TWENTY-TWO

Corny Poetry

The day Jordan came home was the first day it truly felt like spring. The temperature climbed up to seventy-five degrees. I wanted to meet him at the airport in the worst way, but there were critical issues preventing me, such as not knowing the name of the airline, the flight number, or the time of arrival.

I spent the day writing small poems. I never write poems, but there must have been a muse bewitching my every thought, turning it into metered rhyme. I felt like Emily Dickinson, scribbling small lines of verse on small scraps of paper, on the back of a receipt, and on a strip of newspaper.

Only my poems were corny. I was corny. Emily Dickinson never would have produced the fluff that I churned out.

While pouring a cup of coffee: *I'm filling my love-cup with feelings so pure; I'll sip you so slowly, each drop I'll adore.*

While outside, smoking a cigarette: *Tulips are bursting right out of the ground, as children are 'ringing the rosy' around.*

While taking a shower: *Love rains down on me sweet and free; and grows in my heart like a blossoming tree.*

Gazing out the window: *On this beautiful day, I am*

waiting for you; the one love for me who has always been true.

Folding the laundry: *I can't wait to hold you and smell you again, Jordan my soul-mate, my love, my best friend.*

I was pathetic. I even tuned up my violin and played a sappy romantic concerto. My father was in his glory when he heard it.

After I had switched majors, and stopped practicing my violin regularly, he was devastated. I knew how he felt, even though he didn't say so. His parental refrain had always been: *"You do whatever makes you happy."* No matter the case, the Arts were the fabric of his life. That's what made *him* happy. So whenever I rosined up the bow and extracted the holy wood from its case, he couldn't hide his excitement. He kept shouting from the kitchen, "Play it again!" each time I finished. So I did. I had nothing else to do while waiting around for Jordan to call or show up.

The fourth time I played it, my fingers were warmed up and back in business. I sounded good, almost as if I had never really quit. I smiled to myself in silence, waiting for my father to say *play it again*, but he didn't. Still smiling, I turned around to take a break … And there he stood, open-armed, smiling across the continents. "Jordan!" I put down the violin, flew into his arms, inhaled the Downy.

"Your violin sounds great," he said.

"You sound great," I whispered.

"Let's go outside."

Setting on puffy clouds, the sun was red and looked like the cherry on top. It was getting late, but still warm enough for short sleeves. We took a ride in Jordan's father's car back to his house on Darlington Road where he showed me the sketches of his ménage à trois, and some scenic paintings. We ordered pizza and got drunk on red wine.

Then we went out for a walk. He put his arm around my shoulder. I slid my arm around his back. We had never been this close before. We came to a stop sign, and before we crossed the street, I turned to face him and tilted my head. In a burst of desire, I pressed my lips against his. We kissed ... a long, wet kiss ... He pulled away before it was over.

"Are you kissing me because you're *drunk*?" he asked.

"I love you, Jordan. I'm kissing you because I love you."

"Are you sure it's not because you're *drunk*?" He seemed overly cautious.

"Let's go to my house," I insisted. There's something I want to show you." We took a ride back, and I gave him the corny little poems I had written earlier that day. "I wasn't *drunk* when I wrote these ... See? ... I wasn't kidding, Jord. My feelings for you have really changed —"

"Why? Why did they change?"

"I don't know. It was like I had an epiphany out of nowhere, and things became clear. I haven't stopped thinking about you since that moment."

"Bree ... I swear to God, this is the best day of my life!"

That week I took time off from the go-go bar to engage in an array of activities with Jordan: Frisbee in the park ... Hiking through the woods ... Foreign films at The Ritz. We visited our favorite places in the city: museums, restaurants, galleries. We talked, hugged, laughed, and kissed. But we didn't have sex. We were busy upgrading our friendship into the realm of romance. We were both content with just kissing each other, just being together and getting closer.

When it was time for him to return to Rome, I whined like a cat in heat, "Can't you stay a little longer? School doesn't start for another two weeks."

"I know, but I have to get back. I bought a motorcycle before I left, and I have to take care of things."

"A *motorcycle*? Do you even know how to drive a motorcycle?"

"Yeah, it's easy."

"Come on, Jord. I want to be with you."

"The semester'll be over before we know it. I'll come back then. I *have* to get back to work, or I'll lose my job ..."

"So what if they fire you? You can get another job..."

"It's not as easy as you think for an American to find work out there."

I wanted to keep him at home with me. I wanted more time, more adventure, more romance. He was like candy. Like a drug. Like an angel. I wanted to soar above the clouds on his wings, but he flew back to Rome alone.

CHAPTER TWENTY-THREE

The Name Game

Beavis and Butthead are regulars at Studio. They work next door at the supermarket and come in when their shift is over. Their real names are Charles and Paul, but they look, talk, act, dress, and think exactly like Beavis and Butthead. It's true. Charles is Beavis. Paul is Butthead. All the dancers call them by their real names to their faces, but always refer to them as Beavis and Butthead and laugh at them behind their backs. Nonetheless, they're serious about the dancers.

Paul has his heart set on Virginia. He brings her pint-sized baskets full of ruby-red, perfectly plump strawberries from the produce department, and doesn't let anyone else eat them. He honestly believes he has a chance with her because she talks to him and eats his strawberries. But really, we all want to eat his strawberries. I find it pretty funny how he gets so serious when I ask him for one: "No ... *Uh-huh, uh-huh* ... They're *only* for Virginia!"

I'd been sitting at the bar with Beavis and Butthead, sipping a glass of red wine, waiting for my set to begin when Virginia approached us while making her rounds.

"That guy over there is such an *asshole*," Virginia complained.

"Who's an asshole?" I asked, eyeing the

strawberries, waiting for a chance to pop one into my mouth when Butthead wasn't looking.

"Ya see that guy?" she said, pointing. "The one with the comb-over?"

"Yeah, I see him."

"He acts like he's gonna give ya a tip. Then he insists ya tell him your *real name*. So I told him, 'My real name's Virginia.' Well, he refused to believe me and wouldn't give me a tip after I wasted my time dancing for him on the bar. And he's doing it to all the girls tonight. What an *asshole*. Don't even bother trying to get a tip outta him." She popped a strawberry into her mouth. Butthead grunted, "*Uh-huh, uh-huh, uh-huh.*" I sneaked a strawberry during his grunting session. "Hey! I saw that!" he whined.

"Stop being so selfish, Paul. It's not nice," Virginia reprimanded.

The stage names at Studio were ridiculous: Cinnamon, Sassafras, Venus, Dakota, Montana, Madonna, Chicklet, China, Star, Leather, Lace, Lady Dee, Bubbles, Blackie, Butter, and more … including mine … *Barbie*.

Doogie Houser was still the Thursday night DJ, but everyone talked about Junior coming back. I was kind of concerned because Doogie always knew exactly what to play for me, even though I had never even made a single request. He just took control of the music, and his selections were spot-on every time. I worried about the task of asking Junior for specific song titles. It was nice having someone who did the thinking for me.

I danced my first set to the Steve Miller Band, *The*

Joker. I don't know why, but I felt more confident on stage that night, like a paintbrush gliding across a canvas. In all the time that I'd been dancing, I could only make turns to the right. For some strange reason, I couldn't turn to the left. My body refused. But that night, somehow, it happened. I found myself turning leftwards, spinning around with ease, and I wasn't even trying. Some kind of magnetic force had mysteriously entered my realm of balance, setting me in motion on an even path. Wonderment filled my mind. *How is this possible? ... This is amazing!* I thought, and immediately attributed the miracle to Jordan. *His love balances me.*

My spirit soared far beyond the walls of Studio as I painted the stage with my turns, sweating up a storm.

After cooling down at the ice bin, I went right over to the guy with the comb-over hairdo. "Hi, my name's Pussy. What's yours, Dick?" He got hysterical and handed me a twenty. *Virginia takes the customers way too seriously*, I thought.

If a guy doesn't believe a dancer's real name is what she says it is, then she should make up a different name. She should say it's Jennifer or something. Get the money. That's why we're here, to go-go get the money.

I was good at talking to the customers. In fact, I was great. I made them laugh. That was my forte. Everyone wants to feel good. Laughter does the job. Even for a loser with a comb-over who argues with the dancers in a go-go bar, nothing is better than a good laugh, and I knew it.

"So, what's your *real* name?" he asked. I wasn't

sure if I could get any more money out of the guy, so I didn't bother trying. "My real name's Pussy. My parents were cats, and that's what they named me. *Meow*," I purred, prancing away.

CHAPTER TWENTY-FOUR

My Father's Laughter

Jackie and I stopped for a bite to eat after work. We always stopped at Tiffany's Diner on the Boulevard, and always ate the same thing: two orders of French onion soup, potato pancakes with *extra-extra* sour cream, one house salad (to share) with Russian dressing, and two cups of hot tea with lemon.

The living room light was on when Jackie and I pulled up to the house. It was 3:30 in the morning.

"I wonder why the light's on," Jackie said, turning off her headlights, shutting down the car. Deep within my gut, I got a sick feeling that struck me hard and instantly swelled like an ocean, wrapping my head in dizziness.

My father was sitting on the sofa with a pale and tired face, reading the paper.

"What are *you* doing up so late?" Jackie asked him.

"I have some very disturbing news," he said, using his low, serious voice. I started sweating again. "We got a call from Jordan's father –"

"*My* Jordan?" I interrupted. *How could he be talking about* my *Jordan*, I wondered.

"There was an accident … Jordan was in an accident in Rome … On his motorcycle…"

I knew what was coming next. I knew it.

"He won't be coming home … alive …" My father

burst into tears. He loved Jordan. They got along great. Whenever Jordan stopped by the house, he and my father would always sit and talk and laugh a while. They enjoyed each other's company. *He's such a nice boy*, my father always said after Jordan would leave.

When he burst into tears, something hit me hard and brought the reality of Jordan's death into focus. It was the third time in my life I had ever seen my father cry. It sounded awful when he cried ... because it sounded like laughter.

A tidal wave crashed down on me. Then another. Then another. I couldn't breathe. Like I was going down, going under. Drowning. And although it was the news of Jordan's death that collapsed my frame into what felt like a pile of splinters on the living-room floor, it was the laughter-like crying of my father that somehow transported my thoughts, far in reverse. I passed out cold on the living-room floor, yet I wasn't there at all. My subconscious mind traveled back to a time when I was seven years old:

It was 1977. My father had just gotten home from a month's stay at Hahnemann Hospital. Open-heart surgery was fairly new at that time, and he had been certain he wouldn't survive. When he returned home, alive and well, we all gathered around his bed, examining his brand new scar that looked like a long, silky worm running the length of his torso. My sisters and I were thrilled. Our daddy was home! Then the phone rang. It was his sister, my Aunt Libby, calling from Florida. He told her, "I didn't think I was going to make it home alive. I thought I'd never walk through the front door again. I thought my life was over." Then he laughed. It was a strange laugh, unlike his usual snort-ridden laughter. Mona, Jackie, and I started laughing, too. Laughter can be contagious. Then we realized he was crying. It was horrifying. So we began to cry. Tears are also contagious. We might have been young, but we understood. His life was our life. Our past. Our present. Our future...

I could feel Jackie sitting on top of me. Shaking me. I tried to move, but couldn't. I was a paralyzed blob. The stench of the go-go bar was still on us, and I could smell it, but I couldn't hear a thing except the sound of my father's laughter-like crying. And once again, the sound encapsulated me in a cloud of fog. And I drifted again, far away in reverse, back to 1979. We were at a funeral. I was nine years old:

A woman my father worked with had just died. She was a court stenographer, just like him. We all got dressed up and went to a funeral where everyone was Black – everyone, except for us. It seemed as though there were a million people at the service. I was fascinated by all the shades of brown skin. I liked the way the women's silver or gold earrings shined against their dark skin. My silver earrings don't look as nice against my skin, *I remember thinking.*

The funeral was quiet. People sat quietly, respectfully composed. Then, as if from the depths of a hidden well, my father's laugher-like crying erupted, loud and long, spewing out a horrifying sound. All the brown faces turned to see the only olive-skinned man in the place. One woman came over to him, gently patted his back, and said in a Southern-like accent, "There's no cryin' here, sir. Betty's in heaven now.

She's with God. We should be happy for her."

Jackie poured a cup of water over my head. I opened my eyes as if from a dream.

"Do you want me to take you to his mother's house?" she asked.

"Whose mother's house?" I asked.

"Jordan's," she said.

"It's like 4:00 in the morning or something. I can't go there now."

"Oh yeah, I forgot," Jackie said with confusion.

"He went before his time … He was just a boy … It's just not fair," my father said, shaking his head in disbelief. Then he wiped his tears, blew his nose, took a deep breath, and let out a long sigh. "You know Bree … It's part of life. You have to be strong now. Don't get crazy or do anything foolish."

"I'm okay, daddy. I'll be okay. You don't have to worry about me. I love you so much."

"I love you too, baby."

We hugged. I fought back my tears until I got into bed.

Puddles of pain seeped through my pillowcase in silence. I cried for Jordan. I cried for myself. I cried for his parents. I cried for the world.

CHAPTER TWENTY-FIVE

The Prom

I woke up in a stupor some time around five in the morning and took a shower. All the while I thought of Jordan – on his motorcycle – crashing to his death.

Honk! Skid. Crash! ... Honk! Skid. Crash! ... Three distinct sounds echoed through my mind, over and over.

Then came the thought of the passersby – stopping in their tracks – eyes widening – mouths gaping – gasping. They turn to speak to one another in low Italian rumbles, rising and falling in disbelief. And then – shortly after – there's the distant wailing of the *ambulanza* – racing through the streets of Rome – approaching sirens – disturbing dissonance – louder and louder – and still louder yet – arriving – *"Un studente Americano"* – *"Morto"* – Dead.

These ideas washed over and disturbed me as I soaped and shampooed.

A little while later, I stood by the stovetop in the kitchen – waiting for the water to boil – watching the blue and orange flame under the kettle – thinking about orange and blue and how they're complementary colors.

Jordan was the orange to my blue ... He was my complement ... He gave my life harmony ... and balance ... Now I'm just completely blue...

My mother watched me from behind for a few seconds. I sensed her there and turned around. She embraced me. She has the most comforting hugs, real soft and warm. She started crying a lot. She knew how much I loved him.

"I'm okay mom ... I'm okay," I insisted, but I started crying, uncontrollably, into her shoulder. We sobbed together until the kettle whistled.

I drank a cup of tea with lemon, and thought about playing my violin. So I got it out ... and held it a while ... but there was no music in me. The thin silence that filled the air was not to be disturbed. So I put it back in its case.

I thought about drawing something. So I reached for a pencil, opened my sketchbook ... and stared at an empty page a while ... but there was no stroke in my hand, no expression in my mind. The clean sheet of smoothness was not to be disturbed. So I closed the book.

My mind was numb, but my body felt crampy, like I was about to get my period. I started crying again. And even though crying was the only thing I could do to make myself feel better, I ended up giving myself a massive headache. So I just gave up and went back to sleep.

A few hours later, Jackie tiptoed into my room. She tapped on my back and whispered firmly, "Bree ... Bree ... Wake up." I opened my eyes as I turned to face her. She held a large manila envelope that had a bunch of Italian stamps stacked haphazardly in the corner next to a postmark from Rome. "The mailman just delivered this ... Open it. It's from Jordan. He must've sent it before he … you know."

She didn't want to say *died*.

Inside the envelope was a drawing of me playing the violin: a loose sketch in blank ink and lots of bright color. He drew me standing on a mountain ledge, wearing fringy-hippie clothing that revealed my naval. Musical notes and a dreamy rainbow poured out of the instrument.

A small message on pink notepad paper was also included:

Dear Bree Baby,
I love you so much.
Thinking about you all the time.
Can't wait to see you
and listen to you playing your violin again.
I'll call you soon.
              Love,
                 Jordan
p.s. I hope you like the drawing.

"This is amazing!" Jackie said, studying the drawing. "I'm getting it framed for you tomorrow. I'll take it to the Framer's Workshop on Castor Avenue. It's so beautiful—"

"It's unbearable," I said. "How could Jordan be here one day … and gone the next? It's so fucked up!"

"Yup … It sure is." Jackie sat down on my bed and began rubbing my back, real motherly. "Just be strong. You'll get through it ... I wish I could stay with you today, but I have to get ready for work." She gave me a reassuring smile and left the room.

I looked at the drawing again and cried and cried until I was all cried out. Then I knew what I had to do.

I put on my favorite pair of worn-out Levi's and the Guatemalan shirt that Jordan loved. I grabbed my keys, my cigarettes, and my bag and headed over to his mother's house on Darlington Road.

*

The house was sheathed in funereal energy. I quietly entered and quickly lost my sense of purpose. It was the first time that Jordan wasn't there. I was confused and started feeling sick again. Luckily, I knew my way around pretty well, so I ran upstairs past the older adults, and slipped into the powder room. I drank fistfuls of water from the faucet and splashed some on my face. Then I sat on the lid of the toilet until the dizziness went away.

I entered the family room where most of the visitors had gathered. There were a few adults that I recognized from past events, like Jordan's Bar Mitzvah and other occasions. But I didn't know any of them by name. I stood alone, the youngest person in the house, the first friend of Jordan's to arrive.

So many people surrounded Jordan's mother Becky, offering their condolences. Others waited patiently in a line that twisted around the room. Becky sat in her wheelchair, unable to move an inch even if she wanted to. She was quadriplegic. All four of her limbs were paralyzed. She lived her life the best she could while suffering the extreme effects of the fourth stage of Multiple Sclerosis.

It was the first time I'd I seen her since the night of Jordan's senior prom. Back then she could still use her arms. I remembered how she held the camera and took pictures of us before we left. She was smiling then. But now she was a childless mother who bore a grave expression, and I realized that Becky could never be truly happy again:

Jordan was her only child ... He was her happiness. Her joy. Her fountain of laughter ... He was her strength. Her reason for getting out of bed and into that wheelchair everyday ... He was her blossoming artist. Her pride. Her hero. Her hope. Her everything... He was her life.

I wanted to jump through the crowd and land by her side. I wanted to hug her, cry to her. I wanted to share the pain of this unimaginable tragedy. I wanted so badly to make my way over to her. But the moment I aimed to step in her direction, I got scared. My knees began to shake. I cowered and hid behind the crowd; it was like stage fright.

So I tried to think of something to say to Becky:

'I'm so sorry for your loss. Jordan was such a good person and—'... Wait ... I can't say that ... The word 'was' sounds weird ... 'Jordan was' ... I can't speak about him in the past tense? ... It's too disturbing ... I don't want to disturb Becky ... What if I say something that makes her feel even worse than she already does? ...

Panic-stricken by these thoughts, I sat down on the floor in the nearest corner of the room and felt like a child. I just sat there, looking at Becky's thin, unsmiling lips. I had a good view of her through the legs of the people standing in front of me. Her body was so frail, but her face was so strong – chiseled with a high set of cheekbones. The way she held her chin up reminded me of a Native American wise woman. But the pain in Becky's eyes revealed her tortured soul. I wondered how she managed to remain so completely composed in the midst of cruel misery. I wondered if she wanted to escape from the crowd – and hide in a corner – alone – like me.

As time carried on, grim matter set my mind on a downward path to deeper levels of low. And just when I felt trapped in that shadowy place, my imagination emerged like a superhero, rescuing me from my dismal reflections.

All at once I envisioned another scenario, one filled with a series of developments that would change the present mood – not just for me, but also for all who loved Jordan:

I imagined how happily surprised Becky would be if Jordan suddenly entered the room. I pictured him returning home from Rome – standing in the doorway – holding his bags and bundles. He'd smile and say something like *Hey! What's going on?* – I saw myself springing up from the floor – running over to him – jumping into his arms – planting my face into the nape of his neck – breathing in his fresh scent. I saw myself passionately kissing his lips and running my fingers through his thick, brown hair. I imagined everyone in the room sighing with relief, especially Becky. I saw her smile returning to her face.

Upon these thoughts I grew full of excitement and allowed myself to drift away in the wonder of it:

Could this really happen? ... Anything's possible ... Jordan might still be alive! ... Maybe this is all just a big mistake! ...

A surge of adrenaline coursed through my body. I reeled from the feeling and turned towards Becky again. At first I thought she had a cigarette in her mouth, but it was a straw. She was sipping water from a cup that someone had to hold for her. In the middle of a sip, her eyes darted towards the patio door as it opened, and the straw fell from her lips. A large bouquet of tropical flowers filled the doorway. I held on to my fantasy of Jordan's surprise return and quietly begged God to bring him home.

That's when Becky spotted me. I must have looked crazy sitting in that corner, because she was startled by my presence.

Our eyes interlocked and she gasped.

The entire room seemed to vanish the moment our eyes connected. I felt as though in a trance. And through the silent stare we held together, there was an acknowledgement, a strong communication, a bond of understanding. Her eyes kept growing wider and wider in size and intensity. They appeared as two flickering lights encoded with meaning, signaling a message that said: *I'm crushed. I'm exploding. And I know you are, too.* My eyes filled with tears. Becky smiled at me. I tried to smile back. Then she motioned for me to come over to her.

At Becky's side, I didn't feel scared or worried anymore. I felt closer to Jordan. The wheelchair made it difficult for me to give her the kind of hug that I wanted to, so I had to get creative and twist myself around some. My tears soaked my face and ran all the way down to my neck by the time the hug was over.

Becky's voice was weak like the rest of her body, so I had to read her lips as she spoke. She told me that my Guatemalan shirt looked like something Jordan would wear. Then she called me *Bree Baby*, which really surprised me. "Did Jordan tell you he called me that?" "Jordan told me *everything*," she beamed. "He loved you … He was *crazy* about you."

I felt so damn good at that moment. I wanted to stay with Becky and talk about Jordan all night. But so many people were waiting in line to see her. And my turn was over.

The house began filling up with more and more people I hadn't seen since high school. It was strange to see some of them crying. I had never seen these people cry before, especially the guys. It was the saddest of reunions. We shook our heads in disbelief and comforted each other.

Then this girl Andrea – who I used to be friendly with (but *not* friends with) – showed up. She flew into the room and instantly captured everyone's attention with her overdramatized wailing. She carried on and on in an endless series of soprano shrieks, piercing the restrained quiet of the household. Even the people upstairs could hear her. Many came down to see the spectacle, and, as her audience thickened, Andrea's cries of agony intensified. Then she threw herself on the floor and launched into some sort of manic monologue: "Jordan's *dead*! Jordan's *dead*! … No, he *can't* be dead! ... It *can't* be true! ... He was the love of my *life*! ... He was *always* there for me! ... Now I have *no one*! ... No one! ... ... My life's over now that he's gone! ...

Andrea acted as though *she* had been Jordan's girlfriend. I started wondering if there was something I had missed. Some relationship they had had that I didn't know about. Jordan had never mentioned anything to me about Andrea.

She introduced herself to Jordan's mother as *AHN-dree-ah*, pronouncing her name as though she spoke with a British accent. In all the years I'd known her, she never pronounced her name that way. No one did. We all pronounced it ANN-dree-uh.

As if by instinct, I escaped the unbearable clamor and went outside to smoke a cigarette. On my way out to the patio, I passed by a few of Jordan's mother's friends who were smoking near the door. There was a wrought-iron bench at the far end of the patio. I took a seat and hoped that no one would notice me there.

I heard the ladies talking in hushed tones. Their words were almost impossible to decipher, but something stood out, loud and clear: "They won't send Jordan's body until he's been officially identified. So Richie got Jordan's dental x-rays this morning and sent them to Rome..."

Overhearing this made everything seem so surreal. I looked up at the sky and focused on the beauty of the rising moon, the brightness of light, the perfection of creation. I enjoyed the moment of blank thought. My mind had been working overtime, so it was nice to finally give it a break and relieve the tension.

213

Unfortunately, it didn't last too long. Andrea came out for a cigarette and planted herself on the bench right next to me. She started again: "Do you believe Jordan's *dead*? Do you believe it, Bree? ... Our Jordy's *dead*?" she cried.

Our Jordy? I thought. He's not *ours*. He's *mine*!

"No ... It's unbelievable," I said.

"I wanted to go to Rome and visit him this past winter, but I was avalanche hunting in Colorado." Andrea held and smoked her cigarette as if it were a joint.

"You were avalanche hunting?" I asked with surprise. It sounded absurd. I didn't exactly know what avalanche hunting was, but acted as though I did by not asking any more questions about it.

"Yeah, it was awesome ... I really loved Jord. I can't believe he's gone."

"I know what you mean." It was a dead-end conversation. Might as well be over. I prepared to go back into the house as I readied the filter of my cigarette for the final flicking.

"When's the funeral?" she asked.

"Nobody knows yet. They're having trouble getting his body back because he hasn't been officially identified. His father sent his dental x-rays to Rome for a final confirmation. I guess these things take time."

"His dental x-rays! That's so weird – *Ugh*! I feel nauseous – I'm going in to get some *water*. Want some?" she asked. I could tell that she had lost her Philadelphia accent. She sounded like a California girl or something. In Philly we say WUH-ter. Andrea said

WAH-ter. I hate when Philadelphians lose their accents.

"No thanks. I'm not thirsty," I said. I really was thirsty, but didn't feel like hanging out with her any longer. She went into the house. I decided to stay outside and smoke another cigarette. By my fourth drag she was already back out, drinking a bottle of WAH-ter, standing by my side, ready to resume her endless chatter.

"I'm *so* glad I'm here for this," she continued. "I mean ... I'm not glad about the situation ... obviously. It's just that ... I'm *like* not even supposed *to be here* right now. I was planning on heading out to Washington State from Colorado, but the avalanche hunt didn't pay off. I just did it for the experience. So I *had* to come back. And now, I'm like *totally* broke." Andrea had so much to say in her non-Philadelphia way of speaking. She could have chosen any number of people to rattle off her current life story to, but she chose me. I was the loser lottery winner.

"Oh," I said. I had to say something.

"Right now I'm living with some friends out in Fishtown. They're like *totally cool*. But I feel trapped. Philly *sucks*. It's so predictable here. I need to make some fast money, so I can head out West again. I hate it here –"

"I love it here."

"You do?"

"Uh-huh. Philly's great ... It's home." I declared this with the pride of a native. People from Philly usually have a strong attachment to it and cherish their city roots, from near or afar. So the fact that I was

215

having this particular conversation with someone who grew up in my neighborhood was awkward. It didn't make much sense. I chain-lit another cigarette as I considered it: *Saying that she hates Philly is like saying that she hates herself.*

"I wish *I* loved it here, she continued. "I'm just like Jordan. I have to live on the run. That's how he was, you know … Hey, can I bum a cigarette? I'm all out. I started smoking again the minute I got back to Philly, but I can't really afford them, so I just bum when I run out. It really sucks."

I handed her my pack and told her to take a couple extra for later.

At that point I found her character to be more entertaining than annoying, probably because I started analyzing every little thing she said. I wanted to figure out what was wrong with her and why I felt so uncomfortable in her presence:

Andrea presents herself like some kind of sophisticated adventurer … like Philly's not good enough for her – and never was … She won't even say WUH-ter … I guess she's ashamed of who she really is … She just returned from an amazing experience, an avalanche hunt, but she hasn't said anything interesting about it … She just complains about being broke and how much she hates it here … Telling me this was rude and obnoxious, considering that I live here! … Rude people are attention getters … Why does she want my attention? … She's probably so lonely and desperate for attention that she'll take it from anyone who'll give it … Then she says, 'I'm just like Jordan,' living life 'on the run.' … So what does

216

that imply? What's she really trying to say? ... That she and Jordan were in on something that I'm not? ... That she understands Jordan's life better than I do because I still live in Philly? ... How pathetic ... She talks herself up and acts like her life-on-the run is meaningful beyond my comprehension ... But here she is, stuck in Philly, fooling no one, rambling on and on, revealing her miserable inner self. And then, to top it all off, she can't even afford a pack of cigarettes.

I started feeling sorry for her. I wanted to rush her off to Egos Anonymous and sign her up right away. That's the crazy thing about myself. Someone can annoy the crap out of me, and in the turn of a thought, I start enjoying their company. I think it's a form of masochism.

"So, what are you up to these days, Bree?" I guess she ran out of things to say about herself.

"I'm a painter," I said.

"Cool. Are you taking classes?"

"Yeah, I'm at Temple. Jordan really turned me on to the whole art scene there. He begged me to model for his painting class. At first, I didn't want to. But, you know Jordan. When he wanted something, he always got his way. So he convinced me to model for his class, and we had so much fun in the studio. I loved going to school with him. After he left for Rome, I registered for a painting class, and it was the best move I ever made. The studio's awesome. It's like a playground of images in an ocean of color. And, it might sound strange, but I really learn a lot about myself when I'm emerged in the process. I can't really explain it, because I don't really understand it myself.

217

Jordan understood it though."

I felt more confident about my relationship with Jordan at that point. He was like *me*. Not like *her*. He wasn't chasing avalanches. He was chasing images, inspirational images to draw and paint. He was my best male friend. He was my boyfriend. And I was the last girlfriend he would ever have. I was the subject of his final drawing. I was the last letter he ever wrote.

"You're so lucky you got to be with him, Bree. I was secretly in love with him, ya know?" Andrea said this with a wide smile. I had forgotten just how big her horse teeth were.

"I guess it doesn't matter now," I frowned. I didn't want to share the details of my romance with Jordan. I didn't want to open up to Andrea any more than I already had.

"I know what I'll do," she decided. "I'll write a eulogy and read it at his funeral!"

"That's a great idea," I said, even though I thought it was a lousy idea. It was bad enough having to listen to her face to face. But the thought of listening to her ramblings-on at his funeral was even worse.

"I really need to make some fast money. It's like, I want to get out West in the worst way. I'm so ready to do something drastic, like sell my body for cash or somethin'," she giggled. The more she spoke, the more her Philadelphia accent slipped back into place.

"Why don't you go-go dance," I suggested. I wouldn't normally make so bold a suggestion, or even tell anyone that I was dancing in a go-go bar, but Andrea seemed desperate. I wanted to help her get out West. That would put a whole lot of distance between us. I wouldn't have to bump into her at funerals or other unexpected reunions. She certainly had the right body for go-go. Her boobs were always bigger than the other girls. She woke up one morning in seventh grade, and her training bra was replaced with a support bra. We were all fascinated by her transformation.

"Are you serious?" Her face lit up in a smile of bronco choppers again.

"That's what I'm doing … part time. There's a bar out in Princeton. It's not even topless, and the tips are great. I dance there two or three nights a week. Talk about fast money … it's a money marathon. It'll get you out West in no time."

"How much can you make a night?"

"A lot. Anywhere from five hundred to a thousand, depending on the night."

"Cool. What do I need to do? Should I just call the bar and ask for a job?"

"I'll talk to the manager on Thursday night and get you an audition. Just make sure you have something to wear."

"You're so cool, Bree. Here's my phone number." She took out a piece of paper from a burlap sac and scribbled numbers with a pencil that looked like the bark of a tree.

And in my attempt to get as much distance as possible between us, I unwittingly pulled her into the epicenter of my life.

"I guess I better shave my legs and my armpits. There was never any time while I was avalanche hunting. I just got used to being hairy." She pulled up the bottom of her jeans, revealing a flesh-colored cactus plant. I imagined a miniature lawn mower rolling up her leg.

We went back inside and talked about Jordan's life for the rest of the day. His mother introduced me to her family and friends as "Jordan's Prom Date," or "The Girl in Jordan's Prom Picture." She told everyone a story about the prom. About how Jordan had a girlfriend named Abby who he didn't want to take to his prom. About how he only wanted to go with Bree Yeager.

Hey, Bree, can I ask you something?
Sure.
Will you go to the senior prom with me?
What about your girlfriend Abby? Don't you want to take her *to your prom?*
No. I want to go with you. *I want to have fun.*

CHAPTER TWENTY-SIX

Stiff as a Board, Light as a Feather

On Wednesday morning Jordan's body arrived at the airport. A Thursday funeral was planned. Services were scheduled at *Goldstein, Raphael and Sacks* in the suburbs; then everyone would proceed to *Shalom Memorial Park, Section Elijah.*

I couldn't sleep. It was warm enough to keep the windows open that night. The thought of the funeral held my eyes open as wide as the windows.

I rummaged through the basement for my old sleeping bag, the one I used to take to sleepover parties when I was younger. Made of red cotton on the outside, the inside was made of soft flannel, printed with peacocks. I find things made of two different materials particularly exciting. My violin is special, like the sleeping bag, because it's made of two different pieces of wood. The bottom piece is a caramel-colored maple. The top – the belly – had been replaced with a piece of cherry wood in 1918, right here in Philadelphia, by a violinmaker named E.J. Albert. And when you peek through the f-hole on the left, there's a small piece of paper glued to the inside that contains all the historical details. As soon as the salesperson at Zapf's music store said the words *cherry wood*, I knew it was the violin I'd be taking home on my sixteenth birthday.

My father paid two thousand dollars for it. He was usually frugal with money. But he spared no expense when it came to music or any of the arts in general, often securing opera tickets, box seats at the ballet, record album collections, instruments, and more. He'll pay top dollar for top quality, but a little thing like turning on the central air-conditioning on the most unbearable summer night was deemed "unnecessary" and even "irresponsible" according to his financial standards. My sisters and I had to drag our sleeping bags into my parents' bedroom to cool down under the only economy window unit he'd purchased. It was like camping out in our own home! The only good thing about it was that I got to use my sleeping bag. It's so soft.

I threw it into the back seat of the Jeep and headed over to the cemetery at the silent hour of three a.m.

I turned into the cemetery driveway and turned off the headlights. It was spooky all right. The moon had gotten fat again, lighting the strange path before me. I didn't even know where Section Elijah was. I slowed to a stop.

What if I get lost in here? What if I start freaking out and dead bodies rise up from the ground, like in the Thriller video? I'll just drive around the sections near the exit, in case I have to beat it.

I took a right at the first fork in the road. *Section David ... Section Elijah ... Found it!* Excited to have accomplished the mission with ease, I grabbed my sleeping bag and set up camp near (but not close enough to fall into) a freshly dug hole in the earth.

It was good being there. I wanted Jordan to feel comfortable once he arrived. He would find it easier to adjust knowing that I had checked it out first.

The sleeping bag kept me warm, but I forgot to bring a pillow. I can't really sleep too well without a pillow, so I just dozed in and out of sleep on my elbow.

At some point, during one of those in-and-out intervals, I recalled what we used to do at sleepover parties when we were younger. We'd always have a séance: one of the several northeast-Philly-sleep-over-party rituals. One of the girls, usually the birthday girl (unless she was too scared), would lie in the middle of the basement floor, as all the other girls knelt beside her, all around her, placing two fingers from each of their hands under her body. Someone would call upon the spirit of Elvis or a dead pet or a grandparent. I don't remember too much of the incantation except for the last part: "Stiff as a board, light as a feather." All together, all at once, we'd lift the body off the ground with our fingers and chant: "Stiff as a board, light as a feather ... Stiff as a board, light as a feather."

When I finally did get some sleep, I dreamed of a flannel-soft peacock, wandering around the cemetery, looking for me.

He was magnificent.

CHAPTER TWENTY-SEVEN

Lost and Found

Andrea used her phony California accent while delivering her eulogy. But I have to admit that her words were brilliantly poetic. I enjoyed the way she inverted each line and compared Jordan to several birds:

"Like eagle, he was powerful, sacred, a leader. Like hawk, he was intelligent, keen, a thinker. Like sparrow, he was gregarious, handsome, a traveler." I liked it best at the end when she compared him to a peacock: "Like peacock, he was colorful, an artist, displaying his flair for beauty and truth."

I believed he was there with us the whole time. Andrea's bit about the peacock, coupled with my dream in the cemetery, added up to more than a coincidence in my cosmic calculation of all things.

At his graveside, I held two fistfuls of earth and threw them in. I wanted to touch the earth that was to be eternally touching him. I wanted my fingerprints to mix in, like the ingredients of a recipe. I wanted to lower myself into the grave. To die. To feel what it was like. To see what he was seeing. To be where he was.

After the funeral part of the day, my own thoughts ate away at the lining of my brain. I didn't want to stay home, sitting around, thinking, and crying. I didn't want to go back to the *shiva* house either and listen to Andrea again. I wanted to lose my mind. Go-go dancing's good for that.

I decided to tuck the aqua string of my OB tampon way up my crotch (just like Jackie had taught me to), and go up to Studio. I always danced with the Thursday night Dream Team. They were expecting me, and I hadn't called out or anything. I mean, I didn't *have* to go. It's not as though they'd fire me if I didn't show. No one really cared. As long as you showed up most of the time and didn't act like a total idiot, Studio management was cool about things that other employers were not.

*

"Are you sure you want to go up tonight?" Jackie asked.

"We're already on our way, so what's the difference?"

"I'll turn the car around right now and take you back home if you're not up to it. I mean, God Bree, you just buried your best friend. How are you going to get through the night?"

"I'm fine. Stop worrying."

"It's not just that. I didn't want to tell you before, but this is probably my last night working at Studio."

"Why?"

"I found a salon for sale in the city, and it looks promising. The salon is *grrrreat*." She sounded like Tony the Tiger. "The previous owner's in jail for some type of fraud charge. It's all happening so fast. The paperwork's supposed to go through early next week. Omega found out about it through his gay community network, thank God! I'm taking him with me. Tyler's coming, Laura's coming, Kathy's coming, Tina L. and Tina T. are both coming, and I'm trying to convince Jeff to come, too. He feels bad because of Christina. She's gonna have a heart attack when she finds out that half her staff is leaving, but that's what she gets for being a bitch."

I found it hard to believe that Jackie had made so many plans without my knowing. "Jackie! Why didn't you tell me?"

"You've been so busy in your own world. I didn't want to bother you with the details of mine. I know how much you loved Jordan. My plans seemed so little compared to your troubles."

"It's not like I'm a total basket case," I assured her.

"Well, you've surely been acting like one lately. You camped out in the cemetery last night. In case you didn't know, that little stunt of yours has the words 'BASKET CASE' written all over it."

"Okay, I guess I've been deeply affected, but now that the funeral's over, I think I'll be alright." I took a deep breath. "What's the name of the new salon?"

"The one that was there before was called Barry Leonard's. Mine's going to be called Hair Tea ... *The Hair Tea Salon.*"

"Hair Tea! That's awesome. I love it. Did I give you that idea – from that time when Nanette made tea out of my hair?"

"Yup ... that's where I got it ... but there's more to it than what you think. *Hair Tea* is actually a product. There are a bunch of teas that are really healthy for

226

your hair."

"Where's the salon?"

"That's the thing – it's in the *best* location – right on Rittenhouse Square ... Everyone wants to work there. Christina's really gonna freak out."

"Wow, Jackie, I'm so happy for you."

I was happy for her, but couldn't help resenting the fact that I'd be working at Studio without her. Now I'd have to drive myself up and back forty-five minutes each way. It just wouldn't be the same. Nothing would be the same. I was standing on the edge of a life I didn't know.

The usual Thursday night, three-deep crowd was there, but Doogie Houser wasn't. Everyone was so damned excited about Junior being back in the DJ booth. That's all they talked about in the dressing room as they crowded together on the Simpson's cartoon sofa, straightening and counting their money: *Junior's back ... It's such a shame ... How's he holding up? ... He seems fine.*

I didn't know what they were talking about and didn't pay too much attention at first. Most of the dancers had their own secret language, which didn't include the vocabulary of my world. They'd say things like: "I just worked a *double* over at Heartbreakers." Or: "I'm going *on tour* next month." Or: "*Lap dances* at The Dollhouse pay the best." Or: "I'm gonna be a *feature*." Doubles? Tours? Lap dances? Features? I just didn't beat to their rhythm of conversation.

Then I remembered that Junior was the regular Thursday night DJ, and that I had contributed ten dollars to a funeral fund for his newborn when I first started dancing. It struck me as strange that his first night back at the bar coincided with the date of Jordan's funeral. The coincidence produced an unmistakable feeling, like that of déjà vu.

Just as the goose bumps tickled my skin, I spotted a dancer I had never seen before. She was changing costumes in her snow-white skin. Her name was Pinkie. I couldn't stop staring at her. There was something odd about her body. It looked out of shape. But not the out-of-shape figure of a person who really is out of shape. It was the figure of a woman who had just given birth. Her guitar curves had mushroomed. Her breasts were full of milk. Her nipples were softly swollen, as Niomi's had been from nursing, only Niomi's were dark-brown circles. Pinkie's nipples were pink.

I slipped into a pair of pink leather thigh-high boots as I imagined this unfamiliar dancer delivering her baby. My vision included a black-skinned infant exiting her red-haired, snow-white vagina. I don't know what prompted me to imagine that, but my foresight was confirmed a little while later when she passed around a set of photos of her newborn, black baby boy.

"He's beautiful. How old is he?" I asked, handing the picture back.

"I just had him eleven days ago."

"You're back to work so soon, aren't you?" I asked. I had heard of women taking a leave of absence from work to recover from childbirth for at least six weeks. Eleven days seemed too soon, *much too soon* for go-go dancing.

"I know it's way too soon, but we really need the money. I *have* to work," she said.

I didn't know what to say, so I ran down my mental list of cliché conversation-enders, and chose: "What doesn't kill you only makes you stronger."

How did I know that the baby was black? I wondered. *How did I see it before I saw it?* The déjà vu strangeness filled the air like thick soup. I could taste it.

"Your boobs look bigger," Jackie said as she inserted her favorite hoop earrings.

"Mine?" I asked.

"Yeah, look at them."

They do look bigger. And, come to think of it, my costume feels tighter, I thought, observing the difference in the mirror. "Oh, I have my period," I remembered.

"They still look a lot bigger. You look great, especially for someone who just went to a funeral."

"Thanks for reminding me." I gave her the I'm-Gonna-Kill-You look.

"I'm sorry. I didn't mean to bring it up." She bit her lip.

I walked all the way around the bar over to the DJ booth to discuss my repertoire of music. It still felt awkward covering that length of distance in high heels. There was a short line of dancers waiting to talk to Junior. I was last in line. Waiting there felt silly.

Each time I walked up the three steps of the DJ booth, I felt as though I was entering a time capsule. The DJ booth was dimly lit and small, like a cockpit.

Tiny red and green lights on the equipment sometimes flashed, sometimes didn't. Junior had earphones on and was announcing the next dancer's name into the microphone. "Next on stage is Blackie Fox. Time to get excited fellas." His voice was nice, like low and distant thunder. Removing the earphones, he turned around. "Come on in," he said, fitting a CD back into its case, checking a hand-written list on a small notepad.

The déjà vu strangeness reached a climax. Junior was big like Jordan, *exactly* like Jordan. The closer I got to him, the fresher the scent of Downy became. Junior was a Puerto Rican version of Jordan, or so I thought. He wasn't brown-skinned Puerto Rican. He was light-skinned with dark, piercing eyes and a thin moustache. Right away I could tell he sensed something about me. Maybe he sensed that I was sizing him up. Or maybe it was something else. I had just been to a funeral. He had just spent the past three months mourning his newborn. Our energies connected like Velcro. I wanted to run far away from Junior, but instead I just told him what kind of music I danced to. The way he looked into my eyes felt comforting and frightening all at once, a two-toned feeling. "Do you like Latin music?" he asked.

"I like all kinds of music," I said.

"What's your name?"

"My stage name's Barbie, but my real name's Bree."

"It's good to meet you. I'm Junior." He took my hand and kissed it, keeping his eyes fixed on mine. I felt like I was about to be bitten by Dracula, like he would release my hand, take me in his arms, and suck the blood out of my neck. "My real name is Daniel Carlos Sosa-Rodriguez, Jr." I could tell he was fluent in Spanish by the way he pronounced his name.

"That's quite a name," I said.

"Pleasure's all mine," he smiled with Jordan's dimples. I got the hell out of there.

The bar seemed larger. I changed my Regular-Flow tampon before my set began. My period was heavier than usual. I should have brought a box of Super-sized tampons along, but it was only my first day. Regulars hold me over for two days, and then I switch to Super. Nothing was as usual ... the bar ... the de'ja vu strangeness ... my menstrual flow. Everything seemed big on me – everything except for my super-tight costume.

While on stage, Junior's voice came through the speaker, soft and low. Every once in a while, I'd hear him moan, "*Oh, yeah ... Oow ... Ahh ...*" I figured it was his style of DJ-ing. I didn't think he made those noises specifically for me. Then I paid attention to what he did for the other dancers. Nothing. Not an *oow* or an *ahh*. I knew he liked me, and I avoided him because I liked him, too. Somewhere in the universe, a chemistry beaker heated and oozed over the top.

In the back room, the Russian woman was selling costumes again. I bought a hundred-dollar's worth.

"Why are you spending money on costumes?" Jackie asked.

"Why wouldn't I?"

"Because I'm giving you all my costumes after work tonight."

"Oh, yeah. This is your last night. I completely forgot."

"You're such an idiot."

"Well, it's not like they'll go to waste."

The fact that the place was packed and money was plenty put my mind at ease over the hundred I'd just wasted. Thursday nights were wild, but so much was over-exaggerated that night: the money, the smoke, the music, the tippers, the dancers, the excitement. All the big tippers were there. Frank and his driver always got the girls keyed up. Frank was some kind of an investment broker who had an endless stream of bills to spare. So did his driver.

The *White Shirts* from Merril-Lynch made their impossible-not-to-notice appearance as well. The dancers called them the "white shirts" because they'd come into the bar straight from work in their starched whites and cufflinks.

During my fourth set, some guy motioned for me to come down and get a tip. I did my usual dirty dance for him. He handed me a bill. At first glance I wasn't sure if my eyes were out of focus. But Benjamin has an unmistakable face. *My first hundred-dollar bill!* The experience was shocking.

He said his name was Roger. I had a drink with him between sets. He looked like an FBI agent wearing a plaid shirt, rose-colored glasses, and a thick moustache. He passed out hundred-dollar bills to the dancers as if they were trick-or-treat candy. He wasn't very good-looking, but his money sure was. "Do you do private parties?" he asked.

"Not really. I'm just a college student paying my

way through school. I don't work outside of Studio." I felt bad saying it because a few of the dancers really were using their earnings for college tuition. My father paid my bills.

"They're opening a private room in the back for lap dances next week," he said.

"Here? – At Studio? – I haven't heard anything about that."

"I know Joe – the owner. He told me about it."

"Sounds exciting." I didn't know what else to say to the hundred-dollar man, and my mind drifted back to a nighttime series called *The Six Million Dollar Man*. I wished that Roger looked more like Steve Austin. Then I'd have more to say, more questions to ask: *What was it like being an astronaut? I know that your eyes, your legs, and your arms are bionic, but is there something else the secret agents are hiding about you, handsome?* I would have had a slew of things to ask if only he wasn't plain old Roger.

"Maybe you could do a lap dance for me next week," he suggested.

"Sure, I'd love to." I smiled as he handed me another hundred.

I was late for my next set and forgot to change my tampon. I slipped into a white one-piece made of cotton lining and lace that I bought from the Russian lady. It was a one-piece (but more like a two-piece) that connected with little white bathing-suit hooks on both sides of my waist. It made my boobs look great and exposed my stomach and ass as if it were custom-designed just for me. My body was at its peak. Dancing had cut the edges of my muscles like a sculptor chisels marble.

I danced to AC/DC's *Hell's Bells* and was pulled by the undercurrent of Junior's subliminal mating calls. Roger was busy chatting up the girl in the mummer's costume. Not wanting to appear desperate for his hundreds, I tried not to look at him too much and just danced my heart out, sweating through a series of spins and turns. I bent over to show off my ass, spreading my legs into an upside down letter V. While my head was way down at my ankles, I looked directly up at a fearful image: a perfect red circle in the crotch of my costume. With a rush of adrenaline, I sprang out of the upside down V right into the letter I. Looking around to see if anyone had noticed, nothing appeared unusual. I finished my set with my legs glued together like Z's and S's.

I had to get back to the dressing room to change my costume and my tampon. On my way out of the bar, I collected a bunch of tips, squeezing my legs together so that no one would see the ruby circle. Roger gave me another hundred while I iced down at the ice bin. "I love your little ice act. It's so sexy," he said. "You must be delicious. Your nipples are great."

"Thanks. I'll be right back." I ducked under the bar in a perfect zigzag. Roger's comment about my nipples made me want to puke, and I imagined him choking on silver dollars. The dancers always described nipples in terms of coins. I had dimes. Some had silver dollars. Most had quarters or nickels. I'd never heard the term pennies used.

I rinsed out my costume in the bathroom. Alone in there I began to cry. I had gone to Studio to lose my

234

mind, and my plan sort of worked, but not well enough. Jordan was dead and buried. *DEAD AND BURIED!* I ached with the thought. There was a Puerto Rican version of him in the DJ booth *oowing* and *ahhing* every move I made. There was a hundred-dollar man who looked like an FBI agent to whom I'd promised a lap dance. And to top it all off, there was blood running out of me in a heavy flow. I sat down on the toilet.

After I peed a little, a surge of blood flushed out of me in a way I had never seen, felt, or heard of before. If you can imagine the force of a toilet flushing on an airplane, then you can imagine the surge of blood that flushed out of me. *Whoosh!* I sat still.

What the hell was that?

I waited – panted – tried to breath – and finally relaxed for a moment …

Then *Whoosh!* It happened again … *What the hell is happening to me?*

*

Jackie was busy saying goodbye to her generous investors. It was the end of the night. The crowd thinned out. Pinkie, whose breasts were full of mother's milk, was busy milking Frank the investment broker and his driver for every dollar they had out on the bar.

There's an unspoken rule in the go-go business among the dancers: You simply can't be too greedy with a big tipper. And that's exactly what Pinkie was being. Let's say for example, I was getting money from Frank, and Pinkie had passed by once on her collection route, then I would have to move on the second time she made her way around the bar. I'd let her get a stab at the money. It's the considerate thing to do.

But when a dancer named Candy made her way around the bar twice, Pinkie didn't move on. And she didn't budge the third time either. Well, Candy got right up on stage, screaming and cursing at Pinkie like a madwoman: "WHY DON'T YOU LET SOMEONE ELSE HAVE A TURN WITH FRANK, YOU GREEDY FUCKING BITCH. LET SOMEONE ELSE HAVE A TURN, YOU WHORE … FUCKING BITCH …"

The bouncers escorted Pinkie – the milky mother of an eleven-day-old, black baby boy – off the bar, and she got fired. She was the second dancer to get fired in the time that I worked at Studio. You'd think that Candy would've gotten fired for screaming and cursing and causing a scene. But after the arguments had been deliberated over, the judge – Joe the owner – sided with Candy. He said, "The girls have to share the profits. The Dream Team works as a team."

At the end of the night, I handed Junior one of the three hundred-dollar bills I'd accumulated. "I can't take this," he said, handing it back to me.

"Yes you can – just like I did." I shoved the money into his front pocket.

"Beautiful Bree – you're so beautiful – inside and out –" His eyes pulled me in like the tide.

"So are you –"

We kissed until we were both completely lost … and found.

CHAPTER TWENTY-EIGHT

Medicine Woman

"You're pregnant," Dr. Dufner said, his rubber glove way up my crotch.

"That's impossible. I have my period."

"It's not a menstrual period – It's a miscarriage."

Dante Arrigucci, I thought.

"You're about ten or eleven weeks along."

I had called Dr. Dufner's office early Friday morning as blood surged out of me, saturating every pad or plug I used to absorb it. Something was wrong, but I didn't tell my mother or Jackie – no sense in alerting the troops.

"I have to remove the rest of the tissue," Dufner said. "It's going to hurt a little – so just count to ten – and it'll be over."

He began. It was the pain of death. I counted:

One ... Pools of tears swelled in my eyes. *Two* ... I pulled away from Dufner as hard as I could, writhing in anguish before I even got to the count of three. Left with no other choice, he stopped the procedure.

"It hurts too much! I can't do it." Tears rolled over my temples.

"Do you want me to get the nurse?"

"Uh-huh." I didn't know what good the nurse would do, but it was all Dufner had to offer.

He came back into the room with a pregnant nurse

who appeared to be nearing her ninth month. *Is this reverse psychology?* I wondered. *Is the sight of a pregnant woman supposed to scare me still?* She held my hand and smiled, looking straight through my eyes. "You can squeeze my hand as hard as you like. It'll be okay," she said.

One ... Two ... Three ... pain in my abdomen ... Four ... Five ... pain in my chest ... Six ... Seven ... pain in my throat ... Eight ... Nine ... pain in my mouth ... Ten ... Ten ... He's not stopping ... Still in pain ...

"Ten!" I screamed, "I counted to ten! You said to count to ten!"

"Almost done," he assured.

I started counting again from one. By four, the pain was out of my mouth.

I left Dufner's office and drove down to Chinatown, praying all the way that Jessie would be home. Thankfully, she was. The scar on her arm looked exactly like the map of Israel.

"I just had a miscarriage."

"I didn't even know you were pregnant."

"Neither did I. It was awful. The doctor told me to count to ten while he removed the rest of the tissue. I've never felt that kind of pain before."

"You were awake?"

"Wide awake, counting to ten."

"Why didn't he give you anesthesia or something?"

"I don't know. It hurt so much. I can barely move. I need some painkillers. Between Jordan's funeral and this, I think I'm going insane." I broke out in a sweat.

Jessie made a pot of herbal tea: Cramp Bark and

Dong Quai. The medicine tables had finally turned. It was always me who took care of Jessie. Now she was treating my pain, throwing herself wholeheartedly into the task. She applied slices of cold, wet tofu to my fiery forehead to cut the heat. She massaged lavender oil into my feet, hands, neck, and back. She burned sandalwood incense and beeswax candles. She placed healing crystals around my body while quietly humming – and working a miracle. She was a medicine woman. She was her mother.

I felt complete comfort for the first time since hearing the news of Jordan's death. There was nothing in my mind more than the image of a window full of raindrops, like a sky full of stars. There were no thoughts of fear. Nothing of desire. Nothing but the sound of Jessie's sweet cherry voice, humming a healing tune.

CHAPTER TWENTY-NINE

A Braid in the Wind

The antibiotics made me sleepy, but somehow I remembered to get Andrea an audition. And in doing so, I got myself a ride to work.

"Who's picking you up?" my father asked.

"Some girl named Andrea. She was a friend of Jordan's. I saw her at his funeral, and she wants to dance at Studio."

"Is she good looking?"

She was gorgeous when we were younger, but she kind of lost her looks since then ... I *guess* she's still cute, but definitely not like before. Her hair used to be long, blond, and beautiful. I don't know why she cut it so short and went back to her natural mousy brown. It doesn't suit her. She really lost her looks ... She became some kind of naturalist or something ... And she hunts avalanches in her spare time –"

"She sounds like a nut ... Send her to Jackie's salon when it opens. They'll fix her hair ..."

The doorbell rang, and Andrea came in, spreading her horse-teeth smile all over the place ...

"I am so happy. This is definitely my lucky day," she announced.

"Why's that?"

"Well, I'm auditioning tonight for one thing. And for another, I got a part-time job as a Penis Tucker at the T.L.A. –"

"A penis tucker?" I looked at my father. He started laughing. "What the hell's a *penis tucker?*" I asked.

"It's so exciting … I get to tape the performers penises between their butt cheeks before they get dressed in drag." She acted as though she had landed the dream job of a lifetime.

"Cool," I said. "They can screw themselves and perform at the same time." My father and I burst out in laughter. Andrea was laughing, too. She laughed in such a way that my father and I began laughing at the way she was laughing. She had an operatic-soprano-jingle-bell laugh with big horse teeth. She, of course, thought we were laughing *with* her, not *at* her. The more we laughed, the more she laughed, which made us laugh even harder, which made her laugh even harder. My father was in tears. Andrea almost peed herself.

"I need to use your bathroom …" she laughed.

"It's right down the hall, second door on the left."

"Do you think she's pretty?" I asked my father while she was out of the room.

"She's a *dog*. But I guess she'll get the job if she can dance."

"She'll get the job because she's with me. Everyone at Studio gets hired if they can get an audition. All you need is someone to get you in the door. Then it's a free-for-all."

"Well, she's a *dog* ... And those *teeth* …"

Andrea drove me to work in a white Ford Escort. It was decorated with Native American memorabilia. A dream catcher hung from the rear-view mirror, a peace pipe was displayed on the dashboard, a bear claw dangled from the cigarette lighter. It was a theme car. Tacky, but definitely interesting.

At Studio, I introduced Andrea to Joe the owner. Joe the night manager wasn't around.

"Hi – I'm Andrea and my tits are real!" She pulled up her shirt and shoved her chest way out like a sergeant-at-arms in front of at least three dancers who were sporting either saline or silicone implants. Andrea had been in Studio for a total of twenty seconds and was already getting the evil eye. Joe the owner, on the other hand, started to blush.

"Oh yeah? ... Good for you," Joe said. "Have fun with your tits on stage. And ... eh ... come see me in my office if you need anything." Joe rarely invited any of the dancers into his office. He must have thought that Andrea would be a lot more interesting in private.

Speaking of private, Studio opened a private room in the back for lap dances. There were four chairs in there, high off the ground like bar stools, interspersed around the crowded space for the customers to sit on. There was a small refrigerator, like the ones in hotel rooms. And from a speaker in the ceiling, the music the DJ played in the larger bar entered the private room. The other end of the room was strictly for the bouncer who was to maintain order from a reclining leather chair and a matching ottoman.

Only four dancers were allowed to work the room at a time, for a maximum of two songs each. That way everyone could get a turn. Joe the night manager showed up and explained the back-room procedures to

Andrea and me while we waited for our sets to begin.

"I am so excited! I can't wait to get up there!" Andrea declared, in anticipation of her turn on stage. I had thought that she was going to be nervous about dancing, like I had been on my first night at Studio – but she wasn't. She was confident. *Over* confident.

"Have you ever danced before, or is this your first time?" Bobbi the Bartender asked her.

"This is my first night ... I've never even been in a go-go bar before ... It's so amazing here. I can like *totally* tell I'm going to love it. Everyone's so nice ... At first I was worried that the owner would be mean, and wouldn't like me, but he's *so* friendly. He told me to come see him in his office—"

"Who told you that? Joe the manager, or Joe the *owner*?" Bobbi asked with all seriousness.

"Joe the *owner* ... He's kinda cute ... Don't you think?"

Bobbi was Joe the owner's girlfriend. He had a wife and two kids, but Bobbi was his girl on the side. She was crazy about him – territorial and protective, like a tiger. Her claws sharpened as she threw down the rag and stormed out of the bar. I didn't bother explaining the situation to Andrea – didn't want to get involved.

Just then, a dancer named An'yee, who we nicknamed "Onion," was collecting a tip from the customer seated to my right. Onion was Korean. She had long, silky black hair that covered her glass eye whenever she spoke to the customers. She was absolutely beautiful ... except for the glass eye. I listened to their conversation:

"You're gorgeous – What are you? – Chinese?" the customer asked.

"No, you idiot! I'm KOREAN!" she shouted, in a thick Korean accent. "All you Americans are alike. You think everyone Asian is Chinese –so STUPID! – That's all I ever hear from you people. *'You Chinese?'* *'You speak Chinese?'* Ugh!" Onion flipped her hair around to the other side of her head, revealing her big, round, glass eye. It wasn't slanted like her other eye. I could tell the customer seated to my right was totally freaked out from her glass eye as she moved in closer. "I'm not Chinese, you dumb ass! I'm KOREAN! I'm from KO-RE-A! – Asshole!"

The guy apologized and gave her another tip. She grabbed the money before stomping on to the next customer. I was laughing. The way Onion would yell at the customers, and glare at them with her glass eye, always gave me a good laugh.

I took Andrea into the DJ booth to pick out her music. Junior was there. His moustache twitched as our eyes did a dance.

"Hey, Barbie. How've you been?" he asked.

"Great," I lied.

"Barbie?" Andrea interrupted. "Is *Barbie*, like, your stage name?" Her tone was thoroughly Valley Girl.

"Uh-huh," I admitted.

"It doesn't really, like, fit you." She started to annoy me, and I got the feeling that bringing her into my world wasn't such a great idea.

"I think any name would fit her. She's more than a name," Junior said. My heart flew like a butterfly into my throat. Not only did he look like Jordan, but he also spoke with eloquence.

"My stage name is *Chancy*," Andrea declared.

"Chancy? ... That's interesting," I said.

"Do you have that song *Take a Chance on Me?*" she asked.

Junior searched through his collection of CDs with a small flashlight. He looked like a clever detective hunting for evidence. I caught him sneaking a peek at my legs from the corner of his eye. "Let me see ... Abba ... yup, here it is." Junior found the song and was able to resume his lusty look my way with both eyes straightforward. "Cool," Andrea clapped. "This is so exciting." Her horse teeth looked even larger in the DJ booth.

"And what would you like to dance to, beautiful?" Junior licked his lips like a hungry animal.

"Surprise me," I said and hurried out because I got the feeling he was going to devour me if I hung around for a second longer.

"That DJ's so hot for you," Andrea said as we made our way back around the bar. "He reminds me of someone, but I can't, like, place it."

How could she not see that he was the Puerto Rican copy of Jordan? I didn't say a word to her about it. I knew that the less I spoke to her, the better off I'd be. She was too *chancy*.

Junior played some sexy, Latin song during my set. He *oowed* and *ahhed* through the speakers way too much. It was such a turn on. My dancing moves became smoother, better rounded. I spent a lot of time at the end of the stage across from the DJ booth. I danced for Junior. I flew around the pole like a braid in the wind, light and fresh.

Then the hundred-dollar man came in, and just as I had promised, I went into the back room to give him a lap dance. My nerves shook my confidence, being that it was my first time back there. Every chair in the room was occupied except for one. Roger sat down in it and pulled out his wad of hundreds. I tried to keep my cool, checked out the moves of the other dancers, and imitated what they were doing. It was a lot like being on the bar. Nothing to be nervous about.

I took one of Roger's hundreds in my cleavage. He took a while giving it to me, though. He was a talker, and he liked to get real close to my ear whenever he said something. "It's too bad there isn't any ice back here. I'd really like to see you butter yourself up," he whispered.

Just then I realized I hadn't been sweating like usual. It must have been some type of pregnancy symptom. I wasn't hot at all. In fact, I was kind of cold.

"Let me see that ass," Roger demanded. I turned around and took a step forward to create a little distance between us. I didn't want him rubbing up against me the way some of the dancers were allowing the customers to do. I had my standards, lap dance or not.

Swaying my ass from side to side, I spread my legs into an upside down letter V (as usual). Then I bent the rest of my body way down so that my hands touched the floor. It was kind of difficult balancing myself on the carpet in there because the tips of my heels kept getting snagged on the rug. I had gotten used to dancing on the wooden stage.

Roger placed another hundred behind my G-string. Excited about all the money, I was quick to spring back up to eye level again, but I barely made it to knee level when I felt a bang and heard an awful cracking sound. I didn't know what I had hit, or what had hit me. "Ouch," I whispered, holding my head. I looked around. There was nothing out of place, until I spotted one of the dancers, faced-down on the carpet. She didn't make a move. She looked dead. I imagined the police outlining her in white chalk.

The other dancers in the room looked down at her too – Then they glanced at each other – then at me. "What the fuck?" I said out loud, looking at Onion for an answer. "Who is she?" Onion just shrugged.

I bent down and spoke into the girl's ear. "If you're okay – will you say something?" She got up slowly. I had never seen her before.

"Wow – What a rush!" she said with a smile, rubbing a spot on her head. Her eyes were completely crossed.

Holy shit! I thought. *Did I just knock this girl cross-eyed?*

"Are you okay?" I asked.

"I don't know – I was bending over backwards – then I heard a loud *crack* – I guess I blacked out."

"She might have a concussion," Roger murmured. I thought about how many more hundreds I could've been making in the time that this distraction was taking place.

"I'm so dizzy … What a rush!" The way she kept

saying *what a rush* gave me the distinct impression that she liked the pain. I couldn't stop wondering if she had been cross-eyed before we cracked heads. The bouncer came over.

"Do you want to go to the hospital?" he asked her.

"I don't know. I'll go sit at the bar and see if the dizziness goes away," she said.

I sat with her at the bar. "What's your name?" I asked.

"Valentine," she said. I thought of my favorite violin teacher whose cat had a heart-shaped tag on its collar, inscribed with the name Valentine.

"I've never seen you here before –" I said.

"I usually work the day shift. I just started working nights last week – That was so *intense* back there – Are you okay?"

"I have a little headache, but it's not too bad." It was the first time I'd considered the pain pounding in my own head.

"I think they're going to have to take me to the hospital – I don't feel right – I think something's wrong with me," Valentine decided.

"Shit – I feel so bad, Valentine – That was my first time in the back room. I feel like a dancing disaster. I can't even believe this happened."

"It's not your fault. The room's too small to do any real moves."

They didn't call an ambulance – just wrapped Valentine up in her regular clothes and took her to the hospital.

"Is she really cross-eyed?" I asked the bouncer.

"No, Barbie – You did that to her. Wait till she sees

herself in the mirror – She'll probably sue you."

"Are you lying?" I asked, horrified.

"Just kiddin'," he chuckled. For a second he had me fooled.

No one could believe that it was Chancy's first time dancing. She was so forward and outgoing like a pro. Bobbi the Bartender didn't like her. "You better tell your little friend to stay the fuck away from Joe. I saw her coming outta his office."

"She doesn't know anything about you and Joe," I said.

"You better tell her that *I'm* his girlfriend – if you care anything about your friend. Joe's gonna hear it from me tonight."

Bobbi was serious about Joe. She cut her hair real short and got a tattoo of three naked women on her back, just because he told her to. She would do anything for him – except share him. He seemed like a real screwball, and so did she.

Before leaving for the night, I tipped Junior again. This time I only gave him a twenty. I didn't want to seem like I was coming on too heavy.

"I'd rather have a kiss," he said.

"You can have both."

I kissed him, but I pretended I was kissing Jordan – and got back to feeling like I was a braid in the wind.

CHAPTER THIRTY

A Vigorous Painting

The wind swept trash around in circles the following day. It was Saturday. Mr. Mault had given the class a weekend assignment, so I drove down to Temple to use the painting studio. Mini twisters sprang up in the corners of campus life, dancing to *The Symphony of the Howling Winds*. I could actually feel the wind whirling around inside my right ear as my eyes teemed like waterfalls. I think I had a slight concussion from bumping heads with Valentine.

Mault left the key to the studio in one of the lockers and gave all his students the combination for easy access. When I exited the elevator, a few other committed classmates had already opened the studio. I love getting my homework done.

But the assignment seemed impossible: *Fold a white piece of paper into a three-dimensional triangle, like a tent. Place it on top of (and in front of) a white background. Paint the image onto a small- or medium-sized canvas. The image should appear to be white, but don't use a drop of white paint. Use any or all the other colors to create the illusion of white. But remember: no white paint.*

I arranged my palette and attempted the task. The figure in the center of the canvas didn't look white, didn't even give the illusion of white no matter how much I squinted my eyes or blurred my vision. It looked exactly like the other colors I had used.

I decided to cheat and use white. *Maybe Mr. Mault won't notice.* But that didn't help either. Rather than get frustrated over it (like some of the other lip-sucking, cursing-at-the-canvas students who were working on the same assignment), I quit trying and just allowed myself to wallow in the joy of slapping paint on the canvas.

An air vent in the art studio was busy flapping open its lid, like a mouth that has something to say, then decides not to say it, then opens again to say it, then closes, reconsiders, and so on. When the lid was open, the air vent allowed passage to the whistling winds. The sound echoed and mixed with the swelling cyclone in my ear, pulsing and driving me slightly mad.

But once my painting was complete, it satisfied me like no other had before. It didn't resemble a folded white piece of paper on a white background at all. It looked more like an ancient Chinese sampan, helplessly moving through a stormy river current, pulling and pushing between two worlds.

At the critique the following week, the paint was still wet. Mr. Mault held it up from the edges, turning it this way and that, like a doctor examining an x-ray. He made the decision to place it at the end of the gallery spread. I wondered why my sampan was to be the last one for the final analysis:

Could it be that he saved the best for last? ... No way. It's awful ... He probably hates it ... It's not even white! ... A failed attempt ...

Still, I loved my painting. It looked crazy, yet composed. It may not have given the illusion of white, but it was special, like a Van Gogh … only better … because it was mine.

A few of my classmates were able to achieve the white effect with success. I reacted as though they were geniuses, *oowing* and *ahhing* and *wowing* at each of their accomplishments. After all, I wasn't able to do it, no matter how hard I had tried. Mr. Mault never acted as though any of his students were geniuses. He had a dinosaur ego – completely in love with himself and in lust with me. It was a little embarrassing the way he didn't even try to hide his bawdy attraction somewhere in a closet, not even a little.

"Now this – THIS – is a vigorous painting!" He was holding my sampan, critiquing it passionately while flaring his nostrils. I was impressed by his use of the word "vigorous." I said it over and over in my head. *Vigorous. Vigorous. Vigorous.*

Later on, I could feel him breathing down my neck again.

"What were you thinking about when you completed the assignment? It's brilliant." His breath smelled like too much coffee.

"Well … uh … I wasn't thinking about making it look white. I don't think I was thinking about anything at all. I had a concussion the day I painted it. There was wind stuck in my ear … I felt crazy. Something was seriously wrong with me that day."

"How did you get a concussion?"

"I bumped heads with some girl the night before."

He said "IN-ter-est-ing" as he walked away. I could tell he wanted to say more about it, but he had a class to teach.

*

I saw Valentine the following week at the bar. She approached me with a crooked smile under her crooked eyes.

"Thank you *so* much!" she exclaimed, sounding as though I had won her a free trip to the Bahamas or something.

"For *what*?" I asked, bewildered.

"For *this* ..." She held out her forearm, revealing a large purple mark the size of a plum. "I was on I.V. Demerol *for three days straight*, in the hospital. It was *amazing*. Thank you *sooo* much."

"You're welcome ... I *guess*."

Knowing that Valentine was the kind of total freak I'd rather not associate with, I tried to avoid her from then on. But she always seemed to find a way to sneak up behind me while I was dancing on stage or working the floor or getting changed in the dressing room. I felt bad giving her the cold shoulder because of the injury I'd caused her, so I acted as pleasant as I possibly could towards her. She acted as though I was her hero.

I hated being her hero.

CHAPTER THIRTY-ONE

Caught Between Stations

I was already twenty minutes late for the grand opening of Jackie's salon when I finally found a parking spot on Walnut Street. I felt pressured to get there at once, but it took me another two minutes to parallel park, squeezing the Jeep in between two cars, bumping all four bumpers at least four times. Then I almost slammed the Jeep door on my own foot while getting out, which was pretty frightening, considering that I needed my feet to dance. I had to slow down. I wanted to be there for Jackie, but I didn't want to break my legs trying.

Darting down Walnut Street, I lit a cigarette, and within a few moments' time, I began to notice how bright and beautiful the city had emerged from winter. So I slowed my pace to a stroll. The spring weather was perfectly fragrant, delicately revitalizing. It captivated me. I wanted to wallow in the feeling of being outdoors, alone in an urban crowd – once again.

But I already felt guilty for being *unintentionally* late for Jackie's big day. To fight the guilty feeling of being *intentionally* late would be much harder. So I began to rationalize. I figured that everyone at the salon was content with the excitement of opening day. They didn't need *me* there anyway. What was the difference if I arrived half an hour late, or an hour late? It's not like I was a part of the business. I didn't work there. I was just Jackie's little sister. No one would probably even notice I was missing.

I entered Rittenhouse Square Park as though I were entering paradise, gazing around in a state of bliss. I imagined what it would feel like to be one of the trees, happy and tickled by the squirrels running up my trunk, to my branches overhead, which were newly thickened by the fresh leaves of spring – like a new hairdo (*oops ... guilty feeling ... don't think about hair!*). There were so many trees – maples, locusts, and oaks – all swaying gracefully above the elaborate flowerbeds and the blooming shrubs.

I closed my eyes. A gentle breeze filled my senses with pure satisfaction. I was high on life, floating while standing still. I unclosed my eyes. Splashes of color saturated the scene. I wanted to paint all that I saw. I thought about coming back to the park another day with my art supplies. Upon this thought – ever so slowly, yet all at once – the image of Jordan entered my mind, quietly coating my joy with pain, subtly stinging my happiness with sorrow. I tried to shake the feeling of disenchantment as I continued on towards the reflecting pool.

I stopped to look at a sculpture of two cheerful, naked children who were triumphantly holding up a sundial that had been formed as a giant sunflower head. As I marveled at the beauty of it, a hidden memory thrust its way to the center of my mind – a memory that sparkled like sunlight on water:

We were here together. Right here! Jordan and me. It was that day – in springtime – senior year. We cut *school. Planned it all out: We met at Bridge and Pratt, rode the El, got off at 15th Street, wandered around the city, and ended up in Rittenhouse Square Park for the rest of the day. I tuned up my violin and played it for Jordan – right here – on this very spot! Jordan pulled his tattered sketchbook from a brown leather case. He set up his watercolors and painted his version of the giant sunflower head. I watched him paint as I played my favorite pieces of music upon that precious piece of wood. I watched every motion his hands had made. Watched every emotion his face had formed. We smiled at one another because our souls were content. We shared a day. We expressed our happiness. We celebrated our mutual love of art and nature. We danced together in time, yet our bodies never touched.*

This memory was like a bucket full of saltwater buried deep in a well, rising quickly to the surface, spilling over with the tears I'd been carrying deep inside. Tears I needed to cry.

I found a patch of grass nearby and collapsed on my back, facing the cloudless sky. With my left arm I covered my left eye and looked at the heavens through the other, ready to release my tears. A single droplet formed and bubbled, and, through it, another world appeared. Yes, another dimension, a world of prisms, revealed itself through a single tear. I gazed at the celestial sight through my watery eye. My heart hammered against my chest as I witnessed this other dimension. There were mountains of rainbows – prisms upon prisms – encircling me – from the earth to the sky. I beheld rainbows running together –

spectrums running apart – surrounding everything. The vision enthralled me. I kept looking – seeking – searching … And then he appeared.

"Is that you, Jordan?" I asked out loud, with no hesitation.

"Hi Bree," he replied, smiling through an indigo mouth. "It's me." The sound of his voice vibrated the inner strings of my mind.

"I see you, Jord … I can see you … I love you …"

"I love you too." His voice sounded like sunshine.

"Why did you leave? … Why did you have to go?"

He didn't answer my question. He just smiled.

I blinked. The tear broke into a stream, and the rainbow-less world returned. But in less than an instant, another tear bubbled up in its place, and I could see him again, right where he was before – up high in the rainbows – Again!

I fixed my stare upon his indigo smile. It filled me with bliss. Through a single, saltwater tear, I saw my friend Jordan, living in an ocean of color … living in heaven. I couldn't hold the tears that followed, so I sat up, and let them flow …

I returned to the sculpture of the happy children and reviewed it again with new eyes: They faced each other holding the giant sunflower that rose up between them. The sunflower head – the sundial – divided their perspectives. One child stood on one side of time, and the other stood on the opposite side. They were standing together, yet they existed in two realities. I decided that Jordan and me were just like them: I was the child facing the sundial because I was on the side of time that the sun provides for us here on Earth.

Jordan was the child facing the back of the sunflower head because his perception of time was a mystery to me – I could neither see it nor understand it. But one thing was for sure – he was with me. He stood before me as clear as day. I saw him. I heard him. Certainty stood firmly in my mind.

After the ethereal event, I headed over to *The Hair Tea Salon*. I felt as though I had just witnessed a miracle, as though I had just heard the voice of God. I felt like Moses.

*

A long, narrow staircase lead up to the salon. It was located on top of a flower shop. The scent of the stairwell was mystical – like freshly turned soil from the Garden of Eden.

Inside the salon, the first thing to gain my visual attention was the focal-point fishpond. Large koi fish swam around and around – gold, orange, and white. I watched their graceful bodies sway.

"Where the hell have you been?" Jackie grabbed my arm and turned me around to face her. "I've been worried *sick* about you! – You're over an hour late."

I wanted to jump in with the koi and enter the blissful world of water life.

"I was in the park, having a conversation with Jordan! – I swear to God, Jackie. I saw him! – I saw heaven! – It looks like rainbows!"

"Do you even *hear* yourself? – You sound *crazy*. You better see a psychiatrist or something – It's time you got some professional help – I don't even know what to say to you!" Jackie scolded me through clenched teeth. Her abrupt concern quickly alarmed me into thinking of the right words to say – to put her mind at ease – and put her back in her place:

"Okay, okay – just calm down. Nothing's wrong with me – I'm fine. And anyway, this isn't the first time you're calling me *crazy* – Remember when Nanette cut off a chunk of my hair? – To make *hair tea* out of it? – To save her life? – You said that *that* was *crazy* – So why did you named this place The *Hair Tea* Salon? – I guess it wasn't so *crazy* after all."

"I'm sorry, honey," Jackie said, her voice full of guilt. "I know you're having a hard time dealing with Jordan's death – I shouldn't have yelled at you – or called you crazy – I'll never do it again – I was just worried because you were so late – You know I love you more than *anything* –"

Jackie hugged me so hard that she cracked my back in three different places. We both laughed about it for a while, and enjoyed ourselves for the rest of the opening event.

The salon was rustic looking. Dark wooden floors lined the place in large planks. All the furniture looked old and distressed. Dressers full of drawers housed the best-quality, high-tech equipment of the trade. The waiting area had a big wicker chair like the one Morticia Addams sat in. Clients sipped wine and nibbled on fancy cheese. All the female hair stylists wore bell-bottom jeans and belly shirts. The males wore whatever they felt like wearing. Jackie might have invested a hundred grand, but it was a million-dollar salon – completely upscale.

My mother sat behind the receptionist's semi-circle

desk as content as the fish in the pond. She has a natural knack for organization when it comes to business. It's in her blood. She grew up in South Philly on bustling 7th Street, and lived in a house on top of *Austin's Gift Shop*. It was her parents' business, but my mother kept the books, guided my grandfather through the ordering, and helped the customers with their selections. She's a real people person.

I spotted Mona. Her eyes were wild with envy. I went over to her. "Hey, Mona – Where's Steven?" I wasn't used to seeing her without Steven by her side.

"He's still at work – but he'll be here soon."

"Well, what do you think about the salon?" I asked.

"It's unbelievable – I'm totally amazed – I can't believe that Jackie came out of the go-go business and ended up *here* – It just doesn't make *sense* – I mean, people like me work our asses off. We get up everyday at the crack of dawn, put in endless hours, and can't seem to get ahead financially the way we want to—"

"Wait a minute," I interrupted. "It's people like Jackie who literally dance their asses off. Don't knock it, Mona – it's a job like any other. There's just more money, more fun, and fewer hours. And don't forget that Jackie was working *two jobs* when she saved the money for this salon – You can't compare people who work *one* job, to people who work *two* jobs. You're miscalculating."

"Well, I've always dreamed about opening my own shop in the city –" she said.

"You have? – You never said anything about it before."

260

"I never told anyone about it – except for Steven."

It was nice speaking with Mona over the humming of hairdryers that blended with upbeat background music. It was like talking to someone else. And for a moment I thought that the people from *Invasion of the Body Snatchers* had taken over her existence. "So, what kind of shop would you like to open?" I asked.

"Well – I'd really like to sell the things I make."

Mona made all kinds of clothing and accessories. She also loved to paint and decorate household items: mirrors, rocking chairs, flowerpots, picture frames … She had all kinds of projects simultaneously evolving in action. I loved her hand-woven beaded jewelry.

"I even know the exact location," she continued. "My friend Lori's mother has a little cheese shop on 18th and Pine – It's perfect – She's retiring next year and moving to Florida, and she said she'd let me rent the store – The good thing about it is that she owns the property and isn't even considering selling it. So I'd run the cheese shop and add my own merchandise to sell."

"That sounds great. Your store and Jackie's salon would be within walking distance. She'll get you a lot of business."

"The only problem is money. I've been saving, but the figure that Steven and I have projected is not in our budget. So I won't be able to save enough start-up cash by the time that Lori's mother retires."

"I *told you* to make go-go costumes. All you have to do is walk in the back door of any go-go bar with your bags and your racks. Just act like you belong there and set up shop in the dressing room. It's that easy … What's your problem?"

"Steven's the problem. He said it's absolutely out of the question – that I should wait and start my own business with *clean* money."

I couldn't believe what I was hearing. Mona was actually considered selling go-go costumes! And she had even discussed it with Steven!

"Come on, Mona – all money's dirty. Tell Steven to lighten up. He's so uptight, like a tampon!" I laughed like a hyena at my own joke.

"Don't *badmouth* him! At first I agreed – I can understand his point of view. But now … being here today and seeing how far the money has taken Jackie … well, it's a real eye-opener. I just have to find a way to make some more start-up cash. Maybe I can try selling my stuff at the craft shows." Mona tried to sound enthusiastic, but she didn't look too hopeful.

Jackie gloated in her glory the whole day. She highlighted my hair again. I didn't really want her to, but she insisted: "The new growth is too long." It was fun sitting in *her* chair, in *her* establishment. I walked out of *The Hair Tea Salon* feeling like I had Keebler fudge stripes on my head.

Mona got highlights, too. They weren't as obvious as mine, but they were there. Jackie and I couldn't believe it. Mona had actually stepped out of her Billy Joel wedding song. She was changing her tune – caught between stations – not knowing which lyrics she agreed with – and which she didn't.

We never thought it would happen. But it did.

CHAPTER THIRTY-TWO

Chatting With You

Where's Chancy? ... Where's your friend Chancy? ... Is Chancy working tonight? ... Is Chancy here? ... Does Chancy still work here? ...

All along the bar, everywhere I turned, customers were asking about Andrea. This new pattern of inquiries was highly suspect, and I wondered what it was, *exactly*, that had inspired it. Although she'd been dancing at Studio for several weeks, I rarely saw her. She'd gotten some kind of promotion as head of the penis tuckers at her other job, which required her services most weeknights. In lieu of these events, Joe the night manager scheduled Andrea's dancing hours during the day. I never worked at the bar during the day. In my mind, the place was strictly for night creatures, like vampires and owls.

Bobbi the Bartender was working with one arm. Her other arm was broken, wrapped in a cast that ran the entire length of her arm.

"What happened to you?" I asked.

"Me and Joe were fooling around in bed ... and he got a little too rough." She tried to crack a smile.

"Wow," was all I could say.

A-little-too-rough doesn't break an arm. Maybe sprains it, or slightly fractures it. Bobbi's crazy. Everyone in Studio's crazy, I thought.

I spent more and more time in the DJ booth fooling around with Junior, always imagining he was Jordan. Always.

Other than his large physique and the scent of Downy fabric softener in his clothes, he was *nothing* like Jordan. He wasn't an artist. He wasn't interested in travel, poetry, or anything sophisticated. One time I shared my favorite Shakespearean sonnet with him, and he said, "I don't get it." So I read it again and explained the extended metaphor, the allusions, and all the imagery to help him understand the exploding beauty contained and released in just fourteen short lines of verse. But all he said was, "I still don't get it. Whatever you just said … I didn't understand any of it. Honestly, that stuff doesn't interest me, Bree. I can't figure out why people even read it."

I, on the other hand, can't figure out people who aren't interested in Shakespeare's sonnets, but I didn't say anything about it. I just kept myself locked inside a bubble of delusion and pretended that Junior was Jordan when my eyes were closed, when our bodies touched. I kind of felt bad about it though, especially when Junior said, "I really like you, Bree … I – I love you."

"Aren't you *married?*" I asked. It was the first time I had asked Junior about his personal life.

"My wife and my son live with my mother in New Jersey."

"Okay, but aren't you married?" I didn't understand.

"Yes, we're married. We just don't live together."

"Oh … I get it," I said, even though I didn't get it.

So I just gave up, threw my arms around him, inhaled the Downy in his clothes, and imagined he was Jordan. But my conscience was beating me. Junior had just told me that he *loved* me. My guilt forced me into a confession: "Listen. There's something I have to tell you. I want to be honest – because the way I've been acting, really isn't fair," I said.

"What's not fair? You're the fairest of them all. Mirror, mirror on the wall ..." Junior was being as poetic as he possibly could.

"I never told you this, but my best friend died a few months ago. His name was Jordan. His funeral was on the same day that I met you." I was speaking of death, hitting a soft spot. Junior's expression grew serious.

"I'm still a little crazy from the whole thing because I was in love with him."

"I'm so sorry to hear that," he said with empathy in his voice, in his eyes.

"I hope you're not going to hate me after I tell you this, but the *real* reason I like hanging out with you is that you remind me of him. Every time I kiss you, I imagine I'm kissing him. I feel crazy for doing it. And that's why I have to tell you." Junior's expression hadn't changed. I was expecting a small or large jolt – some kind of immediate reaction – but there was nothing. "Do you hate me now?"

"No ... I don't mind. You can think whatever you want." He smiled and started kissing me.

I had believed that Junior would be disgusted by my honest confession, that he would reject me, and it would all be over. Maybe that's what I wanted. Being inside of a bubble of delusion, and knowing you put yourself there, is completely destructive. The bubble will burst. Someone will get hurt. I just couldn't snap myself out of it. I handed Junior the popping pin, and what did he do? He dropped it. He pumped in more air, sending me adrift into who knows where.

*

Beavis and Butthead (Paul and Charlie) were sitting at the bar. Paul had his strawberries, but his favorite dancer Virginia wasn't there. "Hey Barbie. Want a strawberry? *Uh-huh, uh-huh ...*"

"Sure. Wow (chewing), these are great."

"I bought them for Chancy. *Uh-huh, uh-huh.* She's my *new* favorite dancer."

"That's wonderful," I said. I felt like I was on an episode of The Twilight Zone. Everyone was fascinated by Chancy – who was *okay* at best – but nothing to get fascinated over – nothing to switch favorite dancers about.

"Is she, like, uh, working tonight?" Beavis asked.

"I don't think so."

"I wanted to go into the back room with her. *Uh-huh, uh-huh.* Why don't you go into the back room with me instead ... since she's not here."

"Twenty bucks," I replied.

"Chancy takes me back for five."

"Well, I'm not Chancy."

"Oh, come on ... Dance for me for five ... I'll be good ... I won't even touch you."

"Fine." I gave in. I felt bad for Paul even though he was Butthead.

The dancer who looked like Eddie Murphy was in the back room surrounded by a bunch of white shirts. I never liked the white shirts. They were too high on themselves, and I could tell they were total scum. They lined up all the chairs on one side of the back room. Four sat. Two stood.

There was nowhere for Paul to sit. I called the bouncer out into the hall. "What the hell's going on? – I thought this room was for one-on-one lap dances – not six-on-one."

"The white shirts are tipping especially well tonight. They gave me a twenty for this song. Just imagine what they're giving her."

"Does Joe know about it?"

"No."

"Well, there's nowhere for Paul to sit." Everyone in the bar knew Paul by name.

"I'll tell ya what, Paul can sit in my chair, and I'll stand –"

"I'm not sitting in your chair," Paul interrupted. "It's probably full of cooties. *Uh-huh, uh-huh.* I'd rather stand."

It was uncomfortable dancing in there while Paul leaned against the wall – and six white shirts got rowdy in the corner. The ugly dancer was the object of their desire. *What do they see in her*, I wondered. I kept trying to peek their way, out of the corner of my eye. A lot of money changed hands – or so it seemed. It was hard to get a good look at what was going on. There were so many of them and only one of her.

"So what're you going to do for five bucks?" Paul asked me.

"I'm *dancing* … What did you expect?"

"Well, Chancy danced for me for five bucks, and it was a lot more fun than this."

"Oh, yeah? What did she *do* that was so exciting?"

"She showed me her tampon string. *Uh-huh, uh-huh.*"

"Are you lying?"

"No. She really did. *Uh-huh, uh-huh.* It was awesome."

Paul wasn't lying. He was too dumb to make up such a creative story. It then made sense that everyone was so fascinated by Chancy. She was acting like an idiot – breaking the unspoken rules of go-go – kind of like Eddie Murphy's evil twin over in the corner.

*

One of the dancers was putting on a wig in the dressing room. She wrapped her own hair into a tight swirling bun, and fixed the wig over it. Her name was *Cinnamon with an S.* That's how the DJs announced her to the stage: *And next up on stage is Cinnamon with an S.* I liked her name. I hated my stage name – Barbie. It seemed so dull. The guys found it exciting, but I liked the dancers' names that sounded like racehorses: Cinnamon, Thunder, Heroine …

I had worked with *Cinnamon with an S* before, every once in a while, but we never had occasion to speak. Mostly, she just kept to herself. The name didn't fit her image. I think a dancer named *Cinnamon with an S* should sweeten everyone up. She wasn't a sweetener. I hardly ever knew she was there.

I sat on the Simpsons' sofa trying to figure out why

she wore the wig. Her auburn hair was long, full, and beautiful. She was long, full, and beautiful – kind of like a birch tree. She adjusted the black wig and misted herself with scented body spray. *Maybe she doesn't want her hair to smell like a go-go bar when she gets home*, I thought. I hated the way I smelled after a night's work. The first thing to do after work (besides eat) is scrub, scrub, scrub.

"Your hair's so beautiful. Why do you wear a wig?" I decided to ask.

"I can't let anyone recognize me. I'm an undergrad student at Princeton, and my Psych professor comes to Studio pretty often."

"Wow. That's pretty tense. Do you think he knows it's you?" I asked.

"I can't be sure. – It's not like he takes notice of any of the students in class. – He's completely aloof."

"Do you ever raise your hand, during the class discussions?"

"No way. Whenever he poses a question, I refrain from volunteering and just kind of hide behind this tall guy George who sits in front of me ..." She was still arranging her wig in the mirror as she spoke. It was a nice wig, but it had lots of bangs. I hate lots of bangs.

"I get the feeling he knows it's me, though," *Cinnamon with an S* continued. "It feels like a little game whenever he comes into the bar. Last week he asked me if I do private dances, and I scheduled him for Sunday afternoon at the Marriot. At first I was a little nervous, but I've calmed down about it. He's just another customer. And besides, he's got a lot more to lose than I do."

"I'd be scared to be alone in a hotel room with *any* of these guys. How do you do it?"

"I never go on a job alone. My boyfriend comes along and acts like a bouncer."

"Oh, so *that's* how it's done. That's much safer than being alone. Does your professor tip you well?" I felt like I was earning a Masters Degree in Go-Go Antics.

"Pretty well."

"Does he ever do anything weird, you know, to let on that he's curious about you or make you think twice?"

"When class lets out, I catch him staring at me as I'm leaving the room. I try not to look directly at him, but sometimes I can't help it."

"If my painting teacher ever saw me dancing here, he'd go crazy. He's in lust with me. He'd be in here every night."

Cinnamon with an S adjusted her wig with lots of bangs for the last time, and slipped into a pair of studded five-inchers. "It was nice chatting with you," she said, before heading out to the bar.

"You too."

Dancers didn't usually use phrases like *chatting with you* at Studio. It was pleasant to have met one who did.

*

After work, Jordan and I ... I mean *Junior* and I were in the back parking lot, making out, leaning against my hunter-green Jeep, pressing our bodies

270

together. The male crickets made noises, rubbing their special body parts together, singing out into the night to attract the sexually ready females. I was a sexually ready female, but Junior didn't have to sing to me. He rubbed my special body parts, and I rubbed his. I was so hot for him. Well ... not really for *him*.

Just then a cop car pulled around the end of the shopping center by the supermarket. It made its way slowly. Junior and I continued our love game a bit less enthusiastically until it passed. "What the hell's that cop doing back here?" I asked.

"It's probably one of Joe's friends checking up to make sure everything's cool." Junior smiled and nodded politely as the cop passed by.

The police car stopped in front of the dumpster at the far end of the shopping center. There was a guy standing behind the dumpster. It was one of the white shirts. The officer didn't get out of his car, but the two men had a brief conversation. As the "white shirt" spoke, his wedding band reflected specks of golden light. He was the type of guy who coordinated a hand movement to every word he said. It was impossible to hear any of it with Junior's tongue in my ear.

After the cop pulled away, the dancer who looked like Eddie Murphy came out from behind the dumpster, still in costume, wearing a short skirt and thigh-high boots, still working. She got into a white Lexus with the white shirt and buried her head in his lap. I then realized that she was more than a just a dancer – She was a prostitute.

At that very moment I felt like I was part of something much larger than myself. The underbelly of the world had fully exposed itself in the back parking lot of Studio, and there I was, watching it from afar, yet somehow a part of it.

I imagined a genteel, loving housewife waiting for her husband to come home after her long day of looking after their kids. Waiting for a little companionship from the man who had convinced her with diamonds and pearls to marry him. Waiting for a compliment on her new hairdo. Waiting for him to walk through the front door, wearing the white shirt that she had taken to get dry-cleaned and pressed. Waiting and waiting and waiting. And all the while, the image of a hooker giving her husband a blow-job is reflecting in the gold of her husband's wedding band, bobbing up and down in their new Lexus, parked next to a dumpster in the back lot of a go-go bar.

I thought of Junior's wife.

CHAPTER THIRTY-THREE

Better Than Sex

The spring semester ended. And even though I hadn't officially registered for courses, I continued taking Mr. Mault's painting class. He taught the summer sessions, and invited me to set up and sit in as often as I wanted. So I joined the class everyday like a regular student.

The summer schedule for the course was much more concentrated than it had been the previous semester. Classes began in the morning and were scheduled five days a week, rather than just two afternoons. I enjoyed the intensity of the new time frame. The focused practice and daily discipline heightened my painting skills and gave rise to my visual awareness. I felt on the verge of a major artistic breakthrough.

The model was different, too. I was accustomed to painting older men who had angles. Now there was a middle-aged, curvy woman named Amy on the stage. The same stage upon which I had posed for Jordan's art class. The same stage upon which I had uncovered my naked self to the world. I had gone from that stage … to the health food store … to the go-go bar … to the easel. The more I thought about it, the more I saw myself completing some kind of small circle. But I knew I was nowhere near completing a *full* circle. I didn't feel settled. I barely felt *semi*. I was more like a point on a little arc, just starting out, wanting to travel onwards, to accomplish more, but I was stuck on the edge of a little arc, and it had something to do with Jordan. I was stuck on a stage in life where the curtain neither rises nor falls, and it had something to do with Jordan. I was waiting in the wings for something to happen. I missed him. The feeling was sick, like I needed to vomit but couldn't. So I just lived with it. The art studio kept me connected to him. It was my favorite place to be.

The summer class was small and intimate, sprinkled with students rather than loaded to maximum capacity, as I was otherwise accustomed. Amy the model was an old pro. She cracked jokes all day long. And just to be nice, I bought her a cup of coffee at the start of each session. She couldn't believe how *kind* I was. "You're the *kindest* art student I've ever met, and I've been posing for well over fifteen years." Amy acted as though I was giving her gold instead of coffee – but I guess that's what it all comes down to. Then I got worried that she was in love with me – or even *worse*, that she thought I was in love with her. One time she asked me to join her for a salad after class. I said I couldn't – that I was busy. Then I started feeling funny about treating her to coffee, but it was too late. It had already become a routine. I tried my best to set my paranoid thoughts aside, and figured it was a small price to pay for free access to the studio. I didn't realize that my kindness could be interpreted as flirting, especially with a woman. It's like a curse or something – because everywhere I go, homosexuals love me.

Midway through the first summer session, Mr. Mault gave the class another weekend assignment: *Choose a simple object that appeals to you. Paint the object 10x on a large canvas; paint the object on 10 smaller canvases; or choose another arrangement of 10. But be sure to change perspective at least 3x.*

I chose an egg. And once again, I visited the painting studio on a Saturday. I liked the whole weekend vibe on campus. There weren't any time schedules or instructors – no tensions or worries. The setting liberated my mind, and I was free to be me.

On my way over, that Saturday morning in June, half a dozen eggs nestled neatly in half a cardboard egg carton in my backpack. Although I only needed one egg for the assignment, I packed a few extras in case of breakage during transit. And when I arrived at the studio, it was a relief to find all my eggs intact.

After setting up my palette at the easel, I placed one of the eggs on a piece of white cloth. It was white on white again – but without the restrictions this time.

The first few paintings looked pretty much the same, except I varied the size of each egg, and the tone as well, careful not to make them look like Easter eggs. I was satisfied with the results, but became increasingly bored with the assignment. I had to paint the same exact egg seven more times. To change perspective and liven things up, I placed an egg way up high on a shelf, and painted it from that angle. But when the air conditioner started up again, the egg rolled off, and its inner contents splattered onto the floor. So I painted it that way. The assignment became more and more interesting once the egg had opened.

I took out another one, cracked it slightly, and found pleasure in a thin fissure marking its length. I decided to reproduce that sixth image larger than the others, real close-up, almost appearing as though you were looking at it through a magnifying glass.

The seventh painting was a lot like the sixth – but the crack in the egg was larger and deeper. For the eighth canvas, I only painted the cracked area with just a bit of yolk running out. I tried to make it look like a black and white photograph, without any real color at all. It turned out good – but the ninth painting was better.

The remaining eggs looked perfectly snug in their individual compartments. I reached for another one, held it in my palm, and enjoyed the feel of the cool, smooth shell.

As if suddenly possessed by the ghost of a baseball pitcher, I threw the egg against the nearest studio wall, and repeated the act with equal momentum until all the remaining eggshells were smashed in an angle between the wall and the floor. Thick yolk ran slowly down the wall. I painted the image of the mess and even mixed some of the slimy whites and yolks in with the oil paint. I didn't know how the mixture would dry, but the sensation of incorporating the subject matter into the image was irresistible.

The assignment was complete. Ten egg paintings. I stood before them and felt satisfied. I had traveled far from my first attempt by the time I was finished. I bummed a cigarette off one of the other students and smoked it as though I just had sex.

It was better than sex – Paint is sexy.

CHAPTER THIRTY-FOUR

Studio Material

"Do you want to go out for Chinese food?" My mother asked.

"I'd love to, but I'm going to work," I said.

"On a Monday? Since when do you work on Mondays?"

"I decided to take on an extra night a week now that summer's here."

"Oh good." My mother never knew what to say when the topic of go-go dancing came up, so she didn't say anything and changed the subject. "Your sister Jackie fired me."

"Why?" I asked, surprised.

"I wanted to set up a small television set at the receptionist's station, but Jackie said, 'Absolutely not.' – I only wanted to watch when it wasn't busy – to see my shows or catch the news. Well, we ended up arguing over it, and she fired me."

"You don't seem very upset. – You seem happy. – Are you?"

"Of course I'm happy. I don't want to work. I only took the job because Jackie made me."

"No, mom. You made her. Get it? You *made* her." I laughed like a nut.

"Yeah, yeah – I get it," she half-smiled.

"I would *never* fire you, mommy."

"I know you wouldn't. You're my *baby*. But I'm glad she did. She also said that I talk to the customers too much."

"I'd pay you double if you worked for me." We embraced in a big, cozy hug. I loved being her baby. She always called me *The Baby*. Whenever we were out, and she'd bump into someone she knew, she'd say, "This is Mona. This is Jackie. And this is *The Baby*."

"There's a jar of maraschino cherries in the fridge," she told me. She always indulged my cherry addiction. I could usually eat an entire small jar in one sitting. But for the first time in my life, the cherries didn't appeal to me.

We all left the house at the same time. My parents turned right onto Roosevelt Boulevard. I turned left. The Boulevard has two big sections to travel on that run in the same direction, north or south. All four of the three-lane sections are divided by median strips. I'd been driving in my lane for only a few seconds when I realized there weren't any cars around. None behind me. None next to me. None in front of me. I got the harshest feeling that I was advancing in the wrong lane, imagining a herd of cars charging toward me. There was a biting in the mouth of my stomach. My palms and forehead heated up as an intense fear whistled fiery steam throughout the survival part of my brain.

When I finally caught up to the other cars ahead, I began breathing regularly again. At the next red light, I smoked a cigarette with a shaky hand. *Was that an anxiety attack?* I wondered.

Joe the day manager approached me. I had only met him twice before, and was impressed that he knew my real name.

"Bree, let me ask you something. Exactly how good of friends are you with Chancy?"

"Not good at all. Why?"

"I'm afraid she's not Studio material. We're going to have to let her go," he said with all seriousness.

"Studio material? – Why? Did something happen?"

"A lot of things happened. Yesterday it all came to a head: She was sitting at the bar in clothes that were totally inappropriate. Her tank top was cut so high that her tits were literally hanging out of the bottom. All the guys moved in to get a closer look. Then she shook up a beer bottle, gave it a blowjob, and let the foam run down her chest so that her shirt was soaked, and her tits were full of beer. After that, she got up on the stage in a pair of denim shorts that were just about as shredded as her shirt, and she didn't have anything on underneath. Every time she spread her legs – pardon my expression – her beaver popped out to say hello."

"Holy shit! I didn't know she was such a pig, but I had my suspicions about her when Paul told me that she showed him her tampon string during a lap dance."

"There's more than just that," he continued, "But I didn't want to fire her because I knew you brought her up here. So, if you don't mind, I'd like to stop giving her hours."

"I don't mind at all. I don't really even know her."

I couldn't believe he actually asked my permission to fire her. It felt good knowing that I was *Studio material*.

Chancy was the third and final dancer to get fired from Studio during the time that I worked there.

I went into the dressing room. The scent of Downy jumped out like a surprise party. It smelled like the dryer vent behind a house when a Downy dryer sheet is surfing through waves of warming garments. There was no one in the room except for some girl named Jazz who was fixing her make-up in the mirror. "It smells like a Laundromat in here," I said.

"Can you keep a secret?" she asked.

"Sure."

"Check this out." She picked up the cardboard cylinder of an empty paper towel roll, and stuffed a few Downy dryer sheets inside. Then she filled a smokeless pipe with a hit of pot, fired it up, and blew the smoke right through her little invention. Smoke came out the other end of the cardboard cylinder, but it smelled like laundry.

"Well? What does it smell like?" she asked. Her eyes were pink and glassy with happiness.

"Smells like my favorite fabric softener. I love Downy!" I got so damn excited every time I smelled it.

"Do you want a hit? I have tons of this stuff. It's really good." It had been a long time since I'd last smoked. So long, I couldn't even remember how it felt to be high. The zipper on Jazz's make-up case revealed the mother load of nickel bags. "My boyfriend sells it. I stole these from him," she laughed. "Want some?"

"Sure," I said. "One hit'll do me good."

Jazz locked the dressing-room door and opened a tiny zip-lock bag. I love zip-lock bags. They remind me of the fluffy white Wonder Bread sandwiches my mother used to pack for me in elementary school. Jazz packed the pipe. I inhaled a little bit at a time because I didn't want to start choking all over the place. The scent of Downy delightfully filled the air as I blew the smoke through Jazz's clever gadget. "This is a great idea. Did you come up with it yourself?" I asked.

"Yup. I should have it patented," she laughed.

"You should. Then you could advertise on one of those infomercials. We could shoot the whole thing right here in the dressing room." Jazz laughed at everything I said. Someone pounded on the door.

"Who is it?" Jazz sang.

"Is that Barbie?"

"In the flesh." I sang.

"You're on in ten minutes."

"Cool," Jazz beamed. "I'm going up on stage in twenty minutes. Our sets are back-to-back."

Just then, I realized that I didn't have much time to get ready. I usually like to take my time before going up on stage. Smoking pot confuses the concept of time. I knew that Junior was in the DJ booth, and I always anticipated our good time together, rubbing our special body parts together before my set. Strangely, all I wanted to do was breath in the Downy and talk to Jazz who was watering her eyes with Visine. I had worked with her before on nights when there were tons of dancers, but we never had the opportunity to meet or connect. When she first started dancing, she was a lot heavier. Her thighs had been as thick as tree logs, and she had worn braces. Now her braces were off, and she was as thin as me. *I wonder if she's on coke.* Whenever people lose a lot of weight, I always think they're on coke.

I felt high. Sexy. Good. I pulled out the fishnet one-piece and slipped into my thigh highs. Jazz handed me the Visine. "Thanks." I put two drops in each eye and applied my mascara. We were both busy fixing ourselves in the mirror. Jazz kept staring at me. I pretended not to notice and made casual small talk.

"Did you lose weight?"

"Twenty-five pounds."

"Wow. How did you do it?"

"I stopped eating so much. I figured that a dancer should have the figure of a dancer."

I was getting higher from the pot. Jazz's words sounded fuzzy. My head felt like it was wrapped in cotton. "Well, you look great."

"So do you. Your body's awesome. Your boobs are so perky. Mine just droop when I don't have anything on. – Look." She pulled off her costume, and her boobs went down two flights. "I should get them fixed." I wanted Jazz to feel good about herself, so I started putting myself down, just to bring her back up a little.

"Well, at least your nipples are normal." She had silver dollars. "The tips of my nipples always stick out like missiles, even when I'm wearing a bra. It's so embarrassing."

"Your nipples are hot. I'd like to bite them."

Oh no! I thought. *She's coming on to me. Shit. I better get out of here.*

Joe pounded on the door again. "Hey Barbie! What the fuck're you doing in there? You're late for your set!"

Saved by the manager, I thought. "Coming!" I flew out of the dressing room and had to get right up on stage without any time to give a lusty hello to Junior. Nonetheless, his animal grunting sounds could be heard at intervals through the speakers.

The hundred-dollar man entered the bar. For a Monday night, the place was pretty crowded. I had expected much less.

I liked the feeling the pot inspired, and sneaked back into the dressing room for another hit. Jazz's stuff was scattered on the counter: the empty paper towel roll, the box of dryer sheets, the nickel bags shined though an open zipper on her make-up case. She hadn't even bothered zipping it up. I grabbed the one-hitter pipe and a pack of matches.

Others dancers had entered the dressing room by then. Most of the women who worked that night were what I like to call *The Good Girls*:

First there was Janina, a real classy dancer, and the mother of two teenage girls, who worked as a part-time stripper, as well as a full-time interpreter for the government. She was fluent in both Spanish and Chinese. Real smart and young looking for her age. She claimed the secret to tight skin was cold water. "I only shower in cold water," she would say. I tried it a couple of times, but always turned the hot water on in the end. Janina was proud of her work. One time she brought her fifteen-year-old daughter in to meet everyone. It was kind of awkward.

Then there was this plain-style woman who was an elementary school teacher in New Jersey. She never said much and called herself Cricket. I always thought of Jiminy Cricket camping out in the peg box of my violin every time the DJ announced her to the stage. Although her name was silly, she was serious. She came in, did her job, and earned extra cash to support her son, "to give him a better life." A lot of the single mothers were there that night.

Shelly, the mother of a seven-year-old girl, saved her dancing dollars to move to Hawaii. A spot had been discovered on her daughter's lung in a medical exam, and Shelly wanted to relocate to a place with better air quality. She was a carpenter by day, a dancer by night, and constantly worried about her daughter in between.

I didn't want to smoke the pipe in front of them, so I filled it and brought it into the bathroom along with the Downy air filter. I smoked real fast, blew it out through the dryer sheet contraption, and placed all of Jazz's things back where they belonged. Within five minutes I was back collecting tips around the bar.

Roger had already given me three C-notes by the time my first set was over. That was more than he usually tipped, and he didn't even ask for a private dance. I went into the DJ booth and did a private dance for Junior. We were getting hotter and hotter for each other. It was the boiling point, time to explode, and we both knew it. "What are you doing after work tonight?" he asked.

"You," I replied.

"You're doing *me* tonight?" He smiled at the thought.

"Definitely. Let's get a room somewhere," I said.

"Why don't you just come back to my place?"

"Your place? I can't. You're married for God's sake."

"So what? My wife's in North Jersey with my mom."

"I can't. Let's just get a room."

"Then a room it is."

The thought of unleashing my lust for Junior in the house where he and his wife had conceived their babies seemed like blasphemy. And anyway, it wasn't really Junior I was lusting. It was Jordan. A hotel room would be better, less personal.

After my second set, I had practically earned an entire night's tips. My good buddy Roger had given me four hundred dollars in all. That, plus whatever else I managed to make around the bar was enough. I just wanted to be with Junior in the DJ booth.

I looked around for Joe the manager to ask him if I could call it quits, but I couldn't find him anywhere. Not in the bar. Not in his office. Not in the kitchen. Not in the back room. I knocked on Joe the owner's office door.

"Who is it?" Bobbi the Bartender shouted.

"It's Barbie."

"Come in."

I opened the door. A dancer named EnShante was lying on the leather sofa in there while Joe and Bobbi hovered over her ass.

"What are you doing?" I asked.

"EnShante got a splinter in her ass. We're trying to get it out," Joe explained.

"How did *that* happen?" I asked.

In her thick Chinese accent, EnShante explained: "I was slidin' off da fuckin' stage, to get a tip, and big-ass *splinner* go in my fuckin' ass. Mudda-fucka bitch hurt!"

"Stop moving," Bobbi demanded. "I think I got it … Shit! … It won't come out."

"What the fuck do you want anyway?" Joe asked me in his usual arrogant tone.

"I was wondering if I could call it a night. My feet really hurt and I'm tired. I'm not used to dancing three nights a week—"

"You look tired. Look how red her eyes are, Barb," Joe said.

Bobbi looked up from EnShante's ass. "She looks high. Are you high?"

I was high, far away in space, like Pluto. "No," I slurred, "I'm tired."

"Well, you look high," Bobbi said again.

"Dance one more set and then you're done," Joe smirked. "And get the fuck outta here. And stop smoking that shit!"

"*Owww!*" EnShante shouted, and I quickly closed the soundproof door.

I didn't even change for my next set. Junior played Bob Dylan, *Lay Lady Lay*. I danced effortlessly, yet the whole bar seemed to be taken by my performance. Dollar bills waved my way, but I couldn't stop to collect. For the first time, the dance had become more important than the money. I was flying down a mountain, soaring above a sea. I had perfected my act when I wasn't trying at all. I didn't dance to the music; the music moved me. Music plus passion plus marijuana leaves very little room for greed. However, the magic wore off when the song ended. I got down to collect, and the extreme sense of freedom I had experienced on stage quickly faded.

There was a guy sitting at the bar who was neither a regular nor a new face. He came in every so often, but just how often was unclear. Grungy looking in his late twenties, he played it cool. "You were fantastic up there."

"Thanks," I smiled.

"You have beautiful teeth."

"Thanks." I was still high, hence not the best conversationalist. I just wanted to finish the set. Then Jazz got down from the stage and grabbed me from behind. She rubbed my chest. The customer tipped us each two bucks.

"How do you feel?" she asked.

"Like I'm on a cloud."

"Isn't it good stuff?"

"Yeah."

Jazz did something sexy with her mouth and went back to dancing.

"Are you guys high on reefer?" the customer asked.

"Yup."

"Do you know where I can buy some? I've been jonesin' all day."

"Actually, I do. Wait here." I ran to the dressing

room and grabbed two of the nickel bags from Jazz's make-up case, then ran back to the bar, holding them tightly in my fist. I was a little out of breath. "Here you go." I placed the stuff in his hand.

"How much?" he asked.

I wanted to say *It's free. Don't worry about it*, but instead I held out my palm and said, "Twenty bucks." He paid. I walked over to Roger.

"How come you never put on a lesbian act for me?" he whined.

"I don't do lesbian acts. That girl attacked me," I assured him.

"It didn't look like you minded it too much." His moustache twitched as he reached for his wallet. "I'll give both of you girls one of these if you do a private lap dance for me – together."

I wanted to say no, but felt bad about it. Roger had given me so much money. Thousands it seemed. "I'll ask Jazz if she's into it," I told him.

Jazz was on the other side of the bar. I passed by EnShante's ass on stage. It had a big red mark where the splinter had been.

Jazz agreed and we all entered the back room together. I was nervous. I had never done a lesbian act before, and Jazz was really into me. I wasn't in the habit of making back-room dates with dancers who were into me. I avoided them like a mouse avoids a cat.

Before Roger took a seat in the back left corner, he tipped the bouncer. I couldn't see how much, but I bet it was at least a fifty. Junior played that erotic Prince song *Darling Nikki* from the Purple Rain album. I was getting nervous, so I gave myself a silent pep talk: *Just go along with whatever Jazz does. It'll be over in less than five minutes.*

We were only fooling around for the start of the song, mostly teasing, rubbing, and pressing our bodies close together here and there between beats. It was no big deal. Nothing I couldn't handle. Roger sat in a chair. The rest of the room was empty (Yes, that's right, no bouncer). Jazz and I were so focused on each other, we kind of forgot about Roger. But the hundred-dollar man needs a lot of attention. That's why he's the hundred-dollar man. "Why don't you girls give each other a kiss for Uncle Roger?"

Jazz smiled and leaned on me. She was quick to start *frenching* me, and I felt I had no other choice than to give in. I had never kissed a girl before. I'd seen it happen over and over at Studio: at the bar, on the stage, and in the back room. But I managed to stay away from that aspect of the business, never got involved. At first it was shocking, but it wasn't horrible. I kept thinking, *I can't believe I'm kissing a girl*, the entire time. It was sort of like the I-Can't-Believe-It's-Not-Butter commercial.

Roger was really into it. I could hear him moaning below us. I was first to pull away and end it. The kiss had lasted long enough. Jazz looked like she had just been given the keys to her dream car. The green light was lit, and she floored the gas pedal. She moved my fishnet costume over to the side and wrapped her lips around my nipple before I even had a chance to consent. My head felt like it had been lit on fire. I was confused. She was biting my nipple, and I had an orgasm in front of the hundred-dollar man. I wanted to get out of there. I couldn't breath. The song ended. Roger paid us for our services.

In the dressing room, I put my regular clothes on and packed my suitcase. "That was awesome," Jazz said, packing her one-hitter again.

"I had an orgasm," I confessed.

"So did I."

"You did?"

"Yeah. We should do that again."

I wanted to say *no way*, but didn't want to offend her. "I'll do it for a hundred, but nothing less."

"I'd do it just to do it. You're incredible."

"I'm really only in it for the money."

"Oh, too bad." She offered me the pipe. I took another hit and blew the smoke through the Downy sheet.

Jordan, I thought. *Where are you? Why did you have to die?*

I went out the back door. The summer sky wasn't completely dark yet. I chucked my suitcase into the back of the Jeep, turned the ignition on, and pulled out. By the time I made it around the building to the front parking lot, I realized that I wasn't ready to go home. I had plans with Junior to get a room. The orgasm and the pot left me in a state of confusion. It was as if my logical brain system had a Temporarily-Out-of-Order sign pinned to it. I slowly gathered my marbles and rolled them back into place.

Once again, I entered Studio. But this time I entered through the front door, empty handed. No big lumpy suitcase to drag in. I was wearing a sundress, free as can be.

I slipped into the DJ booth without being seen by Jazz, Roger, or anyone else who was erotically connected to me. Junior closed the door of the little space capsule, and 3, 2, 1, blastoff! Our libidos took off. We hugged and grinded. He kissed my neck and ate my ear. Soon he was traveling south. I imagined Jordan, alive, making passionate love to me, and it was okay because Junior knew. I had told him the truth, and he was okay with it. His head was under my sundress. He kissed the creamy space between my legs. I wanted to come. I almost came, but there was a knock at the door.

"Just ignore that," Junior said from under my sundress. My eyes opened slightly, then wider, and even wider yet. My mouth gaped. There were cops all over the place. The banging at the door continued. I pulled away from Junior.

"Look at this," I gasped in disbelief.

"What the—" Junior cut off the music and turned on the house lights. "Wait here," he said. "Don't let anyone in." He exited the booth and locked the door with his keys from the other side. I could see everything that was going on in the bar because the big window in the DJ booth was really a one-way mirror. No one could see me.

They handcuffed Janina, Cricket, and Jazz. They rounded up all the other girls from the back room and the dressing room and cuffed them too. Customers were ordered to leave. Bartenders looked lost. Bouncers stood confused. Junior put as much distance between himself and the DJ booth as he possibly could, way over on the other side. Joe the owner wasn't even around at the time of the bust. He was already on his way back home to his nuclear family. All the dancers were arrested and charged with prostitution.

I kept thinking that they were going to get me every second. I heard keys jingling on the other side of the door. I hid under the big panel where the sound controls were. There were a million wires down there. I felt like a child, scared and alone, surrounded by snakes. It wasn't a very good hiding place. The door opened. I closed my eyes tight to disappear. "Come out. They're gone," Junior said.

I stepped down from the booth. Bobbi and the rest of the bartenders stood together behind the bar talking to the bouncers who were standing together on the other side of the bar. Tension vaporized above their heads. Junior and I walked over, holding hands. His palms were clammy, just like Jordan's.

"How the fuck did you get away?" Bobbi the Bartender asked me.

"I was in the DJ booth."

"Where's your stuff? They went through the dressing room, and your stuff isn't there. They made sure they got a dancer for every suitcase – fuckin' assholes."

"I was already done for the night. Joe said I could finish early. Remember?"

I explained to her how I was tipping the DJ when the cops came in, how they just hadn't bothered to search the booth. And even if they did, I was dressed and done for the night. No suitcase – no arrest.

"How on earth did they get the dancers for prostitution?" I asked.

"Who the hell knows," Bobbi replied. "EnShante's getting charged with prostitution *and* resisting arrest. She shot pepper spray right in the cop's face. The whole dressing room stinks like it."

Bobbi looked nervous. She and the others started cleaning up the bar for the night. Olives, lemons, and cherries. All cleaned up and put away.

CHAPTER THIRTY-FIVE

A Wet Sock

I followed Junior's blue Trans Am south on Route One. He pulled into a diner. I parked next to him.

The menu was the usual. "What are you ordering?" I asked him.

"Pork roll with cheese."

"What's that?"

"You never had pork roll with cheese?"

"No. What is it?"

"It's a sandwich."

"What's pork roll?"

"Pork."

"Oh, sounds good." It sounded disgusting. Junior and I were about to consummate our relationship, and he was ordering a pork roll with cheese sandwich. I thought he would have ordered something sexier, like French Onion Soup or Eggplant Parmesan. Maybe Spaghetti with Clam Sauce or an order of Shrimp Cocktail. Anything that sounded sexier than *pork roll with cheese*. The thought of making love to him became less and less appealing by the second. He wasn't Jordan. That was for sure.

"What are you ordering, sexy?" he asked.

"French Onion Soup, Potato Pancakes with Sour Cream, and a House salad with Russian Dressing."

"What are potato pancakes?"

"Jew food. We eat them at Chanukah."

"Is it Chanukah?" I laughed at the thought of Chanukah in the summer.

"No, but I like to eat them all year round."

"I'd like to eat you all year round." He rubbed my leg under the table.

We had nothing in common. The less we spoke, the better. I tried not to watch him eating his pork roll.

After he paid the bill, we got a room at The Marriott, and I soon discovered that Junior wasn't circumcised. I had never seen a real foreskin before. I had seen the difference between the two varieties of penises in a textbook picture in health class in ninth grade. We were actually tested on identifying the similarities and differences using a Venn Diagram.

Junior wanted me to give him a blowjob. "Would you like to taste my lollipop?" he asked.

I couldn't bring myself to do it. Instead, I jumped on him, and he rolled on a condom. The sex was all right, but I couldn't have an orgasm no matter how hard I tried, so I faked it. Junior came *with me* and it was over.

Standing in the middle of the room, he stretched his arms way over his head, practically touching the ceiling. He was a big guy. But he wasn't Jordan. He was an uncircumcised Puerto Rican man who enjoyed eating pork roll with cheese and cheating on his wife. As he stretched his arms upward, the condom he wore hung off his dick like a wet sock. It looked awful. Up until that point, I had been trapped inside an episode of magical realism. It was all about Jordan. After having sex with Junior, the magic disappeared. All that remained was realism.

"Let's do it again," he said.

"I don't feel so well."

"What's wrong?"

"I think it's the onion soup. I better go."

I got dressed and left while he was in the bathroom. I knew it was rude, but I had to leave.

The whole way back down Route One, my anxiety resurfaced. The feeling was gastrointestinal, like a small volcano starting to erupt. I knew it could only mean one thing: It was time for me to get a doctor. To seek professional help, like Jackie had advised.

The professionals will know how to handle my situation. It can't be anything they haven't encountered before. Death is common, the most common source of anxiety known to humankind. They'll know how to cure me.

I don't know why I was thinking in plurals, as if it would take an entire team of doctors to analyze and treat me. But I was able to calm myself down with these thoughts. Knowing I was about to enter through the doors of self-help gave me a feeling of hopefulness. I hadn't felt that hopeful since before the time of Jordan's death.

After my mind cleared a bit, I kept thinking about the go-go bar and the police. How many laws had I disobeyed? How many moral codes had I violated? How many hearts had I broken?

One, I knew, was shattered for sure –

Mine.

CHAPTER THIRTY-SIX

Mama Tropicana

It was a sharp summer morning. All the a.m. shadows were in place. Freshly watered gardens scented the air between morning sips of coffee. Before leaving for my painting class, I gave my father my earnings to take to the bank.

"How come your bag's so empty?" Wasn't there any business last night?" he asked.

"Oh, there was business. The hundred-dollar man came in and gave me four or five hundred dollars. I can't remember. And I only danced three sets. So there's probably around seven or eight hundred dollars all together," I said. The birds were chirping loudly by the window, competing with me to be heard.

"Sounds pretty good for just dancing three sets," he said.

"It was a good night ... until the cops showed up and arrested the dancers for prostitution!"

"What?" Jackie barged into the room upon overhearing the soap opera go-go news. "Who got arrested?" she asked.

"All the *good-girl* dancers: Janina, Cricket, and Shelly. Jazz got arrested. And so did EnShante."

"Did *you* get arrested?" Jackie asked.

I explained the situation and how I saw all the

action from the other side of the one-way mirror in the DJ booth.

"What were you doing in the DJ booth?" my father asked.

"Giving the DJ a tip."

"Oh." The way he said *oh* made me nervous. Like he could see right through me, into my mischief. He can sense it when I'm up to no good. And although he'd been picking up on it all my life, it's always a surprise when it happens.

"I wonder why they were arrested for *prostitution*?" Jackie said. "The owner's a cop. He must've pissed someone off."

"Someone was probably jealous of him," my father decided.

"Are they allowed to keep the bar running?" Jackie asked.

"I don't know. I'll call there later and find out."

"Was any prostitution going on there that you're aware of?" my father asked. His question painted a picture in my mind of the dancer who looked like Eddie Murphy.

"Not really. Everything's pretty kosher in there, but a few weeks ago I saw one of the dancers giving some guy a blowjob in the back parking lot. She definitely was a prostitute, and she dances at Studio."

"Who's a prostitute?" my mother asked as she entered the room, sipping decaf from a coffee mug with the Tropicana Casino Hotel logo printed on it.

"No one's a prostitute," Jackie and I answered in unison.

My father changed the subject to protect my

mother from the ugly truth of last night's goings on.

"Tell Bree where you're moving to," he said in his showing-off-proud-happy voice.

"You're moving?" I said in disbelief.

Jackie found a townhouse in Society Hill. The news was bittersweet. I was happy for her, but letting go of our morning-noon-and-night encounters would take a lot of getting used to.

"Why're you moving?" I asked, suddenly saddened.

"I need to be closer to the salon. I can't stomach the traffic everyday, and I keep getting anxiety attacks on the way downtown when I'm driving on I-95."

"You do?" I asked. "You get anxiety while you're driving?"

"Yeah, it's horrible."

"So do I! I get anxiety in the car, too! But not when there's traffic. It happens when I'm alone on the road. I freeze up and then I break out in a sweat. I keep thinking I'm going the wrong way. And when the fear takes over my mind, it feels like an invisible person is choking me. Then another car comes into view to assure me that I'm in the right lane, and it ends."

"You better call Dr. Cohen right away. He'll know what to do," my mother advised. I was skeptical.

"What could Dr. Cohen do to help?" I asked.

"He can write you a prescription, or refer you to a specialist." She retreated into the kitchen.

"Society Hill sounds nice. When are you moving?"

"The house will be ready at the end of July." Jackie sensed my emotions. "You can live with me if you want to."

"Thanks. I'll think about it … Can you do my hair today, around two?"

"Call the salon. See if I'm busy. I don't even know my own schedule anymore. I'm so damn busy."

My mother came back in holding a small piece of notepad paper with Dr. Cohen's name and office number scribbled under the Tropicana logo. I'm sure she wrote it with a Tropicana pen, after she drank her morning brew from her Tropicana coffee mug, after dissolving some sugar from a small white packet that had the Tropicana logo printed on it, too. Everything in our house had that logo on it. My parents went to Atlantic City pretty often, and always stayed at the *Trop* and participated in all their promotions. My mother likes to gamble there. My father visits the health spa.

There were Tropicana bathrobes in our house, Tropicana jackets, t-shirts, sweatshirts, sweatpants, sun visors, coasters, and more. So many things said that word: *Tropicana*.

"Call Dr. Cohen today," my mother said, handing me his phone number. "And don't forget."

My mama loves me …

CHAPTER THIRTY-SEVEN

The Loving Teacher

Although it was the last week of classes, the smell of the painting studio inspired me as though it were the first. Mr. Mault geared up to give his final critique of our paintings. He strolled alongside the gallery setup he had arranged of our paintings, and inspected the results, scratching his chin and adjusting his glasses like some kind of art detective. The glasses he wore were way too big for his Clint Eastwood face. You could tell that he felt very important in his role as our painting instructor. Or maybe it was I who felt he was very important in his role as our painting instructor. I tend to view teaching professionals as demi-gods and goddesses. I used to view them as *total* gods, until my violin teacher sexually harassed me. That was the real reason why I had dropped out of the music program. I kept the whole thing to myself and didn't tell *anyone* about it. Not even Jackie.

I had always loved being a music major. But during the second semester of my freshman year, I grew frustrated. All the music students were so competitive. And when I was named second-chair of the university's symphony orchestra, I felt as though the other violinists were plotting my death – like someone was going to push me down into the subway tracks or something.

Maybe they resented me because I really didn't deserve to get second-chair. I knew it was a fluke. I had accidentally performed exceptionally well at the audition. If the judges had asked to play my audition piece again that good, I couldn't have. For some weird reason I perform better at auditions than I actually am.

The violin teacher who sexually harassed me is a member of The Philadelphia Orchestra. I can't say his name because I don't want to disgrace him – even though he deserves it.

At the time, I had been working on the Bruch Concerto in g minor. It was about three weeks before final exams, and I had to prepare myself to play the concerto in front of a panel of judges. I loved the piece and really threw myself into my practice.

At the end of my private lesson one day, I was chatting with my teacher as I packed up my violin. I guess I ramble on too much because it was then that the whole thing started:

"I read an interesting article last week about a violinist named Midori," I said to my teacher.

"Oh, what interested you?" he asked.

"When Midori was a little baby, she would caress the strings of her mother's violin—"

"You're so cute. I'd like to caress you," he said, cool as could be. And his eyes flashed into mine.

What the fuck did he just say? ... Did he just say that he wants to caress me? ... Maybe my ears are full of bow rosin? ... I must be crazy ... He's my violin teacher – a renowned member of The Philadelphia Orchestra ... He would never say that to me ...

I let out a nervous laugh and left my lesson in a

state of confusion.

At my next private lesson the following week, my teacher told me that I needed to concentrate on my bow arm. He said that I wasn't getting the most out of my bow.

There was a dark-green chalkboard hanging on the wall in the small room where we met for my lessons. He walked over to the board and drew a large crescent moon on it with yellow chalk.

"Your bow should follow the shape of the curve," he instructed. Then he drew a great big yellow number eight next to the moon. "When you arrive at the tip of the bow, imagine you're creating an invisible figure eight as you make the transition from up-bow to down-bow. Then make the same action again at the frog. Think in crescents and eights. Here … let me show you …"

He made his way around to my back, and stood closely behind me in order to demonstrate the bowing technique. He instructed me to start playing my concerto from a particular passage. I began to play:

The piece started out on the G string, and progressed high and hearty to the E string. My teacher held on to my bow arm with his, and showed me how to form the crescent moons and the figure eights. The technique was the miracle cure to my awkward attempts. I had developed bad habits in bowing that held me back from achieving the sound I wanted. But my brilliant teacher knew exactly how to unfold my wings and set me free. And just as I got really excited about the sound that was rising up from the f-holes in the violin, I could feel my teacher's penis swelling in the f-holes between my butt cheeks.

When I fully realized what was happening, I froze – but just for a few seconds.

Functioning on instinct alone, I quickly pulled away from my teacher, flew across the room, and opened my violin case. I started mumbling as I packed up in a panic:

"I – I just remembered. I have to go. I – I have a doctor's appointment."

I got the hell out of there and ran down the hall to the exit sign.

It was the only time in all the years that I had been studying the violin that I didn't wipe the excess rosin off the fingerboard or the bow when I packed it up.

My next private lesson with him was scheduled during evening hours, at The Academy of Music, in one of the practice rooms. I arrived at the long, empty twists of turns in the corridors that led to the remote room in which we were supposed to meet. I sensed danger. It was creepy down there. I instinctively reversed my steps and left the building.

After that night, I completely stopped practicing my violin, and completely stopped going to all my classes. I really should have officially dropped the courses before I failed them, because that semester really messed up my college transcript.

Painting proved much less frustrating than playing the violin. Classes were held in a studio. The competition wasn't half as intense. Artists are very supportive of one another. Mr. Mault might have had the opportunity to breathe his hot, coffee-cigar breath down my neck every once in a while, but he couldn't harass me to an extreme and get away with it. Painting class was more like being in an orchestra – everything was public.

*

"Here we have another psychological approach by Bree Yeager," Mault announced, stretching out his bony chin towards my egg paintings. Once again, he saved my work for last.

During the critique, I enjoyed viewing the paintings that my classmates' had completed. I found they had chosen very interesting objects to include for the assignment: an oil lamp, a tennis ball, a telephone, a rose, and even a pickle.

Mault really liked my eggs, and he produced a lengthy philosophical lecture about the theme:

"The legendary egg … An interesting choice of subject … All life comes from it … The egg is known to symbolize new growth, new potential, fertility and eternity." Mault slowly paced as he considered, and rubbed his chin as he spoke: "The egg is a container for the universe … It contains within a miniature sun … The Chinese decorate a baby's crib with egg designs to attract good luck …" Mault seemed to be in some kind of a trance as he spoke about the mighty symbolic egg, and I worried that his lecture would never end. He just went on and on: "The egg represents the four elements … the shell is the earth … the membrane is air … the white is water … and the yolk is fire … To put it simply, the egg is everything … And I'm not even going to mention the role of the egg in the Resurrection of Christ …"

305

Jesus Christ, I thought. *What the hell is he talking about? It's a bunch of stupid egg paintings. I didn't set out to inspire an oration on the role of the egg in the universe. I eat them. That's all.*

Mault's attraction to me was embarrassing. When the other students looked my way to offer their sympathy, I just rolled my eyes and smirked.

"In this arrangement of paintings ... of color ... I see destruction." Mault stopped pacing and looked directly at me. "Are you experiencing episodes of darkness in your life, Bree? ... Has death paid a visit to your door? ... Heartbroken, maybe?" Mault slid his oversized frames down his nose.

I clapped my hands and applauded yet another of his spot-on analyses of me.

"Well done, Mr. Mault. You know everything. In fact, I'm calling my doctor today about the very thing you're seeing in my eggs." I reached into the pocket of my cut-offs. "Here's the number." I held up the piece of Tropicana Hotel and Casino notepad paper that my mother had written it on.

"Artists are all alike," he said. "The canvas is an undeniable snapshot of our mental states. Whether we like it or not, we expose our inner selves to the world without even knowing it."

I had to argue his point, even though his summation was correct:

"Yes, but some people might look at my work and just see a series of eggs. Like Victor's pickle. What do Victor's pickle paintings say about him?" I was done being the center of attention and turned the spotlight on someone else.

306

Mault was more than willing to play along. He said, "Victor's pickle speaks to me in two ways. First, he's getting way too much sex. And second, he smokes way too much pot." Victor and the rest of the class laughed. Everyone knew that Victor was a stoner. And his love hickies were a focal point anytime you looked at him.

"But the pain isn't there," Mault continued. Emotional torture shrieks in your work, Bree."

In the end, I liked Mault's analysis. He was right. I owned my emotional torture. I loved my eggs. They were outstanding. They told a story, and they sparked a discussion. They were more than eggs. They were me.

I took the elevator down to the first floor because I had to load a few heavy canvases into the jeep. The doors were about to close when Mault hopped in.

"Hey, Bree. You're so beautiful. And I can *safely* say so, now that you're not officially my student."

"What do you mean, *officially*?" I asked.

"You're not registered this semester –"

"But I'm still your student – officially or not."

CHAPTER THIRTY-EIGHT

Happily Ever After

Terry Tarri didn't have a Ph.D. in psychiatry. She was a licensed professional with an impressive address at 17th and Sansom Streets. I had called Dr. Cohen earlier that week regarding my situation, whereupon he gave me a list of professionals to choose from. The ring that Terry Tarri's name produced had prompted my choice. But even more, I liked the sound of the location: 17th and Sansom. Something about it was oddly familiar.

On the way over, I passed by a frosted glass door with the words *The Ballet Studio* encrusted on it, immediately recognizing the root of my choice. My sisters and I had studied dance there when we were still in the single digits of our youth. I stood before the door, recalling how we were introduced to the study of ballet under the instruction of three retired dancers of The Pennsylvania Ballet Company who had founded the school. I wanted to go in and see if the same people were still there: Missy, Anye, Yonic, Ruth the receptionist, and the pianist. But my appointment with Terry Tarri required immediate attention.

A long, narrow staircase gave me the feeling that therapy wasn't going to help my condition. The world of psychology didn't have a place in it for me. I was certain. And once I entered Terry Tarri's office, my suspicions were confirmed. The office didn't resemble anything I'd previously imagined. My vision included a long, leather sofa, enormous bookcases, framed degrees from ivy league universities, and a Doctor of Psychology taking notes from the comfort of a high-back leather chair in a room where one can not see the ceiling.

Stepping into Terry Tarri's office was more like stepping into a medicine woman's hut, or Andrea's (Chancy's) Native American Ford. The smell of aromatic candles was the first of several sensory devices to be detected. I inhaled the scent – *Fig Leaf?* I wondered.

Terry Tarri sported a crew cut of thick, silver hair. And when her back was turned, a silky braid extended down the length of her spine. There was a deep purple dream-catcher with lavender feathers hanging from the ceiling. Healing crystals were scattered about. An ionic air filter purred in the corner like a happy pet.

She was a full-bodied woman who I could tell must have been a real looker in her youth. She greeted me with a smiley hug before excusing herself to a telephone call I'd interrupted. Seated on some kind of magnetic cushion, she swiveled around after ending her conversation. I sipped lukewarm coffee from a paper cup that I'd brought along for my first hour of therapy.

"So, Bree. What brings you here today?" She clapped her hands together. A variety of chunky silver rings on her fingers produced a pleasing tympanic sound.

I gave her the outline of my year in brief: the health-food store, my Shakespearean romance with Dante, my short-lived romance with Jordan, the go-go bar, my miscarriage, painting class, Jordan's death, my delusional relationship with Junior and, lastly, my pathetic attachment to the scent of Downy. She quickly scribbled words on a yellow legal pad of lined paper. I enjoyed the scratching sound of the pencil.

"Let's back up to your relationship with Jordan," she said and asked me a handful of questions before arriving to the one that would spark the remainder of our discussion: "Did you mourn for him?"

I was an English major who had spent an entire semester dissecting Greek and Latin word roots, prefixes, and suffixes, but the simple word "mourn" became a sudden mystery to me in such context.

"What exactly do you mean by *mourn*?" I asked.

"Grieve," she explained. "How did you express your grief after Jordan's death?"

"I'm not sure I did – I slept at the cemetery one night, and cried at the funeral the next day ... And then I met Junior –"

"You slept at the cemetery!" she shrieked. Her eyes appeared as though she were looking at a tarantula.

"It was the night before they buried him ... I wanted to check it out before he got there ... just to make sure everything was okay." I tried to make it sound like camping out in the cemetery was a normal thing to do, and hoped that my nonchalant tone would set her at ease. But I could tell it wasn't working. I couldn't even convince myself.

"Well, how did you express your love for Jordan

while he was alive?" she asked.

I had to think about it for a moment.

"The last time he came back from Italy, I waited all day at my house and wrote some corny little poems while I waited. I guess that was my way of expressing my love for him."

"Do you still write poems?"

"No, I just paint. I used to play the violin ... Oh yeah! The day I wrote those poems, I also played my violin." Upon this point I got excited. I was making breakthroughs, and it occurred to me that therapy was a game I could play.

"Bree, you have to *mourn* for Jordan. You haven't mourned for him as of yet. It's a very important step when dealing with the loss of a loved one. You've missed that step. That's why you're tripping all over the place."

I was impressed by her insights. She was on to something. She was wise and deserving of her professional license. I don't believe a Ph.D. would have made any difference in the situation. I listened to her advice with hungry ears:

"I want you to write. Write a poem to Jordan about how you feel. Or just write him a letter. I believe it'll benefit you to write on a daily basis. Tell him what you're thinking, what you're feeling. Ask him any questions that come to mind."

"Then what should I do?"

"You can do whatever you like. You can go to his grave and read what you've written to him. You can keep your writings in a special place, like a box or a drawer. Whatever you want. That part's up to you.

The important thing is that you communicate with him. A visit to the grave, a letter, a poem. Play the violin if you want. Just stay away from that DJ at the go-go bar. You're with him for all the wrong reasons. That affair is heading down a dead-end street. It has nowhere to go. It's completely destructive."

"Then why did it feel so good for so long?"

"Because relationships are tricky. People are perplexed by the choices they make, *after* they make them. It's just bad judgment."

"I feel so stupid."

"Most of us are guilty of making stupid choices. It's not just you. I married my ex-husband because his last name was Tarri. I wanted to be Mrs. Terry Tarri. The marriage lasted for twenty years. Now we're happily divorced."

I laughed at her confession. "Is that what the quote on the wall is all about?" There was a framed quotation that read *"And they lived happily ever after…"*

"The majority of my clients are here for marriage counseling. People are trying to live with their mistakes. Be careful while you're still young and single. A fantasy is just that. There's no fairytale ending. Life goes on. Junior was a fantasy. Leave it at that. *Never* marry your fantasy."

My eyes were a bit more open. It was as if the world had suddenly gotten so small that I could examine it under a microscope. The world of relationships was never my strongpoint. All of my boyfriends were fantasies. But I wasn't quite sure if Jordan was a fantasy boyfriend or not.

"How do you know what's real and what's fantasy? And what if it's real for you, but it's just a fantasy for the other person?" I asked.

"Unfortunately, I don't have all the answers. Love's a gamble. A risk. There are no guarantees. You just have to be careful with the things that *are* in your control. Write down your thoughts, communicate with Jordan, and come back to see me in two weeks."

Terry checked her watch. It was her way of saying that our time together was up. She slid back over to her desk, which was located under a fairly large window. The view of Sansom Street was almost the same from her office as it had been from The Ballet Studio. A sense of relief washed over me. A sense of satisfaction bounced off the dream catcher, the healing crystals, the fictitious quote about marriage, and filled my mind with longing: *I will come full circle some time in the future. For now, I'll just have to crawl along the arc.*

"Same time, same day?" she asked, flipping through the pages of her appointment planner.

"Sure. That'll be fine."

She gave me the same smile and hug of an hour ago. Her clothes were loose and flowing and silky.

"One more question," she said. "Where do you get your hair done? It's fantastic."

"My sister opened up a salon on Rittenhouse Square. It's called *Hair Tea*."

"I'll have to check it out. My hairdresser just moved to New York."

"Ask for Jackie. She'll take care of that beautiful silver braid of yours."

313

"It used to be blond … I'll never cut it off. It's my way of staying connected to my youth."

"You must've been gorgeous with long blond hair." It was supposed to be a compliment, but gorgeous in the past tense always sounds like an insult.

"I have to admit, I was very lucky in the looks department."

"You still are," I assured her.

"Oh, get out of here before my ego inflates. And make sure you buy yourself some Downy fabric softener. Drench your clothes in it."

CHAPTER THIRTY-NINE

The Winter Of My Summer

I had rattled off so many details of my recent life to Terri Tarry, but purposely left out the part about the rainbow vision in the park. I wanted *something* to remain intimate. It was the most intimate moment I ever shared with Jordan. It was like Demi Moore and Patrick Swayze in the movie *Ghost*. Telling Terri would have ruined it. She probably would have said something like: *Most people have similar experiences when they're grieving.*

Not wanting the encounter to be chalked up to a statistic or reduced to a medical term, I filed it in a safe place near the base of my brain.

Although I'd left that first session in good spirits, my mood quickly swayed to sadness while walking down Sansom Street. The thought of visiting my former ballet school ceased, and I did what I usually do in the throes of indefinite emotions: look for Jessie.

The weather was perfectly hot. August in Philadelphia always is. The only thing we can hope for is less humidity so that the heat is bearable. Since the maximum humidity was only forty percent that day (which equals zero clamminess), a local rarity, I left my Jeep in the parking garage and walked over to the Academy. Jessie had to be either there, home, or working in her garden plot.

Upon the approach of Cherry Street, the thought of

entering another brick building on such a perfect day was insufferable. *Jessie would think so, too. She'd take to her garden.* The assumption shifted my gears and set me on another course through town.

Jessie involved herself with a program that was financed by the University of Pennsylvania. It aimed to bring natural beauty back to some of the trash-infested areas of the city. Great efforts were made to clear and divide one such abandoned lot on Spring Garden Avenue. When Jessie heard about it, she applied and was granted access.

On both sides of her oversized, cut-off overalls, two large watering jugs spit water on the ground as she hauled them along a path. She appeared especially radiant with a considerable amount of hair growth. No more blond. Her simple brown and sun-kissed highlights looked a lot like mine, except hers were natural. Mine were from Jackie.

"Hey Jezebelly!" I shouted, walking past the other plots. "Need some help?"

"Sure," she smiled. I could see that her arm was healing. The map of Israel had shrunken down to half its original size. She wasn't surprised to see me. It's as if we're always expecting each other.

"Your arm looks much better," I said.

"Comfrey salve is a miracle. My mother insisted on it."

A big barrel of water sat along the path. Jessie handed me a four-gallon watering jug, and we spent the early afternoon soaking vegetable plants and flowers. The edibles were fattening like well-fed babies. Varieties of peppers, eggplants, tomatoes, and more burst into color. She even had garlic growing in there. I had never seen garlic growing before. The scent of the garden was as heavenly as childhood.

"I feel like writing ... My therapist says I'm supposed to write a lot ... I'm in therapy now ... Dealing with Jordan's death and crap ... Do you have any paper?" I asked. She pulled a few sheets out of her bag and handed me a sketching pencil.

"Your therapist sounds smart. Writing is a great way to work things out – but listen, I promised Sylvester I'd check out his dill. He's only two plots down – Why don't you get started writing, and I'll be back super soon," she said. I agreed and she wandered off.

As the heat of summer sizzled on, I sat in a lotus position in the center of the garden thinking about Terry Tarri's advice. Flowers opened a bit wider. Insects enjoyed their healthy snacks. I wanted to feel at one with nature, but there was a large distance between my desire and my reality. I was in a funk. Alone, I composed in couplets:

> *The winter of my summer has arrived,*
> *Among the leaves of green, as flowers thrive.*
> *Cold icicles have formed around my soul,*
> *Which only you can melt, to thaw my woe.*
> *As berries burst in bloom and fruit trees bear,*
> *The kiss that gave me life's no longer here.*
> *Soft roots of my desire have turned brittle;*
> *A promise once so grand, shows not a little.*
> *The tree of love I climbed – no longer living;*
> *The winter of my summer's unforgiving.*

317

I stopped writing because I couldn't see too well through my tears. Jessie was standing behind me, reading over my shoulder.

"Aw, Brie Cheese … I love you." She sounded like a song. I soaked her suntanned shoulders with my tears and watered the garden once again.

Jessie walked with me to the parking garage. On the way, we stopped in front of a Feather and Leather Shop, studied the contents of the store through the vast window, and were inspired to enter.

Inside the store, the scent of suede massaged my senses. A pair of baby moccasins caught my eyes, reminding me of a shoe I had lost as a child. I picked up the moccasins and decided to buy them.

A woman in the store looked exactly like Mona from behind, except the woman's hair was much longer, looser. She picked out a good length of black, buttery leather. As the salesperson cut the material, the woman turned to look around. "Mona!" I shouted. It was the first time I had ever bumped into her while out and about in the city.

"Hi, Bree. What are *you* doing here?"

"I'm buying these." I held up the moccasins. "Didn't we have shoes like these when we were little?" I asked her.

"*You* did … Mine were different … I think you lost one," she said.

She remembered my lost shoe. The fact that she remembered it was a relief. Mona usually concerned herself with only herself as an adult (and with Steven, of course). But as a child she had concerned herself with me. I was her baby sister. And she remembered.

"I think I lost it at camp and cried for days. I guess it's silly, but I'm buying another pair just for the fun of it. I probably have Cinderella Syndrome or something like that," I said.

"I don't think it's silly at all," she said. And just then, the saleswoman asked Mona if she needed anything else. "Yes ... uh ... I need the same amount of leather in light pink ... natural ... and white."

What's she doing on 11th Street purchasing yards of leather? I wondered. It seemed odd for her – out of character. Mona was the frilly floral type of material girl, not the leather type. She made quilted baby blankets and matching bibs, lacey covers for photo albums, quaint kitchen curtains with corresponding placemats. "Why are you buying all that leather?" I asked.

"I'm making *something* ... Just trying my hand at a few new things." Her tight-lipped tone implied that it was top-secret information.

"Like what?" I pressed.

"You'll see ... If it all turns out the way I want, then I'll show you." I looked down at the moccasin and played around with it a little.

"I hardly recognized you from behind. Your hair got so long – You look different," I said.

"Jackie's responsible for that ... She wouldn't cut my hair the way I wanted her to ... She's so bossy when I'm in her chair ... She definitely likes having the upper hand."

"I know. She got me started on these highlights, and now I'm addicted."

"So am I ... I *never* thought I'd get highlights ...

319

Never … and now I love them." Mona spoke about Jackie without the condescending tenor I had grown accustomed to. They had been at each other's throats for the longest time – decades it seemed.

"Does Steven like your highlights?" I dared to ask.

"At first he was upset – *very* upset. He doesn't want me to change anything about myself."

"They're not *that* drastic," I assured her. "They're really subtle."

"I know … but you know how he is."

The woman behind the counter handed Mona four cumbersome rolls of freshly cut leather. I felt differently about Mona then. Something was different – changed for the long haul. It wasn't awkward seeing her. It was nice. For the first time in a long, long time it was nice.

Jessie and I parted ways with our usual hugs and kisses and I-love-you's and I'll-call-you's.

On the way home, I followed the instructions of my new therapist, and stopped at the market to buy a season's supply of Downy fabric softener. It felt like a mission.

*

"What did the doctor say?" my mother asked. She was busy in the kitchen setting the table for her Mah Jong friends. The clinking of the chunky ivory tiles delighted me as she mixed them up.

"What did *the doctor* say about what?" I asked, clueless. *Terry Tarri isn't even a real doctor*, I thought.

"What do you mean *about what*?" she asked in

320

frustration. "About your panic attacks in the car?" The clinking of the tiles diminished as her French manicure slowed the mix.

Realizing that I hadn't even mentioned my anxiety to Terry Tarri, I felt like an idiot. That was the reason I originally set out for therapy in the first place. I spent an entire hour in her office, but completely forgot to tell her about the way I reacted each and every time I turned onto Route One.

"I guess I forgot to mention it," I admitted.

"How could you forget to mention it? That's why you went there … What's the matter with you?" She shook her head in disgust as her hands mechanically stacked the four tile walls of the game.

The kitchen went through a metamorphosis every third Wednesday of the month, from heart-of-the-house, to side-room-casino. A different tablecloth was laid out. Four ivory-tile walls – that reminded me of the white keys on my father's piano – were built and assembled against four colorful tile holders. Porcelain lotus cups filled with cashews sat beside each holder. Snack tables were opened and loaded with tasty treats that my sisters and I were forbidden to touch: "Don't eat that … it's for *Mahj*," she'd remind us. We always did though. A chocolate pretzel here – A potato chip there. She never noticed, but we had to be careful. It was her sacred ritual.

My father usually spent Mah Jong nights in town at the opera, or he'd go to the local Y center and sit in the steam room. My mother never paid much attention to my sisters or me on Mah Jong nights, so it was with great effort on her part to concern herself with me in the midst of setting up.

"You better call and tell the doctor that you forgot." I thought it was funny the way she kept saying *the doctor*.

"I have another appointment scheduled in two weeks. I'll mention it then."

She turned her back to fill the Mr. Coffee with measured water. Jackpot! I sneaked a bit of raspberry pastry and got out of the kitchen with a puffy mouth.

I was ready to douse my clothes in Downy, and write another poem. This time – Free Verse:

Downy
What other kids' clothing smelled like
'cause mom used Solo
What your mom overused
What I buried my nose in, with each April-fresh
hug
What I buried, when I buried you
What I buy, inhale, and overuse to remember
What lifts me up
What knocks me down
Down to knees
Downy

CHAPTER FORTY

Good and Plenty

"No more walking around with your tits out!" Joe the manager announced from the dressing room door.

In spite of the bust, not much had changed at Studio. Rumor had it that the dancers who were arrested were fighting the charges. Joe the owner was given some type of violation and had to pay a fine. It was business as usual except for the strange feeling I had regarding my situation with Junior. The whole time I was changing in the dressing room, I tried to rehearse what I would say to him once we were face to face. The only problem was, I couldn't concentrate too well. A dancer named Shari was having a problem with her crotch – a very distracting problem:

"Look at this!" she shrieked. "My whole pussy fell out!"

All dressing-room eyes were on her. She stood by the mirror grossly displaying a medical condition between her legs. Shari was the identical twin of Kimmy, but everyone at Studio secretly referred to them as *Dumb and Dumber*. They looked exactly like taller versions of Bette Midler – only their faces were much longer than Bette's. They always worked together. Shari was the one whose crotch fell out.

"Oh my fucking God!" Kimmy shouted. "What the fuck happened to you? That is the most horrifying thing I've ever seen in my life!"

"I'm calling my doctor right now," Shari panicked. "I can't go on stage like this. Everyone's gonna think I have a dick in my panties. They're gonna think I'm a she-male!"

Shari rummaged through her pocketbook for change, dumped it into the payphone, and frantically pushed the numbers with her golden polished daggers. Every dancer in the dressing room couldn't help but take in every word that Shari shouted into the phone.

One girl who was drawing on her lip liner kept messing up and had to wipe it off with a tissue and start over three times until she got it right. Another dancer was rushing into her fishnet stockings and caught her toe in the net, ripping a big hole in it. She gave Shari the evil eye before the phone call was over.

"Hello? ... I need to speak to the doctor! ... I know it's after hours. But I have an emergency! ... It's personal ... Fine ... If you have to relay the message then here it is: My boyfriend was fucking me really hard today, and my whole pussy fell out! And I can't get it back in ... So tell Dr. Seidman that Shari Rivers is having a serious medical emergency! ... What? ... This isn't Dr. Seidman's office? ... This is my dentist's office! ... Dr. McKenna? ... Are you sure? ... Oh Shit! ... I must've called the wrong doctor ... But wait a minute. Has anything like this ever happened to you? ... Hello? ... Hello? ... Bitch! ... *Click* ... That fucking bitch hung up on me!"

Most of the dancers were laughing. Kimmy laughed too.

"It's not funny," Shari panicked. "LOOK AT ME!

What am I gonna do? – Stop laughing, Kimmy!"

"I can't help it," Kimmy said. "That was so funny. You're such an idiot – You called the dentist and asked the answering service lady if her pussy ever fell out – Now that's funny," Kimmy said, still laughing.

"It is not! … I hope the same thing happens to you. I hope *your pussy* falls out!" Shari shouted.

"I can't believe you'd wish that on me, you bitch! I hope you get hit by a Mack truck and your guts spill out all over the road and the vultures peck at your half-dead body –"

"Oh yeah? Well I hope you get cancer and die a slow miserable death and get chemotherapy and all your hair falls out!"

"Oh, whatever … Just give me some mascara."

The twins would get real ugly whenever they argued. They'd say the most horrible of things to each other; then they'd act perfectly normal again. Their carryings on were absurd, but I found them very amusing. They really should have their own show: *The Kimmy and Shari Show.*

There was a new girl in the dressing room that night. She was gorgeous: tall, blond, and built like a brick house. She came forward and introduced herself to Shari:

"Hi, I'm Natasha. I just started working here tonight, and I don't mean to intrude, but I couldn't help overhearing your conversation. I'm pretty sure I can help you out, but first I have to tell you a little secret: My name used to be Scott. I wasn't always a … well … ya know … a woman."

"No fucking way!" Shari gasped.

"I've had a lot of surgery … but I haven't gone through with the *big one* yet, if you know what I mean."

"Wait, I don't get it … what do you mean?" Shari wasn't too quick to pick up on things while applying electric-blue mascara to her eyelashes.

"Okay," Natasha continued, "I'll spell it out for you: I'm getting a penisectomy in two weeks. That's the *big one* –"

"You mean you have a dick? … You're a *man*?" Kimmy asked, screwing the mascara stick back into the container.

"Well, there's still some *man* left on me – but not for much longer. I can't wait to finally get it removed. Keeping it concealed when I'm dancing on stage is such an ordeal. I have to tape it up really well and keep this cheerleading skirt on. But pretty soon, I'll be able to dance like the woman I am – and spread my legs wide open on stage."

Just then I thought of Andrea, and wondered if she was still working her job at the T.L.A. as a penis tucker.

I studied every centimeter of Natasha. There was nothing – and I mean *nothing* masculine about her. No Adam's apple. No harsh jaw line. No broad shoulders. No facial hair. No faint trace of a deep voice. Nothing. It was amazing. All the dancers stood in awe of her, wishing they could transform themselves into their own images of perfection.

"So why *exactly* are you telling me this?" Shari asked Natasha.

"I just wanted to show you how to dance and make

326

tips while you have that load hanging out of your cootchie. Keep your cover-up on and don't spread your legs tonight. It'll probably be back to normal by tomorrow. It's only swollen."

"Oh my God! You're so smart! Thank you so much!" Shari gave Natasha an enthusiastic hug, and got ready to work without a care in the world. Natasha gaited out of the dressing room like an exquisite diva. I got a big kick out of the whole scene. It was like something right out of SCTV.

Junior was particularly affectionate towards me in the DJ booth – grabbing me, kissing me, hugging me. The wet-sock-hanging-from-his-dick image flashed like lightning in my mind. "We have to talk," I said, but he continued gnawing on my neck. And even though the smell of Downy in his clothing was bewitching, I pulled away and managed to spew out my semi-rehearsed lines: "Just listen to me for a minute … We can't be together anymore … This has to end." He frowned like a puppy put out for the night.

"Why?" he asked, raising one ear a bit higher than the other.

"Don't you remember when I told you that I was only interested in you because you reminded me of my friend who passed away?"

"Yeah – I think I recall something about that."

"Well, it was a really bad thing for me to do. It isn't healthy. I started seeing a therapist, and she told me to cut it out – She said it's destructive." Junior's ear was still raised.

"It feels healthy to me," he said with a smile.

"I'm sorry. I really am. But whatever we've started

has to stop. I have to deal with the death of my friend in a more realistic way…"

"But, I love you." His eyes widened.

Holy shit! I thought. *This guy knew from the start that he was my fantasy boyfriend – I was honest with him, and now he's acting as though I'm breaking his heart.*

"Why are you talking about love?" I asked. "What did you think, that we would get married or something?"

"I just want to be with you?" he whispered.

"I'm sorry, Junior – I just can't do this anymore."

Another dancer entered the booth to select a song. I used the opportunity as an exit cue, and avoided the thought of Junior for the rest of the night.

I chose to focus my thoughts on the fact that Natasha was really a she-male. I entertained myself by watching the customers who were especially interested in him/her.

Deception was good and plenty at Studio 67 – Good and plenty.

CHAPTER FORTY-ONE

Ecstasy

The horoscope for Gemini called on all the early summer babies to *buy several pairs of shoes suitable for a variety of moods and functions*. This cosmic shopping spree for new soles was rooted in the belief that footwear had *the potential to bring a person all the way down to earth and become as well grounded as possible*.

I immediately blew the seven hundred bucks I'd earned the night before.

Wine-red cowboy boots, powder-blue hiking boots, and licorice-black motorcycle boots were a good start. Roller Derby roller skates with orange wheels, and a pair of pink ballet slippers were a good finish – except the salespeople always hated it when I paid in ones. They'd give a look of horror as I extracted the loaves of cash from my bag. "You don't mind if I pay in ones, do you?" I'd innocently ask. They'd take the cash, of course. That's their job. But it's always slightly embarrassing – as if the money has the words GO-GO DANCER stamped all over in bold capital letters. Nonetheless, I had to fulfill the prophesy of the week. With that kind of horoscope, it's easy to get carried away.

*

"Do you have anything for me to take to the bank today?" my father asked.

"No," I replied. "I spent it all on shoes."

"On shoes!" he shrieked. "All of it? – How much did they cost?"

"A lot." I didn't volunteer the receipts. He hates when I'm irresponsible with money. I might have been making a fortune, but most of it was sitting in the bank, responsibly earning interest. A lot of the dancers didn't know how to manage their cash. They'd say things like, "I need to make at least six-hundred dollars tonight, so I can make the rent by tomorrow. My landlord's been on my case for two weeks." It was hard to believe how any dancer at Studio could be in desperate need of money when there was so much of it. I was able to save practically all my earnings. But even if I *had* to pay for rent and school combined, I still wouldn't be hurting for cash.

"I bought some roller skates, some boots, a pair of ballet slippers –"

"Ballet slippers?" he interrupted. "What're *they* for?" His curiosity climbed like a cat on an oak.

"I'm thinking about taking ballet lessons again … at The Ballet Studio," I said.

"No kidding! That's terrific! You should *definitely* do that." He was suddenly short of breath. "Sign up as soon as you can … right away. It'll be a wonderful experience … I *mean* it."

Anything that had to do with the arts lit his internal chandelier and sent him beaming. The arts were his passion. The mere mention of ballet slippers had the

330

same effect on him that the lotus flowers had on Odysseus' men. One bite of the spellbinding blossom and they'd forgotten why they were on the island in the first place. One conversation about ballet, and my father's focus of origin was blurred into oblivion. Nothing else mattered. Not money. Not religion. Not time. Nothing stood before the stage – any stage. Whether it was the stage at Carnegie Hall, or the stage at Studio 67, it didn't matter. A stage is a stage is a stage. A gateway to higher meaning. To higher life. An elevated existence. Pure expression. Ecstasy … That's just the way my father thought.

"I have another appointment with my therapist next week … Her office is on the same block as The Ballet Studio. I'll stop in there and make arrangements right after my session," I assured him.

*

We had gone to see The Nutcracker ballet at The Academy of Music on Broad Street when I was a six-year-old, bell-bottom-wearing, shit-kicker-sporting tomboy. The ballet spectacle was an icebreaker in the Yeager household, a turning point in the artistic life of our family. My sisters and I hadn't been the frilly taffeta-and-lace variety of little girls. We were more like boys – rough and tough – passing away the hours of the day piggybacking and punching, wrestling and screaming *Uncle!* We'd play air-hockey, bottle caps, wire-ball, and two-touch with the boys who lived on our street. But when the magical performance of The Nutcracker was over, we had transformed into instant wannabe ballerinas. As soon as we returned home that day, my father went straight to his record album collection and found The Nutcracker Suite. He played it for us on full volume. My sisters and I were entranced. Drunk on the genius of Tchaikovsky – full from the eye candy that fattened our imaginations – we turned spins around the living room – took turns flying up as our father *swooshed* us off our feet and into his arms – into the dreams of angels, fairies, and prima ballerinas.

He signed us up for lessons almost immediately. And for a good many years, we traveled into center city every Saturday morning past the *cloud factories* on Interstate 95 to our destination: The Ballet Studio.

I was probably the most ungraceful ballerina in the whole class. Bored with my cursed inability to dance, I yawned a whole lot during the lessons. Just to keep myself awake, I'd focus on the upright piano in the corner of the studio. A live pianist played all the practice music for the class. I enjoyed watching his fingers skipping along the keys, and I imagined his fingers were little legs, dancing upon an ivory stage.

My skinny legs never did what I wanted them to do, but my sisters were great at it. While practicing leg exercises at the barre, their legs would kick up much higher than mine. Mona's legs would shoot off the floor like fireworks on the Fourth of July. They flew up so high that it appeared to me as though an invisible line connected her foot to her face. Jackie was just as good as Mona. I, on the other hand, could only raise my foot off the ground as high as my knee. I was awful. My sisters were awesome. They eventually went on to point shoes. I went on to replace

Saturday morning ballet class with violin lessons. I was never a dancer – not until Studio.

*

The next time I drove to work, I had my usual panic attack. Only this time, I really was in the wrong lane! A stream of headlights twinkled ahead, growing brighter by the millisecond, and for some strange reason, I was reminded of the lights on Boathouse Row, reflecting in the Schuylkill River against the night's sky. I instinctively slammed on the breaks and turned the steering wheel around so fast and hard that I felt it might fly away. A small antique lamp that I had purchased as a house-warming gift for Jackie was in an open cardboard box on the back seat. The lampshade was made of pale-pink glass and had strands of little glass beads, dangling all around it. The lamp spiraled out of the box and onto the floor, miraculously surviving the fall. I was glad it didn't break, but it took a while for my jitters to subside.

It wasn't a very good night at Studio either. Right before my first set, Sheila offered me some Ecstasy.

"Wanna do some X?" she said.

"Some *what*?" I asked.

"X ... Ecstasy ... Haven't you ever done it before?"

"No ... Never tried it."

"Really? ... It's *great* ... Wanna try some right now?" She reminded me of the kid from the Just-Say-No to drugs commercial: *It'll make you feel good ...*

"What does it do?" I was actually considering.

"It's fantastic! It makes you feel like the world

333

isn't really suffering – like the world's full of love – *exactly* as it should be." Sheila looked kind of sad after delivering her advertisement for Ecstasy. The way her beautiful eyes had changed from shine to mud played a role in my decision about experimenting with a drug named X.

"No thanks – maybe some other time. Right now I *need* to feel the suffering in the world – It enhances my creativity," I said, satisfied with my explanation.

"Suit yourself ... Valentine and the girls should be peaking in about half an hour, but I'm just getting started." Sheila popped a big white pill into her mouth and washed it down with a glass of orange juice.

Beyond marijuana, I never ventured too far into the world of drugs. I had tried cocaine a few times back in high school, but hated the way my nostrils felt after the high was gone – all those rubbery little boogies in exchange for all that cash – it just didn't seem worth it in the end. And there was also the summer of the hallucinogens after eleventh grade: LSD, mushrooms, and peyote buttons. The first time I tripped that June, I was with Jessie. We laughed the entire night. The last time I tripped that August, I sobbed until the night was over. And that was that. Pills, I believed, were strictly for sick people – and Ecstasy was a pill. Sheila was nice, I *guess*, to offer it. She always felt the need to include me in everything because I was Jackie's little sister. And even though Jackie didn't work at Studio anymore, many of the dancers traveled to her salon for all their grooming needs – hair, nails, waxing, make-up ... The Hair Tea Salon had it all.

The Ecstasy Girls were completely preoccupied

with each other on stage that night. They spent more time up there kissing and caressing each other all over the place, than they spent on the floor collecting their tips. It was great for me and the other dancers because the less inhibited the Ecstasy Girls became, the more generous the patrons grew. The more they licked each other up and down, the looser the guys held on to their money. The more they straddled and humped, the larger the wad of cash grew in my hand.

After my fourth set was over, I sat at the bar with Roger, sipping a glass of wine. As Ice-T's vocals sliced the smoky air with rap music, the thunderous rhythms and lightening beats seemed to possess the customers into releasing their money even faster. The energy was pulsating.

As I observed the bacchanalian scene from my barstool, I could see that something was wrong with Valentine – the slow uneven steps of her shoes caught my attention. Exotic dancers usually strut and glide across the stage, but Valentine's heavy-footed limp was more like the walk of a zombie. And just as I noticed it, she came to a complete stop and stood motionless upon the stage. Her eyes crossed even more than usual. I smiled at her, but she didn't smile back. *That's weird. I thought I was her hero. She always smiles at ...* But before I could even finish my thought, Valentine's eyeballs turned up and rolled back into her head. It was a horrifying sight. Her eyeballs looked exactly like the outer whites of two hardboiled eggs. And about a second later or so, she fell straight back ... and passed out. Or so we thought.

Six ecstatic dancers stopped what they were doing

335

on stage and ran over to Valentine. They gently shook her shoulders and tapped her cheeks, but they hadn't yet realized that Valentine wasn't even breathing. Bobbi the Bartender was the first one to figure it out.

People respond differently to death. Some of the girls were screaming. Some were crying. Sheila ran out of the bar. After checking Valentine's pulse, Bobbi's body shook with fright, and her six-inch, dagger-studded fingernails quivered uncontrollably as she placed Valentine's lifeless arm back down. There was still a faint mark on her arm from the IV Demerol. Or maybe it was my imagination.

In the ensuing chaos, Bobbi fainted. She passed out cold on the stage next to Valentine who was getting colder by the second.

I usually spent most of my time at Studio making a conscious effort to avoid Junior. But there I was, guided solely by instinct, running straight into the DJ booth. "Stop the music! Turn on the lights!" I huffed and puffed.

"Are the cops back again?"

"No, it's not the cops." The moment seemed motionless. I felt like I wasn't really a person made of human flesh. Like I was animated – Plastic.

"Is someone dead?" Junior had a sense for death. That's what connected us in the first place. Ever since his baby had died, he knew the signs. He could smell the fear and taste the bitterness in the air.

"It's Valentine … She just *died* … on the stage."

"Shit …" Junior turned off the music and flipped on the house lights. I wanted to close the door and hide inside the DJ booth, just like I'd done when the place got busted. But instead, I returned to my seat at the bar and finished the glass of wine I had started earlier with Roger. He hung around until everyone cleared out. Before he left, he handed me the rest of his wad. "Here you go, hon ... Don't spend it all in one place." He gave me fifteen bills, fifteen hundred dollars – in my hand.

All in all, it was the biggest paying night in my experience at Studio 67. Over twenty-four hundred dollars in just four sets. That's called *Go-Go money*.

*

The back parking lot behind the bar smelled like a skunk. I love the smell of skunk and couldn't resist a quick meditation on it while sitting in the Jeep with the windows down. So I smoked a cigarette and sat in silence and tried to clear my mind before the long ride home ...

Just as I was about to start the engine, the back door of the bar flung open, and Valentine's body came out. She was sealed inside a big black bag. Two men who I didn't recognize held her body high above their heads. I released my fingers from the car key and lit another cigarette ... I thought about Jordan. It pained me to think that he too must have been sealed up in a bag, somewhere in Italy.

I wondered if anyone had noticed the smell of Downy in his clothes. Or if maybe there had been a skunk around, secreting fluid from its anal scent glands. I wondered if someone had been smoking a cigarette nearby. Watching. Thinking about someone they had known ... and loved ... and lost.

CHAPTER FORTY-TWO

Out of Character

Terry Tarri often seemed to get run over by the words that dashed out of my mouth during our sessions. Her extended neck. Her gaping mouth. Her look up to heaven as if to say, *Dear God, please help this suffering soul!*

I thought that therapists were supposed to act as though their clients are perfectly normal – even if they're not – to avoid the potential development of an inferiority complex or something. Terri didn't make me feel normal at all. When I told her about the seven months I'd suffered on Route One, she remained pretty calm, jotting down words on the yellow notepad, nodding to show she was paying attention. But when I spoke of the event where I had finally faced my fear and survived the threat of oncoming traffic, her eyes popped out almost as far as her jaw had dropped below her chin.

"I'm not saying that you need a new job, Bree," she explained. "Exotic dancing has its place in the world, obviously. But I'd like you to consider doing something out of character. Something you wouldn't ordinarily do."

"Dancing is something that I already *do* out of character. I'm totally out of place at Studio."

"Then why are you there? Why do you choose to

earn your money that way?"

"My sister Jackie danced there before she bought the salon. That's where she got the start-up cash. I'm there because of her. Because of the money." I wondered if I sounded like a whore.

"Are you saving the money?"

"Every dollar ... practically. My father hauls it to the bank every week. He did the same for Jackie, and she ended up with a nice piece of chump-change in the end. It's all about the money, really. The smart girls get out of the business as soon as possible." I avoided mentioning the downside of dancing that affects people like Sheila and Valentine, people who don't know how to handle it. The glamorous side of the business was much more appealing. "One girl opened a bridal shop not too long ago. I hear she's doing very well."

"What are *your* plans for the money?"

"I don't know – Jackie didn't know either. But when my father told her how much had accumulated in the bank, she figured it out right away. She knew exactly what to do with it. I guess I'll figure it out too one day. I just don't know yet. I haven't even thought about it."

"What does your other sister do?"

"Mona?" Not in the habit of discussing Mona with anyone, *ever*, I was surprised by the question. "Mona works in a marketing agency and pretty much keeps to herself. Her whole life revolves around her husband Steven ... and that leaves her at a distance. She won't even let me try to get close to her. The one time I tried to confide in her, she freaked out. She wouldn't even listen to what I had to say. She hung up on me."

Discussing Mona, even the slightest bit, stirred a hot pot of emotions. I could feel my balance tilting like someone about to fall off a tightrope. It was obvious that Terry Tarri sensed it as she leaned in a little closer. She had hammered the dysfunctional family nail right on the head – right between my eyes.

"I take it that Jackie has always been your role model."

"You can pretty much say that. But don't get me wrong. I'm my own person. Jackie and I aren't *exactly* alike. We have different taste in men and music and other things, too. But we've always been very close, like peanut butter and jelly. Mona's more like grilled cheese."

"I know this is going to sound strange to you, but I want you to do something that Mona would do. When you're faced with a choice … when you have to make a decision sometime in the near future … think of Mona. Think about what Mona would do, and do it. But try not to think about it too much. Don't work your mind into a quandary. Let it happen naturally."

"Why? Why should I do what *Mona* would do?" It didn't make any sense. I started feeling really uncomfortable, disgusted.

"It's an out-of-character exercise," she explained. "The reason for doing it doesn't matter right now. The important thing is that you stay on the right side of the road, away from oncoming traffic."

What does driving in the wrong lane have to do with Mona? I wondered. *Terry Tarri's a quack. This therapy crap is bullshit.* "Okay, I'll try," I agreed. She

340

sensed my discomfort and quickly changed the subject.

"Have you started communicating with your friend, Jordan?"

"Oh, yeah." I had almost forgotten. "I wrote this poem last week." I pulled out *The Winter of My Summer* from my army bag and handed it over. The paper had gotten crumpled by then. As Terry read it, her mouth kept opening and closing like subway doors letting passengers on and off. I could tell she read it twice, as my eyes followed hers and their place on every line. Once again, she gave me the You're-Not-A-Normal-Person look.

"This is sensational!" she gasped.

Bullshit, I thought. *You're so full of it. You're only saying that to keep me happy. To keep me coming back for another session so you'll get paid.* "Really?" I asked, examining her nautical-blue eyes, trying to detect the tails of deceit swimming around in them.

"Yes, really. I've read a lot of poetry. I've got volumes full of it." She pointed at the bookshelf to her left. "Actually, I used to write some when I was younger, much younger. Especially around the time I was going through my divorce ... What was it like for you while you were writing? What did you feel?"

"It felt good to write," I admitted.

"Keep writing. You're a natural."

"Okay."

I couldn't tell if she was lying or not. I'd make a horrible FBI agent.

CHAPTER FORTY-THREE

Pressure

The Ballet Studio still smelled fresh, like Murphy's Oil Soap. All the same people continued to work there except for Ruth the receptionist and the guy who played the piano. I remember Ruth well because she had commented on my chin. "You have a perfect chin," she would say. "Your sisters aren't as lucky as you because they don't have your chin." I didn't know what a perfect chin was, but it sure sounded good to have one.

Even though there was another guy playing the piano, it was still overflowing with sheet music. I watched the way this new pianist's fingers danced along the keys. The little legs I used to imagine were no longer there. Instead, a set of tan, muscular fingers put me into a kind of trance. They were thick with hair. But not the hairy fingers of a werewolf, sprouting thin straggly hairs under a full moon. His finger hair was thick, short, black, and cottony. And the sight of these particular fingers had such an effect on me that I could not remember anything else I had seen in The Ballet Studio thereafter that morning.

Were the mirrors the same as they had been? Had the instructors aged much? Did the floors remain in good shape? Were the little ballerina teddy bears still for sale at the front desk? I tried to recall.

I filled out some papers and signed up for Tuesday night adult-beginner classes. But other than that, my memory cabinet only filed his piano fingers. His strong, tan, hairy, fingers.

*

I drove over for a quick visit to The Hair Tea Salon. It was well worth the trip because, in addition to a meal of sushi that Jackie and I shared for lunch in the back room, she treated me to a spa pedicure (*ahhh!*). It was heavenly. Then I drove over to Temple University and entered the hellish task of registering for my fall semester courses.

The eyes of summer were about to blink into autumn while my eyes were tangled in a long list of college courses. It took me the rest of the afternoon to register. I had waited much too long, and every time I submitted my schedule, the person on staff would inform me that this or that course was already full. Then I'd have to start the whole process over again. I submitted five or six different schedules before I was able to complete my roster.

Since I couldn't sign up for all the classes I had originally wanted, a small dilemma crept in on me. I had to choose from a hodgepodge of courses with which I was completely unfamiliar, and make a quick decision. Terry Tarri's assignment had edged its way into my life much sooner than I anticipated. To *deliberately* do something that Mona would do was as great a task for me as shifting the mighty stones of the ancient pyramids. But somehow a butter knife found its way in between, and I did it. I registered for a course in marketing: Marketing Strategy, an act completely out of character. Even though I had my doubts about Terry's assignment, I was never one to avoid homework.

I thought hard about it and wondered if I'd gain anything of value from this strange selection of courses. Was there any merit in trying something new that seemed to be totally futile? I thought about the time that Nanette drank a cup of hair tea to cure her leukemia. How on earth did making tea out of hair prove to be the solution to her problem? Drinking hair tea seemed to be as ridiculous a task as my registering for a course in Marketing Strategy. Upon these thoughts, I concluded that anything could be a potential cure for any problem. Nanette didn't question it. She just did what she was told to do. No matter how absurd the assignment seemed, she took a leap of faith and did her homework. She made the hair tea and drank it up. Did she really think it would work?

I decided to give my out-of-character assignment a wholehearted chance. Maybe Terry Tarri knew where the unlikely solutions were hiding. Maybe a Marketing Strategy class would be the key to my future.

*

It was Tuesday night, and because the ladies had decided to switch evenings, the kitchen was set for *Mahj*. The Mahj Jong crew focused on the tiles, calling out their random names in their northeast Philly accents: "Two Bam" … "Five Dot" … Flower"

... "East" ... "Red" ... "That's it!" ... "Mahj!" ...
"Oh shit!" ... clink, clink ... shuffle, shuffle ... rotate
seats around the table ... pour the coffee ... grab a
snack ... run to the bathroom ... start all over ...

I always got a kick out of their staged routine.

My father came into the kitchen. "I'm taking a ride over to Mona's. Want to come with?" he asked me.

"Sure," I answered. It had been ages since I'd been to Mona's house.

We arrived and were immediately enchanted by the pink and red roses in bloom on the fence by the entrance, sautéing the air with wide-open daydreams.

Inside the house, Mona was the gracious hostess. She served tea with lemon slices (that's how everyone in my family drinks tea) and Pepperidge Farm assorted cookies. For some reason, her high school yearbook was on the kitchen counter. I picked it up and thumbed through the pages.

There she was – Mona Yeager: Feature Majorette – leading the marching band around the football field at half time, wearing a skimpy, sequined bodysuit in the middle of winter. I had forgotten how bold she had been. "How did you stay warm?" I asked.

"I just didn't think about it. I was so worried about doing perfect cartwheels and keeping the baton up. The weather wasn't an issue."

It was a different Mona in those black-and-white yearbook photos. A Mona who had faded away, it seemed. At one time, her hands had had an intimate relationship with her baton, weaving it in and out of her fingers so fast that the intricate action was not detectable by the human eye. The baton was an extension of her enigmatic character. It had been a weapon the time she got into a fight with our neighbor Paula. Mona had kept it in the umbrella stand, and Jackie and I weren't allowed to touch it. The baton was her sacred object, her instrument, her magic wand. And now – it was just a piece of her past.

In her yearbook photos, wearing her sexy little costume, she looked good enough to be up on stage at Studio 67. *It could be her gimmick*, I thought. *I had never seen a majorette gimmick on stage. The guys would go wild for it. A dancer with a baton would certainly rile the crowd.* I was really enjoying my thoughts, the tea, and the conversation when all of the sudden, all attention was thrust upon Steven.

"Look at your husband," my father beamed. Steven was sipping tea from a hole in the nipple of a ceramic mug that was shaped like a giant tit. As we sat around the kitchen table, discussing Mona's baton, Steven had been standing by the stove, nonchalantly sipping the nipple mug, waiting for someone to notice.

Mona giggled. Her laughter sounded like a succession of hiccups.

"Nice mug," I said.

"It's for those long, lonely nights when Mona says she has a headache and won't put out." Steven got such a kick out of himself. Mona did as well and started up the hiccup laughter again. My father shook his head while snorting through his laughter. He gets a bang out of any joke that involves a sexual reference.

But humor is a double-edged sword for Steven. He has his own ideas about what's funny and what's not. He sure didn't think that go-go dancing was funny when it hit so close to home. According to him, *it's not a way to earn* clean *money*, and I can understand his point to some extent, but I'm opposed to the way he judges the people who earn it honestly, the dancers who rely on it to give their children a better life, like Janina and Cricket. I can't accept the way that Steven stereotypes all go-go money as dirty. Every situation is different. I mean, what if the world were to shrink down to just Steven, at that very moment, sipping tea from a tit mug? Would anyone truly have the ability to judge his character? Of course not. It's the same thing, really.

Steven thinks very highly of himself and looks down his nose at others. He thinks he's better than everyone. I hate it when he brings up the fact that Jackie used to be a go-go dancer (which he manages to do at the most inappropriate of times) and makes comments about her salon and how she got it by "shaking her tits."

When the subject of Jackie's salon came up that evening, Mona impressed me by arguing on Jackie's behalf: "What's the difference where the money came from? Jackie earned it. And now she has something to show for it. It's not like she committed a crime …"

Unbelievable! I thought. *Absolutely unbelievable!* Mona had actually disagreed with her husband. Ever since the day she met him, she had conformed to his idea of perfection. But here, on this point, on the honor of her sister, she seemed to be unraveling.

And there was Steven, drinking tea from a tit at the kitchen table. I felt uncomfortable, probably because I was a go-go dancer, so I made small talk (Steven style) to mask my frustration.

"Hey Steven. Maybe I'll get you a blow-up doll for your next birthday, for those long lonely nights you were talking about –"

"Make sure it's a blond ... With big boobs," he replied.

"Bigger than Mona's –" I asked.

"My boobs aren't *that* big." Mona had always hated her large D cups. When her breasts started developing, she wore oversized sweaters and brought her shoulders forward so that no one could see them. She even wore a T-shirt over her bathing suit in the pool at the swim club.

It was all right kidding around with Mona and Steven on *their* terms, as long as *they* initiated the fun. Tit mugs and big boobs were topics that Steven had brought up. But as soon as I had something to say about it, they didn't enjoy it so much.

"Well, they look pretty big to me, Mona ... Don't you think so, dad?" I loved plowing into her sensitive issues. She really brings out the worst in me.

"I don't know," my father muttered.

"Well, they're the same size as mommy's –"

"Could we *please* talk about something else?" Mona screeched. It was fun watching her freak out, but she never knows how to snap out of it and start having fun again. She's a real nut sometimes. I swear she is.

I tried to smooth things over by asking her to show me the stuff she'd been working on. Mona usually loved to show off her latest projects in her workroom in the basement. But she wouldn't show me anything.

"*Come on*," I whined, "Let me see what you're working on."

"I'm not ready to show *anyone* my new line –"

"I'm not just *anyone* – I'm your sister," I reminded her.

"I didn't even show Steven yet." Mona started to whisper.

"*Oh*," I whispered back.

I wanted to be closer to Mona. I wanted to tell her all about my marketing class. About The Ballet Studio and the painting studio. About Studio 67. About Terry Tarri. About everything. But I couldn't. She was a woman, but she was more like a child – like someone who needed to be shielded from the realities of adulthood. She acted as though she had grown up in some type of enchanted fairyland where pain didn't exist – as though roses didn't have thorns – as though she was a stranger to the ways of her own family.

She's not a stranger … She's not the stranger … She's just gotten *stranger*, I thought, trying to convince myself that we really were sisters. There was so much distance between us, like we were on opposite sides of a pole. The more I thought about it, the more I remembered that we had been close during a special time in our lives – during childhood. We had bathed together, slept together, even shit on the same toilet together. We played house, library, and doctor. We rode bikes, hopped on pogo sticks, and raced on roller skates. We had a pure closeness then. Now she wouldn't even show me what was in her closet. Now she was older, hiding behind her big tits. Hiding from her role as my sister …

349

… But then again, there was that one instance that evening when she came to Jackie's defense. It made me wonder if she might also be in therapy, completing an out-of-character assignment.

Is she trying to emerge from her shell? Will she ever be the bold and beautiful feature majorette again?

Steven popped a Billy Joel cassette into the stereo. The Nylon Curtain. *Pressure* was on.

CHAPTER FORTY-FOUR

A Broken Doll

There was a fight at Studio. A dancer named Joelle had just returned from a trip to Cancun. Joelle was a half-Italian, half-Black Philly chick with a perfect body and cute little Shirley Temple dimples. When she wasn't suntanned, she looked more like the Italian side of her heritage. But after she got back from cooking her skin to a dark brown in the Mexican sun, everyone noticed the change.

"You look just like a *nigger*!" shouted Tex in her southern accent. The word *nigger* rolled off her tongue as smooth as metal.

"I'm Black!" Joelle retorted, reddening through her tan.

"You are?" Tex asked.

"Yes ... my father's Black."

"I'm so sorry. I didn't know," Tex apologized.

"Sorry for what? For calling me a *nigger* to my face instead of behind my back, you fucking bitch!"

I really din't mean anythin' by it, honest."

"Oh, so you use the word *nigger* as though it doesn't mean anything. You know what you are? You're a white bitch. A white racist bitch!"

"Fuck you, Joelle. I said I din't mean any harm by it."

"Fuck me? FUCK YOU!" Joelle's tropical tan

mixed with the red of her blood, boiling just beneath the surface. I pulled her out of the dressing room before it got really ugly.

"She's not worth it, Joelle. Forget her. She's a stupid redneck."

"I really wanna mess her up, right now … I'm raging! … She makes me sick … How *dare* she talk like that? … Who does she think she is? … No one around here talks like that …"

"Just ignore her. Remember why you're here. Get the money and get out. Everything else is just bullshit." I sounded just like my father.

"Yeah? Well, you say that now, but if she made a nasty comment about Jews, then it would be me, pulling you, off her."

"Please do – if it ever comes to that."

I loved Joelle. She was funny. We always had a good time working together.

A little later on, I finished a set early because my ass was killing me. I had worn my red cowboy boots when I came into work, and decided to dance in them. I wanted to look like a cowgirl. It was an obnoxious thing to do because Tex was the one who dressed like a cowgirl on stage. Other girls would wear western-style costumes from time to time, but Tex was the only dancer who sported the boots. It was her Texan gimmick.

I went up on stage in Jackie's cowboy hat, a fringy two-piece, and my new red boots. Not used to dancing in almost-flat heels, I did a high kick and landed exactly on my ass. *Ouch!* Amazingly enough, no one seemed to notice – except Joelle.

"Are you all right?" she asked.

"I am … but my ass isn't."

"Let's get high," she suggested. "I have some pot in my bag."

"You do?"

"Yeah … it's the Mexican goods. Let's go in the dressing room."

"That's not really a good idea. Ever since the place got busted, Joe's been nuts. Sometimes he barges in there just to see what's going on. We should smoke in my Jeep."

"But we can't just *leave*. Can we?"

"I'll talk to Joe."

I knocked on the office door. Joe opened it. Bobbi the Bartender sat in the corner, filing her daggers.

"Can I leave for a few minutes … to get some McDonalds? … I'm starving," I said.

"Why don't you just order something from the kitchen?" Bobbi suggested.

"I was thinking about doing that … and then I was talking to Joelle. She just got back from Cancun and she's craving McDonalds. She's going through fast-food withdrawal, big time. And while she was talking about it, she put me in the mood for it, too … So, can we go? … *Please*?" I was begging.

"Oh, first it's *Can I go*? Then it's *Can we go*?" Joe was on to me.

Just let 'em go," Bobbi said, still focused on sharpening her claws.

"Fine. But do me a favor … Pick me up a burger and some fries … And hurry the hell back!" he yelled.

"We will," I said.

353

Joelle drove. She had a little red Corvette from the '80s. It was low to the ground, like a racecar. A dancer named Katie wanted to buy it from Joelle in the worst way. Katie collected Corvettes. That's what she did with her dancing money. Her husband built a whole bunch of garages on their property to protect her collection. She had wallet photos of her Corvettes, and she'd show them off like a proud mother of octuplets.

Katie looked exactly like a heavy-metal poster child with teased-out blond hair that exuded the horrible odor of too much Aqua Net hairspray. She wore stonewashed stretch jeans that had matching vests. She wore blue eyeliner, blue eye shadow, and blue mascara in shades around her eyes. At first, I thought it was an '80s blue gimmick or something, but then I came to understand that it was her style (or lack thereof). She was stuck in a fad that had come and gone, and she was addicted to Corvettes.

"Are you selling this car to Katie?" I asked.

"She made me an offer, but I'm still thinking about it. I love this car. I never thought I'd have a little red Corvette." Joelle started singing the Prince song like a maniac. I accompanied her the best I could. Singing is not my talent. My mother is completely tone deaf, and I believe I inherited a fraction of her disability. But I'm not as bad as she is because of all the aural theory training I'd had in music school. At least I could hit Prince's *Ooh - hooh – hoohs* in tune.

Joelle handed me a small wooden pipe. I puffed on it two times before entering inner space, high as a twinkling star. Each slight motion was magnified. The pattern of my breathing and the beating of my heart intensified. I lit one of Joelle's Parliament cigarettes. I normally hate Parliaments, but, at the time, it tasted just like a Marlboro. That's how high I was.

We probably should've gotten the food *before* we smoked the Mexican goods and mixed up the puzzle pieces of our brains, because neither of us could remember where McDonalds was located. We had already taken a wrong turn. Joelle didn't want to get lost, so we returned to Studio empty handed. No burgers. No fries. Joelle pulled into the back lot.

"Do my eyes look high?" she asked.

I gave a look. One eye was open, glassy and pink. The other was more than half-closed, glassy and pink. She looked like the broken baby doll I got as a gift for my fourth birthday. The doll came along with a swinging wooden cradle, and it had big blue eyes that opened and closed. I played with "Dolly" so much that it broke, and one of the eyes wouldn't open up all the way unless I forced it to.

"Your eyes look fine," I lied. I couldn't tell Joelle that she looked like my broken doll. I didn't want to make her paranoid about her cockeye.

I knocked on Joe's door again. Bobbi was still in the corner.

"Where the hell's my burger?" he asked in his pompous way.

"We couldn't find the McDonalds," I confessed.

"Whaddya mean? It's right up the road. You can practically see the golden arches from here," Bobbi said.

"Joelle was driving, and I didn't pay attention to

where she was going."

"Are you *high*?" Bobbi asked, focusing on my eyes.

"No?" I answered, unsure.

"She's high," Bobbi decided. "Look at 'er eyes."

"I am not," I laughed. I must have looked higher than the Eiffel Tower.

"Just get back to work," Joe said. "And stop smoking that shit!" He smacked my ass. It hurt like hell because he smacked it exactly on the spot where I had fallen earlier.

By the time I returned to the dressing room, it was too late to save Joelle again. Tex had her finger firmly rooted in a dispenser of mace pepper spray, aimed directly at Joelle's broken doll face. It was a mess. No one got fired though, only sent home for the night.

The rest of us had to move all our stuff into the storage room downstairs. The dressing room was off limits. No one could breath in there. The storage room wasn't much better. It was cold and there weren't any mirrors.

Nonetheless, I still enjoyed my high for the night.

CHAPTER FORTY-FIVE

Sigmund Freud Lives On

A local weather station reported it to be the coldest November in over forty years. Not only was it cold on the outside part of my life, it was pretty iced up on the inside as well. No matter how many tasks I engaged to remain upbeat, something was missing. I had been enjoying my courses, writing inspirational poems and letters to Jordan, making pocketbook loads of cash at Studio 67, and dancing with grace at The Ballet Studio. But none of this truly warmed me.

Then one day, just as I had accepted my frozen state of being, my hot spot was hit in the strangest of places by the oddest of people. It was the pianist – the piano man. I had never spoken to him, or heard his voice, or even looked past his fingers. So when our eyes finally did meet, the spark was startling. His dark piercing eyes were like laser beams, slowly melting my frozen core.

An hour of adult-beginner ballet classes, followed by an hour of therapy, had become the pattern of my Tuesday night schedule on Sansom Street. Thanks to all the dancing experience I'd acquired at Studio 67, my performance reached a crowning point in ballet class. My kicks and jumps were higher than ever. My posture was poised with precision. But above all physical means, my spirit soared out of the cold place it had been lurking. I reached new heights, and strangely, it had something to do with the pianist in the corner. I couldn't keep my eyes from wandering his way every ten seconds. It was history repeating itself, only better.

There was also something else I couldn't help staring at in The Ballet Studio. One of the male students only had one arm. Whenever the class was doing barre exercises facing the window, he'd hold onto the barre with his long arm while his fleshy nub stuck out of his shoulder, moving around in whatever position the teacher directed us to follow. I couldn't stop myself from focusing on the nub. A pattern of synchronized arms, all moving gracefully together in a row – up, down, in, out – was broken by a fleshy nub, creating the appearance of a giant wounded octopus. Whenever I caught myself staring at the nub for too long, I'd look at the place in the mirror where I could see the pianist. Sometimes he'd be looking at the place in the mirror where he could see me. Our eyes would lock. I'd always turn away first. It was awkward. Warm and awkward.

Back in the dressing room, a small refrigerator was stocked with green bottles of Perrier, just as it had been over a decade ago. As a child, I felt as though its purported "50 million" tiny bubbles were biting my throat, and I couldn't drink it. Now the Perrier revived me. The change was strikingly satisfying.

This wonderful sensation is part of my coming full circle, I thought. *There are small signs along the quest of making sense out of chaos, of finding meaning in my life. It's like reading a treasure map, and I have to decipher the clues. Water - even carbonated water - has a way of transporting the soul...*

Upon this revelation, one of my classmates decided to jump-start a conversation. The trouble with me is that someone will be speaking, and I won't even know that it's me they're talking to because I'm too busy talking to myself (but not out loud, of course.) It's just that there are times when my thoughts are screaming. After the last of the 50-million bubbles was cruising down my throat, I realized that she had been asking me the same question three or four times: "How long have you been a dancer?" she repeated.

"Who me?" I spun around, pointing to my chest.

"Yes," she smiled.

"What makes you think I'm a dancer?" I grew paranoid. When she said the word *dancer*, I interpreted it *as go-go dancer*.

"Your leg muscles are so cut," she clarified.

"Oh," I sighed, relieved. I wasn't about to start advertising my secret profession. It's not something you want people to know about you, especially people you've just met.

"I'm not really a dancer," I lied. "I do a lot of roller skating." I hadn't even taken the skates out of the box yet.

"Well, I hope that these classes will get me in half the shape you're in," she said.

"Thanks. You'll get there." I felt bad saying it, but she really was out of shape. Her legs were full of spider veins, and she looked so soft and doughy.

"My name's Vera." She extended her doughy,

white hand.

"I'm Bree. Nice to meet you."

I rushed out of there because I didn't want to be late for my appointment with Terry Tarri. I practically broke my neck on the way up to her office. Not very graceful for a ballerina.

"I want him *sooooo* bad," I whined, plopping onto the sofa.

"Who?" she asked.

"The piano player, who plays for my ballet class."

"Oh yeah? What's his name?" she asked.

"I don't know. It doesn't even matter. All I know is that when he looks at me, I'm on fire." I closed my eyes and imagined his eyes in the mirror.

"Hold on. Slow down. Let's be realistic for a moment. You don't know anything about him, starting with his name. Take away the fire, and what are you left with? That's what you need to ask yourself when you enter a new relationship. You're not a teenager anymore, Bree. If you want to build meaningful relationships, you're going to have to look beyond the fire. Start by finding out his name and whether or not you have similar interests."

"Oh, that's easy. He plays the piano. We already have classical music in common," I said.

"That's a good start. What else?"

"I don't know. I've never even spoken to him."

"The best advice I can give you is this: Turn down the flame! I know it sounds difficult, but your prior record in the world of relationships is a hazard zone … a burnt piece of toast …" Terry Tarri wasn't yelling, but she sounded like a preacher. "It's time to

360

be wiser. Time to avoid making the same mistakes."

"So, what should I do?"

"First of all, get to know him. Find out his name. What he wants in life. See if you have similar goals. Find out about his childhood. What his family is like? What was his mother's role in the house? His father's? Did his parents get along? Or did they co-exist out of habit rather than love?"

"I need to know all that? It seems like too much. I just want to feel my skin melting under his piano fingers," I said dreamily.

"If you don't follow my advice, then I can't help you." She was giving up on me. I looked at the dream catcher on the wall.

"I'll try my best," I said.

"If you don't, you probably end up where you started, and we'll have to begin *all* over again."

"Are you sure you know what you're talking about? What does his childhood have to do with anything?" I asked.

"Bree," she explained, "We size up the people we meet, and we're not even aware of it. There's a hidden computer in the base of the brain called the subconscious mind. It's working all the time, even while you're sleeping. You're just not aware of it. Every single moment of your life is recorded and stored there. It's where your memories live, but you just can't access them.

"Think about the colors of the spectrum. They surround us all the time, but we don't see them. Then, every once in a while, a rainbow appears in the sky. Or the colors are reflected in a gasoline puddle. Or a crystal chandelier throws prisms all over the place when the sun hits it just so. The subconscious is present all the time like the colors of the spectrum that surround us. Just because we don't see it, doesn't mean it isn't there."

I recalled the vision I had seen in Rittenhouse Square Park: the numerous rainbows, Jordan's voice. Terry's words fed my theory about noticing the signs on the way to discovering one's self. It was the same feeling I had earlier while drinking the Perrier. I perked right up like a dog anticipating a bone.

She continued, "The piano player, so far, fits your subconscious notion of family and companionship. He already reminds you of either your mother or your father for some reason. That's what we humans do. We fall in love with the people who enable us to recreate our own families."

"Holy shit! That's incredible! My father plays the piano. He's been playing my whole life."

I was amazed by the truth of Terry's insight. It was the first time during all our sessions together that I felt completely intrigued. It was the type of therapy I had expected from the get go. I'd been craving this moment. I'd been yearning to cross over bridges in my mind, to connect the present with the past. She was giving me the groundbreaking news report I'd been waiting for. But what was she saying?

"Are you saying that I'm subconsciously in love with my father? What is this, therapy or mythology?" I asked.

She laughed a bit. "Let's just say that all the positive and negative characteristics of *both* your parents are what your subconscious mind seeks out while sizing someone up, *after* you're already physically attracted. The physical attraction comes first. If it turns out that this pianist happens to be addicted to game shows, it won't be a characteristic that will turn you away from the relationship, even though it's a quality you find annoying in your mother. It'll actually make you feel safer and more at home."

"Wow. This is really wild stuff," I said.

"It's also sad stuff. Why do you think women who were abused by their fathers often end up with abusive husbands? And it goes the other way, too. Men who were pushed around by domineering mothers often end up with bossy, nagging wives?"

"Okay, but why would anyone *choose* to recreate a painful past, on purpose?"

"Because it's not a conscious choice!" Terry beamed. I could tell she was getting off on all this enlightening information. "The subconscious mind desires to reconcile the problems of childhood. And the only way to reconcile a situation is to recreate it."

Wow!" I said the word *wow* in a way that strangely reminded of Niomi from the health food store. "Wait ... Let me get this straight," I continued, "I can analyze every little detail of someone's life and possibly gain a deeper understanding of what attracted me in the first place, but how will I know if that person really loves me? How will I know if they dig me for who I am? What if I'm just a part of a painful past that they'd be better off without?"

At this question Terry's eyes widened. "That's the

catch, Bree. There's always a catch. Unfortunately, you can't know it all. Love's a risk. That's the bottom line. You can only try to make sound choices and avoid disaster."

I left her office more confused than ever. It was as if a thousand-piece puzzle scattered in front of me, and only two pieces had been connected. I had nine hundred and ninety-eight pieces to go. That's what I was thinking about when I walked past The Ballet Studio on the way to the Jeep, and strangely enough, the pianist was standing on the corner. My ears turned red when I spotted him. My air supply snapped in half.

"Hey," I said. "I'm Bree. I dance in the class you play for."

"Hello." He spoke with a slight Russian accent. "I'm Dimitri. Nice to meet you."

"Are you waiting for someone?" I asked.

"My sister was supposed to pick me up half an hour ago. I guess she is running late. She teaches violin over in Jersey," he said. I liked the way his lips formed each word, spraying steam into the space between us. I tried to focus on what he was saying. I needed to control myself.

"I used to be a violin major," I said, casually. "I recently changed majors."

"Why is that?"

"I had a bad experience with my teacher. And anyway, I wanted to learn about other things. The music curriculum's so limited. I need more in my life right now. Maybe I'll get back to it one day. Who knows?"

"What other courses have you taken?" He seemed genuinely interested.

"Painting with oils was a blast. And Shakespeare 101 was phenomenal." My senses were doing a tango as I spoke about these subjects.

"Did you study any of Shakespeare's sonnets?" he asked.

"Of course!" I gleamed.

"Which was your favorite?" I couldn't believe I was having this particular conversation with this particular piano man. I had waited so long to hear his voice, but I never imagined what words would come out of his mouth.

"I have a lot of favorites. Do you know the one about the piano player?" I asked.

"I'm not sure. Tell me about it," he smiled. *Nice smile. Nice teeth*, I thought.

"Well, it's about two people. The speaker's a woman, and she watches a man as he plays the piano. She starts wishing she could trade places with the keys of the piano, so that he would touch *her* rather than the keys. It starts off with the lines, 'How oft, when thou, my music, music play'st / Upon that blesse'd wood whose motion sounds...'" I quoted these specific lines. And knew it was a flirtatious thing to do, but that's the point. And anyhow, it really was the sonnet that naturally came to mind at the time. It's not as though I had planned this conversation. But I knew that Terry Tarri would probably tell me that I was being too forward, to tone it down a notch.

"Shakespeare wrote in the voice of a woman?" he asked.

"Uh-huh. That's why some people think he was gay … but wait a minute. Hmm. I might be mistaken. Now that I think about it, I can't honestly remember if that sonnet was in the voice of a female … or if maybe it was another one. I have to check."

I immediately recognized my Freudian slip. I had internalized the poem. I was the female who watched a man playing the piano. I was the female who wanted to change places with the piano. To be touched by his fingers. To be the instrument upon which he created music. I wondered if Dimitri could sense it.

"Do you still play the violin?" he asked.

"Sometimes."

"What was the last piece you worked on?"

"The Bruch Violin Concerto in g minor."

"You must be good. That is a challenging piece."

"It sounds impressive, but Bruch really knew how to write for the violin. The runs are actually quite natural for the fingers, so it's not as challenging as it sounds."

There was a brief comfortable silence between us, and I was on fire again. It was worse than it had been in The Ballet Studio. Now it was more than his eyes and more than his fingers that fueled my fire. Now it was his voice and his interests, his mannerisms, and the way his loose curls bounced a bit when he spoke. My heated attraction multiplied by the second. I had to break the silence before I lost control, before I turned into an animal in heat.

"So, where do you live?" I asked.

"In the Northeast."

"Oh yeah? So do I! Is that where you're heading?"

"Yes, I am on my way home."

"I can give you a ride if you want. I'm parked up the street."

"That would be great."

"What about your sister?"

"Oh, she will figure it out."

On the way home, I learned that Dimitri was twenty-eight years old. His car was being repaired. He had come over from Russia when he was fourteen. He still lived with his parents and his sister. He loved his mother's cooking. He never used contractions when he spoke. (For example, he said *I am* but never said *I'm*.) His family isn't particularly religious, but he has a Jewish background. He impressively graduated from the Curtis Institute of Music and has mastered several instruments. He currently composes contemporary music, teaches music at a few private schools, and plays for The Ballet Studio (obviously). He volunteers as the conductor of a local orchestra that rehearses at the Y center in Northeast Philly – the same Y center where my father goes to swim and exercise. And, most surprisingly, he lives about ten minutes from my house.

Intense word play and a bit of playfulness went a long way in the warm space of the front power seats. The chemistry between us began to freely run its course. It was a good thing I had to concentrate on driving; the road kept me focused on Terry's advice.

When I got home, my father was sitting in his underwear, playing the piano. I couldn't even look.

CHAPTER FORTY-SIX

Deathday Cards - Notes To The Grave

By the time Dimitri finally asked me out on a date that semester, I had already written twenty-four poems and thirty-eight letters to Jordan. I thought that Dimitri would have asked me sooner, and my patience tested me from time to time. Twice I'd been on the verge of inviting him to join me for dinner or a movie, but I always stopped myself at the very last minute. There was no need to push it for a few important reasons: For one, I continued to experience immense satisfaction from the feeling that flared up every time our eyes met in the mirror during ballet class. And each time I stared at his strong dark fingers dancing along the keyboard, I was content. But above all, I didn't want to scare him away and ruin it all by coming on too strong. I guess that Terry Tarri had convinced me to be a patient mental patient at last. It wasn't until fall semester midterms had concluded that Dimitri finally asked me out on a date.

I waited by the living-room window and watched as he approached my house. I grabbed my jacket and ran out before he had a chance to get to the front door. I wasn't ready to let him into my house for fear that I'd take him into my bedroom and lose all control of my libido.

We ate dinner at my favorite restaurant, *Kawabata*, the only Japanese restaurant in my neighborhood. We sat comfortably on floor cushions and started our meal with Ikura; black seaweed rolls filled half with rice and half with caviar. The plump little salmon eggs sparkled like red and orange lights on the table. Dimitri did most of the talking. I enjoyed listening to his voice, as his rhythmic phrasing sounded like a musical masterpiece to me.

I couldn't figure out what I liked more, listening to his voice, or watching him speak. The way that he wrapped his soft, full lips around the food – and the way that a tiny trace of a single fish egg clung to his lower lip and glistened as he spoke – made me want to kiss him in the most passionate way possible. But even more than these things that physically attracted me to him, I was interested in what he had to say. I was taken in by all of it.

He spoke about the salmon. He said that the fish itself is associated with wisdom, and he told me a story about an old Irish myth that claims the salmon fish would grant wisdom to anyone who eats it.

In between bites, he continued, "The salmon swims upstream, against the current, to lay its eggs ... *these eggs* ... that we are eating ... It is really pretty impressive because it takes a powerful fish to do this ... and the salmon makes the trip upstream many times in its lifetime ..."

I felt just like the fish that Dimitri described. I had been fighting my own desires, swimming against my own current. But I knew I couldn't do it much more. I longed to be myself again, to flow with nature as I was used to flowing. I wanted to act according to my instincts, to stop fighting the current. So I beat around the bush a little:

"Have you ever heard of the notion that caviar is one of the most powerful aphrodisiacs in the world?" I asked.

Perhaps it wasn't the wisest thing to say at the moment – and I could almost see the image of Terry Tarri frowning at me in the corner of my mind – but I wasn't eating the *salmon's flesh* – hence I wasn't granted the wisdom of the Irish legend. I was eating the *salmon's eggs*. There aren't myths about gaining wisdom from eating caviar, only tales of sex and fertility. Dimitri smiled and I could tell he was turned on by my comment.

He said, "It is never guaranteed that a fisherman who is trying to score some caviar will find it. The fish that produce the best caviar are not as abundant as they used to be. It is hard to get them. Maybe that is why eating caviar is considered an aphrodisiac – because the fish are playing hard-to-get – Now that is a pretty sexy game, *Hard-To-Get*. – Don't you think?"

I wanted to crawl out of my skin right then and there! Dimitri was aware of the game I had been playing. And he was playing it too – playing by the rules. I wasn't fooling anyone.

We went back to playing Hard-To-Get, but it was only a matter of time before it would end and we'd both lose – and win.

We finished our meal and decided to check out the movies at a local theater nearby. We made it just in time to see *Stargate*. The interstellar theme of the film aligned neatly with my own feelings about Dimitri. We held hands the whole time. It was perfect.

The weather remained frigid, and the fire that was heating up between us, had we allowed it to blaze, would have created the perfect system of heat. But containing it was the right thing to do. Dimitri spoke and behaved like a perfect gentleman.

He gave me soft kiss on my cheek after we said our goodbyes, before I got out of his car. I began to melt. He held his lips upon my face for an interval of time that was significantly longer than a typical peck on the cheek. And even though he was right there, right in my face, pressing his lips against my cheek, he was still playing Hard-To-Get. I wanted to turn into his mouth and rest my lips upon his lips and settle there a while. But I continued to play the game. I swam against the current. I controlled myself. It was the first time in my life that I had ever controlled myself in that way – ever!

When I went into the house, I felt like a firecracker exploding all over the place. I knew I wouldn't be able to sleep, so I didn't even try. I took on a project to keep myself busy. I folded and glued pieces of wax paper into envelopes and stuffed each one with a letter or a poem that I had written to Jordan.

When I was through, I stuffed the whole pile into a backpack. And without much thought, I grabbed a small memorial candle from the dining-room breakfront, got into the Jeep, and drove to the cemetery.

Jordan's headstone had a small opening carved into

the back of it for placing a candle. I ignited the wick, placed the candle inside, and closed the little gate that protected the flame. I didn't know the graveside prayers, so I read each card out loud to him instead.

It was easy to see the words because the moon was full. Greatly affected by the low temperature, I read through my teeth, which chattered like a wind-up toy.

If Mona could prance around in a little body suit while twirling her baton in the middle of the freezing cold winter on the football field, then I can handle the icy air, too, I thought.

After reading each card, I'd look around the cemetery for a rock or a stone to place on top of the envelope – to weigh it down. Otherwise, they would have all blown away. An icy wind shot around every so often. Sometimes it took a while to find a stone, but I was determined with an abundance of adrenaline and insomniac energy.

After the final reading, his grave was full of sixty-two rocks and stones on top of sixty-two wax paper envelopes that contained thirty-eight letters and twenty-four poems. I originally planned on leaving it that way, but I experienced a change of heart in the end. His grave looked a mess. I figured that someone would most likely come by in the morning and trash all of my hard work. I gathered the envelopes into a bundle, leaving the sixty-two rocks and stones instead.

*

Earlier that week two important things had happened. First, I was given instructions for a final project in my marketing class. I had to come up with a product and market it. The entire proposal was to be outlined, executed, and summarized in a report. Coming up with an original product wasn't easy. Nothing I thought of seemed achievable: ballet slippers that transformed into point shoes and back again; a self-cleaning art box (like a self-cleaning oven); mop-socks to clean the floor. I wasn't thrilled with any of them.

The second important thing that happened earlier that week had to do with a book I checked out of the library: *The Art of Dream-Thinking*. It was like a guidebook of some kind. The author claimed that a person could work out a solution to any problem, simply by focusing on it during the time before sleep. In this way, a solution would reveal itself in a dream.

I had been thinking about a product to market for my final project for three consecutive nights. Each night I asked the same question, over and over, as my mind entered the deeper stages of sleep: *What product should I market? ... What product should I market? ...* My dreams revealed nothing. Still, I tried. I was desperate. The night I returned from the cemetery marked the fourth night of my dream quest.

As I slept I dreamed of a peacock. It held a waxy envelope in its small beak. I opened it up and pulled out a black card that was completely blank and wordless on the cover. But inside the card, there were strange characters of an ancient script that seemed to dance across the page from right to left. At first it looked like Hebrew letters, but I couldn't identify a single symbol. About midway down the page, one line boldly stood out in English, from left to right. It said,

"One day, a day will come, and all you can do, is blame that day."

I woke up, reached for the pen on the night table, and scribbled the words onto a piece of paper before I forgot them. The dream book had suggested that the reader keep a pad of paper and a pen next to the bed in order to jot down anything of significance, when awakening in the middle of the night, in between dreams. It said that any information may be vital, and may be lost, because people tend to forget the important details of their dreams by the time morning arrives.

I stared at the words on the paper … imagined them in their place on that strange and magical card. I closed my eyes again and thought about the dream: *The sky was full of moonlight ... There was a peacock messenger in full plumage ...*

I recalled the time I had slept in the cemetery on the night before Jordan's funeral.

I dreamed of a peacock that night, too! ... Another peacock? ... That's strange ... Was it a message from Jordan? I wondered.

I had read sixty-two cards to Jordan at his grave before I went to sleep that night. Could it be possible that he had corresponded by entering my dream?

As the sun rose up like a ball of truth in the sky, the light was clear. I sat straight up in bed and sorted it all out: Aside from the thoughtful inquiry I'd recently made for the past four nights, concerning my marketing project, there had been a far deeper question itching my subconscious mind – every night before I went to sleep, everyday while I was awake,

374

and many moments in between – itching to be scratched since the time that Jordan had died. This particular question was a part of my subconscious desire to reconcile the past – a subconscious question relating to the matter that Terry Tarri had been talking about. The question was *Why? Why did you have to die, Jordan? Why did you leave?*

It was the same question I had asked Jordan in Rittenhouse Square Park when I saw him through my teardrop – when I saw him above in the sky, smiling in the rainbows.

Relief had come at last. The answer had arrived in the beak of a peacock. Jordan died for no other reason than it was his day to die. It was his turn – his moment in time. There was nothing to blame. Nothing other than the day – the day he died.

As I thought about it, I realized that there was more to this dream. Somehow the dream card was also connected to my marketing project. An idea drizzled upon my thoughts:

I will create and market a line of greeting cards. But not ordinary greeting cards. They will be death day cards. I'll call them "Deathday Cards - Notes to the Grave." People visit their loved ones at the cemetery all the time. How practical it would be for them to stop at a local card shop on the way to the cemetery, and purchase a special greeting card – preprinted especially for the occasion – with a message of love – a message of longing for their dearly departed – maybe a message of forgiveness for some event that had gone unresolved – that still remained open like a festering wound upon one's soul. People have a hard time dealing with death. People have a hard time expressing their grief. Not everyone seeks help from others. Not everyone spends an hour each week with Terry Tarri. People need guidance. They need help just like I needed help. But they don't know where to turn. So many mourners aren't even aware of it. They can't easily verbalize their emotions – I can help them – Yes! – Practically everyone shops for greeting cards at one time or another. They'll see my "Deathday Cards – Notes to the Grave" and they'll grieve – and it'll feel good.

The possibilities that this idea inspired stretched out before me like the birth of the new day. I felt as though I had connected the dots of my mind. I felt as though the sun had risen two times in one morning before the day had even begun. Two mysteries had been solved – I got to work right away.

There were already twenty-four poems I could tweak for my new purpose. In addition to those, I would create *Deathday Anniversary Cards* that would start with phrases on the cover, such as: *It's been ten years now since you passed away ...*

I spent the day sketching different scenes on the cover of each card, using a variety of mediums: pen and ink, pastels, colored pencils, and charcoal.

First, I sketched a sun setting on a mystical landscape. Then I sketched a set of empty hands ... Then a single teardrop ... A soaring blue bird ... A tree full of sparkling icicles ... A violin surrounded by sunflowers ... A drifting sampan in a river of hope ...

I was unstoppable and found it challenging to keep my hands in step with my ideas. Tiny thought bubbles popped all over my brain. Some ideas came so fast that I couldn't even catch them.

Nonetheless, I illustrated twenty-four poetic *Notes to the Grave* and twenty *Deathday Cards* before the sun had set for the night. I celebrated my victory by playing my favorite sleeve-piece on my violin: *Russian Fantasia No. 2,* by Leo Portnoff. The expression "sleeve-piece" is an informal way of referring to a musical composition that a musician plays to impress people. Most musicians have a "piece" of music "up their sleeves" for those unexpected, on-the-spot performances.

The *Russian Fantasia No. 2* is a one-page composition that has four distinct parts. And it is those four distinct parts that summed up my emotions and gave me a sense of accomplishment, of closure. Somehow those four parts translated my life: *Slow and Sad; Fast and Confused; Fearless and Bold; Warm and Bittersweet.* Playing the *Russian Fantasia No. 2* was like eating a juicy piece of fruit for the hundredth time, but truly tasting it for the first.

My father muted the volume on the television set in his bedroom when he heard me playing. I expected him to come in and accompany me on the piano, like he usually did. He loved that piece. He made me play it so much that it became my sleeve-piece. But that night he left me alone. He only listened.

CHAPTER FOURTY-SEVEN

... And Jessie Came Tumbling After

Jackie was having a housewarming party on the Friday before Thanksgiving. Many of the dancers from Studio 67 were going. I wanted to invite Dimitri to go with me, but there was too much tension involved. I still hadn't told him about my job at Studio. I hadn't figured out a way to tell him that I earned my money by dancing around half-naked in a go-go bar. We were just getting to know each other. He was refined. He seemed so innocent. I didn't want to rock the boat. I mean, I planned on telling him about it, one day, but it wasn't the right time. So I invited Jessie instead. We were due for a night out together anyway.

Her hair was still her natural color. She was the first person I pitched my line to about *Deathday Cards - Notes to the Grave*.

"It's *fanfuckintastic*! I love it!" she shouted.

"Do you really think it can work?" I asked, smiling from ear to ear, totally amazed by her enthusiasm. Jessie was a true artist. If she *thought* it was a good idea, then I *knew* it was.

"Sure. The concept's totally unique," she insisted.

"I'm afraid that people might think it's too

morbid," I said.

"They will. And that's exactly why they'll be turned on by it. How did you come up with the idea anyway?" she asked.

"I got the idea from a dream I had."

"That's so cool."

"Yeah, but what about production? And distribution? I made over forty different cards. How do I reproduce them?"

"Just go to a print shop," she said, making it sound so simple.

"There's so much more I have to figure out. I want the cards to have texture and dimension. And where do I start with distribution once everything else is in place?"

"Ask some local card shops to give them a try. They'll do it. They have nothing to lose. Students from the Academy sell their stuff like that all the time, especially at this time of the year ... *'Tis the season* ..."

"I guess I'll figure it out. Let's go get a drink."

Jackie had prepared several pitchers for her guests, filled with laughter and margaritas. Jessie and I drank until our tanks were loaded with rocket fuel. Spending time with her always propelled my spirit into another galaxy.

Jackie's house was a rustically elegant replica of her salon. The beaded antique lamp I had picked out for her added a splash of pink to her colorful bedroom. She placed it on a farm-barn vanity right next to an ionic Chi hairdryer. Everything was either super old or ultra new ... or alive! By the night of the party, Jackie had acquired three kittens, two lovebirds, several fish, and an iguana. She's a real animal lover.

Mona and Steven didn't show up because Mona was sick. I'm pretty sure that she was sick over Jackie's recent success. The Hair Tea Salon received rave reviews, and business was like a boom box on full blast. I sensed that the green-eyed monster named Jealousy was in the mix because, for the longest time, Mona had also wanted to open a shop in the city. The handcrafted items in her basement workroom were suffocating her. She needed to spread out of her current station in life and feature herself once again. I tried to imagine what it was like to be her. *What's it like to be Mona?* I wondered in my drunken state. I came up with a series of oxymorons: explosively fragile, aggressively timid, violently peaceful ... Thinking about her not showing up at the party was depressing.

"*Hasshe* been *ta* the salon lately?" I asked Jackie, slurring my words in my drunken state.

"No. She hasn't even called me to schedule another appointment."

"I *sawer ater* house. She *needser* hair done. Her *roots're* down to *herears,*" I said with a thick tongue.

"You're slurring your words," Jackie told me.

"So?"

I enjoyed slurring my words and swaying as I spoke. Life was glorious again, like a Renaissance banquet. Jessie and I climbed the stairs to use the bathroom – to pee the River Margarita.

On the way back to the first floor, I felt as though an avalanche had taken us by surprise. It swept us up

380

and knocked us over and I skied down twenty-four steps on my ass – and Jessie came tumbling after.

Bump ... Bump ... Bump ... Bump ... Bump ... Bump ... Bump ... Bump ... Bump ... Bump ... THUD!

Jessie landed directly behind me at the base of the steps with her legs behind mine in a letter V.

I stood up to check myself for cuts, scrapes, torn clothes, anything. But there was nothing amiss. Jessie didn't have too look far. Both of her palms were gushing blood. She looked like a holy mess, like Jesus. The blood wouldn't stop gushing out of her palms.

Once again we had another emergency room episode – but this one wasn't as bad as the others.

CHAPTER FORTY-EIGHT

"Not By The Hair On My Chinny Chin Chin"

The outline for my marketing project was complete. All I needed to do was market it. *But how?* Jessie had suggested I take my cards to a printer. *But who?* I felt intimidated by the whole thing because I didn't really know what I was doing. I didn't excel in Marketing Strategy. It wasn't even my area of interest. It was an *experiment* for crying out loud. An out-of-character *experiment*. All semester long I'd been skating between a low-B-high-C average. I didn't really understand much at all about retail marketing.

Completely frustrated with the project, I decided to consult the one person I rarely went to for help: My mother. I only sought her advice under dire circumstances. And although she was always my last resort, she always came through.

She'll know what to do, I thought. *She always knows what to do. She's an expert at coming up with quick solutions, like the time when she cured that itchy rash on my ass.*

I knew exactly where to find her at seven thirty on a Monday evening: lying on the sofa in the living room watching the *Wheel of Fortune* spinning around. I hated to disturb her during a game show. It was like interrupting a person during prayer.

"Mom?" I said softly, not wanting to startle her. She immediately grew with excitement as soon as she saw me:

"Come here, Bree. Look at the contestant on the left, and tell me what you see," she said. I looked at the screen, at the contestant on the left, but I didn't know what I was looking for. All I saw was an enthusiastic young woman with brown hair who wore a printed sundress. Even though it was freezing in Philly, it was sundress weather in Hollywood.

"*Uhh* ... I don't know. What am I supposed to be looking for, mom?" I asked, growing more and more frustrated by the second.

"Look at her name tag," she said.

The contestant's name was Bree – just like me. And she spelled it the same way too. There aren't many people named Bree, so my mother and I both get a jolt when we find one. I smiled and seated myself on the sofa next to her.

She continued, "Don't you notice anything else interesting about her?"

"Mom, I came in here to talk to you about something important, and I don't have time for this game—"

"Okay, okay. But just take a good look at her dress. It's full of *cherries*." My mother boasted in a singsong way, proud to have discovered this strange reflection of her own daughter.

"Oh, yeah ... they *are* cherries. I didn't even notice. They just looked like a bunch of dots to me."

That's weird. There's another person named Bree

*in this world who has an affinity for cherries. I
thought I was original. Maybe this other Bree makes
Deathday Cards, too. Maybe she's getting them
printed right now. Maybe she'll sell hers before I sell
mine. Oh no!* I worried.

"Listen to me, mom. I'm going nuts from my
marketing project. I don't know what to do," I
complained in a tone of voice that demanded her
attention.

It was odd for me to approach my mother with a
problem. I usually sought my father's advice. So
whenever I needed her help, she was always on call,
willing to assist. She loved me. I was her *baby*.

"What's the matter?" she asked. "What's going
on?" The expression on her face revealed a true
concern for whatever crisis I was having. (She just
assumed it was a crisis because no one ever
interrupted her game shows.)

"I created a line of greeting cards, and I have to get
them copied so I can sell them. But I don't know what
to do. I don't know where to go, or who to ask. It's
driving me crazy!"

For a second she turned her attention to the puzzle
on the television screen. The contestant named Bree
wanted a letter *T*.

Is there a T, Pat? ... T ... One T! ... Ding! Vanna
White revealed the *T*, and the audience applauded.

"Why don't you just go over to Staples, or one of
those places?" she suggested.

"I have over forty cards, and I want forty copies of
each. I don't think Staples does that kind of printing,"
I said.

384

She turned her attention to the screen again when the contestant Bree found the letter *H*. I could tell that my mother wanted to focus on the puzzle, but she forced herself to consider my plight.

"*Forty copies* of *forty cards*? That'll cost you a *fortune*. What kind of project is this?"

"It might sound like a lot, but I have to think big. It's a huge project. I want a lot of copies, and I don't care how much it costs me. I'm getting an *A*," I stated adamantly.

The other Bree wanted to spend some money too: *I'd like to buy a vowel, Pat.*

My mother turned sharply, looked upward, and bit her bottom lip. That's what she does when she gets an idea. "*Hmm*... I wonder if Cookie Goodman can help you ... Get me my phonebook. It's on the table over there." She pointed her long nail at the phonebook.

"Who's Cookie Goodman?" I asked.

Can I get an E? ... There are 5 E's. Ding! Ding! Ding! Ding! Ding! The contestant Bree was feverishly trying to solve the puzzle.

"You remember Cookie. She's the woman who does the invitations. You have to remember her. She did the invitations for your Sweet Sixteen."

"I remember my invitations, but I don't remember Cookie," I said, surprised that I could forget someone named Cookie.

Is there an S? ... 3 S's! Ding! Ding! Ding! The other Bree had successfully uncovered ten letters.

My mother disappeared into the kitchen with her biblical phonebook. I tried to listen to her conversation with Cookie Goodman, but I got zapped into the *Wheel of Fortune*. I solved the puzzle and said it out loud: *"As Far As The Eye Can See."* The other Bree looked lost. She couldn't figure it out. *She might have my name and my love for cherries, but she doesn't have my brain.* I was relieved.

My mother shouted to me from the kitchen, "Do you want to go over to Cookie's house at two o'clock tomorrow?"

"Okay ... What did she say about the cards? Does she know what to do?" I shouted in response.

"She said it shouldn't be a problem. I'll drive you over to her house tomorrow. Make sure you're ready to leave at one thirty."

My mother quickly ended her conversation with Cookie and went right back to watching the wheel. Within an instant she solved the puzzle and beamed with delight. I didn't tell her that I had already solved it myself. I waited like a good girl until a commercial break before I interrupted her again.

"Thanks, mommy. I knew you'd know what to do." I smiled and gave her a cuddly sofa hug that was three commercials long.

*

At one thirty the next day, I gathered all my cards and was forced out of the house. Even though Cookie lived just fifteen minutes away from our house, my mother wanted to leave thirty minutes before the time of our appointment. She's always early for everything. One time, we were the very first people to arrive at my cousin's bar mitzvah. The doors of the synagogue were still locked, and it was cold outside, so my whole family had to wait in the car in the parking lot. We were there before the maintenance men, before the rabbi, and before my cousin the bar-mitzvah boy! It was so embarrassing.

We pulled into Cookie Goodman's driveway at a quarter to two – fashionably early. We let ourselves in through an unlocked basement door that immediately led us to the smell of stale cigarette smoke mixed with cheap fabric softener and some other odor I couldn't identify. "It stinks in here," I whispered, and gagged for a second.

"Cookie? I'm here!" My mother chanted with her neck outstretched.

There was no reply, so we walked slowly down a narrow corridor, passing by piles of invitation boxes stacked upon one another. They looked exactly like bakery boxes, but it didn't smell like a bakery. It smelled like … like … "What's that *smell*?" I whispered. My mother ignored my question.

"Go in there," she ordered, leading me into a basement-paneled room. It was thoroughly lined with bookshelves that sagged with heavy exhaustion from having supported too many invitation bookbinders, for too many years.

We seated ourselves in leather armchairs that rolled on wheels around a big Formica table in the middle of the room. While we waited for Cookie, I ate four butterscotch hard candies from a ceramic bowl that was shaped like a frog.

Cookie Goodman entered the room on the hour, and cleared her throat with the voice of a man. She was as thin as a brand new Virginia Slim cigarette, but she was wrinkled worse than the bellows of an accordion.

After she and my mother had caught up on all the latest gossip in their circles of Jewish geography, they turned their attention to me. Skinny Cookie examined a dozen or so of my *Deathday Cards*. She looked me dead in the eye and gave me the *Your-Not-A-Normal-Person* look that Terry Tarri had given me from time to time. It was the same look that Mr. Spade had given me during every critique of my work.

"Are you crazy?" Cookie asked me.

"Maybe, but don't worry. I'm in therapy," I joked.

"What made you decide to make these morbid cards?" she asked, continuing her analysis of them.

"It's a project for my marketing class. I have to develop an original product and market it before finals. So I thought up this line of greeting cards. It's called *Deathday Cards – Notes to the Grave*. It's totally original ... never been done before."

"You know what? ... That's pretty catchy ... You might have something big here..." she decided, looking at each card with more and more enthusiasm. "People might just buy these. The artwork's fantastic - *Look* at this!" She leaned over to show my mother the card in her hand. "I didn't know you had such a talented daughter."

"They're *all* talented," my mother boasted. "You should see the stuff that Mona makes – and Jackie's salon is absolutely gorgeous. You have to get down there and see it for yourself. Maybe you'll come with me the next time I go."

Cookie seemed stuck on one of the cards. She kept

388

opening it and closing it.

"So – can you get them printed?" I asked.

"Sure," she smiled. "Absolutely."

"How long will it take? The project is due three weeks after Thanksgiving."

"I can have them ready for you on the Wednesday or Thursday after the holiday."

"You can get them that fast? – I need a lot of copies."

"How many of each one do you want?" Her voice seemed deeper than before.

"Around forty—"

"Of *each*? Are you *nuts*! That's over sixteen hundred cards. Do you have any idea how much that'll cost you?" Cookie grew concerned and a whole new set of worry lines formed above her brow, emerging like rising waves on a troubled sea.

"Money's not an issue," I calmly explained.

She didn't know that I had go-go money in my wallet. My mother gave me a look, as if to say: *I know you have go-go money in your wallet, but Cookie doesn't.* Then Cookie gave my mother a look, as if to say: *I can tell your daughter doesn't know how to spend her money wisely.* Then I gave them both a look, as if to say: *I'll spend my money however I please, so shut up and get back to business.*

Cookie pulled the order forms from the shelf. "This is the largest order I've ever filled in the thirty-five years I've been in business! It might take a while."

Just then, Cookie's husband, Mr. Goodman, came in through the basement door with an overweight bulldog waddling by his side.

"Well, look who's here!" Mr. Goodman shouted in a roll of jolly laughter when he saw my mother, and the dog let out a stinky fart that proved to be the mystery odor I had wondered about earlier.

"Hi *doll*." My mother got up and gave Mr. Goodman a peck on the cheek, careful not to smear her cherry-red lipstick on it. "How ya doin' *doll*?" She had called him "doll" twice in one greeting. And even though he was at least twenty years older than her, she still greeted him like he was a toddler. She calls everyone "doll." I always think it's funny.

"What're *you* doing here? Is someone getting married again?" he asked. In contrast to Cookie's super-low masculine voice, he spoke in a high-pitched feminine voice. He also had feminine nipples protruding through a white winter sweater over what I call *man-tits*.

"Another *wedding*!?" my mother shrieked. "Come on, Sol! Give me a chance to recover from the last one—"

"So, what's the occasion?" he asked as the dog let out another fart …

"You know my Bree," she said, pointing towards me. "She's *the baby*." I smiled and waved and loved being the baby.

"That's one good-looking baby – just like her mother."

"She's here to get some cards printed up for a project," Cookie explained.

"What kinda project?" His voice climbed higher and higher. I thought he might be a castrato and looked for the bulge in his pants. When I didn't see it,

I started to worry.

"I created a line of greeting cards for a final project in my Marketing Strategy class," I clarified. "They're called *Deathday Cards – Notes to the Grave*. I designed them for people who go to visit their loved ones at the cemetery … They can buy one at a local greeting card store on the way, and read the message to the dearly departed once they arrive at the grave."

"That's the nuttiest thing I've ever heard!" Sol gave me the *You're-Crazy* look. Cookie glanced up at him from her triple-carbon order forms.

"It might be crazy Sol, but it's original. And that's what sells: Originality." Cookie started choking on a tar ball something fierce. It gave me the distinct impression that there was black cancer in her throat.

We all waited in silence until she popped a butterscotch candy into her mouth – and her cough calmed down.

*

The next morning I vowed to never smoke again. A crazy nightmare inspired my commitment.

After I had read the dream book, I paid very close attention to the images that occupied my sleeping mind, and was bent on figuring out what they meant. It was somewhat of an obsession of mine at the time.

My nightmare was based on an unwanted hair that grows out of the left side of my chin. Every other month, a single strand of hair emerges (ruining Ruth's perfect-chin theory about me). And as soon as I see it, I grab a tweezers and pluck it out.

After meeting Cookie Goodman and her horrible

choking cough, I dreamed that my chin hair had sprouted out from the surface again, just enough to annoy me. I readied the tweezers, but pulling the hair out wasn't as easy in the dream as it is in real life. It usually takes one good tug or two before it pops out. In the dream, my chin hair wouldn't break off. The more I pulled, the more it emerged – sort of like a handkerchief in a magician's pocket that goes on and on. And the more the hair emerged, the thicker it grew. And the thicker it grew, the viler it became. And the viler it became, the more aware I became that it wasn't a hair at all. It was a tail. The tail of a creature! A black nicotine tar-creature!

I pulled the creature out of my chin! Out of my head!

I woke up from the nightmare, sweating and swearing. I grabbed the pen on the night table, jotted down some notes about it, and vowed to never smoke again.

CHAPTER FORTY-NINE

The "O" In Studio

I longed to be close to Dimitri. To smell his burnt cinnamon skin. To watch his dark spider lashes moving softly around his eyes as he spoke. To listen to his buttery voice. To melt under his fingers as they'd transform me into an erotic sonata. I wanted to be with him in the flesh.

Flying above the wooden floor in the ballet studio, I imagined myself being gently chewed by his mouth. All my thoughts involved sexual acts with him. A triple-X slide show flashed through my mind's eye. My imagination was out of control. *Does it show? Does he sense it?* I thought that the piano sounded happier, more pulsating. Or was it my imagination?

I was practicing my kicks at the barre when another most-embarrassing-moment-of-my-life took place. The instructor directed the class to kick our legs up fast and frequent. The rubbing of my leg muscle up into my crotch combined with my X-rated thoughts, and the combination caused the bolts in my mind to loosen. I had an orgasmic explosion right at the barre! I stopped kicking and doubled over to hide my face. My heart pumped faster then. The vibration between my legs had triggered a total physical blow out. I couldn't move for several seconds. Dimitri ended the piece he'd been playing on the piano. I came up for air, panting like a dog. Dimitri smiled at me in our spot in the mirror.

For a second, I thought about this girl named Marni who Jessie had met at the Academy. Marni was an artist and also a marathon runner. And whenever she ran, she'd build up to a certain speed and then break into a series of orgasms. Both Jessie and I thought that that was totally intriguing. We acted as though Marni had some kind of super powers when she told us about it.

But I felt like a lunatic – like one of those guys jerking off under the bar at Studio. *How could this happen to me?* I wondered. It was positively perverted – freakish.

After class, I decided to skip my therapy session. I had no desire to hear a single word uttered from the mouth of Terry Tarri. I didn't want to analyze another situation with her. I wanted to live and experience my emotions.

I was no longer obsessed with the smell of Downy. Jordan was traveling onward in the heavens, and I was moving towards a different kind of love. A kind of romance I had only dreamed about as a child. Dimitri was the knight of my now, the yin of my yon, the rod of my curtain. One round with Terry Tarri would certainly cure me of that. If love was a disease, then I wanted to be sick.

It was hard to catch my breath and organize my thoughts when I faced Dimitri on my way out of The Ballet Studio. He followed me down the skinny steps.

"What happened to you in there?" he asked.

"It's kind of embarrassing, if you want to know the

truth," I said.

"Tell me, Bree. I want to know the truth," he insisted.

"It's ... *personal*," I laughed, nervously.

"You can tell me – even if it is personal – if you want to," he assured me.

I wanted to say it. I wanted to let him know exactly how I felt about him. How I reacted to him. How I sizzled and steamed just standing there in his presence. What was stopping me? Was it honesty? *If I'm honest about this, will other truths follow? Truths about go-go dancing? Will one truthful word snowball into others and grow and roll and crush my hopes?* I worried. But I knew what I had to do.

I tried to tell him: "I had an ... uh ... an unexpected ... uh –"

"You can tell me, Bree? It is okay. Your secret is safe with me," he said. We were outside by then. He reached for my arm. My face turned hot.

"It was an orgasm ... I had an orgasm," I confessed. Somehow I managed to overcome my fear and blurt it out.

He laughed as a smile lit up his face with redness. "Wow! That is honest –"

"Is there anything else you'd like to know?" I asked, relieved to have been brave enough for honesty – which proved *not* to be such a lonely word.

He looked at me square in the eye. "Yes, there is something else. It is you, Bree. I would like to know you."

I couldn't speak. I was paralyzed. Dimitri was still holding my arm. He slid his fingers down to my hand.

I felt dizzy again, like I was on the brink of another orgasm. I looked up and saw Terry Tarri's office window. It brought me back down to earth. I took a deep breath and lowered the flame.

"Why don't you come over my house for Thanksgiving dinner. My mother makes a big feast," I said, figuring if he wanted to know me better, my family was a logical place to start.

"I would love to, but my mother makes a big dinner too, and she is expecting me to be there. I will talk to her about it. I am sure she will understand." He sounded uncertain.

I knew how much he enjoyed his family and how much he loved his mother's cooking. I thought of a way to balance it out. I thought of Mona and Steven. Whenever there was a holiday, they would eat the main meal with one family, and have dessert with the other.

"We could end up at your house for dessert," I suggested.

"You mean, you want to meet *my* family?" he asked, surprised.

I nodded with enthusiasm. I wanted to build the first sensible relationship of my life, following the sensible map that Terry Tarri had drawn: Honesty, Family, Expectations, Reality ... and then Fantasy. *Fantasy comes last, not first*, Terry had insisted. I finally understood why.

His smile was the smile of happiness. Of a child. Of a man. A smile that unlocked my dreams of love. A smile that was filled with music. And poetry. And laughter. His smile mirrored my feelings. His smile was my smile.

Could he be my soul mate? I wondered. The question frightened me.

Terry Tarri had said that love is a risk. I was riding the roller coaster again. Where would it take me this time?

*

"Come here, Bree!" my father shouted from the living room.

In the kitchen, I smeared some Philadelphia brand cream cheese on my bagel – placed a thin slice of well-oiled nova lox on it – and dashed on command.

"Isn't she the woman you worked with at Natural Foods? – What was her name?"

He pointed at the television set. Channel 12 was airing the premiere of a cooking show called *Nanette's Organic Studio Kitchen.*

Nanette was vibrant. She had the same red hair and the same red smile, only more luminous, more alive. The camera shot a quick view of the studio audience every once in a while. I recognized a few of the faces from the *Natural Foods* lunch counter. Seeing Nanette was a relief. Tears swelled at the sides of my eyes, and I smiled because she was alive and thriving. I had cut off a chunk of my hair for Nanette, and would have willingly cut off more if she had needed it. She had made tea out of my hair. She had drunk the hair tea – and somehow it worked – and she stayed alive.

The simplest of answers can be found in the oddest of places. When people are willing to open their minds and test the solutions, however absurd, anything is possible.

I watched as Nanette taught her viewers to make Orecchiette with Arugula Pesto, Oven Roasted Winter Vegetables with Gremolata, and a desert of Orange Cake with Chocolate-Pecan Streusel. Her jokes were funny. I chuckled in delight.

While devouring the last of my bagel-and-cream-cheese-with-lox, a few thoughts swam around my mind. One was that Nanette cooked with Sea Salt, a *white* product. I thought about the *white* daikon radish that she steamed and ate everyday. I thought about the way she boiled my hair down to a *white* powder to make the hair tea. I recalled what Nanette had said about *white* being bad. About all that jazz she rattled off about white sugar, white flour, white rice – About the white powder that Nick snorted up his nose. But there was so much goodness in so many other white things. I thought of Yin and Yon: a balance of dark with a balance of light. I wanted to call Nanette right then and there and tell her all about it.

When the half-hour show ended, Nanette's recipes flashed on the screen as a kind of summary. I noticed that each dish started with the letter "O" and wondered if Nanette had planned it that way.

I thought of Dimitri and my earlier orgasm at The Ballet Studio.

I thought about the letter O. *It is a circle. A full circle.*

CHAPTER FIFTY

The Kiss That Ends The Story

It snowed the night before Thanksgiving – perfect white snow. Looking out the window, I witnessed the best kind of white on earth. It was the white Thanksgiving where Dimitri would enter my house, and I would enter his. The white of heaven had come all the way down and beautified our otherwise dull neighborhood in Northeast Philadelphia, turning it into a slice of paradise. It was the first snow of the year. I felt safe.

Jackie introduced us to her new boyfriend, Zack. He owned a pro-golf shop out in the suburbs. He was a golf guy. Jackie usually dated heavy-metal dudes who wore tattoos and tattered jeans – who had long hair and leather vests draped over their naked chests. Zack was different. He had been a heavy-metal dude who had grown up and out of the scene. He played the guitar and the keyboards to rock-n-roll music, and he was comfortable in his white golf sweater. He was a trivia guy, a human encyclopedia. He scored higher than the Jeopardy champion (and my mother) during the game show we watched after dinner.

Dimitri wore white as well: a crisp, button-up collar shirt next to his tan skin, which seemed brighter against a white background. The first thing Dimitri noticed upon entering the house was my father's piano, naturally proceeding to impress us with a little Beethoven. During the meal, my father enjoyed telling the story of his first experience with a piano:

"I wanted a piano in the worst way, but my parents couldn't afford one. My aunt Fanny had one; she had a lot of money. And one of my neighbor's had one. Every time I was in either of their houses, I'd play around on their pianos. I used to find excuses just to go there. Then one day, on my way home from school, I saw a piano sitting outside on the curb. Someone had left a piano outside for the trash men to collect. A lot of people started getting rid of their pianos because it became "unfashionable" to have one in the house. Could you imagine that? *Unfashionable?* Well, this piano had a set of wheels attached to its legs. I rounded up a bunch of my friends, and we struggled to roll it three blocks to my house. It took all afternoon just to get it there. Later on, my father and my uncle got it into the house. I was around seven or eight years old at the time. My parents were too poor to afford piano lessons, but I was determined. I figured out some chords and learned to play it on my own, even though some of the keys were missing."

Did you ever take formal lessons, as an adult?" Dimitri asked.

"I took a few, but by then I never had the time to practice. I couldn't read music with any kind of ease because I had learned to play by ear. It's easier for me to listen and find the starting note than it is for me to read. I play to relax. Practicing sheet music took too long, and, like I said, I just didn't have the time. I was always working or taking the girls to their music lessons, ballet lessons, Hebrew school, and so on. Time is a funny thing."

"What do you do for a living, if you do not mind my asking?" Dimitri said.

"I'm a retired court stenographer."

"Is the stenographer the person in the courtroom who types everything on the little typewriter?"

"Yes, but it's not a typewriter. It's a stenograph machine."

"What is the difference?"

"It types in shorthand and uses special paper. I'll show you after dinner, if you want."

"Sure. I would also like to hear you play the piano. I have never met a person who started out by trash-picking his first piano. That is a great story –"

"Speaking of trash," Steven interrupted, "Since when did they start letting white trash move into Society Hill?" He was referring to Jackie. It was his rude way of trying to burst her bubble. It was his way of being *funny* in a not-so-funny way. I wanted to shove a turkey bone down his throat. Jackie gave him the finger when she thought no one was looking. Other than that, she kept herself composed. I assumed it was because she didn't want her new boyfriend to feel uncomfortable.

"Actually," Zack said, "I'm thinking about moving to Society Hill. There's another place I have my eye on in the city that would be perfect for my golf business. My Feasterville shop pretty much runs itself, so if I opened another store downtown, I'd be better off making the city my home for a while –"

"And you'd be closer to *me*," Jackie added. I could

tell she wanted to kiss him.

"Definitely another plus," Zack smiled. I could tell that Jackie was in love.

Steven kept his mouth shut for the rest of the night.

"Well, I might be getting that shop on Pine Street after all," Mona announced, excited to join in the conversation.

"Really?" Jackie asked.

"I don't want to jinx myself, but things seem to be coming together. I'll know in a few weeks."

"Speaking of the city," I remembered, "I'll be down there a lot for the next two weeks, trying to convince the local card-shop owners to let me display my cards." I had to explain my *Deathday Cards - Notes to the Grave* project to everyone.

"That's a little strange," Jackie said.

"No it's not," Zack disagreed. "It's a good idea ... It's new ... It's fresh. You'll probably sell a lot around Christmas. Everyone visits the cemetery around Christmas." Zack wasn't Jewish, and he had inside information on the antics of Christmas.

"They do?" I asked. "Then, I should add something Christmassy to the line."

"That is a good idea," Dimitri added, keeping himself included in the dialogue. I liked that about him. I liked everything about him.

"I could put together some small display stands for you and help you set up. Just let me know what you need," Zack offered. "I'm also a carpenter." He must've really liked Jackie. All her prior boyfriends behaved in a similar fashion: They'd become as available and as helpful as possible to Jackie's family, in order to get in better with her.

"Cool," I said, "I'll sketch you a picture of what I have in mind," I said. I felt like we were the Cleavers or the Brady Bunch or something.

"Okay, but try to get me the sketches as soon as possible. It sounds like you'll need the displays pretty soon," Zack said.

"Why are you taking a *marketing* class?" Mona asked me.

"Because I want to be more like you," I smiled.

"Really? Is that the reason why?" Mona got super excited.

"Yup. That's the only reason. Honest to God," I admitted.

"I'm honored," she beamed.

Dimitri started a sidebar conversation with my father: "I think it is interesting how you chose a profession that allows your fingers to move in a similar fashion to that of a pianist's."

"I never thought about it that way," my father admitted. "But there's probably a connection."

"There's definitely a connection," I interrupted. "It's called the subconscious mind; it's working all the time." I proudly announced my Freudian insights.

The subconscious mind explained a lot that night. It explained Jackie's new golf-playing boyfriend who represented my mother (golf: a game) *and* my father (keyboards: music). It explained Dimitri's interest in me. His mother was a retired professional ballerina. And, like me, she was also a very good listener (a quality I inherited from my father – trained to absorb every word with the keen ear of a court reporter). The subconscious mind even explained Mona's choice in men: Steven also played the piano. He had taken lessons until he was seventeen years old, and he was still able to impress us that evening with his "sleeve piece."

Was it a coincidence that each of our male interests knew how to manipulate the ivory and ebony keys with ease?

Dimitri and I went to his house and gorged ourselves on Russian desserts: cheese blintzes, raspberry pudding, poppy seed cookies, and my favorite: homemade cherry pie. His family was warm and welcoming. They were Russian Jews, but they were dark-skinned and looked more like Spanish Jews. I felt comfortable in his house, surrounded by the symbols and images I was familiar with.

He drove me home when the evening was over, but I didn't want it to end.

"Let's take a walk," I suggested.

All around, the snow was twinkling. I fixed my scarf and slipped my arm through Dimitri's. Being close to him came naturally.

"I had a nice time tonight," I said.

"If it would end with a kiss, I would call it the nicest night yet," he blushed.

*

It was the kind of kissing where time becomes a tunnel, and we were traveling to the melting point of nonexistence. The kind of kissing that could last for five minutes or five hours, and no one would know the difference. It was the kind of kiss that young girls dream of. The kind of kiss that ends the story.

He tasted like Thanksgiving dinner … He tasted like sweet cherry pie … He tasted like home.

CHAPTER FIFTY-ONE

When the Day is Done

A week before final exams, a major greeting card company approached me with an incredible offer. Inglenook Greetings wanted to buy the rights to *Deathday Cards – Notes to the Grave*. Needless to say, it was an unexpected turn of events.

An Inglenook Field Merchandiser named Valerie had stumbled upon my cards during her lunch break, while shopping for holiday gifts at Fresco Secco, an artsy little crafts shop in Old City – the same crafts shop that let me set up my marketing project display. Valerie was intrigued by the novelty of my card line, and later on that day, she discussed it with her boss Sophia, Inglenook's Retail Merchandiser.

Since Fresco Secco is only a few blocks away from Inglenook's headquarters on 2nd Street, Sophia took a short walk over to check out my cards for herself ... She got my phone number from the owner.

At first, I thought that Sophia was some kind of prankster. Her offer seemed way out of my league. *I'm just an amateur – a student in an introductory course, completing my final project – and a quirky project at that*, I thought. So I hung up the phone on her. But she called back right away and suggested that I listen very closely to her proposal before hanging up again. As she explained the details, I understood that her offer was real – It felt like a miracle.

Sophia and I met just once before a twelve-page contract was drawn and negotiated. I had to initial and sign it seventeen times at our second meeting.

There was one part of the contract that struck me as curious: Inglenook Greetings had given my card line its own company imprint: *Celladore Cards*. I asked Sophia about it. She said that "Celladore" is a term that sounds like "Cellar Door" – that the cellar, in a literal sense, is the room within the house that people don't regularly enter as part of their daily routines. And keeping in step with that idea, the cellar has been used for centuries as a symbol in literature to represent an individual's deepest – and often saddest – emotions. Sophia explained that the "cellar door" represents the human need to dig down, to open up and face the emotions that exist beneath the surface. She said the term fit nicely with the message of the cards. And as she spoke, the psychological notions behind the word Celladore filled me with wonder...

As part of the agreement, I was hired under the Creative Director to work as a Designer for the Celladore imprint. Some silly guy from the Marketing Department named Mike, the Associate Product Manager (a seriously fancy title), started the process of putting together a "team" for the card line. I immediately thought of Jessie, and was quick to show Mike my high school yearbook because it features Jessie's paintings and sketches throughout the pages. Mike smiled and said *bring her on board.* Jessie accepted the job – We can't wait to start working together – That's the *best* part of the deal.

407

Mike has all kinds of creative ideas to enhance the series. My answering machine has been full of his messages about his ideas: He has plans to manufacture these little stones engraved with images of hearts, religious symbols, and other appropriate emblems. He wants to include them as part of the whole display – to advertise them as *"Tokens of Love, Carved in Stone"* – for people to purchase along with the cards, and tenderly leave at the grave of a loved one. Mike also plans to manufacture a specially designed utensil made of sturdy plastic that has a pointed end for securing in the ground at the grave, and a special feature on the other end for holding the card in place. He said that people respect the gravesite, so they require a neat and tidy method of displaying their affection for their loved ones. I agreed wholeheartedly – remembering the mess I'd created upon Jordan's grave that night in the cemetery. I never could have imagined that my poetic expressions for Jordan would go where they were going …

The salary that the company offered me was irresistible – almost comparable to my weekly sacs of go-go money. I made sure that the contract delineated my summers off. I'll need them to study. I'm still set on completing a college degree in something – maybe Art, maybe Journalism, maybe Music…

*

I've been tuning up my violin again, rosining the bow regularly, and practicing my scales. I need to keep my fingers in shape because I joined the local symphony that Dimitri conducts. He suggested that I sit in on a rehearsal when the concertmaster died because a chair had opened up in the first violin section.

The orchestra is not the best, but it's a lot of fun. The musicians are mostly returnees. That is, they are players who were once very active with their instruments, then stopped playing for a number of years, and decided to pick it up again later in life. They all have their own stories, but they all end up in the same place: the local symphony. A bunch of sponsors support Dimitri and the orchestra's five annual performances.

At first I was a nervous wreck. Dimitri had never even heard me play before, and I wasn't familiar with the music. Then I met the violin section. There's this one guy named Nick who's ninety-two years old. His son C.P. plays the trumpet and celebrated his seventieth birthday last week. Nick shows me his arthritic hands *every* time we rehearse; and he *always* says, "I hope ya never get like this. It's awful! But don't ever stop playing. Once ya stop, ya dead. Dead!" I laugh, but I know he's serious.

Then there's Rhona. She sits next to me, and quite honestly, I find myself following her lead sometimes. She's fantastic. Her long, red nails sail up and down the fingerboard as smooth as can be. I don't know how she does it with those nails, but somehow she manages. I can only play on the pads of my fingertips. If my nails grow out, even just a little, I cut them off right away. Rhona is twice my age and has never gotten married and has no children.

Then there's Don who sits in the back. Even

thought he's completely blind, he doesn't miss a note. He can "sight read" music better than most of us. He has some type of auditory memory, and he records all our rehearsals on a cassette tape. When Dimitri pulls out sheet music that I've never seen before, I sometimes get lost. But Don doesn't. He can be heard playing out, over all of us. Sometimes he plays the flute part or another part the violins don't have. No one stops him, though. Every so often he'll play a passage forté (loud) when it's supposed to be pianissimo (super quiet). Rhona yells at him then, but not in a mean way. She has to yell because he's playing so loudly that he won't hear her otherwise. You can tell he enjoys himself there. You can tell that the violin is his life. He has agreed to let me interview him next week an hour before rehearsal. I'm going to write an article about him and submit it to *Philadelphia* magazine. His eyes are colorless. I wonder if he knows that I stare into them when we talk. He fascinates me.

Tony was the original concertmaster. He had been the first chair of the orchestra for thirty years. I feel weird sitting in his seat. Sometimes I cry just thinking about it while I'm playing. Everyone loved Tony. They still talk about him a lot. There's pain in their eyes each time his name is mentioned. I designed a special *Note to the Grave* for him and everyone signed it. Rhona took it to his grave and read it to him. She said it felt good.

Being led by Dimitri is nice. He's an outstanding conductor, and he makes us laugh. That's the best part: his subtle humor.

We're completely professional during rehearsals. The hours we spend together after rehearsals are another story – completely romantic.

*

I still feel anxious driving north on Route One. No matter how well things are going in my life, I can't shake the fear.

It is my final night of dancing at *Studio 67*. My time here has ended. Tonight will be my final performance in the House of Burlesque. No more stage names. No more gimmicks. No more tips. I'm moving on to another me, a polished me. But I couldn't have gotten to this better version of myself by any other means. *Studio 67* played a critical role in the carving of my emerging adult self. It was a ride of excitement. A bungee jump. And tonight, it ends.

I'm spending more time each set saying goodbye to the regulars than I am dancing. I'm giving Junior a hug goodbye in the DJ booth. His clothes still smell like Downy, and his breath still smells like pork roll with cheese. Beavis and Butthead are proposing marriage to me. The guy with the foot fetish is giving me a farewell massage. Bob the mechanic is offering me a Winston, one last cigarette together. But I tell him that I quit. The hundred-dollar man is offering me five grand for the night, which I have to laughingly refuse.

The dancers are concerned about their tips, of course. Back in the dressing room, they are secretly dreaming of their own last nights at *Studio 67* when the curtain will close on their go-go dancing days.

The back door opens and a woman enters with a couple of suitcases and a few racks on which to hang the costumes she is selling. Since it's my last night, I don't pay much attention to her. I have no need for new costumes. I am dressing for my next set – only two more to go.

Before I make it out of the dressing room, I decide to take a look at the costumes for sale because they're amazing. The girls are going through the racks as if their lives depend on it. *How much is this one? This one?* I pick up buttery leather one-piece that has fringe and glass beads. I think about buying it. I think to myself: *I love the leather one-piece. I want to buy it and save it for a special occasion ...*

"How much for this one?" I ask, figuring I could buy it and wear it for Dimitri at some point in the future. I haven't shown him any of my sexy costumes yet. I'm always in a rush to take my clothes *off* for him.

"It's forty-five dollars," the woman tells me.

I know that voice! I turn around to look at the saleswoman ... It's Mona ... She is standing right in front of me, selling go-go costumes in the dressing room of *Studio 67*.

"Mona! I can't believe you're here!" I scream.

"Neither can I ... but here I am ... selling the costumes I made. That's what was in my workroom when you asked to see what I was working on. I've been selling these costumes door-to-door ever since you suggested it –"

"You have? ... Why didn't you tell me sooner? I could've been selling them for you all this time. I'm

412

here twice a week."

"Steven didn't want me telling anyone."

"Steven knows? ... Is he mad at you?"

"I didn't tell him about my new business until I made some hard cash. I wanted to prove to him just how lucrative it was. I started selling at *The Lion's Den* and at all the other bars around the city during my lunch break. But there just wasn't enough time, so I began lugging the stuff around at night ... He really freaked out at first – but I stood my ground. "

"What did he say? ... Is he okay with it now?"

"I left him no choice. I told him I wanted that shop in the city ... and I was willing to get the start-up cash by selling costumes. I said, *I'm either moving up, or I'm moving out.*" A Billy Joel song echoed in my head. "When he finally realized how serious I was, he stopped bothering me – and that was the end of it."

"Wow! ... I can't believe what I'm hearing!"

"What about you?" Mona asks. "What are you doing back here in the dressing room? I thought you were a *cocktail waitress?*"

"I am ... in a sense. I shake my *tail* and wait for *cocks* to tip me." Mona's hiccup laughter starts up. "No kidding, Mona ... you caught me here on my very last night."

"Well that figures, now that I'm finally here ... You can have the leather one-piece. It's on me – but why do you want it, if you're not going to dance here anymore?"

"I want to wear it for Dimitri one day –"

"Uh ... Too much information! ... No thanks!" Mona flashes the red light on the conversation.

"Oh, now that I know *your* little secret, you're going to know *all* of mine. Wait till you hear how much I have to fill you in on," I warn her.

"Bree, that's what *therapists* are for."

"No, Mona. That's what *sisters* are for …"

"I'm sorry … You're right … I'll come over sometime this week, and we can drink tea while you tell me all your secrets … Let's invite Jackie, too."

I say, "I love you, Mona." And I mean it. I love the costume designer who is talented and vibrant. I love the woman who has taken charge of her life. I am thrilled because she is back to being my sister.

"I love you too, Bree."

We embrace. We smile. We get back to business.

*

After all the goodbyes are said at the bar, it feels good to be done. It feels better than good. My circle is complete. But I know it's only one circle of many more to come.

There will be more unexpected events in my life for which I won't be prepared. I will crawl along other stages in life. I will stumble and fall. I will find solutions in the oddest of places. I will do an out-of-character experiment. I will analyze a dream. I will drink a cup of hair tea. I will find the strength to rise – and find my footing – and fly with grace.

I will reveal myself through a spectrum of colors in broad daylight, and flash like lightening against a midnight sky – when the day is done.

Painting 101

Spring Semester
Instructor: Mr. Mault

Pedro's Pupka (150)

Pedro's Hat

Sampan - *"Now this ... THIS ... is a vigorous painting!"* (252)

Still Life - *"Is there something you're pushing into the corner of your mind?"* (188)

Summer Semester

Egg Paintings

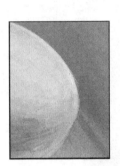

"The assignment became more and more interesting once the egg had opened." (275)

*"**The egg represents the four elements** ... the shell is the earth ...
the membrane is air ... the white is water ... and the yolk is fire ..."*
(305)

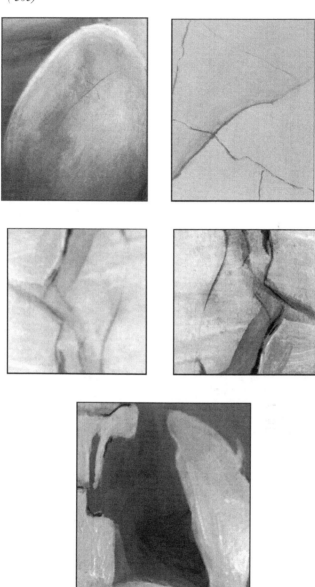

*"**Emotional torture shrieks** in your work, Bree."* *(307)*

Webster's Unabridged Dictionary, (bottom volumes):
"Stopless *isn't even a word. I looked it up in the dictionary."* (30)
The Riverside Shakespeare: *"I have lost the immortal part of myself, and what remains is bestial ..."* (16)
World Religions, Third Edition: *"In my World Religion class, last semester, we learned that the whole 6-6-6 thing is a fluke."* (18)
Utrecht Classic Hardcover Sketchbook: *"I searched through Jessie's bag for a sketchbook ..."* (178)

This arrangement of color shows that **Amy, the summer semester painting model,** had been recently kissed by the sun while wearing a one-piece swimsuit. Just look at the sunburn on her chest, arms, and legs. While posing on stage, Amy warned the class: "Even though I stopped menstruating two years ago, you still better stock up on red paint - I burn all summer long ..."
"Amy the model was an old pro. She cracked jokes all day long." (274)

"But now she was a childless mother who bore a grave expression ..." (209)

The plaque on Jordan's grave.
"Shalom Memorial Park, Section Elijah." (221)

"The Winter of My Summer"
(315)

"Are you kissing me because you're drunk?" he asked.
"I love you, Jordan. I'm kissing you because I love you." (195)

420

Dear Bree Baby,
 I love you so much.
 Thinking about you all the time.
 Can't wait to see you
 and listen to you playing your violin again.
 I'll call you soon.
     Love,
      Jordan
p.s. I hope you like the drawing

Made in the USA
Middletown, DE
06 April 2015